Anatomised

Also by A.F. McGuinness

A Portrait of the Arsonist as a Young Man

Heidi Seek and Other Stories

Anatomised

A.F. McGuinness

Red Sail Press

First published in Great Britain by Red Sail Press in 2018

Copyright © A.F. McGuinness 2018

A.F. McGuinness asserts the right to be identified as the author of this work.

A catalogue record for this book is available from the British Library.

ISBN 978-0-9927121-4-3

In loving memory of

My mother Martha McGuinness

My father John McGuinness

My mother-in-law Patricia Campbell

Anatomise (v): to cut apart; to show or examine the position, structure and relation of parts; to study something in detail in order to discover more about it.

-PART ONE-

There is no health; Physitians say that we
At best, enjoy, but a neutralitee.
And can there be worse sicknesse, then to know
That we are never well,
Nor can be so?

John Donne, *An Anatomy of the World*

A Night at the Opera

On the road to Glyndebourne the sky seemed fragile and spent, dull blue fading to grey and speckled like a fledgling gull. The atmosphere was hot and humid, so Alice switched on the air-conditioning. Even then Jack perspired in his tuxedo and winged collar, hands planted in front of the dashboard blowers. He wasn't an aficionado of opera or a fan of dinner jackets. All he wanted to do was turn the car around, but as Gerry's special guests there was no going back.

The Manns were behind schedule, or as Alice preferred to call it, fashionably late. Jack had grown accustomed to this, yet it sometimes felt like itching powder sprinkled down his shirt; Alice dressing and re-dressing, asking for an opinion at various intervals before rejecting his advice and going back to her original dress. Jack on the other hand, could be showered, shaved, suited and booted in less than half an hour, assistance required only with tricky cufflinks.

Tonight, the order of things had changed. No quibbles over shawl or shrug, which necklace matched what earrings or what heels were best suited to the plush lawns of Glyndebourne. Alice was ahead of herself and Jack was the one pleading for more time. He'd sat on the edge of the bathtub repeatedly flexing the fingers of his left hand and the toes of his left foot trying to shake off pins and needles. In the heat of imminent departure Alice had been the one locking the windows of the rented 1970s bungalow they jokingly called the Bunker. She'd been the one filling Pandora's dog bowl with fresh water. She'd been the one standing by the front door jangling the keys and glaring at the hallway clock.

The strangeness of this role-reversal didn't occur to her until they were clear of the M23, fast approaching the Sussex Downs, and only after something else sprung to mind: 'Jack, did I switch off the hair-straighteners?' Usually, he'd respond with wit: *How would I know? You used them after me.* When he said nothing, she glanced across. 'Are you alright? Do you want some music?'

'No,' he said, stretching his collar.

'No you don't want any music, or no you're not alright?' He told her about his pins and needles and she tapped the days out on the steering wheel. 'A whole week? I told you not to strim the garden for so long. It's repetitive strain injury or carpel tunnel syndrome.'

'I needed to clear it before we move into Seagull House.'

'Jack, we don't move in for months, and we're not moving into the garden.'

'But it's a jungle.'

'It's not now,' she smiled, pressing down on the accelerator.

'God, I can't wait to move out of the Bunker. Floor tiles in every room. It will be an igloo come winter.'

'It's only temporary, and we do have a big garden for Pandora.'

'With a whacking great railway line at the end of it.'

Alice was used to his grouchiness en route to social events. It wasn't that Jack was misanthropic, it was more that he got nervous; a trait she viewed as odd given he'd been a stand-up comedian since the age of twenty. As usual, she'd have to jolly him along.

'It's handy living around the corner from Seagull House, isn't it? We're lucky to rent somewhere that close. Speaking of which, could you take over the project for a while? I'm busy for the next month, and soon you'll be touring the country with *Mad Infinitum*, and then I'll be doing everything.'

Jack nodded, staring out of the window. 'I'm all over the place. Liverpool, Newcastle, Manchester, Birmingham, Glasgow, Leeds, York, and then I'm in Godknowswhere. That's a place you know. There's a regional theatre in Godknowswhere. I'll be done and dusted by Christmas.'

'Christmas in Seagull House!' she squealed like a girl. 'Enormous lounge with log burner, brand new open-plan kitchen diner, bi-folding doors on to the veranda, four bedrooms, balcony off the master with panoramic sea views...'

He looked at her, poker-faced. '*Partial* sea views.'

She pictured them sitting together on the balcony, sipping fresh coffee, eating bagels and reading the morning newspapers, sea sounding in their ears. 'Don't worry about the pins and needles, Jack. You've been overdoing it. Prep for the tour, moving down here, driving up to London to see your mum. Relax. You can drink the champagne. But watch your hiatus hernia. Bubbles mean troubles. You never know, you might actually enjoy the opera.'

'I might understand it too. It's in English.'

'Exactly. The Taming of the Shrew.'

'Alice, this isn't a Shakespeare musical. It's Britten's *Turn of the Screw*? Based on the horror story? It's about about dead people and ghosts.'

'And love. There's always love in a good opera.'

'There's always sex and death in opera.'

She groaned. 'Romantics call it love and tragedy, not sex and death.' She placed a hand on his thigh, squeezing. 'You look so hot in your tux.'

'Hotter than you realise, chickpea. I'm melting inside this chainmail.'

'The Incredible Shrinking Mann!' she blurted.

And finally, he smiled.

Alice parked the car beside a vintage Rolls Royce so it would be easier to spot come the end of the night. Hurriedly, they made their way down from the sloping car park. She wobbled in her badly selected highest heels and Jack strode out, chiller bag clinking with champagne. Parties of ladies in elegant gowns and gentlemen in dinner suits were seated around tables on the expansive lawn. They were quaffing and guffawing. Some older men smoked cigars and waddled like penguins across the grass, partners as bright as peacocks on their arms. A pleasant summer breeze blew over, tinged with laughter and perfume. 'Where are they?' asked Alice, shielding her eyes from the sun. Jack picked out the hulking six-foot-three frame of Gerry Ravenscroft who rose to his feet in a far corner, waving furiously, bald head gleaming, large walrus moustache twitching.

'Slow down,' Alice muttered under her breath.

Jack slowed, linking arms. 'You look gorgeous, Alice.'

They were half way across the lawn when Jack felt a shifting sensation in his left foot and his ankle buckled. 'Careful, hon, it's me wearing the heels,' Alice joked, but Jack was oblivious. Half of his foot felt foreign. A line of numbness ran down the middle of his sole, heel to toe, having a curious curling effect. In his mind it was like one of Alice's dinner decorations when she cooked Chinese: a dissected spring onion soaked in a bowl of iced water curling at the tips into the letter C. His left foot had turned into a spring onion at Glyndebourne. He walked on, stamping his boot down heavily, but the normal feeling didn't come back.

'Here they are!' said Gerry, face aglow from early drinking. He kissed Alice on both cheeks, exclaiming: 'Stunning as ever.' He shook Jack's hand, which had turned into slippery ice. 'Blimey old boy, you must have a very warm heart. This is Francesca. Fran, these are my good friends, Jack and Alice.'

A petite, pretty brunette in a tailored black ball gown stepped forward. She kissed Alice and then Jack saying how pleased she was to meet them. She was in her late thirties, slim and pale with attentive green eyes; most unlike any of Gerry's previous girlfriends who were usually more boisterous and blonde.

They settled down on picnic chairs around a table brimming with Parma ham, smoked salmon canapes, pungent cheeses, rocket and tomato salad, olives, houmous and rustic bread. A half-empty bottle of champagne teetered on the edge of the table. Gerry caught it, poured the remains into plastic flutes and said, 'To health and happiness.' Everyone raised their glasses. Jack pulled a fresh bottle from his chiller bag and planted it on the table. 'Good man,' said Gerry, patting him on the back. 'They'll have to carry us home on stretchers.'

'So, how did you guys meet?' asked Alice.

'In a record shop,' said Fran. 'Gerry was looking for jazz, I was looking for the blues, and we literally bumped into each other.'

'Sounds just like a Woody Allen film,' said Alice.

Jack smiled at Gerry. 'When did you start liking jazz, *daddio*?'

'I don't. I was stalking Fran around the whole of Brighton.'

'That's how we met in San Francisco,' said Alice, 'only it was City Lights bookstore, wasn't it, Jack? You were stalking me too.'

'I don't think it qualifies as stalking.'

'Jack followed me around every nook and cranny of that bookstore.'

'Please,' he implored, 'not the book story.'

'So,' Alice continued, 'when I get to the till with Ginsberg's *Howl*, I turn around and Jack lurches towards a shelf, pulling a book out at random.'

'Well, random is what he's always claimed,' said Gerry, winking.

'And he hurries up behind me in the queue.'

'I honestly didn't know,' said Jack.

'I pay for my poetry and Jack puts his book down on the counter, and we both stare at it.'

'What was it?' said Fran.

Alice patted her husband's hand. '*An A-Z of S&M.*'

'Oh my God!' said Fran, clapping a hand over her mouth. 'You're joking!'

Masking his embarrassment, Jack hunched his shoulders, opened both palms and said in his finest Woody Allen voice: 'And what d'ya know folks, it was the most practical ten bucks I ever spent.'

Sitting in the beautiful grounds of the opera house, sipping champagne and making witty asides, Jack Mann could be forgiven for thinking everything was almost right with the world. Things had been tough these past few months. Not only his mother's descent into dementia, but his own health; an odd mixture of non-specific ailments put down to the stress of selling the maisonette in Fulham, buying a wreck by the sea and temporarily renting the Bunker. Everything had been in flux. Yet sitting here at Glyndebourne, nestled in a splendid bowl of hills, listening to conversations passing blissfully back and forth around the picnic table, life seemed back on track. Preparation for his first tour in seven years was complete. Six months of hard graft on a new set would pay off. Glowing Edinburgh Fringe reviews had bolstered pre-sales. Radio appearances were booked. Work on Seagull House was scheduled to end in a few months too, and everything would come right just in time for Christmas.

Jack took in the quintessential English eccentricity of dressing up in one's finest clothes and dining outdoors whatever the weather. The air was growing damp. The once blue sky was turning grey and speckled as if it had followed him over from Kent. A stiff breeze gusted, whipping gentlemen's jackets into wings, changing them from penguins into crows. Fine spots of rain landed on Alice's bare shoulders. She drew her sparkly shawl over her back. Looking into the middle distance, trying to take his mind off his strange foot, Jack drew the party's attention to the view: an undulating landscape of grazing sheep flanked by mature, manicured trees, topped by dramatic clouds. There was something of a Constable painting about it. He pointed out that there were no fences, suggesting the sheep would soon be joining them for dinner.

'There are ditches,' said Fran. 'They're called "ha-ha's", and the ha-ha is too steep for sheep.'

'Impressive pastoral knowledge,' said Jack. 'So, Francesca, the ditch beyond that first one, is it called a ha-ha-ha?' Alice pretend-punched his arm, but it was gentle and he didn't feel it.

'Ha. Ha. Ha,' said Gerry. 'Excuse my good friend, Fran. Jack has a penchant for puns. *Mad Infinitum, No Mann is an Island, Mann versus Machine, Mann About The House, Renaissance Mann, Mann in Black*...the list goes on. Who was it who said puns are the lowest form of twit?'

'You did,' said Jack, the champagne having a pleasant, loosening effect.

Gerry popped an olive into his whiskered mouth. 'Jack got a first-class degree in English at Oxford, Fran.' She seemed impressed and Jack felt his neck burn. Edgy, alternative comedians didn't like to be reminded of their time at Oxford. He'd prefer to be thought of as one of the people. 'Yes, Jack had a promising future in academia, going to do a PhD on John Donne, but of course he *jacked* it all in for the sake of La Commedia!'

Francesca laughed. She leaned forwards in her chair. 'You're blessed with a name like Mann. Gerry showed me your *No Mann is an Island* DVD.'

'Careful,' said Gerry. 'No one admits to that in public. Waterboarding is a less effective form of torture than watching Jack's old shows.'

Jack pictured the poster Gerry designed for that tour: a cartoonish map of the UK with Jack's trademark hang-dog face planted in the middle. The opening lines of the set flashed through his mind: *No man is an island, said John Donne, the Jacobean metaphysical poet, and with the possible exception of the Isle of Man who could disagree with him?* He remembered the fun he had perfecting John Major, the mannerisms as much as the Prime Minister's strangulated vocal register.

'What I enjoyed most were your impressions,' Fran said, as if reading his mind.

Gerry nodded. 'No one does impressions better than Jack. It's his USP. You should hear his Trump and Obama in the new tour; better than his Bush or Clinton.'

Jack appreciated the praise but his old friend was overdoing it.

'He's the original Mann of a thousand voices,' said Gerry. 'It's a gift.'

'And lots of practice,' Alice added.

'When Major's in bed with Edwina Currie,' said Fran, 'and his soul becomes possessed by the spirit of John Donne, and he recites "The Flea" to her, I nearly wet myself. But my favourite bit was the voice of God, or rather Richard Burton as God. I don't suppose you could do some for me?'

'What? Now?'

'Oh go on, Jack,' Alice joined in.

He looked to Gerry for support who said, 'You're cornered, dear boy.'

Jack cleared his throat. 'I'll recite the Meditation, but if I sound more like Richard Harris than Richard Burton, don't blame me.' He got himself ready, face visibly changing, graver in expression, getting into character. Really, he was trying to remember the lines. Also, it had always been easier doing Burton when he had a cigarette in his hand. Jack hadn't smoked for years but back then he'd puffed so much that comperes introduced him as "London's own Marlboro Mann". He plucked a thin breadstick from the table, using it as a prop cigar. He sucked on it, took a deep breath and began: 'No man is an island…entire of itself…Every man is a piece of the continent…a part of the main. If a clod be washed away by the sea, Europe is the less. As well as if a promontory were. As well as if a manor of thy friend's, or of thine own were.' He paused for effect and also because he was beginning to sound like Anthony Hopkins. For a reason he'd never figured out, the Welsh accent was a devil to master. If you didn't keep a firm grip on the intonation and pitch you could lapse into Ghandi. 'Any man's death diminishes me, because I am involved in mankind. And therefore,' he paused for longer, 'never send to know for whom the bell tolls. It tolls for thee.' He took an exaggerated bow, still sitting in his folding chair. Fran whooped, Gerry slow clapped, and Alice beamed.

'How do you remember the entire thing?' said Fran.

'Jack did that show so many times, never forgot a word, and barely a heckle,' said Gerry. 'Now that's art.'

'And lots of practice,' said Alice, stroking Jack's arm in appreciation. He should've been bathing in the impromptu light but was momentarily alarmed; the place Alice touched wasn't felt.

First bell sounded for the performance. 'That sets the tone nicely for *The Turn of the Screw*,' said Gerry. 'Look, people are clearing their tables. Knock that back, old boy.' He nodded at Jack's plastic flute. 'And could you give me a hand putting everything in the Jag?'

The rain held off a while longer, and all four carried the folding furniture to Gerry's car. Empty bottles and Tupperware containers were deposited in the boot. Remaining food and wine was left in the hamper and retained for the long interval later. Gerry placed the basket in a good spot, on a bench under a large canopy, not far from the main entrance.

It was during the short walk back to the theatre that medical matters escalated. No longer an imagined, decorative spring onion in his sock, Jack's left foot had become harder and less moveable inside his polished brogue; his toes felt like the pinching claws of a crab. It was nothing short of Kafkaesque. If anyone paid close attention they'd have noticed the slight limp he'd developed. Making matters worse, the pins and needles in his left hand were pulsing with greater intensity, as if someone offstage was switching an electrical current on and off. He couldn't say anything about these developments. He didn't want to ruin anyone's evening, especially Alice's, and besides, it might only be the effects of champagne after three weeks of being on the wagon. His anxiety mounted as the operatic performance drew near, the corporeal electricity grew more intense, and the grey clouds mingled and threatened to block out the sun.

The party climbed the stairs, walked down aisle three and took their seats in the upper red circle. Jack was seated in D44. From there, he surveyed the auditorium and watched the throng finding their places.

Waiting for Act I to begin, the party chatted excitedly and flicked through summer season brochures. Alice noticed a slip of paper inserted inside hers that stated a cast change. Ironically, the soprano had been taken ill. The role of Governess would be sung by a replacement. When called upon, Jack joined in the light conversation, leaning across Alice, issuing smart refrains, but his minor contributions were drying up as quickly as his mouth. A knot of anxiety tightened in his belly; the tingling that had been entirely peripheral was now morphing into patchy numbness and spreading up his limbs.

Houselights dimmed, hushing the eager crowd. A bright light shone from the back of the stage behind a tall screen, forming the perfect silhouette of a gnarled and leafless tree, or, as Jack saw it, a giant depiction of human nerves he'd once seen on a science programme. The orchestra started, and a plaintive voice swept over the audience: 'It is a curious story…'.

In that first hour, during the most dramatic and loudest sections, Jack reached down pretending to scratch his shin, unable to feel it. In quieter, more intense moments, he stroked his left arm, unable to feel anything below his elbow. What could he do, except sit there fidgeting, lost in a forest of unfortunate futures: *passing out in the theatre, being lifted down the stairs to a waiting ambulance; going into a coma at the*

*hospital and Alice agreeing to switch his machine off; or dying
ironically in his red circle seat, D44, forever associated with that
comedian's **Death**, aged **44**, his limp body lowered down the stairs to
a volley of weeping; or losing control of his bowels and fouling his silk
and wool mix suit in the upper circle of Glyndebourne, people thinking
he'd been afraid of ghosts.*

Jack had died many times before, on stage as a comedian. He'd
died mainly in his early career: booked for an inappropriate venue,
playing to the wrong crowd, selecting the wrong material or pushing
the boundaries too far. But, as he'd told some wannabe comedians on a
weekend university workshop not that long ago, dying on stage is a
breeze; it's dying in real life you've got to worry about. And that was
exactly what Jack Mann was doing now; worrying about death in real
life. He remembered once, issuing advice to students on the chances of
becoming a successful comedian: 'Always die trying than try dying.'
Ha, ha, ha.

During the 80-minute interval, the friends sat on the bench and
finished the food and wine. Jack could only stomach water, saying he
had a headache. Before the final rays of sun disappeared, Fran took
Alice in search of rare orchids, and Gerry took Jack to the topiary
where he lit up a cigarillo. Amid the long shadows of unearthly box
and yew animals, and the curling plumes of Gerry's smoke, Jack
started to feel nauseous and unbalanced. He realised the sporadic
numbness had crept beyond his left elbow reaching his shoulder, and
up his left leg reaching his groin.

'Well? What do you think?'

'It's good. Who'd have thought it? Gerry Ravenscroft the opera
buff.'

'Not the bloody opera, Jack. Fran? Music tutor. That's why I
invited her to Glyndebourne. I'd never be here otherwise. You think
she's alright?'

'She has a sense of humour, which she'll need living with you.'

'Oh, Fran's not living me with me. She's got a flat in Brighton.'
Jack appeared agitated, shifting his weight from foot to foot. 'Look,
I'm sorry she banged on about your work earlier, Jack.'

'Comedy is a shop that never closes. Isn't that right, Gerry?'

'That's right,' he snorted. 'Nonetheless, it ruffled your feathers.' He stubbed out his cigarillo. 'That's enough milling about the shrubbery. Let's get back to the ghosts.' He clapped Jack on the back.

Before returning to Alice and Francesca, Jack paid a visit to the gents'. He wanted to inspect himself in a cubicle, but Gerry followed him into the room and they stood shoulder to shoulder at the urinals. Relieving himself, Jack realised his penis was dead to the touch. Unspeakable though this was, he couldn't say anything, standing there like a waxwork, agreeing mutedly with Gerry that Act I had been a triumph; the stand-in and the staging just as much as the music and libretto. As if either of them knew much about opera beyond Classic FM, Radio 3, or collections of The Three Tenors.

Ever since childhood Jack had become accustomed to the Mann family maxim at times of worry: *pray to your god and all will be well.* This maxim usually worked, even though no one in the Mann household went to church or believed in a specific god. Jack's father, Jack Snr., had had a strong affinity with Buddhism and occasionally wandered off to the foot of their Muswell Hill garden to speak to a large Buddha statue. Jack's mother, Estella, had an open mind about spirituality in general, without subscribing to any established religion or institution in particular, because they were in her words, or someone else's, "the opium of the masses". Jack assumed that his older brother Ernest and younger sister Lauren were just like him; they called upon an anonymous "god" when in need but rarely gave it a second thought when everything ran smoothly. Rumbling appendicitis in Jack's twenties miraculously abated with indigestion tablets, and prayers. More recently, hiatus hernia had been diagnosed after an endoscopy, but not ulcers, not stomach cancer. Most of Jack's prayers to a god he hadn't truly believed in had been answered, so perhaps there was a god. Although, he remembered with a heavy heart, what benevolent god allows a newborn child to die barely three hours old?

Now, desperately wanting to believe in a higher divinity, praying privately at his urinal, invoking the Mann maxim, Jack knew that no god of any denomination was going to answer.

'Okay?' said Gerry, drying his hands in a paper towel. 'Only you've been standing there a while. I think you're finished?'

Jack washed his hands, forcing a smile, hoping Gerry's question wasn't going to be prophetic.

'I'm worried you might be coming down with something and that would be terrible timing with *Mad Infinitum* around the corner. I don't need to tell you that a lot of time, money and effort have gone into this comeback tour.'

Jack dried his hands unable to wipe away his one-sided numbness. 'Edinburgh took it out of me. I'm 44, not 24. Recovery takes longer.'

A bell sounded and Gerry hooked a giant arm around Jack's caved-in shoulders. 'Come on. Act II is about to begin. The ghosts are waiting.'

And Jack thought, *am I going to die at the opera like Abraham Lincoln?*

Act II was an even greater triumph than Act I, not that Jack noticed. The stand-in soprano's singing was beautiful, powerful and haunting. The drama scarily unfolded reaching a terrifying crescendo and ghostly, tragic climax. Not that Jack consciously absorbed these things. The migrating numbness was beginning to terrorise his midriff. With the exception of his face, half of his body was now dead to the touch. Not quite dead, just almost dead, as if his normal, feeling hand was inside a glove or the unfeeling half of his body was wrapped inside Clingfilm. He could move his limbs, but the feeling of moving them was going; a strange sensation of disembodiment or dying alive, or dying from the outside in. He took a deep breath.

A trickle of applause started, quickly turning to a flood. The lights came on and Alice smiled at Jack, her eyes wide and joyful. He clapped along with her, but with the numbness it was like clapping with one hand.

After the thunderous applause had fizzled to a drizzle, the party returned downstairs. Jack was the slowest down the steps, using the handrail. Alice and Fran headed towards the toilets, leaving the men standing outside. The rain had been and gone, and would come again. 'That was truly creepy,' said Gerry, 'and I can see it's had the desired effect on you. The blood's completely drained from your face. Fancy a nightcap?'

Jack shook his head.

'C'mon, just for an hour? You could stay over.'

'Sorry, Gerry, we need to get back to the Bunker, and Pandora.'

After hugs, hearty handshakes and long goodbyes Alice and Jack found their car and set off along the dark and winding country roads. Alice drove cautiously having had a glass of wine, and the rain was beginning to set in. Over the sound of windscreen wipers, and tyres rolling through surface water, she said how wonderful it had been at Glyndebourne and they should return one day. Fran was just great, she said, and a good match for Gerry. Jack agreed to everything she suggested, even to visiting her parents in the morning when normally he'd put up some in-law resistance. His responses were all grunts and nods. Usually, there'd be an extended post-mortem; who said what about whom. Maybe the champagne had made him sleepy, though it was difficult knowing if his eyes were closed in the fleeting light from oncoming traffic. Although she'd never say it, it was as if *The Turn of the Screw* had cast a ghostly hue over him. By the time they were on the motorway, Jack appeared to be asleep, he was that quiet.

Half way home to the Bunker, the rain eased off. Alice glimpsed a sign welcoming them back to Kent. Jack lifted his chin a fraction, then a hand to his brow feeling with his fingers. He turned to her and said: 'Alice, I'm frightened.'

The car swerved. She recognised the serious, vulnerable, child-like quality of his voice. 'Is it the pins and needles?'

'Something far worse,' he said.

A Night at the A&E

A minute before midnight Jack and Alice walked through the sliding doors into hospital reception. Remarkably for a Saturday night the corridors were quiet and the waiting area was largely unoccupied. The last time Alice visited with her father it had been Bedlam and standing room only. This time, a bare-chested man was holding a blood-stained t-shirt to his eye, trying to focus on a wall-mounted TV that advertised accident insurance. An elderly woman was asleep in a wheelchair. A young man was seated close to the counter with one shoe missing, pressing down on a bandaged ankle and groaning in an exaggerated fashion. The receptionist glanced up from her computer and stared through a glass screen. 'Can I help?'

'It's my husband,' said Alice, breathless.

The woman looked Jack up and down taking in his well-groomed appearance, salt and pepper hair, silk bow tie and tux, saying with a warm smile, 'Aah, did Scaramanga get away, Mr. Bond?'

'What?' said Jack.

'*Man with the Golden Gun*. It was on earlier, before I came on shift.'

'I can't feel half of my face,' he said, but the words didn't sound or feel right. His lips, chin and teeth were frozen on one side as if he'd been to the dentist.

'Did you have an accident or were you attacked, sir?'

'He wasn't attacked,' said Alice. 'It wasn't an accident either, but this *is* an emergency.' She turned to Jack, tutting.

The receptionist looked at her computer again, and back at Jack. 'Name..?'

'Mann, Jack Mann.'

'Shaken, not stirred,' she muttered under her breath. 'One N or two?'

'Two,' said Alice.

'Name of GP and surgery?'

'We haven't registered with a surgery yet.' Alice gave the address of the temporary Bunker and their former address in London.

'What's the name of your current doctor and surgery? It doesn't matter where they are.'

'Dr. Munch,' said Jack, tugging his lip.

The receptionist hesitated, forehead furrowing. 'Munch? As in eating?'

'No, Jack. It's pronounced *Mooonk*,' said Alice, trying to smile at the receptionist. 'He's Norwegian.'

'Who is? Your husband?'

'Look,' said Alice. 'Our doctor in London was Norwegian, and still is I should think. He's called Dr. Munch, pronounced *Mooonk*, spelt M U N C H, like the artist Edvard Munch who painted *The Scream*? And if you've ever seen *The Scream* you'll know exactly where I'm coming from right now.'

The receptionist frowned. She saw an elongated Halloween mask, white and screaming, from Wes Craven's nineties slasher movie, not a painting. 'And where is Dr. *Mooonk's* surgery, madam?'

'Fulham Broadway, London.'

'Right.' She tapped it into the computer. 'So, sir, when did your face start?'

'Tonight at the opera.'

'But he's had pins and needles for about a week now, haven't you, hon?'

'Okay, pins and needles in the face for a week.' She tapped it in.

'No. Not pins and needles in my face,' said Jack. 'In my hand and foot, but now I can't feel my face, my foot, my hand, my arm, my leg...or my bollocks for that matter.'

Everyone in the waiting area jerked their heads around; even the old lady in the wheelchair, by now wide awake. Noticing this, the receptionist rocked forwards on her elbows and said quietly but firmly, 'Now, sir, madam, I don't know what kind of world you live in or what sort of treatment you expect to receive here tonight, but we don't tolerate any kind of harassment. That includes swearing of any kind.' She tapped a laminated sign taped to the inside of the glass screen.

'Sorry,' Jack said.

'Thank you. Now, shall we start over from the beginning..?'

Alice's heart raced. 'We're worried it might be a stroke.'

The receptionist's whole demeanour changed, and she politely asked them to take a seat.

'How are you feeling?' asked Alice, sitting down beside him.

'D'you think I've had a stroke?'

Alice held his hand and tightened hers around it. 'You don't have a stroke over a week. My dad's happened in minutes, not days. Also, he was seventy. I don't know what this is, but it definitely isn't a stroke. They'll do a CT, maybe an MRI. They'll run a full blood screen, monitor your vitals and send you home with a leaflet, a course of statins and a referral to a specialist. Healthy people don't go numb for no reason. They might keep you in overnight for obs.'

Jack's heart sank. *Overnight?* Although he'd visited Alice in hospitals before, his own experience didn't extend beyond Carry On films and sitcoms he'd watched as a child with his father, including M*A*S*H and *Only When I Laugh*. Such was Jack's good health, or good fortune, he'd not spent a single night in hospital since the day he was born. Well, apart from that New Year's Eve in Fulham, at the age of 33, when he'd found himself in a bottomless pit of drunken despair because his accountant ran off with more than £300,000 of his money and he'd tried to kill himself with a bottle of scotch and anti-depressants. He cringed with the memory of it, at the turn of the millennium, how he'd sung that Prince song to the nurses: *I'm gonna die like it's 1999.* Which it was, but he hadn't. His stomach had been pumped and he was forced to eat charcoal, but it'd been a straightforwardly self-inflicted plea for help and he was discharged early the next morning with nothing more than a note for his GP and a list of recommended psychiatrists. Jack, a Hemingway fan, understood that life could be swell again once the hell was over. A man could be destroyed, but that didn't mean he was defeated. In other words, Jack Mann was a survivor.

A nurse arrived pushing a wheelchair and calling Jack's name. On seeing this, the patient with the bandaged ankle leapt to his feet, hopped across the floor waving a fist. He bawled through the receptionist's glass screen, and she tapped the laminated sign with her biro.

The nurse helped Jack into the wheelchair and pushed him through a set of double doors along a short corridor that opened onto rows of cubicles bisected by plastic screens. Most of the cubicles were occupied, voices of patients tempered and whispering, those of nurses comforting and cajoling. The nurse pulled a screen around a spare bed. Jack removed his jacket and Alice folded it neatly over her arm. The nurse asked him to take off his shirt. Alice undid his bow tie, slid it inside his jacket pocket and hung his shirt over the back of a chair. Jack clambered onto the bed, beginning to describe his strange symptoms and sensations. The nurse said a doctor would be along shortly; she was only there to do baselines. She took blood pressure and temperature readings, both of which were normal. She asked him to summarise his medical history (migraines, hiatus hernia, manic depression); if he smoked (hadn't smoked for more than ten years); if he'd had anything to drink (a few glasses of wine); was he on any medication (over-the-counter painkillers); if he'd ever had problems with high blood pressure (no). She said he needed to be hooked up to a heart monitor, and disappeared in search of one.

She returned with a doctor in his mid-twenties, broad-shouldered, tall and swarthy, with a mop of dark hair. A stethoscope hung limp around his neck and his shirtsleeves were rolled up hairy forearms. When he spoke to the nurse in perfect English there was a trace of Eastern European in the vowels. He looked and sounded, Jack thought, like a cross between Croatian tennis player Goran Ivanisevic and the actor who'd played Luka in *ER*. The type of guy Jack used to resemble when he was twenty years younger. The strong-jawed type of man Alice fell for.

The doctor shook Alice's hand, noticing her long sparkly gown and high heels. He saw the dinner jacket over her arm and turned to Jack, for some reason speaking slowly and loudly as if the patient was eighty years old, hard of hearing and had stumbled in his nursing home. 'So, Mr. Mann…what trouble have we been getting into?'

Jack explained. Alice filled in some of the missing information and the doctor asked her if it would be okay for only Jack to answer. That way he could paint a more authentic picture. The nurse removed Jack's shoes and socks and attached leads to pulse points on his ankles, chest and wrists. She connected them to a monitor as the doctor asked a series of questions, including Jack's date of birth and his mother's maiden name. At first, it seemed more like a bank security check, and then a test for dementia. 'And what day is it, Mr. Mann?'

'I don't know.'

'What do you mean you don't know?' said Alice.

'Please,' the doctor said. 'Your husband only.'

'I came in on Saturday, and now it's Sunday,' said Jack.

'That makes complete sense,' replied the doctor, looking at a clock on the wall. 'And who is the prime minster?'

Although petrified of staying in hospital and anxious about his illness, Jack said, 'Lloyd George.'

Alice shook her head. 'He's making a silly joke. He does this when he's frightened.'

'Oh, quite the comedian are we?' the doctor said, tapping Jack's shoulder.

'Jack *is* a comedian.'

'Oh.' The doctor took a step back, screwed up his eyes theatrically and gave him a lingering look. 'If you don't mind me saying, you don't look like a comedian.'

Jack dragged a hand down his face. 'Sorry. I left my fez at home.'

The doctor gave him a physical examination, paying particular attention to his sense of touch. He felt Jack's face, neck, hands and feet noting there was patchy loss of sensation on the left side. Jack said he couldn't feel his genitals, resisting a smile that such a double entendre implied. The doctor flashed a light in Jack's eyes. He asked if he had any trouble swallowing or speaking (no). Was there any loss of sight or hearing? (No). Jack said he felt weak and off-balance when standing, and a bit nauseous. Alice reiterated that the original symptom of pins and needles had started one morning exactly a week before, and that this had turned into numbness.

'I note you suffer from migraine, Mr. Mann.'

'Migraine?' said Alice, half relieved, half unbelieving.

'You say the pins and needles were "just there" when you woke up one morning? Well, it is entirely within reason you had an attack during the night.'

'Can a migraine cause all these symptoms?' said Alice.

'Of course. Some people are paralysed by attacks. I have known a patient not to walk for months.'

'But I've never had anything like this,' said Jack. 'And I've had migraines since the age of eleven.'

'Does migraine run in your family?'

'My mother's side.'

'You get aura?'

'I get this flickering rainbow, then I go blind in one eye.'

'Headache?'

'Pounding, but only mild this time.'

'I'm going to order a scan to rule out a stroke, and run some bloods, but I think it's migraine. You can speak and swallow, are not cognitively challenged. There is partial sensation in the affected parts. You are not physically compromised. You don't smoke, are not overweight. This could be migraine. This is where I put my money, if I was a gambling man.'

Blokes with Strokes

From his bed on bay three, Jack watched the sunrise creeping through a far off window, pink as a grapefruit. It was going to be a red sky in the morning. He'd slept in fits and starts, being woken hourly by a male nurse taking blood pressure readings and checking the heart monitor; steady bleeps interspersed with unexpected spikes that Jack thought might drive him insane. The nurse had been kind. He'd gone out of his way to fetch a cheese sandwich from the canteen, the kitchens being closed at that time of night. Jack noticed it sitting unopened and sweating in its carton beside his mobile phone and a glass of water.

Memories of the previous night were a blur of whispers, cables, adjustments and dimly-lit faces. He remembered being told he was lucky that the vascular consultant, Dr. Richter, had been in charge of A&E that night, spotting an abnormality in his CT scan. He had no memory of seeing her. He remembered having to change into a gown with no back, self-consciously climbing into a different bed and being wheeled along a never-ending corridor called Main Street. And he remembered, with regret, amongst his mindless rambling, making an unfortunate remark to the porter who'd pushed him: 'I once read a murder mystery called *Dead on Main Street*.' To which the faceless porter had replied: 'Yeah, we get a lot of those in here.' Alice had sat by his bedside until she was satisfied medical staff had everything under control. Before leaving, she'd kissed him on his forehead like a mother would a child. And he remembered that just after her departure a man barked across the bay: 'About bloody time! I'm trying to sleep over here!'

And now, here Jack was, on bay three of the stroke ward, fuzzy through lack of sleep, fearful of a flat-lining future and fighting the fierce intensity of hospital heating. The numbness on his left side was unchanged. He tried to examine his foot, though it was difficult because of the wires and cables. It still felt like a crab's claw, though it looked perfectly normal from the outside. He leaned across and opened the drawers. There was nothing there; not even a bible. He realised then that he had no civilian clothes, only this arseless gown.

The machinery of the early morning routine creaked into motion; just like Jack's noisy stomach. The cleaning staff cleaned with mops and buckets and cloths. They swept the floor under his bed, smiling and nodding. Then the nurses started their rounds. One of them checked Jack's monitor and clipboard notes. She gave him a pill saying it was a blood-thinner and he swallowed it with some water. She pulled back the screen, exposing him to the rest of the bay; three male patients opposite, and one to his right. They ranged in age from sixty to eighty, but it was hard to tell because their faces were distorted by strokes; the man to his right most severely.

'So it was you, was it?' called an Asian man from the other side of the bay. Jack recognised his angry voice from the night before. He had a neatly trimmed goatee beard and short-back-and-sides. His face was jaundiced, as if nicotine-stained. He was propped up with pillows, ankles crossed, exuberant blue paisley dressing gown tied at the middle. 'You kept us up all ruddy night.' He shook out a copy of the *Telegraph*.

'What's 'e supposed to do?' said the patient directly opposite Jack; white-haired, red-faced, dressed in green-striped pyjamas that made him look like a tube of toothpaste. Half of his mouth was droopy but his voice wasn't greatly affected. His dropped aitches weren't illness-related. 'You don't pick and choose when to 'ave a stroke, do yer?'

'Still...' the jaundiced patient said, 'damned inconsiderate.'

'I'm Stan,' said the friendly man, 'and the crabby nut next to me is David.' David folded his newspaper and started reading the horseracing section. 'Ignore 'im,' said Stan. 'These Indian businessmen are all the same. And this is Wilfred, the old soldier.'

Jack saw a wiry, short gentleman dressed only in a long Granddad shirt, sitting on the edge of his bed staring out of the window. Hearing his name, he turned and waved.

'He's alright is old Wilf,' said Stan. 'Apart from 'is nightly shenanigans.'

Wilfred looked in Jack's direction, smiling, but soon his expression returned to an idling vacancy as if he was searching for Neverland in the middle distance. It reminded Jack of his mother's senility, now full-blown vascular dementia.

'What's yer name?' asked Stan, and Jack told him. 'Well, Jack. Welcome to the land of the arf-dead.'

'More like three quarters,' David harrumphed from behind his newspaper.

'That's right,' Stan chuckled. 'You might not get outta here alive, Jack.'

'You won't get out of here dead either,' said David, 'the administration's that slow.'

'Oh,' said Stan. 'Not forgettin' The Docta over there beside yer, Jack. We call 'im The Docta because he used to work here for forty years. And you don't mess wiv The Docta.'

'He gets special privileges,' said David.

'Quite right,' said Stan. 'He gave most of his life to the service and now it's payback time.'

'You can say that again,' said David, chortling. His rasping laugh was slightly dirty; unintentionally, quite a fine impression of Sid James from the Carry On capers. 'Wah-hah-hah.'

Clearly, this was the established order of things on bay three: Stan was simply gregarious, David was the cynical joker in the pack, Wilfred was an amiable child and The Doctor was a highly respected Time Lord. The Doctor opened his beady eyes, craned his neck and glanced at Jack. Having summed him up, he rested his head again on elevated pillows. His emaciated, bony features, receding hairline and grave expression gave him the appearance of the first Doctor Who, William Hartnell, crossed with an angry, time-warped John Malkovich.

'The Doc got the worst of it,' Stan said, having no qualms about public frankness. 'All paralysed down one side. I've been here two weeks, but the Doc's been here two months. They have to feed 'im by 'and, and he needs a bedpan.'

'Those are the rules,' said David, letting the paper drop to his lap. 'The four Ss.'

'Four Ss?' said Jack.

David cleared a frog from his throat. 'They won't let you out of here until you can shower, shit, swallow, and shuffle out the door all by yourself.'

Stan laughed. 'That's it. And what can't you do, David?'

'I'm having trouble with the former and the latter.'

'Snap,' said Stan. 'Dr. Richter's reassessin' me later. I'm hopin' I'll get discharged.'

'Good luck,' said David. 'Wilf over there has serious problems in all areas, isn't that right, Wilfred?'

'I think that might be the dementia,' said Stan.

'He needs a nursing home,' said David. 'Wait until tonight, Jack. You'll see what he gets up to.'

Wilfred grinned, saying, 'My son's a police officer.'

'I think he's comin' in to see yer today, Wilf,' said Stan. He turned to Jack again. 'What side did it get yer, mate?'

'You're a bit young for a stroke,' said David.

'You can have one even as a baby,' said Stan.

'Still,' David said. 'Look around. We're all over sixty. He's in his forties.'

'If he...if he's had a stroke,' the old Time Lord said, 'then...then I'm Mary Pop...Poppins.'

Jack's mobile phone vibrated on the drawer beside the bed. A message from Alice saying everything fine at the Bunker, and was he alright? Jack replied saying he was about to have breakfast with Sid James and Doctor Who.

Scrambled egg was on the menu today, much to the delight of David, Stan and Wilfred. 'It's not up to the Hilton's standards,' said David, 'but beggars can't be choosers.' The Time Lord had Weetabix mashed to a fine pulp with milk, fed to him in tiny spoonfuls by a nurse. It dribbled down his chin and she wiped it away with a paper tissue.

Jack was amazed by the colour, shape and texture of his scrambled egg as he shunted it around the plate with his feather-light aluminium fork. He guessed the eggs had gone through countless reforming processes to end up looking like a grey sock semi-dried on a washing line. The other men dug into theirs, taking the occasional break to chew and swallow. 'In the Sheridan you get a sausage, bacon, griddled tomatoes, hash browns and a lovely pot of tomato ketchup,' said David.

'Is there any salt?' asked Jack. 'I can't taste anything.'

'You'll get used to things tasting of nothing,' said David. 'Salt's banned.'

Jack texted Alice: *Breakfast reminds me, I need some clothes? xx*

Alice texted Jack: *Will bring in later. Walking Pan on the Slopes. xxx*

Jack pictured the scene, wishing he were dog-walking this sunny morning along the grassy Slopes abutting the shore, lined for half a mile with colourful beach huts.

Alice: *Spoke to Ernie, left a message on Lauren's answer machine. xxx*

Jack: *Don't tell Gerry, until we know more. xx*

A nurse removed the sticky tags from his chest, arms and legs. 'Sorry, where are the loos?' he asked her.

'Down the corridor to the right, mate,' said Stan. 'Can yer walk then?'

'I think so.' Jack clambered out, holding the back of his gown. He limped past the Time Lord's bed and felt the old man's eyes following him into the corridor.

The bathroom was spacious and included a walk-in shower with numerous grip rails. Beside the toilet was an emergency cord. Looking in a full-length mirror, Jack saw panda rings around his eyes. He prodded and probed the numb parts of his body and face. All looked quite normal, except for his cheeks jutting absurdly out from the gaping gown. He returned to the bay, aware the Time Lord's eyes were not just following, but steadily examining him.

'You're good to go,' said David.

'You can 'ave minor strokes,' added Stan. 'What they called, Doc? Those little ones?'

'Trans,' the Time Lord mumbled, 'attacks...trans ischemic...' He moved his dead arm onto his lap. 'T...I...T...TIAs.'

'That's easy for you to say,' said David, smiling cruelly.

'Maybe you've had one a them,' said Stan.

'Food...fool!' snapped the Time Lord. 'He's no...not had a stroke!'

'Dr. Richter will know,' said Stan. 'The German bird's real clever with the old grey matter.' He tapped his temple.

'She's the vascular consultant,' said David, 'and does the rounds after lunch. Stanley has the hots for her.'

Jack texted Alice: *Come in the afternoon. Will know more then. xx*

'What is it you do?' asked Stan. ''Cos I was a plumber.'

Jack was unsure how to answer. If he said a "comedian" everyone would expect him to play the clown. 'Lecturer,' he said, having taught the occasional comedy workshop at university.

'What subject?'

'English.'

'Oh, I was never any good at English.'

David snorted, 'You surprise me, Stanley.'

'Put a sock in it, Dave. You might be good at language, but you're actually from India, mate.'

'Wrong,' said David. 'As I keep telling you, I'm Hindu but am actually from Uganda. My family was expelled in the 1970s. We don't all look like Idi Amin, you know. I was educated at Winchester and could give you a bloody good lesson in English.'

The Time Lord sighed loudly; a definite signal for David and Stan to call a truce.

When he needed to go for a shower, David rang his buzzer and was escorted by a nurse holding him by the elbow. He could barely lift his feet, as if magnetised to the floor. In his absence, Stan took the opportunity to fill Jack in on David's full condition. 'Poor bugger's got everything. Cancer in all his vital organs, including his brain. His liver's packed in, that's why he's yella. He's 'ad chemo the lot. Then the poor bugger has a stroke. It explains the way he is, you know, grumpy? He just wants to go 'ome. That's all we want to do, ain't it, to go 'ome?'

With great difficulty selecting the order of his words, and shaking his head each time he got it wrong, the Time Lord made a sobering observation: 'David won't…won't go…be going home for long.' He grappled with a book and started reading: *Mind Over Matter*.

After lunch, a baked potato topped with tuna mayonnaise, followed by apple sponge and custard, Jack became aware of activity at one end of the bay. A sturdy woman in her thirties wearing an unbuttoned white medical coat over a pale blue blouse and grey skirt was at the centre of the melee. She strode purposefully towards Wilfred in calf-length boots, behind her a constellation of junior doctors and nurses. One of these pushed a trolley with a computer perched on top. 'Dr. Richter,'

Stan half-whispered to Jack, buttoning his pyjamas as best he could with one hand. He tried to flatten his messy white hair with licked fingers but it sprang up again.

A few minutes later, Richter was at the foot of Stan's bed discussing his case with the junior doctors. She stood with her back to Jack, strands of shiny red hair running down her coat in a waterfall. Stan asked if he could go home and, like Jesus in the Bible, she asked him to get off his bed and walk. Her voice was deep, her English near perfect, but the roots of her German accent showed. Stan got out of bed reasonably quickly and stood upright in front of the consultant. She made way for him, inviting him with a swish of her hand to walk a few paces. The first step was steady, but that was with his good leg. He concentrated hard and managed to drag his left leg a few inches. 'See, Dr. Richter, I can walk.' He took another step, and another, dragging his bad leg behind him like a plank of wood. He stumbled, clutching the rail at the foot of the bed, and was helped up by two nurses. 'My daughter said she'd take care of me.'

'Mr. Waites, you've made good progress.' His face lifted. 'But not enough to go home.' His face fell. 'You know the rules. Up the physio,' she said to a junior. 'Keep working hard, Mr. Waites, and you could be going home in a few days.'

'Thank you, Dr. Richter,' Stan said, a smile returning to his face. 'I won't let yer down, Dr. Richter.'

After a short deliberation, a junior handed the consultant a new case file. Dr. Richter took out a sheet of paper, gleaned essential information and turned to look at Jack, making the blood drain from his face. He was standing beside his bed, heart thumping.

'Mr. Mann,' she said, pulling the screen around for privacy. Three junior doctors stood behind her in a line, listening and learning. There was so little room Dr. Richter was practically nose-to-nose with him; close enough to see the broken veins in the whites of her hazel eyes. 'You may wish to sit down, Mr. Mann, before I tell you the news.'

'God, is it that bad?' He pulled the back of his gown together, perching on the edge of the bed, hands on knees, fingers drumming.

'I've had a good look at your CT scan and I'm sorry to say that there is a focal area of low attenuation within the right centrum semiovale consistent with an acute infarct.' When Jack responded with a dazed expression, as if struck on the back of the head with a cricket bat, she said, 'You've had a stroke, Mr. Mann.'

'I can't have. I'm only 44.'

'Younger than average, but statistically insignificant. We want you to have an MRI to get a better look at the bleed and the damage in your brain. We also want to check your carotid. I'm told you can walk?' He nodded. 'And eating isn't an issue?' He shook his head. 'So I think the damage is minor.'

'When will I have the MRI?'

'Good question.' One of the juniors whispered in her ear. 'Apparently the scanner's down for maintenance, Mr. Mann, but we'll schedule it for tomorrow morning. A backlog is developing, so it could be the afternoon, or possibly the day after.'

'Will I recover?'

'Initial signs are good.'

'How long?'

'How long for what, Mr. Mann?'

'How long will it be until things go back to normal?'

'What is it you do for a living?'

'I'm a professional comedian and have a big tour coming up.'

'You don't look like a comedian,' she said.

'It starts in two weeks, lasting three months.'

'I suggest you delay this tour.' She turned around and said to one of the juniors, 'Simvastatin once a day. Outpatient appointment for ECHO and 7/7 monitor. Bloods for vasculitis screening.' She pulled the screen open again and strode across the bay to David, followed closely by her juniors clutching files, and the nurse who pushed the computer trolley.

Jack lay flat on his bed. *A stroke?* A ball of anger rattled up his windpipe. He turned to the Time Lord and said: 'Did you hear that, Mary Pop Poppins? A stroke!'

Alice arrived at three o'clock, bringing clothes and bathroom essentials. She looked tired and Jack guessed she'd had as little sleep as him. As she bent over to kiss him, her loose bob of light brown hair shone in the sunlight turning it blonde. She opened her bag. Jack never thought he'd be so grateful to see his own pyjama bottoms, t-shirt, socks and slippers, emerging as they did like favourite friends. He told Alice about the stroke. 'Well,' she said, 'at least now we know.' She still hadn't managed to speak to Jack's sister Lauren but had left a few messages. His brother Ernie in San Francisco had sent his love and best wishes.

'I'll text Gerry later. Did you bring the charger?'

'It's in the bag.'

'He'll hit the roof. He's going to have to cancel the first two weeks at least.'

'Gerry will have to deal with it. I think you should cancel the whole thing, full stop.'

'I've worked too hard for this, Alice.'

'I know, hon,' she said, rubbing his arm.

'So much for migraine theories.'

'This makes more sense. You can have small strokes.'

'I know,' he said, glancing at the neighbouring Time Lord. 'TIAs.'

'I'm impressed. One night in hospital and you're already picking up the lingo.' Alice looked around the bay. Everyone had visitors, except for the Time Lord. A tall, stooping man towered over Wilfred, talking to a nurse about care homes; his police officer son. Two women were sitting beside Stan, one about his age, the other younger with his shaped face; presumably his wife and daughter. David was sitting upright, eating grapes brought in by his chatty sister. The Time Lord lay all alone, eyes closed as if sleeping, but something made Jack think he was listening, or possibly watching with his third eye.

After Alice departed, Jack went to the bathroom for a shower and a shave. He changed into his pyjamas, t-shirt and slippers, feeling immediately more human. He limped past the Time Lord's bed and the eyes followed him.

'You *were* a lecturer,' said David, 'but *now* you're a professional comedian?'

'The grape…the great pretender,' said the Time Lord.

'I do a bit of both,' said Jack, glaring.

'Know any good jokes?'

'That's why I never say I'm a comedian, Stan. You're a plumber, but I don't ask if you know anything about boilers.'

'He's got a point, Stanley knife,' said David. 'What kind of comedy, Jack? You look familiar.'

'Stand-up.'

David laughed, 'Wah-hah-hah. More like lying down now, hey? What's your last name?'

'Mann.'

David thought for a while, mumbling to himself: 'Mann…Jack Mann.' He clicked his fingers. '*The Mannologues*!'

'The what?' said Stan.

'A play on words, Stanley, from monologue. I liked it. Highly politicised. Yes, highly current it was. And this stroke has scuppered your tour? You've got a celebrity to compete with now,' David said to the old doctor. 'The Doc has nurses fawning all over him, Jack. Yes, special treatment. Don't think I don't notice, Doc. Now they can fawn all over you instead, Jack.'

'I'd prefer it if they didn't,' he said. 'I'm just a bloke with a stroke.'

David slapped his dead thigh. 'A bloke with stroke! Yes, every cloud has a silver lining. Maybe you'll find new material in here?'

'Well, comedy is a shop that never closes,' Jack sighed, recalling his conversation with Gerry at the opera.

Evening drew in. Dinner was an indescribable mound of shepherd's pie and dayglow mush of carrots, but Jack forced some down. Noise from a wall-mounted TV came and went. Everyone except Jack dozed in the vacuum-packed heat. David opened his eyes and watched the news for a few minutes before nodding off again. Stan snored gently, mouth half open, hands on belly, fingers knotted together. The Time Lord seemed to be sleeping, but it was hard to tell.

Everyone opened their eyes when a trolley rattled by. A Filipino woman poured tea from a steaming pot into plastic beakers. Everyone except Wilfred accepted one. David nodded at Jack. 'Wilf can't hold anything in for longer than a couple of hours.'

'They moved 'im over there just before you arrived last night,' said Stan. 'He was makin' a fuss wiv 'is buzzer. You can't keep anything in, can you, Wilf?' Wilfred shook his head. 'Poor bugger kept pressin' that buzzer, drivin' the nurses mad, weren't you, Wilf? Well, you ain't got no buzzer tonight.'

'I'm moving in with my son,' said Wilfred, but that wasn't what Jack had overheard. Wilf's policeman son had contacted social services who were searching for a nursing home. The detective simply didn't have the time or space for his father.

The night wore on. Lights were dimmed on bay three. The only sounds were of snoring and the damned TV. It was ten o'clock. Jack couldn't sleep. The heat penetrated to his marrow and Wilf was moaning about a toilet. 'Ring your bell!' he called out. 'Ring your bell!'

In the end, Jack reached up and pressed his buzzer, and a nurse came. 'It's not for me,' he said, pointing at Wilfred.

By now, Wilf was skidding around the floor in his own faeces, saying he wanted to go home. The nurse called for assistance. Another nurse arrived and they cleaned Wilf up and put him back to bed. Everyone was wide awake. 'I told you,' David said. 'Every night is Groundhog Day.'

Jack was exhausted. He'd developed a problem with insomnia over recent years, even when conditions were ideal, but this was off the scale. Having not slept the night before, he was almost hallucinating. The sound of the TV was driving him crazy, as was its flickering light. He asked if anyone minded him switching it off. No one seemed to know where the remote was. Jack asked a nurse who was passing by with a bedpan if she could please turn the TV off. 'Not without a step ladder,' she said.

'It must have a remote,' he replied. The nurse asked the other men if they knew where it was. Everyone shook their heads. 'Can't you use that chair? You can reach the TV. I just need to sleep. No one's watching it.'

The nurse looked at the chair and the TV, working out the logistics. 'No, sorry, it's a matter of health and safety.'

'What about *my* health and safety?'

The nurse walked away. Jack got out of bed and limped over to the chair. He placed it directly under the TV and climbed up, reaching higher and switching it off. He got down again.

'Ha! A stroke one day, one…day…chairs…climbing chairs the next!' laughed the Time Lord; the first time in the last twenty-four hours the old doctor had deigned to speak to Jack directly.

'You heard the diagnosis, Mary Poppins,' said Jack, climbing into bed.

'This…this you…this what you were looking for?'

Stan and David stared at the remote-control locked in the Time Lord's hand, and then back at Jack. Stan said: 'I told you. No one messes wiv The Docta.'

Sick of the sight of the old man, Jack pulled his screen all the way around. He tossed and turned. Too much light and heat. Wilfred was on the move again too, grumbling and shuffling. 'Press your buzzer, ring your bell!' This time Jack ignored the pleas. He plugged in the earphones Alice had brought in and listened to the best of Leonard Cohen. At least it blocked out the snoring. His mobile glowed. A text from Alice: *Night night sweetheart. Hope you get a good night's sleep.* A minute later, another text, this time from his brother Ernie in America: *Chin up, bro, enjoy the bed baths!*

An hour later, Jack heard a loud bang from Wilfred's direction. He unplugged his music, heard the steps of sensible shoes and static from fast-moving nylon tights, and then low voices. At first, the nurses whispered, but when Wilfred refused to get back into bed they shouted at him and he started to cry. 'I want to go home!' he wailed.

Soon the sun would be up. Jack willed it to stay down, but the grey fingertips were emerging in the large window. Already gone four o'clock, he hadn't had a slip of sleep on bay three, hadn't slept a single minute since Friday night into Saturday, and now it was Monday morning. He was like the bird on the wire that Cohen sung about. The left-sided numbness hadn't abated. His curling crab foot neither. Tomorrow, or was it now today, he'd have an MRI scan to determine the extent of the damage in his brain. A junior doctor from Sri Lanka had given him a Stroke Foundation leaflet that said almost half of stroke victims died from the attacks, so he'd been lucky. And seeing the severity of its effects on the other men on the bay, how could he disagree? But he didn't feel lucky. In a month's time he'd be forty-five; a stroke victim and has-been comedian, the long-awaited tour having to be cancelled.

Wilf moaned again. A tsunami of smell rose up, threatening to swallow all in its wake. The nurses and cleaners were back again. Mop and bucket. Jack threw a pillow to the foot of his bed and lay upside down, ears facing away from the commotion, but nothing could block it out. He looked up at the ceiling and noticed a metal hook that must have been there for a redundant curtain.

Jack wanted to hang himself from the hook. He imagined hanging limp from a rope or his bootlaces. He closed his eyes and covered his ears but nothing could block Wilfred out. He pressed his buzzer. A nurse arrived ten minutes later, by which time he was ranting in whispers. Jack told her he couldn't stand it; the noise, the smell. He hadn't slept, he told her, for two solid nights. 'I'm bipolar. I've had a stroke, and I haven't slept. Move me somewhere else. Get me out of here, please.'

'There is nowhere else. Too much bed-blocking.'

'If I don't get out of here I'm going to hang myself from that hook on the ceiling.'

She looked up at the hook. 'My shift's over in half an hour, but I'll leave a note for the next duty nurse.'

'She'll come in and find me hanging from the ceiling.'

The nurse repeated that she'd leave a note.

'And so shall I,' he groaned.

The daily routine started over again; cleaners, brooms, cloths, mops and buckets. No scrambled egg. A bowl of cornflakes. Jack's curtain was still pulled across. He wanted to murder Wilf. The infant-man kept everyone awake all night and then slept all day, building the energy to do it all again like a child with colic. But then he thought of his mother in the Muswell Hill nursing home. Sometimes when Jack visited, she'd ask to be taken back to her proper home. She knew where it was but a family of strangers was living in it now. Jack pulled his screen back, saying good morning to the others. Wilf was asleep, his face a vision of cherubic innocence.

Jack texted Gerry: *You won't believe this. I'm in hospital. Stroke. Due an MRI later. Sorry.*

A young nurse came to escort Jack to the MRI room. She asked if he needed a wheelchair but he said he thought he could walk. When she said it was a good ten minutes, he still insisted on walking, but it was becoming harder on his left foot. On the way down, he leaned on her and asked if it was unusual to have a stroke at 44. She told him about a man in his early twenties who'd had a scan after a stroke. The scan showed a tumour the size of a tin of baked beans, she said. And it was a pity as he'd just got married. The young man was taken to London where neurosurgeons cut half of his brain and face out. Apparently, his wife divorced him soon after, saying she no longer recognised the man she married.

Jack removed his watch before going into the scanner room. He lay down on a long table and they placed a brace over his head to keep it still. The brace had small headphones inside and the radiographer asked through them if he'd like any music before they started. It was to block out the sound of the machine.

'Have you got any Beatles?'

'We have a best of The Beatles called *Love*?'

He nodded, hitting his forehead on the brace.

'It's important not to move or we'll have to do it again and each scan is a thousand pounds.' He nodded, banging his head again. The table vibrated backwards, taking him into the heart of the MRI scanner; like a large tumble dryer. 'It makes strange noises but don't move your head. It'll take about twenty-five minutes.'

The Beatles sounded scratchy, like real beetles scuttling around a beer can. They'd been Jack's father's favourite group; his preferred album being *Revolver*. He hadn't thought about Jack Snr. for quite a while, and now here he was. The MRI scanner had turned into H.G. Wells's *Time Machine*. Jack was thirteen, wishing he could cry on his father's shoulder. But Jack Snr. was dead and hadn't died in any ordinary way either, blowing his head off with a shotgun on a country estate. The lace on one of his boots had come undone, investigators said, and he must've bent down to tie it, left the safety off, and boom! But that had been a clever conceit on his father's part because Jack Snr. had wanted to die. He had metastasised lung cancer and hadn't wanted to burden the family, nor compromise his life insurance. Jack Snr. went the way he was meant to go; by blowing his head off with a shotgun, just like one of his literary heroes, Ernest Hemingway.

The MRI machine started; a series of regular, medium-pitched thumps that sounded like minor guitar chords, then the drums of a thrash metal band. They blocked out the sound of The Beatles and the memory of Jack's father. He became mesmerised instead by the strange banging, visualising the convoluted canals of his brain, trying to keep as cool and as still as possible.

After the MRI, Jack found his own way back to the stroke ward. As he passed The Time Lord's bed, he heard him humming "The Great Pretender".

'It makes a right racket dunnit?' said Stan.

'I've got to have another one,' said David, 'and I'm claustrophobic.'

Jack's mobile glowed on the bedside table. Gerry texting: *You are kidding me, right...?*

Later that morning Jack went for a walkabout, trying to shake off the drumming of the MRI scanner and the image it had conjured of his father's face flying through the country air. He took in six bays, some all-male, others all-female. On his way back to bay three he heard sobbing in one of the bathrooms and noticed the door wasn't fully closed. His first instinct was to give the patient some privacy, to walk on by, but as he passed the door he saw through the crack, and the patient was David. He knocked on the door three times. When there was no reply, he slowly pushed it wide and saw David sitting on the floor beside the toilet bowl. 'Are you okay? Have you fallen? Do you need a nurse? Shall I pull the emergency cord?'

'No,' David said, wiping his eyes. His blue silk dressing gown had spread out like a puddle around him. 'No, it's just...just everything.' He tried to get up using a grip rail and Jack helped him to his feet. Jack noticed a grooming kit on a shelf under the mirror. 'Do you want me to put this back in for you?' Jack put an electric shaver, nail-clippers and aftershave into a bag and zipped it up. He put an arm around David's waist and helped him along the corridor and back to bed in very small steps.

After lunch, Dr. Richter and her team started their rounds and she made a beeline for Jack asking him to walk with her to the nurses' station two bays along. She sat him down in front of a laptop. The consultant clicked on some images, expanding one in particular. 'This is your brain. These are your eye sockets and that is where your nose is. And this area here,' she pointed to it, 'is the damage caused by the stroke; in the right hemisphere which accounts for your left-sided numbness. It formally confirms what we suspected.' She clicked another image and the brain started to revolve slowly, like an art installation at the Tate. 'It is well circumscribed. See the ovoid shape?'

'Looks like an egg.'

'It's larger than anticipated but not as big as others we see. In any case, it's not just the site of the stroke that matters but the degree of vascular damage. There are no additional lesions that might suggest an acute plaque of demyelination.'

'Which means..?'

'No MS.'

'You were looking for multiple sclerosis?'

'And the appearance is not typical of a tumour.'

'God. You were looking for a tumour?'

'You never know what you might find in a person's first MRI. In my opinion it is a stroke, and might even be historical. You see here? There's a giant perivascular space, or the site of an old infarct. It is possibly fluid-filled.'

Jack looked at her, bewildered.

'From your symptoms, which are sensory rather than motor, you may count yourself lucky. You work in the creative industry you said?' He nodded. 'I can say that the imagination and language centres have been unaffected. Three or four weeks complete rest and then you can resume work, but gradually I think.'

'What caused it?'

'There are many factors; vascular diseases, smoking, obesity, blood pressure, stress, genetics…many factors. A man your age and physical condition with no underlying health problems, I thought it was your heart. I suggest we investigate that further, but there is no stenosis or abnormality in your common carotid artery on either side, which is good.'

'So can I be discharged?'

'You will be able to go this afternoon.'

'And the numbness…will it go too?'

'Damage is damage. I tell you what I tell all my patients. Everything in moderation, keep a healthy lifestyle, reduce salt intake, and no stress. Okay, Mr. Mann. You may go back to your bay now, and good luck with your comedy tour.'

'Thank you,' he said, shaking her hand.

'You're not out of the woods,' she said. 'We'll send a letter in a few weeks regarding investigations of your heart. You'll need a Doppler scan.'

Dressed in his jeans and black t-shirt, Jack sat by the bed waiting for Alice's text message. Wilfred was asleep, but Stan and David were full of talk. Stan said it must be the fastest ever turnaround for a stroke victim in history. There was a trace of envy in his voice. David wished him all the best with his tour. He was sitting in a wheelchair waiting to be pushed down to the MRI. The Time Lord was cloaked in his usual conspicuous silence, eyes closed but radiating third-eye vision.

Alice's text came: *in car park outside old 1930s entrance.xxx*

Jack shook Stan's hand and then David's. He left Wilfred undisturbed and alone to his sleeping. Jack flirted with the idea of shaking the hand of the Time Lord but changed his mind at the last second. As he approached the corridor, he turned around, clicked his heels together, saluted, and said in his most commanding Alec Guinness *Bridge-Over-the-River-Kwai* voice: 'Good luck, men.'

He turned, and was about to depart, when he heard a loud hum from the Time Lord: *Yes, he's the great pretender.* Jack thought about ignoring it, but couldn't bear the injustice. He walked over and the old man's beady eyes stared up at him. 'You make a lousy patient, Mary Poppins,' said Jack. 'I sincerely hope you were a better doctor.' He held the Time Lord's stare, then he spotted the TV remote on the bedside drawer. He picked it up, crossed the bay and put it down on David's bed.

Jack turned away, only getting a few paces before he heard the Time Lord's retort: 'You'll be back!'

It was delivered with all the gravitas of Arnold Schwarzenegger in *The Terminator,* and those were the final words echoing around Jack's head as he hobbled along the labyrinthine corridors of the hospital, all the way down to Alice's car: *You'll be back!*

At the Bunker

It was five o'clock by the time Alice navigated her way through the city and onto the coast road. The first thing she did before driving back to the Bunker was park outside a fish and chip shop one street back from Tankerton seafront. Jack wanted to take in some fresh air after the stifling fug of the stroke ward, and he craved something with genuine flavour and heaps of salt. He limped to the seafront and sat on one of the benches that lined the grassy Slopes. Sailing boats sliced through the water, creamy waves cresting in their wake. Children skimmed pebbles across the surface and chased each other along the shore. The wind was up, taking heat out of the sun. It was about as pleasant as anywhere on Earth, and a million miles from hospital.

Alice arrived with the steaming booty. 'Not strictly the best food for someone who's just had a stroke,' she said, opening up the vinegary, grease-sodden paper. They ate chips greedily with their fingers, not saying much. Life was once again as simple as marvelling at the luminosity of green mushy peas beside golden batter and pure white cod, like the land meeting the sea.

The Bunker was exactly as Jack remembered it, except his view of it had changed. Two years seemed to have passed in two days, and for the first time he felt genuinely grateful for the tiny rented bungalow despite its many aesthetic failings. Everything worked, didn't it? It had a long garden for Pandora, hadn't it? More importantly, it wasn't the wing of a hospital.

Pandora barked at the door. When Jack opened it she did a figure of eight between his legs before pogoing as high as his chest. He knelt down and buried his face in her long fur, breathing in her unique, woollen smell. She wriggled and snuffled at his cheek in just the same way his first beloved collie Major Tom used to. He fed her leftover cod from the comfort of his leather armchair. Alice put his hospital wear into the washing machine, banishing all scents and traces of the stroke ward.

After a satisfying mug of tea, Jack walked around the garden as far as the railway track. Pandora followed him, sniffing the ground for foxes that came each night. She hopped up beside her master in the arbour, her beard wet and dripping from the water bowl. From here they watched seagulls flying to and from the rooftops of other bungalows. What did the seagulls know of Jack's trials and tribulations? They just went about their daily lives and rituals as surely as the tide. But then, he thought, what does anyone know about the trials and tribulations of a gull, except a gull?

Gerry called to discuss rearrangements for *Mad Infinitum* but Alice batted it back, saying Jack was sleeping. At last, he could finally rest his eyes, switch off, and sleep. He slept for five hours straight, waking at eleven o'clock at night. Alice was watching TV. Pandora was curled up on the sofa beside her. Jack's left-sided numbness was just the same (his foot more suitable for a seashore than a shoe, the crab it had become) but maybe, just maybe, with time these things would abate.

He took a call from San Francisco. Ernest (or Ernie as he preferred to be called) was Jack's older brother by four years, named by their father after Hemingway. Coincidentally, Ernie had been having his own health issues; a pounding, migraine-like headache that'd been going on for more than two weeks. He had gold standard private insurance and was going to have an MRI of his own. His MD had suggested a spinal tap to check the pressure. Ernie thought the coincidence of their illnesses remarkable, until Jack reminded him he'd actually had a stroke, not a migraine. They shared a few jokes. Ernie's humour wasn't the same as Jack's. It was literal and direct, and Jack guessed life might be like that for a real estate lawyer. Jack could weave a joke from a complex web of narratives using wicked wordplay, clever characterisation, insightful impressions and punchline after punchline, but nothing would make Ernie explode with laughter faster than a random fart in a lift full of strangers.

Ernie said he'd be flying over to the UK in a few weeks for their mum's birthday. He'd stay with Lauren, but planned to visit him in the Bunker too. 'At times of stress,' he said, 'blood brothers stick together.' They were brothers by blood, not blood brothers. During their childhood, and especially after their father died, Ernie had become the rock of the Manns, and although thousands of miles away beside the Pacific Ocean, Ernie was still the Commander. He was genuinely a Super Mann, as Lauren called him.

The next day, Jack telephoned Gerry. Between them they decided to cancel the first month of the tour. Gerry said the cancelled gigs would be rearranged for later in the year or in the spring. The most important thing was Jack's health.

Two days later, the numbness in Jack's left hand and foot changed to a new sensation of intense burning. Although it was hard to describe to Alice, who thought it might be a sign his body was mending itself, Jack likened the feeling to being burnt by steam from a boiling kettle, or the worst case of sunburn imaginable. For unknown reasons the pain was worse at night, interrupting sleep. The only way to soothe it was by wrapping his hand in a towel soaked in cold water, but relieving it this way increased the severity of the burning seconds later. If this was his body healing, he told Alice, he was in trouble.

Nonetheless, the Manns persisted. They survived, believing everything would pass in time. They visited Alice's parents and this helped take Jack's mind off his stroke. His in-laws Patricia and Alan, now in their eighties, had more ailments and illnesses than the patients of five surgeries put together. Arthritis, heart failure, prostate cancer, high blood pressure, low blood pressure, stroke, kidney failure, macular degeneration, the list went on. But Pat and Alan persisted. They muddled through. They'd converted an airing cupboard in the hall of their flat into a personalised pharmacy; floor-to-ceiling shelves weighted down with pills, lotions and potions. Jack had once made a joke on stage that come a nuclear holocaust, cockroaches would queue around the block to get antibiotics and painkillers from Pat and Alan.

To take Jack's mind off the recent past and to set it on a happier future, Alice took him to Seagull House. Scaffolding still surrounded it, but the new roof was on, shaped like a sail. Five men were whistling while they worked, listening to a loud radio. All of the spaces downstairs were re-wired. The copper central heating pipes had been fitted. The walls were still a mixture of brick and breezeblock, waiting for plasterboard. The window spaces were waiting for glass. Jack took a walk around the garden thinking of the strimming he'd done the week before Glyndebourne, and how it seemed to have set in motion his stroke. He thought about his old doctor in London who'd said he'd only excited his nerves. Thankfully, Alice had registered them both with a new GP at a local surgery.

It should have meant a fresh start, a new beginning for Jack and Alice Mann.

-PART TWO-

Life is short, art long, opportunity fleeting, experience perilous and decision difficult.

Hippocrates, 'Father of medicine', 5th Century BC

Carry On Kafka

Exactly one week after Glyndebourne, Alice drove Jack to the beach in Whitstable and they swam with Pandora. Unlike their previous neurotic collie, Pan wasn't afraid of the water, and it was fun standing in the sea up to their waists throwing a tennis ball for her. She paddled back and forth between them, chin up, nostrils flaring, puffing the briny water like a dolphin through a blow hole.

Jack first realised he'd lost all sensation from the waist down when one of Pandora's paws caught him in the midriff. An errant claw scratched the skin in a six-inch line, drawing an ellipsis of blood, but he barely felt it. Optimistically, he thought it was the coldness of the water or an aggravation of pre-existing numbness, but the pessimistic part of him feared the worst.

By early afternoon, Alice was thinking about what to have for lunch, calling out suggestions from the kitchen. Jack was in the bath examining his body and face. He knew where he'd be going and wanted to be ready. He sat on the edge of the bathtub, almost in tears, just as he'd done that afternoon before Glyndebourne. This time the numbness had spread up his right leg, right arm and across his torso, joining up with the left side. He couldn't feel the back of his head either. The glove effect he'd first experienced in the Glyndebourne auditorium now encased more than three-quarters of his body.

Alice drove at breakneck speed through the woods to A&E. This time there were no arguments with the receptionist. Jack was rushed straight past triage to "majors". He was assessed by a different doctor who took him through the same protocol and questions as before. This time Jack didn't crack a single joke. He lay on the trolley hooked up to machines and let the nurses get on with their work. With his recent history, he was told it was most likely another stroke or trans-ischemic attack, but they'd need a CT scan to confirm. A stroke nurse came. She assessed Jack with a degree of caution. There was a drug she could use that halted progression, but it had potentially life-threatening side effects. Ideally, the drug needed to be given to a patient within 4.5 hours of the onset of symptoms, and Jack was borderline. The nurse didn't think his symptoms were classic signs of stroke. He was, in her words, "too good" to inject. His heart was monitored, as was his blood pressure. These readings seemed "too good" also.

Another emergency was wheeled in and helped onto the bed beside Jack; a naked man in his late fifties, head close-shaved and coated in jammy blood. He'd had a seizure and fallen from his racing bicycle. He didn't know who he was, where he was, where he lived or how old he was. All he knew was his first name, Freddie. He'd fouled himself and the nurses had cut off his latex cycling gear to clean him up. He groaned incoherently. Having stabilised Freddie, nurses wandered in and out to stare at him through the gap in his curtain. Once, there was even a giggle exchanged between nurses. Jack and Alice realised what the fuss was about when the dividing screen was pulled right back. Freddie had an erection a pony might be proud of, and they too were shocked by the magnitude of the wagging truncheon.

In the cubicle on the other side of foot-long Freddie, an elderly woman had just gasped her last. Her two daughters were weeping, entering the first stages of denial. 'No!' they cried. 'No, Mum, don't go!' Denial turned to desperation as they called for her to come back from the far bank of the River Styx. Then their pleas turned into wailing like the chorus of some Greek tragedy.

Jack couldn't get his head around it: a throbbing instrument of procreation in one cubicle and the daughters of a dead mother in the other, pouring their souls into her chest. There was something monstrous about the extremes, as if the two theatrical masks of comedy and tragedy were melting, being forged into each other. Jack shut his eyes. He struggled to see how he could be splashing around one minute, treating Pan's brave adventure like a toddler's first swimming lesson, and then, a few hours later, lying in a bed bearing witness to such purgatory, drowning in a stranger's tears. Then again, he thought grimly, there's only one second, one letter between humorous and tumorous.

He was wheeled into a CT room and scanned. No one told him the results; not even Dr. Richter, who was again the clinical lead in A&E. He saw her white coat, stocky frame and flaming hair as she darted from corridor to cubicle to corridor, but she didn't seem to notice him waiting to be "moved upstairs". Once again, a porter pushed him along the winding arterial Main Street.

Ten minutes later he was on a stroke ward in a bed next to Freddie; bay one, near the nurses' station. It was the place Dr. Richter had told Jack he'd been lucky. Now, good fortune seemed to have run its course. He spent the long night listening to hushed conversations coming from the nurses. One of them gave him paracetomol, which had no effect on the pain. In the small hours, he unplugged himself and limped to the bathroom with a towel. He soaked it in cold water and wrapped it around his hand, returning to bed, cradling his pain like a baby. And miracles of miracles, he drifted off between the nurses' nightly visits, getting enough sleep to stay sane.

In the morning, just after breakfast, an old woman was wheeled onto the bay, her bed placed opposite Jack's. She was unconscious and covered with wires. 'She's in a coma,' a nurse told him. 'There's no room for the poor lady on the women-only bays.' The nurse left the screen wide open to keep a better eye on her patient, checking vitals every twenty minutes. With no working TV, Jack and Freddie watched the old girl compulsively as if she was the tragic character in a medical drama. They listened to her ragged breathing and the slow bleep of her monitor. They glanced at each other now and then, though neither spoke of the coma patient.

Unlike Stan and David, Freddie was not the talkative sort. Jack overheard occasional words exchanged between him and the doctors. Freddie still didn't know his last name, address or age. He'd gone out cycling without any ID or mobile phone. Foot-long Freddie remained a mystery man with a badly kept secret the nurses joked about. The only other thing definitely known about him was that his seizure had caused lasting cognitive damage. He could swallow and process food, could shuffle to the shower unaided, but he couldn't process verbal information. Asking him to spell "milk" was like asking a Sat Nav for the coordinates to Mars.

Dr. Richter appeared on the bay mid-morning. Jack's bed was the last in a line, closest to the nurses' hub, and he saw the consultant swish down the walkway without turning her head. Jack heard her German accent as she talked to the nurses about other patients and the day's duties. He strained to hear if his name got mentioned. On her way back he thought she might nod in recognition but she glanced the other way, pretending to look out of the window.

Not long after her departure, a tall, straight-backed man with a long neck and full grey beard strode down the corridor. Not so much strode, thought Jack, as glided purposefully. The nurses went into a mad flutter, straightening and smoothing their uniforms. Junior doctors flooded from an adjoining staffroom, standing to attention.

This towering man was the God of consultants; someone commanding respect if not fear among staff. He leaned on the counter of the hub discussing something with the assembled, and Jack noticed a small black bag in his hand. Locked in deep conversation with one of the doctors, the consultant turned around and looked in Jack's direction, nodding. He stroked his beard, thinking, looking over at Jack again, then at the floor, then at the doctor, listening intensely. 'Right,' he said, having heard quite enough and tapping the counter, 'shall we get on with it? I'll show you how this is done properly.'

The consultant strode over to Jack's bed. Five junior doctors gathered around him. 'Hello, my name's Mr. Swan. Senior neurological consultant.' He shook Jack's hand. 'Can I call you Jack?' His eyes were the darkest brown, so dark it was hard distinguishing iris from pupil. They looked like the penny eyes of Officer Dibble from *Top Cat*. 'I'm here to ask a few questions and establish a few things,' he said. Jack's heart started to race. 'Please, can you tell me in your own words what's been happening, when the symptoms started et cetera.'

At last, he thought, *someone who might know what's really going on*. Jack told him everything from the very beginning and Mr. Swan was patient, listening, nodding at his colleagues.

When Jack's story came to its natural end the consultant said, 'I'm afraid you might be on the stroke ward under false pretenses. I'm sorry about that, Jack. You haven't had a stroke and didn't have one last week either.' Mr. Swan placed his bag on the bed. His hands were not large but the fingers were long, the nails short and clean. 'You're suffering from neuritis.' Seeing Jack's confusion, he added, 'Inflammation of the nervous system. And if it's okay with you I'd like to undertake a short physical examination. Is it alright for my colleagues to stay and see this? They might learn something.' He winked. 'That's it. Good fellow.' He pulled the screen half across, blocking Freddie out.

Mr. Swan unzipped his bag and took out metal instruments. He lined them up on the bed. Some of them were pointed, others rounded, including a small gavel. His colleagues, four women and a man, jockeyed for position at the foot of the bed watching closely as he tapped Jack's knees and elbows. 'You see?' he said, and they nodded. He scraped a sharp instrument down the soles of Jack's feet, saying, 'See that reflex?' They nodded. He lifted Jack's t-shirt and guided the point over his stomach, and then his arms and back. He turned to his colleagues and they nodded as if they were all on the same page. And then Mr. Swan asked if Jack would be kind enough to slip his pyjamas and boxers down to his knees. Noticing hesitation, perhaps acknowledging that his patient was lying prone before a group of mostly female strangers, Mr. Swan leaned across, whispering in his ear: 'We'll let the hounds see the hare, what?'

For a split second, Jack didn't know what the consultant had meant, but understood by the smile immersed in Mr. Swan's beard. It was a sad attempt at banter, designed to put the patient at ease before the public unveiling of his genitals. It had the opposite effect. As Jack slowly drew his garments down to his pallid knees he realised his sleeping penis had the overall appearance of a mouse he'd once found asleep inside a wellington boot in his garden shed, curled up sweetly in its nest of straw.

Mr. Swan prodded and scraped his cold instruments along Jack's inner thighs from testicles to knees, remarking with a raised eyebrow on the reflexes and responses. 'Did you see that?' he said to one doctor in particular. She nodded. Jack recognised her as the young woman from Sri Lanka who'd given him a leaflet from the Stroke Foundation. She had long dark hair and her name badge said *Dr. De Silava.*

'Okay, thanks, Jack,' the consultant said, putting his equipment back into his bag and zipping up. 'We'll get to the bottom of this mystery. Don't worry about that. You may get dressed now.' Mr. Swan turned to Dr. De Silava. 'I want an LP, VEP, SSEP and an MRI.'

'Yes, Mr. Swan,' she said, writing these down on a notepad, 'but the patient's already had an MRI.'

'I know. I want one of the spine as well as the neck and head. The VEP and SSEPs need booking weeks ahead, but get the LP and MRI as soon as possible. Tell them Mr. Swan insists.' The consultant pulled the screen back, revealing Freddie who was still staring ahead at the coma patient's monitor.

Jack told Mr. Swan about the burning pain which was keeping him awake at night. The towering consultant turned to his colleagues, some of whom were clearly in training, and said: 'Anyone? What's good for neuropathic pain?'

'Gabapentin,' one trainee said.

'Lyrica?' said Dr. De Silava.

The consultant shook his head. 'Pregabalin is an expensive first line of pain protocol. C'mon…anyone? Pain is worse at night. Anyone heard of amitriptyline?'

'The old anti-depressant?' said De Silava.

'We don't use it for depression anymore but it works wonders on polyneuropathy, and more importantly it's cheap as chips. Ten milligrams to start with, treat empirically up to sixty if necessary or until the pain is bearable.'

'Thank you,' Jack said.

Mr Swan glided out of bay one.

'What a relief,' said Jack. 'Just inflammation.'

'Yes,' said Dr. De Silava. 'Mr. Swan's excellent with neurological mysteries. He's one of the best consultants in England. You're lucky he's here. He's off to the Bahamas tomorrow.' She walked away before Jack had time to ask what VEP, SSEP and LP were.

He texted Alice: *Yippee! Not a stroke, chickpea! Inflammation. More tests. xxx*

Lifted by Mr. Swan's diagnosis, Jack limped down the corridor to bay three to say hello to David and Stan. Of course, he'd have to suffer the presence of the Time Lord and accept that he'd been right all along. *After all, Time Lords see the future.* As he turned the corner it was obvious everyone had been replaced by new stroke victims. In fact, it was now a women-only bay. He started making his way back to bed, imagining the old Time Lord had run out of regenerations and was dead and buried on Gallifrey, David was in a hospice receiving palliative care, Wilf was in a nursing home and Stan had finally made it "ome".

He passed bay two, glancing in out of interest, and picked out the Time Lord's miserable old visage. At first, he was tempted to ignore him, but realised something and walked in. 'Is this chair taken?' he said, and the old man made no response, turning his eyes away. Jack sat down noticing the name *Dr. Skelton* written on the board above the doctor's head. Still a patient without a first name, but no longer a Time Lord; far more mortal and just one letter away from skeleton. 'I have to give it to you. You were right. I'm back.'

Dr. Skelton rolled his eyes, placing a book down on his sheets: *No Laughing Matter*, by Joseph Heller. 'What…what have you been diagnosed with this time?' he said. 'Leopard…leprosy?'

Jack talked about Mr. Swan's conclusion of nerve inflammation. Skelton was keen to hear more. Jack told him about the ascending numbness on one side, and then the other.

'Mr. Swan is an egg…damn this stroke…an *excellent* remedial…*medical* man,' Dr. Skelton said, thumping the bed in frustration. He was thinking the correct words but they slipped through the fingers of his mind like wet bars of soap, translated en route into things that were similar in sound but incorrect in sense. He tried to explain that he'd worked at the hospital for forty years and still remembered the first time he met Mr. Swan some twenty years ago.

'Came from King's Lynn. No damn it! *King's* in London. Ambitious manner. *Man*. Had a rod complex. *God* complex. An eye for the ladies. Good rapper...damn this thing! Good *rapport* with patients. Rarely puts a wrong foot in diagnosis.'

'So, if not a stroke...what?'

Dr. Skelton shrugged one shoulder and tapped his Heller book. 'Gillian Barry syndrome? G...B...S? Look happened...what happened to Joseph Helicopter...*Heller*. The mind,' he said, grabbing Jack with his good hand, 'is a mirror ball... oh God...*miracle*. A miracle-worker. It can heal toes,' he shook his head and thumped his bed. 'It can heal, *if you keep it on its toes*.'

'I hope so,' said Jack. 'Before I go, do you know what SSEPs and VEPs are?'

'Evoked potentials,' said Skelton. 'They test the curry...*currents*, electrical currents in the brain and the botty...the *body*. S is for sensuous...sweet Jesus...S is for *sensory*, V is for visceral...*visual*.'

'So what's an L potential?'

'A what?' he said.

'An L potential?'

His whole expression changed. 'Not potential. Punch...*puncture*. Lumbar puncture.   Who's doing it? Swan? No, wouldn't be a consultana. He'd use a junior. Don't worry, the neuroses...*nurses*, they know what they're doing.'

As Jack was leaving, the Time Lord called out: 'Of course, there's a chance of total paralysis when a six inch nail...*needle* is stuck in your spyhole...*spinal cord*, but you're in good Hansard...*hands...hands*.' He crumpled again on his bed, exhausted from the effort of mining for words.

When Jack got back to his bay there was a new patient beside the coma lady; an irritable-looking potbellied man in his fifties. Jack said hello and the man replied with a cursory nod.

'Where have you been?' said Dr. De Silava, fussing around him. 'There's a chance of an MRI slot. Can you walk or do you need a wheelchair?'

'I don't think I can walk that far,' he said.

A nurse wheeled him to the scanner room. This time he looked down a list of music and chose *Revolver*. He asked the radiographer via the headphones why there was so much Beatles on the list. She said patients brought music in. Someone must have had a Beatles obsession.

When the bed rolled into the machine and the music started he asked if it could be turned up. He listened and heard about lonely people, and others who lived in a dream, and others who died in church, and understood that no one was saved.

Jack started to fidget. The chamber was turning into a coffin, not the time machine it had been the first time around. He listened to the music and the words, thinking he might only be sleeping. He imagined he might be a dead old man. This was about as close as he could get to being buried alive. He wanted his love to be there. He knew what it was like to be dead. Who put all these things in his head?

Forcing his head to stay still had the opposite effect, tensing his neck muscles, causing his skull to vibrate side to side. The radiographer said: 'Please, Mr. Mann, relax. Focus on the music. We're already a quarter the way through the procedure.'

The prospect of staying locked in the head brace and machine for just one more minute, let alone another thirty, made his heart race and the small of his back sweat. He tapped a finger along to the beat. 'Mr. Mann, be still, please.' His neck muscles tightened again and he was about to scream: Let me out! Stop it now!

The music became a jumble, the words swimming in his head. And in the melee he found the mantra he thought he'd lost for good: *This is nothing*. His father had taught him about mantras on his first visit to the dentist. He was kicking and screaming and Jack Snr. took him outside to calm him down. His father said: 'Whenever you're in a fix, kid, and you see no way out, say the mantra over and over like a chant. You'll be okay. You can face any music.' *This is nothing. This is nothing. This is nothing.* 'And what's your mantra, Dad?' Jack had asked. 'Now that would be tellin'. You lose the power of your "Manntra" if you reveal it. It's yours, no one else's, kid.' *This is nothing. This is nothing. This is nothing.* Attending his father's funeral at the age of fourteen, sitting between his big brother and little sister watching the velvet curtain close around the coffin, listening to the Beatles' "Here Comes the Sun", *this is nothing, this is nothing, this is nothing, this is nothing, this is nothing.* When it had been everything.

Jack focused on the large stone Buddha in his mind. He'd asked his mother for the statue when she decided to sell their old home in Muswell Hill. There'd been a family feud over that statue. Ernie didn't care. He was already living in America. Transporting it would cost thousands. Transporting it just ten miles would cost more than its material worth. But its true value was intrinsic and personal. Lauren had fought Jack passionately over the Buddha. It had been Jack Snr.'s prized possession. It was carved from solid limestone and stood more than three feet tall; or should that be sat? His legs were folded beneath him, eyes closed, right hand raised and facing outwards like a shield. The left hand rested on his lap, palm up. His father told him this was a "Protection Buddha" or "Overcoming Fear Buddha". Buddha had sat prominently in one corner of their garden and Jack used to run around it singing nursery rhymes. Later, at secondary school age, he'd kick a ball back and forth from the Buddha's belly. In the end, Jack had to pay Lauren £500 for it, which she needed to buy a clapped out VW Beatle. *This is nothing. This is nothing. This is nothing.* Now the Buddha was sitting near a railway line in the corner of the garden of the Bunker near the sea, in an east-facing position, just as it had been all those years ago in London.

Jack focused on the image of this statue now, using his secret mantra and consciously slowing each breath. He listened to the music and told himself to relax. It wasn't dying. It was be-ing. It was know-ing. It was believ-ing. It was the end of the beginning.

The scanner stopped. *Revolver* finished. The table vibrated out of the machine and the radiographer said, 'Well done, kid. You made it through.' She didn't say this, of course. Jack only imagined the words, and that was good enough for him.

Alice texted a dozen times during the day, sending her love and asking when the lumbar puncture was going to be done. The truth was, no one knew. Having researched the subject online, Alice reassured Jack the procedure was quite simple, but if he could text her when he knew the exact time she'd leave work and be with him. Ernie texted from America: *Are u becoming addicted to bed baths, Jack? Take care, bro. Thinking of you, will see you soon. Love, E*

That night on bay one, the coma patient died. Jack was alerted by the alarms. When nobody responded, he'd called out and pressed his buzzer. Two nurses had rushed in and examined the old lady. One of the nurses walked past Jack's bed to make a telephone call. The old girl was barely alive by the time the doctor arrived. Just before she died, the nurses attempted to move her out of the bay to a more private space, one of them saying, 'I won't have a lady patient dying on a ward full of men.' She flat-lined in the centre of the bay instead, at the foot of Jack's bed. He saw her skeletal remains, the closed and sunken eyes of a corpse, her toothless mouth wide open. He bore witness to her lonely demise, lungs with no breath, mouth with no words left, hands with no hands to hold, no family or friends to mourn her. She died with nothing and no one to cling to; no one to weep and wail over her passing. No chorus from a Greek tragedy. As she was wheeled out of the bay, Jack feared for his future, seeking out and finding his own perfect loneliness in the shadow that fed the dark folds of his curtain. He struggled to sleep, a towel soaked in water wrapped around his left hand. When he eventually drifted off, well after 2 a.m., his dreams were warped and meaningless, fueled by amitriptyline and anxiety. It went without saying, just like any other mortal, Jack was statistically far more likely to die in a hospital bed than in any other bed, and he prayed to the Buddha in his mind for strength, protection and an early discharge.

The next morning Dr. De Silava told Jack his lumbar puncture would be undertaken in a few hours and she got him to sign a form. He texted Alice: *Gulp! LP today! Xx* . She texted back: *Okay, hon. Let me know when they're taking you down to neurology. Xxx*

An hour later, the telephone on the table near his bed rang out. A nurse answered it and Jack heard every word. 'Yes, this is the stroke ward,' the nurse said. She listened and nodded a few times, writing information down on a scrap of paper. 'Me neither,' she said, laughing.

'We don't normally do LPs up here.' Jack's ears pricked. 'Okay, so what else do we need? Uh-huh, uh-huh. Okay, how many needles? Uh-huh. And *the big one*, how *big* must it be? How many inches?' She wrote it down and Jack's heart started to thump. 'Uh-huh, uh-huh. And how many vials? Uh-huh.' She replaced the receiver and returned to the nurses' station.

Jack's hands were clammy. He saw Dr. De Silava passing and asked when the LP would be done. She still wasn't sure. 'And when are they taking me down to neurology?'

'They're chock-a-block in neurology,' she said. 'We'll be doing it up here. It's not complicated. I've done lots, and supervised even more.'

Fifteen minutes later, a large man wearing a doctor's coat arrived at the foot of Jack's bed, pulling a trolley. He smiled, Jack thought a little nervously. With enormous hands he picked something up from the trolley; a needle in sealed plastic. Trying to remove the needle, he fumbled and dropped it onto the floor. He picked it up, replaced it on the trolley, still smiling. He picked up another sealed needle. There was a slight tremor in his hands.

'Are you from neurology?' asked Jack, already sweating in his t-shirt and pyjama bottoms. The man shook his head, continuing to take things out of packets, placing them neatly beside each other on the trolley. He resisted eye contact. 'You're not doing the lumbar...are you?'

The man nodded, mumbling, 'Sorry.'

Dr. De Silava introduced him as Dr. Emba, a doctor in training. 'You know what to do now, Dr. Emba. Just as we discussed, count down the vertebrae to L2 or L3, find the correct place, numb the site, wait a while, and then insert the needle, gently but surely.' She turned to Jack. 'Dr. Emba has done this before, haven't you, Dr. Emba?'

The trainee doctor nodded.

'Mr. Mann, if you can please remove your t-shirt,' De Silava said, 'and pull your pyjamas down over your hips.' She dragged the screen around the bed and stood to one side, watching the trainee doctor. 'And if you can assume the foetal position, Mr. Mann. That's it. Lie on your side and pull both of your knees up to your chest. Good. Squash a pillow between your arms and legs if you like. That's it. Try to relax, Mr. Mann. You might feel some discomfort, but not any pain. ' She patted him on the arm. 'Look at me and don't think about what's happening on the other side of you.'

Jack's mental universe was now entirely focused on what was happening behind his back. He felt the cold fingers and thumbs of the trainee doctor pressing down on his spine top to bottom, and he heard Dr. Emba whispering to himself, counting the vertebrae in Nigerian, like a chant. He felt something cold dabbed onto his lower back, smelling bromide.

'Okay, you'll feel some small stings,' said Dr. De Silava, looking over the top of Jack's exposed hip. 'That's the anaesthetic.' Jack felt three in quick succession. *This is nothing*, he thought. *This is nothing. This is nothing.*

The Sri Lankan doctor shook her head. 'Count once more to be sure, Dr. Emba, before inserting the needle.' Jack felt the fingers again, heard the Nigerian numbers, and his back tensed into a coiled spring. *This is nothing. This is nothing.* He was in the flush of a fight or flight adrenalin rush. The counting went on for what seemed like forever. There came a pause, and then Jack felt the needle make a cold entry into his back, changing the pressure in his spine and what seemed like his stomach too. He groaned. It was as if someone was trying to pop a balloon with a spoon, and that balloon was Jack's spinal column. *This is nothing. This is nothing. This is nothing.* 'Are you all the way in, Dr. Emba?'

'Jesus Christ!' A bolt of lightning flashed down Jack's leg, fanning from groin to toe, streaking like electricity through every nerve fibre, burning like hellfire.

'Tttt, you've hit a nerve,' Dr. De Silava said, shaking her head.

The needle was withdrawn. Jack felt a slow ache with the pressure change as if his stomach and leg were being sucked through a keyhole in his back. He mopped his brow with the edge of the pillow, aware that every pore in his body was perspiring. He repeated his mantra: *this is nothing, this is nothing, this is nothing.* When it failed to have any calming effect, and all he could think of was what the Time Lord had said about a small chance of complete paralysis, he reverted to images of his stone Buddha; Protective Buddha or Overcoming Fear Buddha. He closed his eyes and imagined Pandora running around it in the garden of the Bunker. He saw seagulls flying blissfully high above her head. But now the gulls were looking down on a hospital bed; a bed with Jack lying on it curled up in the foetal position, and another man was crouched behind him with a six foot needle quivering in his hand.

'Count along the spine again,' De Silava said, and Emba did as he was told. When he took too long about it, she asked rhetorically: 'How many lumbars did you say you've done before?' This was to bolster the confidence of a junior doctor in the last year of training; someone who'd already told her he was familiar with the procedure and protocol, but it was ticker-tape news to Jack.

'Six lumbars,' Dr. Emba said.

'Good,' she said, nodding reassuringly at Jack. 'Six you see, Mr. Mann.'

'But,' said the trainee, 'all six were on cadavers.'

In the shattering silence that followed, Jack looked the Sri Lankan in the eye with piercing horror. Dr. De Silava glared at the Nigerian trainee in disbelief. Dr. Emba stared at the English patient's back as if it was a Rubik's cube.

With relief Jack watched Dr. De Silava step around the bed. She asked Dr. Emba where he'd inserted the needle. She counted the vertebrae herself with warm fingertips. 'This should be easy,' she whispered. 'There isn't much fat. You can feel the vertebrae. Now try again.' She returned to Jack's side of the bed, and once again he felt the uncomfortable pressure change, and clutched his pillow. *This is nothing. This is nothing. This is nothing.*

A fork of lightning shot down Jack's other leg. 'Jesus Christ!' he screamed, so loud it bounced off the walls. His ears were ringing. He was close to vomiting. 'Jesus, help me,' he groaned. 'God.'

'You've overcompensated,' De Silava said to the trainee. 'You moved too far to the right. Remove it carefully and we'll give it one more go. Third time lucky, hey, Mr. Mann?'

'I'm not a dartboard! I'm a human being!'

'We have to do this. Mr. Swan's orders.'

'Oh my God,' said Jack, as the needle came out again, the pressure changing again. 'Oh my God,' he said when it punctured his skin a third time.

'In,' said Emba, sighing.

'And are you getting any cerebrospinal fluid?'

He nodded.

'Good. So, now collect it in a vial.' When the trainee hesitated, De Silava paced around the bed, picked a vial from the trolley and collected the fluid herself. 'You're coming out very slow,' she complained to Jack. 'We don't need too much though, Dr. Emba. Too much can affect the meninges, too little and we'll have to do this all again. No visible blood. Good.'

Jack stayed still on the bed, curled in the foetal position, bed sheets soaked. After fifteen minutes, he felt the pressure changing as the needle came out, and he groaned. Dr. Emba taped a small bandage to the puncture site.

'You can straighten up now, Mr. Mann,' said De Silava. She pulled the curtain back and issued a set of instructions to Emba regarding the sample as he pushed the trolley away. Jack noticed an exclamation mark of sweat on the back of his white coat.

When De Silava had gone, Jack lay still in a barren psychological wilderness. Before the lumbar puncture he'd have said physical torture was a thing that happened to prisoners of war or innocent victims of totalitarian regimes. But lying there, traumatised, he understood it could happen to anyone, anywhere, any time. He looked up at the ceiling and then around the bay as if for help or counsel. Freddie glanced over, saying nothing. The pot-bellied stranger opposite pretended to read a magazine.

A woman appeared at the side of Jack's bed. At first, he thought she was imagined; a vision brought on by trauma. If so, she was quite an ordinary illusion: sensible shoes, plaid skirt and black shirt. Quite ordinary, except for the white dog collar. She was middle-aged with a round, kind face and a long straight fringe. Her oversized brown spectacles made the top half of her face appear wider than the bottom half, like Velma in *Scooby Doo*. 'Hello,' she said. 'May I join you?'

Without thinking, Jack nodded, and the woman sat down. 'I heard you calling out for Jesus,' she said. The patient across the bay ruffled his magazine. 'I'm a chaplain from the cathedral. I visit patients in hospital once a week,' she said. 'Sometimes it's good to talk. What are you in hospital for, if you don't mind me asking?'

'Inflammation of the central nervous system, cause unknown.'

'And what happened to you just now? We heard you two bays down.'

'I don't even have words to describe it, except Nazi experiment.'

'Do you have any religious beliefs?' she asked. The man opposite put his magazine down and glowered.

'More spiritual than religious. More disorganised than organised.'

'But you believe in God?'

'Take your bible-bashing somewheres else,' the man shouted across the bay.

The chaplain ignored him.

'I want to believe in God,' said Jack ,'but he abandons me at critical moments, like when I lost most of my savings, then I lost my son Hunter.'

The chaplain placed a hand on his, squeezing, and he thought he'd burst into tears. He turned his face away, not wanting to be seen doing it. The chaplain understood and sat there quietly for a minute or two, holding his hand. 'Do you want me to say The Lord's Prayer? We could say it together if you like?'

'Take your bible and stick it!' the man yelled across the room. 'We don't need medieval witchcraft! Nurse! Nurse! Get this charlatan off my bay!'

He reminded Jack of the worst kind of heckler who sits close to the stage waiting for an opportunity to be funnier or louder than the stand-up. Jack glared across the room. 'Hey, mate. This is a private conversation. You heard of freedom of speech?' The man huffed, picked up his magazine and pretended to read again.

'Thank you,' the chaplain said.

'I might not believe in a particular God but would be grateful for any prayers right now.'

'That's fine. I'll recite and you can listen.'

'Here we go,' the man grumbled behind his pages. 'Hocus fucking pocus.'

'Our Father who art in Heaven...'

Jack listened in wonder, or stupor, or astonishment, and his eyes welled up, almost spilling. After the prayer was complete and the chaplain bade him good luck and farewell, he thought to himself: *What are the chances? During the worst agony of my life I call out for Jesus Christ, and when the torture is over one of God's representatives on Earth comes to console me; a bit after the event, but better late than never.* He wondered if this could be the theme of a comedy sketch for radio, or a stage routine, but it was all too serious for these. This chaplain, this dowdy angel, this Velma in plaid who owed him nothing and came from nowhere, had offered comfort and solace, not expecting anything in return. *If I have faith,* he thought, *I might not be alone in my darkest hour.*

Dr. De Silava returned. The mere sight of her had Jack thinking of angels of death, like Mengele. He was gasping for water and had the inkling of a headache. There was no water in the glass on his bedside table. Dr. Silava sat down for a chat as if they'd bonded during a spinal rite of passage. She said how she couldn't wait to finish her practical year at the hospital and fly back to her home in Sri Lanka. She was aiming to help the poorest people around her village. They had very little food and disease was rife. 'You might think the lumbar was bad, Mr. Mann, but let me tell you it is nothing in comparison to my native Sri Lankans. No state health system. Only the richest afford health care. You're privileged to receive free treatment. It would never happen in my village, or even the nearest town.' She got up to go.

'I'm thirsty, but I can't get anyone's attention.'

'I'll ask a nurse,' she said, and walked away.

He texted Alice: *LP done. I'm still shaking. xx*

Alice arrived forty-five minutes later, having cancelled a meeting. She was wearing her black trouser suit and looked like she meant business. She raced over to Jack, shocked by the exhausted heap she found on the bed. He asked for water and she gave him a small bottle from her handbag. She looked around the bay for a nurse, but they all seemed to be doing things at the station. She was angry no one had thought to give him any water after a lumbar puncture, furious that his sheets and pillows were soaking. She asked him why he hadn't phoned or texted and he told her the LP had been done on the stroke ward, and if he ever had to go through it again he'd throw himself out of the nearest window. 'Here?' she said. 'Not in neurology? Who did it?' He told her about the trainee, the procedure, and how he'd been terrified of being paralysed. 'Oh, Jack, you shouldn't have let them do it.' He told her he'd signed something and the Sri Lankan doctor said he should feel privileged to have such a procedure done for free. 'What's her name?' Alice said, and marched over to the nurses' station. Jack watched from a distance, a helpless spectator.

At first, Alice spoke calmly to a nurse. Dr. De Silava was called from the staffroom. She trudged out, tired-eyed, with Emba at her side. He appeared horrified when he discovered who Alice was. She asked them to explain why the LP had been done on the ward and listened to their explanation. She folded her arms, eyes shining like steel, mouth set firm.

Dr. De Silava showed Alice the consent form, pointing to Jack's signature. Alice's voice ratcheted. 'He didn't know what this form was. He's never had an LP before. Do you always use these forms?' De Silava rolled exhausted eyes. 'Judging by your reaction, no. This was an opportunity for you and your trainee to tick a few boxes.'

Dr. De Silava shook her head. 'It's clearly stated on the form, Mrs. Mann.'

'He was too frightened to read it, let alone have a lumbar on a ward that doesn't routinely do them.' She glared at Dr. Emba. 'It should have been done on a neurology ward by a specialist. My God.'

'You're overreacting,' said Dr. De Silava. 'There was a minor complication but we retrieved the sample and it wasn't contaminated. Doctors have to train sometime, somewhere.'

Alice unlocked her arms and wagged a finger. 'We put our faith in you. What did you do?' She pointed at Jack. 'You put my husband through hell. His clothes and sheets are soaked. Then you leave him without water. A patient must drink a litre after a lumbar because of pressure changes in the brain. If my husband suffers any ill-effects from your farce, so much as a mild headache, I'm coming back. Do you hear me? In fact,' she said, 'you'll be hearing from my solicitor.' Not that she had one.

She made to turn when a comment rose out from a knuckle of nurses: 'Your husband should experience genuine pain, love, like childbirth.'

'Who said that?' said Alice sharply. No one replied. 'Whoever it was, they're ignorant.' Her face was thunderous. 'They don't know that we have no children because of a hysterectomy, and before that I had two miscarriages. Then I lost a son just hours after birth. They should know pregnancy is usually a choice, not an illness.' She looked at Dr. De Silava. 'And as far as I know, neither is pregnancy misdiagnosed twice as a stroke!' She moved her eyes back to the nurses, one of whom was reddening on the neck. 'When a pregnant woman screams out for Jesus Christ she ends up with a little miracle in her arms, not a head full of unanswered questions as to why she can't feel three-quarters of her body.' She pointed at Jack again. 'His mother campaigned in *support* of the NHS. At the age of 72 she lobbied her MP over the reduction of midwives. And he...' still pointing at Jack '...he climbed Kilimanjaro for Age Concern and does charity gigs to raise awareness about cuts in public services. To support people like *you*!'

She turned to face Dr. De Silava. 'I've heard you've been giving my husband a lecture on how lucky he is to have the NHS?' Jack dragged a hand down his face. 'Well, let me provide a footnote to your lecture; a footnote the size of Godzilla. The NHS wasn't a gift from God. It was created more than 70 years ago by socialists for democratic, philanthropic reasons. And for more than 50 years my parents, Jack's parents and everyone else's parents have paid for it in tax and national insurance contributions. Now, if you can kindly process Jack's discharge notes, I'm taking my husband out of here.'

'Of course,' said Dr. De Silava. 'But please accept an apology. It's been so busy. We are short-staffed. Dr. Emba and I have been working 24 hours without a break. I am genuinely sorry.'

In the car on the way back to the Bunker, conversation was slow to materialise. Jack guessed it had been the digging up of sacred ground;

the rekindling of terrible memories: the death of Hunter, followed by Alice's hysterectomy. He remembered visiting her in hospital in Chelsea the afternoon after that surgery. It was a Saturday and he'd decided to go smart, wearing his best linen suit. He'd brought flowers from a proper florist, the biggest and boldest he could find. Alice was woozy, semi-hallucinating on morphine, telling the nurses how her husband was a useless loveable lump, and then she threw up over his chest, her half-digested breakfast hanging from his lapels. But a suit can be dry-cleaned as if nothing has happened. Alice's reproductive organs could not. The surgeon had cut out ovarian cysts the size of pomegranates, thankfully benign. He'd taken the extra precaution of removing her Fallopian tubes and uterus too.

'Thanks for rescuing me, Alice.'

'I don't know how they get away with it,' she said.

'Are you really going to complain?'

'No. That doctor was dead on her feet. It's not her fault, is it? I shouldn't have said those things.'

'Thanks for saying what you did about Mum.'

'It all just came out.'

'I know,' he said, smiling. 'Came out like a footnote the size of Godzilla.'

The Seagulls

There was an unexpected visitor waiting for them outside the Bunker. Gerry's giant frame and gleaming bald head gave him away from a distance, and Alice panicked about the messy state of the bungalow. He was standing beside his Jag smoking a cigarillo. 'I had your post code, but not the number. All these bungalows look the same.'

'How long have you been here?' said Alice. Pandora heard her voice and started barking behind the front door. Jack hauled himself out of his seat and Gerry eyed the slow movement.

'Let's go in,' said Jack, fumbling with the house keys.

Pandora leapt up at Gerry, weaved herself around Jack's legs before sitting down in front of Alice pleading with her nutty eyes for a walk. 'You go through,' said Alice. 'I'll take Pan along the Slopes. She's been stuck in all day. Crack open a bottle, Jack!' she shouted above the noise of the barking. 'I know it's not six o'clock yet, but you deserve it!'

Gerry and Jack made their way through the dark hallway into the kitchen; a much brighter room with a view over the garden. They heard the front door bang and sat down at the farmhouse table. Jack filled Gerry in on what had happened over the past two days. He was very sorry to hear it and was obviously worried about the tour as well. Jack retold the ordeal of the lumbar puncture. As that story unfolded, Gerry started to fidget. He looked grey around the gills and his moustache seemed to droop. 'Alice is a long time,' he said. Jack told him that the feeling of the needle going into his spinal cord was like trying to pop a balloon with a spoon, and that the pain was like being shredded by lightning. At that point, Gerry said, 'Gosh, it's damned hot in here. Do you mind if I go outside for a smoke?' As he stood up he lost his footing, his chair screeching across the tiles. He ran into the garden, and Jack followed.

Gerry was bent double, head down, hands on knees, puffing his cheeks that were whiter than shells. 'I'm sorry,' he said, pulling himself up straight. 'I've never been good with needles, even in secondhand stories.'

'Same goes for Dr. Emba. When he hit my spinal nerve the second time -'

'Jack, Jack, I get the picture. Change the channel.' A train rattled past at the end of the garden and they both looked at it. 'You poor sod,' said Gerry, shaking his head.

'I'm going to drown my sorrows. You've already had two glasses, you can't drive, do you want to stay over?'

'Well…I could, but only if you promise not to mention another damn needle.'

'About *Mad Infinitum*,' said Jack, as they returned indoors. 'My symptoms are bad. If anything, they're getting worse.' He flexed his left hand. 'Maybe we should cancel the first half of the tour?'

'It's supposed to start in less than a fortnight, Jack. You need to find out what's wrong. This is serious. You don't have time to fanny about on stages. The comeback is cancelled. I mean *postponed*.'

Dejection was etched on Jack's face, eyes cast down to the ground. Initially, he'd been annoyed by the tag "Comeback Tour", but in hospital he'd realised it would've been a comeback. He hadn't performed live or made appearances on radio or TV for nearly seven years. It had all started with the death of Hunter, then Alice's operation and the psychological fallout. He had to be there for her, hadn't he? And somehow this turned into a year and then two, and then three, and then four. He gave up the circuit and made do with freelance teaching at university and a few commercial voice-overs. Gone too long and you're forgotten.

Seeing the resigned look Gerry clapped an arm around Jack's shoulders. 'It's not the end of the world. We'll postpone until spring. By then you'll be better and everything will work out fine.'

'I can't thank you enough, Gerry. You didn't have to drive all the way over here.'

'That's true. I could have hired a helicopter, or a limousine, or jet-skied around the coast.'

Jack laughed. 'A time machine would have been faster, and I know a good Time Lord.'

Alice returned from the seafront. She'd assumed Gerry would stay for dinner but there was nothing fresh to cook at the bungalow so she'd come home with takeaway chicken tikka, lamb Rogan josh, three portions of special rice and vegetable naan bread. Hearing the news that Gerry was actually staying overnight, she panicked. The Bunker had only two bedrooms and the second was full to the rafters with boxes waiting to be moved to Seagull House. No room to swing a mouse, let alone the six-foot-three frame of Gerry Ravenscroft. She thought about phoning her parents to ask for the Z-bed they kept in their garage, but then her dad would have to dig it out from under the debris of eighty years of life, lift it into his Mondeo and deliver it in person. Just this process would involve five phone calls, three arguments, a slipped disc, and potentially four hours. To make matters worse, her father would then enter the Bunker and work out that three grown adults had drunk three bottles of wine before nine o'clock, discovering that his only daughter had turned into a goofy teenager again, or worse, a raging alcoholic. No, Gerry would have to make do with the sofa, but it was long enough and there was plenty of clean bedlinen.

As the evening wore on, and the fourth bottle of wine had been consumed, the sleeping arrangement wasn't a problem for anybody, and neither were Jack's medical issues. He had the same patchy numbness, his left foot filled his slipper like a crab and he could barely feel the back of his head, but surviving a bodged lumbar puncture, still able to walk and talk had turned him into a legend in Gerry's drunken eyes. When Jack said A&E was like an episode of M*A*S*H without the jokes, everyone laughed. Jack played some of his favourite CDs and they reminisced about old haunts, comedy gigs, all-nighters, accidents and funny disasters.

Alice insisted that in the morning she'd show Gerry around the new house; their dream home by the sea. Seagull House.

'I've been thinking about that,' said Gerry. 'Should a comedian really live in a house called Seagull?'

'Why ever not?' said Alice.

'Well, firstly, as a former twitcher I can tell you there is no such thing as a "seagull", only different types of "gull". Secondly, it's all a bit Chekhovian, isn't it…*Seagull* House? Why can't you call it Pebble Palace…or Shingle Mansions or Dun Roamin just like everyone else?'

Alice slapped his leg.

'My mum once played Nina in *The Seagull*,' said Jack. 'Dad took me to see her in the West End on my tenth birthday. Mum didn't know I was in the audience.'

'You must've been bored out of your wits.'

'I really enjoyed it, but it could have been in Russian for all I knew.'

'Quite right,' said Gerry. 'Don't forget, everyone's miserable in *The Seagull*…and the seagull dies in every show.'

Jack remembered the opening and closing lines (curtain lines his mother called them) and conjured up a Russian accent he stole from Nikolai Gorbachev in the 1980s: '"Vy do you always vair black?"' And in a higher register, '"I'm in mourning vor my life."' Gerry fell about laughing. 'And Dr. Dorn says right at the end, "The fact is…Konstantin Gavrilovich has shot himself." Chekhov was a doctor before he was a writer you know.'

'You see, Alice?' cried Gerry in delicious pain. 'It's all too depressing. Anyway, and I've never got this, who or what is the seagull in *The Seagull*? Is it Nina, Konstantin, Trigorin, or everyone…?'

'Don't go all postmodern, Gerry,' said Alice. 'It will bring you out in a rash.'

'It's like *Spartacus*,' he said, leaping to his feet. 'No, I am the seagull!'

Alice leapt up beside him. 'No, I'm the seagull.'

Jack rose to his feet, thrusting his chest out. 'No, I am Jonathan Livingstone Seagull.'

'Trust you to be different,' said Gerry, slumping back down.

'My dad used to read me *Jonathan Livingstone Seagull* in bed,' said Alice.

'Exactly, to send you to sleep,' scoffed Gerry. 'And there's a recurring theme here. The seagull dies.'

'Maybe we should think about another name,' Alice said to Jack.

'Don't listen to that old fart,' he said. 'Seagull House it is and Seagull House it will remain.'

Last thing at night, Jack popped his head around the lounge door to say goodnight to his old friend and felt a pang of sadness and self-pity. It was seeing the sofa with someone lying on it wrapped up in sheets. Jack had been the last person to sleep there. Because of the stifling heat that summer, Jack had slipped out of the marital bed, dragged a spare duvet into the lounge and curled up on the sofa. And he'd awoken the following morning with pins and needles, and that was that. The beginning of what he hoped would soon come to an end.

Before going to bed, he went to the kitchen to make himself a cup of herbal tea. Alice had got him into the habit of drinking it instead of coffee late at night. By now, Alice and Gerry were sleeping. Gerry's snoring from the lounge was audible; Alice's from the small double bedroom was a light snuffle. *Alice in Slumberland*, he thought. Pan was upside down in her bed, piglet pink belly facing the ceiling, hairy legs limp and akimbo, freckled gums and white teeth showing under sagging, relaxed upper lips. How he loved her. She was like a strange person, this dog. Like his previous collie, Major Tom, only different. How he loved all the other persons present in the Bunker too. He was going to have a hangover in the morning.

Standing at the sink, staring out of the window, he saw a train pass by, its only trace the rumbling of the tracks coming down a redundant chimney breast and the lights from each carriage flickering through a canopy of trees. The effect reminded him of a magic lantern he had in his room as an infant; perhaps his first-ever memory. Had it been a boy running away from demons, or a man towards angels? And this current flickering through the trees: was it a man running into the woods, or a demon coming out?

Last tea bag in the box. The box said *Night Time: a dreamy blend of organic oat flower, lavender and lime flower*. He smiled because Alice preferred to give things new names and had renamed it "Sleepy Tea". He opened the sachet, put the bag in a mug and poured water that was just off the boil for a taste that was less harsh. Waiting for his tea to brew, he noticed there were some fancy words printed on the floor of the box; marketing people trying to entice customers to sample other teas in an extensive range. The writing was calligraphic, intertwined with ornate tracery; really too beautiful for the *inside* of a box, he thought, too pretty for people in too much of a hurry to notice. He wished he'd been in too much of a hurry to notice, because the words struck him cold, as if a sign of things to come: *this is not the end; only the beginning.*

In the morning, Alice heated pains au chocalat and they devoured them with filtered coffee. Despite hangovers, they managed to show Gerry Seagull House before he drove back to Sussex. He was genuinely impressed. From what Alice had told him, it was all a bit too contemporary compared to his rambling Georgian pile in the country, but he could appreciate what would eventually become spacious, whitewashed interiors, and he could actually see the sea from the proposed master.

Gerry noticed that Jack was unable to climb the ladders to the first floor, his friend rooted to the drive looking up and waving. He'd noticed over breakfast too, how haggard Jack looked, and suspected it wasn't just booze. Gerry had regarded the no-frills kitchen of their rented little Bunker with some regret. Why now, when so much was going well for the Manns, had this mysterious illness come to stay? Why, when Jack's most important tour approached was Gerry having to cancel everything? It wasn't the disappointed theatres and wasted publicity costs running into thousands that concerned him. These could be recouped. It was the production company who'd seen the previews at Edinburgh and agreed to record and sell it to mainstream TV and make DVDs. That's where the real money would have been.

Then again, one doesn't pick and choose when to be ill or what to be ill with. It wasn't as if Jack had a chronic drink or drugs problem like some of his other comedy clients. Jack's manic depression was under control as far as Gerry could see. In fact, Jack's diagnosis and public openness about that illness had been positively lucrative, providing material for his brave and iconic *Mann in Black* tour. *Mad Infinitum* would've been the belated follow-up. Maybe, one day, after all of this had settled down, Jack might be up on stage adding the lumbar puncture story to his repertoire, and they'd die laughing at the madness of it all. But when Gerry looked into Jack's eyes upon leaving, he recognised fear. When they parted company at the roadside, Gerry squeezed his old friend to popping point, saying, 'You bloody get better, dear boy.'

The Phone Call

Jack and Alice had just finished their lunch in the conservatory when the phone call came. The door was open and they were watching Pan nosing around the rose bushes. Jack was the first to the phone, which was most unlike him, and for some reason he noted the time on the answer machine: *15:28*. He checked the number displayed. The machine indicated *0* which meant number unknown or unrecognised; usually from abroad. He set himself for a conversation with his brother, who he expected would call, and the time was right to be morning in California. 'Hello, Ernie,' he said. 'This is a nice surprise.'

'Hello. Can I speak to Mr. Jack Mann, please?' He instantly recognised the voice of Dr. Richter, the vascular consultant. 'Hello? Mr. Mann?'

'Yes, speaking,' he said, mouthing "hospital" to Alice, and she stood up.

'I'm sorry to call you at home but I have some new information.'

'New information...?'

Alice's eyes widened and she took a step closer.

'Yes, it concerns your second MRI scan.'

'The MRI that Mr. Swan requested?'

'Correct. The radiographer's report has now come back, and we had our MDT meeting this afternoon...'

'MDT?'

Alice drew closer, a hand pressed to her cheek.

'There was a long discussion, and we agreed your results should be sent to a radio-oncologist at King's College Hospital in London.'

'Oncologist? King's?'

Alice's eyes grew even wider.

'Look, Dr. Richter,' Jack said, 'can I be straight with you?'

'Yes, by all means.'

'Are we talking about a *brain tumour*?'

Alice took a sharp intake of breath, clapping both hands over her mouth.

Jack had only asked the question as a deft double bluff to allay fears it could actually be a brain tumour. He'd deployed a similar tactic in many difficult circumstances over the years and it always worked. *If you don't want to dance with the devil*, he understood, *you ask him to dance, and he always turns you down.*

'Can I be straight with you in return, Mr. Mann?'

'You can.'

'Yes, we're talking about a brain tumour.'

Well, he thought, *you don't get straighter than that.* His legs buckled. 'How bad is it, Dr. Richter? I mean, what are my chances?'

'There's no reason to panic.'

'But what are my chances?'

'Pretty good,' she said.

'*Statistically* how good?'

'There is a one-in-five chance this is a tumour.'

Jack pictured himself in a waiting area outside an oncologist's room, sitting alongside four other patients all of who looked just like Jack. One of this gang of five Jack Manns would be told he has a brain tumour. One-in-five was worse odds than Christopher Walken playing Russian roulette in *The Deer Hunter*.

'You must not panic,' she said. 'There is an eighty percent chance it is not a tumour. And even if it were, it doesn't mean it is malignant. People can walk around without knowing they have a tumour, until it causes havoc. You wouldn't thank me if I had done nothing about this irregularity on your scan and it turned out to be malignant and was too late to intervene.'

'I'm sorry,' Jack said, 'I don't think I can take all of this in.' He handed Alice the phone, sat down, staring at the tiles, looking at the cracks between them.

Alice was as calm as possible under the circumstances, though Jack could hear in her feathery breathing that she was flustered. She wanted to be told everything. Then she wanted to know more about the statistics. And then she asked: 'Does Mr. Swan know about this?

'He's on holiday, Mrs. Mann, but he was present at the meeting.'

'Did he agree with you about the tumour?'

'Possible tumour, Mrs. Mann. This is precautionary.'

'Did Mr. Swan agree with you about the tumour?'

'No, he did not, but we took a show of hands and came to the view it would be remiss not to have a second opinion. Your husband's scan was unusual.'

'When will we know what they think at King's?'

'They have their meetings every Friday afternoon. I have already emailed them attaching the MRIs. I shall telephone you when I know what they think, at about 5:30 p.m.'

'You will definitely call us in two days' time with the verdict?'

'Of course, but it is not a *verdict*. It is not a *firing squad*. You must not worry.'

Alice replaced the phone and embraced her husband. Tears flowed down her cheeks and Jack held her shaking frame. 'Why?' she cried. 'Why us?'

'Guess it has to happen to someone,' he said, rubbing her back. 'And like Richter says, I'm a good bet. I'm 80% in the clear.'

Pandora trotted in as if to share the emotions and sat at their feet looking up, tip-tapping her paws on the tiles. They got down on their knees and folded their arms around her, and each other.

The next 48 hours were interminable. Each in their own way tried to push the uninvited guest out of their mind, but it crept back in like a bad smell. Watching TV, not absorbing details, making phone calls, not mentioning the unmentionable. They made the decision not to tell anyone anything until they had confirmation. This decision was wise and unwise. Wise because a tumour was unlikely; unwise because they were burdening themselves without the comfort of friends or family. When Alice's parents called she affected normality, but they guessed something was wrong by her voice. She said it was just too much overtime on the theatre she was helping to build, and they accepted it.

The Manns occupied themselves with strange activities, like going to a local wilderness park to see semi-wild animals in the woods. It was primarily an educational facility for young children, not adults, and they found themselves surrounded by a kaleidoscope of kids who squealed with excitement at seeing animals or whined with disappointment at empty cages and enclosures. For a while, Jack and Alice stood holding hands in front of two sister ravens perched on a branch, eyeing raw meat scattered across the ground. They were magnificently proud and black, their feathers glinting in the sunlight. Flies swarmed around their bloodied beaks.

They walked to the wolf enclosure at a fortuitous moment, a siren wailing on a nearby road setting off not one but two howling wolves, their heads thrown back unleashing their call of the wild through vibrating larynxes. They saw deer, and foxes, and badgers and red squirrels. And by then Jack was exhausted. His head began to feel as heavy as a medicine ball on his shoulders. He was anxious that it could be the extra weight of a tumour weighing him down like an anchor and making his legs unstable, as if he'd just stepped ashore from a ship long adrift in an ocean, leading to a rolling pattern of walking; a sailor's gait.

Alice took Pandora on more walks than the dog was used to. Jack stayed in the Bunker trying to sleep through increasing neuropathic pain; pain he now believed to be caused by the ticking tumour.

Come Friday, time seemed to slow down even more; seconds were minutes, minutes were hours, hours were whole days. Each looked at their watch not saying anything, though communicating the same thing: Doomsday. At 5 p.m., Alice found herself pacing the lounge and then the conservatory where the phone was. Jack stood by the kitchen sink looking out at the garden towards the large stone Buddha. *This is nothing*, he thought.

At 5:30, he moved to the conservatory where Alice sat hunched over the phone, rocking back and forth. At 5:35, she got up and went to the kitchen. She paced and paced the tiled floor, feeling sick in the pit of her stomach. A train passed at the foot of the garden and Pandora charged at the far-off wire fence, barking beyond the tall trees.

At 5:40, Alice came into the conservatory complaining about Dr. Richter; Jack reminded her that King's might still be in their meeting. At 5:50, she felt like pulling her hair out, her pacing circles ever decreasing. 'That's it, I'm calling her,' she said.

'How? We don't have her number. If you phone the hospital they'll send you around the houses. It will take ages and our phone will be engaged when she calls.'

'*If* she calls,' said Alice, scowling. 'Anyway, I'll use my mobile.'

At 6 p.m., Alice telephoned the hospital and was put through to Dr. Richter's section. The secretary said Dr. Richter had already gone away for the bank holiday weekend and wasn't due back until the following Tuesday. She knew nothing about any request to King's College or Jack's MRIs. 'You've got to be kidding me,' said Alice, explaining their situation, but there was nothing she could do. She banged her phone down on the dining table. They'd just have to wait until Tuesday; though how, she didn't know. She was beyond crying; only thinking how she might slap Dr. Richter's face.

'This is so wrong,' she said. 'It doesn't feel real. Maybe Dr. Richter's just getting back at Mr. Swan, because he disagreed with her diagnosis?'

'Which she did get wrong.'

'Yes, that's it,' said Alice, perking up. 'She's trying to trump Mr. Swan.'

'And now they're both on holiday.'

'I don't know how you can stay so strong,' she said. 'Look at me, I'm in pieces and I'm not the one with the brain tumour, I mean waiting to discover if I have a brain tumour.'

'I'm finding hidden depths,' Jack said, kissing her ear. 'You're amazing, my little Alice in Blunderland.'

Saturday was nothing. Sunday was nothing too. By Monday it was even more nothing. It was all nothing, except torture. During this time, both imagined the worst things that could happen: A) King's College Hospital say it's a tumour. B) a neurosurgeon cracks Jack's skull open, fishes around his brain, hooks out a sample and determines whether it's benign or malignant. C) it is malignant. D) it is too big, badly situated and inoperable. E) Jack is dead within six months. It was only a small chance, but not outside the realms of reality. People die every day, and they never come back.

Alice phoned at 8 a.m. on Tuesday, hands shaking. The administrator didn't have a clue what Alice was talking about. King's? MRIs? Tumours? 'I'm afraid you'll have to wait to speak to Dr. Richter. She's doing her rounds.'

'Please tell her this,' said Alice. 'She promised to call us about Jack Mann's *tumour* last Friday, but failed to do so. We are out of our minds with worry.'

'I'll leave a note for her. She's a very busy consultant.'

'With respect,' said Alice, trying to contain herself, 'have *you* ever waited five days to discover if *you* have a brain tumour? No, I didn't think so. Please tell Dr. Richter that we are still waiting to hear. She has our number, but here it is again, and here's my mobile number.'

At 12:15 precisely, Dr. Richter called on the landline, and the news wasn't good. 'Something went wrong with our computer system last Wednesday and the email to King's was never sent. I've just re-sent it.'

Alice said, 'So when will we find out from King's?'

'Friday, I'm afraid.'

'So we wait another three and a half days because of an admin error?'

'Listen, Mrs. Mann, as I told you last week, there's no reason to worry.'

'I shouldn't worry whether my husband has a brain tumour?'

'I'll call you on Friday, after 5 p.m.' Dr. Richter hung up.

'This is a nightmare.'

'One that Kafka couldn't even dream,' said Jack. 'Pinch me. Pinch me, so I wake up.'

The next three days were a repeat of the previous four, except that Jack was now feeling the pressure. Whenever he went to the bathroom his thoughts turned to his brain, convinced there was a tumour nesting. What else could explain his weird, continual symptoms? No, he didn't have pounding headaches or nausea in the mornings that brain tumour sufferers commonly complained of. Neither did Jack smell an odd burning upon waking. These were the signs Alice had gleaned from internet searches. He gently pressed his temples and felt all over his skull, back to front, imagining what might lurk inside. What colour was this tumour: grey, yellow, green or black? Was it the size of a pea, a golf ball or a tin of baked beans? He relived his trip to the MRI scanner that first time, when the nurse told the story of the unfortunate young man who lost half of his brain, half of his face, and all of his wife.

Alice went back to work. Jack had insisted, and she'd agreed that it might take her mind off the impending phone call. In any case, she really did have her hands full of the theatre. As project leader, and control freak extraordinaire, she couldn't be absent for too many days or the new building might collapse after years of hard work.

Jack rested most of the time. The weather was good, so he took Pan on short walks along the Slopes. He became a creeping figure silhouetted against the deep blue water and pale sky. Fatigue made each walk shorter and shorter, and he took breaks on benches lining the seafront.

The call came shortly after 5 p.m., just as Dr. Richter had promised. Alice had left work early hoping to avoid the Friday rush hour, but she was on "Alice Time", as Jack fondly called it, always cutting it fine. She bibbed, hooted and yelled at slow drivers en route to the Bunker. A bottle of champagne she'd bought at lunch time, chilled in a fridge next to her office, rolled about on the passenger seat. She'd been in two minds whether to buy it, given the circumstances, but positive thinking had won the wrestling contest between tempting fate and hope of a long, healthy future. Whatever the outcome, she thought, Jack and she would need a drink. It was "Fizz Friday" too; what they called the start of most normal weekends. But this one wasn't normal. As it turned out, she arrived with minutes to spare and sneaked the bottle into the Bunker fridge. She found Jack pacing room to room, Pandora following like a third leg.

When the call came it was Alice who answered, and despite desperately wanting to hear the news she suddenly wished it was a wrong number. Dr. Richter said she'd only speak to Mr. Mann, so Alice handed the phone across, whispering, 'Good luck, sweetheart.'

His heart pounded. He sat down in his tatty leather armchair and crossed his legs. Alice sat on the sofa opposite, glued to every word, and wise to any shift in facial expression. She felt a flutter in her stomach. Jack listened without speaking for a long time, his face strained and hard to read, and then he looked confused, brow furrowed. He half-smiled across the room, but without his usual thumbs up. 'So, they are saying it's *non-specific* in appearance, and *not likely* to be a tumour?' He nodded at Alice whose shoulders relaxed a little. 'The radio-oncologist at King's doesn't know one hundred percent if it is or isn't a tumour…okay…and he wants interval imaging. What's that? Okay, another MRI in six to eight weeks' time.' His free hand seesawed in a fifty-fifty motion and Alice's shoulders bunched up again. 'With gadolinium contrast. What's that?' He listened some more. 'Okay, so that they can see any inflammation. So, they don't think it is a tumour, but can't confirm this until they've seen another MRI over time. I understand. Well, thank you for phoning with the news, Dr. Richter.' He put the phone down and Alice jumped across the room to embrace him. 'I'm not out of the woods,' he said, locked in her arms. 'We have to wait another two months to be sure.'

'If it was a tumour they'd have seen it, Jack.'

'It's not definitive.'

'It's better than it could've been. Christ, you sound like you *want* it to be a tumour!' She felt his back stiffen, and squeezed him tighter. 'I'm sorry; I didn't mean that, Jack. I didn't mean it. I won't let anything happen to you.' She covered his face in kisses.

-PART THREE-

Everything may die, nothing may be regenerated.

Ramon y Cajal S, *Degeneration and Regeneration of the Nervous System*

The Importance of Being Ernest Mann

As promised, Ernie flew over from America. He had flowers and chocolates for Alice and wine for Jack. He stayed just one night in the Bunker and it was wonderful to see him after so many years. Ernie hadn't changed much, perhaps weight gained around the middle, a little less hair on top, a little more Californian in accent, but he still looked and sounded remarkably like his younger brother Jack: lively grey-blue eyes, lop-sided smile, same mannerisms, and *that laugh*. At times, when they were sitting side by side on the sofa, or standing shoulder to shoulder in the garden, Alice thought Ernie looked like a fast-forward version of Jack. But, she thought, compared to her husband there was something too safe about Ernie, the real estate lawyer; too conservative. Ernie was a planner, a plodder, whereas Jack was creative and spontaneous.

Ernie waxed lyrical about his two sons, Ryan and Gus, but wouldn't be drawn on his wife Ariel. They talked in detail about their illnesses, but Jack didn't mention the tumour conundrum, not wanting to place an extra burden on his brother who was having a miserable time of his own with unexplained headaches. The pain was carved on his forehead in crooked lines. Ernie had spent a small fortune on investigations that involved an MRI and spinal tap, but nothing was abnormal about his scan, bloods or spinal fluid. Perhaps it was just stress headaches, suggested Jack, watching his brother gobbling painkillers. 'Weird though, isn't it?' Ernie said. 'We have MRIs and spinal taps at about the same time but on different sides of the planet? Could they be related?'

'Maybe we're just getting older. Things go wrong in your forties and fifties. Alice's dad told me if you can get to fifty without anything major going wrong you're set to live a long, healthy life; unless you get blown up by a terrorist, run-over by a bus or struck down by lightning.'

'How old is he?' asked Ernie.

'Early eighties, but he had two major heart attacks in his mid-forties.'

'Maybe he's the exception to his own rule then?'

'He said a squeaky gate hangs the longest.'

Ernie asked if Lauren had come down from London, knowing full well she hadn't. Jack's sister hadn't visited him in the hospital or the Bunker. She'd phoned and sent a get well card. Ernie advised Jack to cut her some slack. She had a lot on her plate: visiting their ailing mother four or five times a week in the nursing home, with all the distress that brought, and another one of Lauren's short-term relationships had collapsed.

'Why didn't she come down with you tonight, Ernie? You're actually staying with her.'

'She sends her apologies, bro, but teaching came up. It's the start of a new school year; a whole term's work. She's broke, and needs the salary.'

'I'm sorry I couldn't get up for Mum's birthday,' said Jack. 'I was too sick.'

They talked about their mother's dementia, how fast it had accelerated over three years. Apparently, Estella had remembered Ernest and Lauren at first, but after twenty minutes she'd drifted off to sleep in front of them, waking to a room full of strangers.

'It comes and goes,' said Jack. 'Good days and bad days.'

'And now the bad days are winning out. Lauren's really cut up over it. She'd never say, but Mum's starting to feel like a burden.'

'She's in a good nursing home, Ernie. I'd visit more, but with moving down here, the house-build, my tour prep, now this damn illness…'

'I know, bro,' he said. 'But when you're feeling better, I'm sure Lauren would appreciate a bit of help, emotionally if nothing else. If I wasn't in America I'd do more, but I am in America so it's impossible. Maybe Lauren thinks you've jumped ship by selling your place in Fulham and moving down here to the seaside?'

'Don't lay a guilt trip on me, Ernie.'

'All I'm saying is that Lauren feels a bit…well…abandoned.'

'Abandoned? Ernie, you chose to live thousands of miles away in California. Don't talk to me about abandoned. I go when I can, but right now it's impossible.'

'Okay, I get it, you're ill, but you were going to come and see us in San Francisco too, and we've been waiting years. You and Alice are Ryan's godparents, but he doesn't even know what you look like. Gus gets his memories of you from looking at old DVDs!' Ernie laughed when he said this, to deflect the seriousness.

'If you hadn't noticed, Ernie, Alice was ill with possible ovarian cancer. It took a year for her to recover. She lost a baby, survived a cancer scare and had the menopause by the age of forty-three, and I didn't see you running to help, or even calling at the time.'

'I know, I know,' he said, holding his hands up. 'I'm sorry. I shouldn't have mentioned any of this.'

Everyone went to bed early, Jack knowing that his older brother was pulling his strings or pressing his buttons just like he used to when they were kids; mentioning things he was then sorry for mentioning. Like dropping a bomb and walking away.

Ernie left mid-morning, after they'd driven him through Whitstable to soak up some of the atmosphere. They walked the length of the high street, all the way down to the harbour, and back to the seafront where they sat together on the Peter Cushing bench. Of course, it couldn't compete with Fog City, the bustling bay of SF, Ernie said, but it was quirky and "kinda cool". Alice showed him around Seagull House in Tankerton too. Jack stayed on the ground, dizzy and leaning on a skip full of rubble and render, dead wood and spent cabling. Ernie was impressed with the house, saying Alice had "vision" and a wonderful imagination. Ernie had always been good at pumping an ego shortly before popping it. So when he questioned her idea of having an attached garage instead of another bedroom, Alice bristled with irritation, and he adjusted, saying garages were always good for storage. 'It's a prime location, though a direct sea view would have been better.' He said that if it was in San Francisco it would be worth a couple of million bucks. He shouted down from the would-be balcony: 'Jack! I'm living on the western seaboard of America and you're living on the east coast of England! How we ever goin' to meet up?' *There he goes again, probing and pushing and planning, and mentioning things that have an edge to them.* But maybe he was just trying to make the point that time races forward, boys grow into men, and men are middle-aged before they realise they're even born.

They parted with customary bear hugs. Ernie was due to fly back in two days' time and said he'd call when he got back to the States. Before he departed, Alice gave him a couple of envelopes for their godson Ryan, and Ernie's teenage son Gus. Not knowing them well, she had put money in the cards that Ernie could change into dollars at the airport. Jack gave his brother a prototype poster for the cancelled *Mad Infinitum* tour; something Ernie had hinted his eldest would like for his bedroom wall. 'Sometimes, I look at Gus,' Ernie said, 'and I swear I'm staring straight at you when you were fourteen. He's naturally funnier than you, though.'

Mid-September, and Jack's birthday came and went without celebration. The Bunker wasn't the right size to accommodate the guests he'd usually invite, and besides, fatigue had now become one of his worst enemies. It could strike at any time, worsening in the evenings when he'd collapse onto the sofa. On his birthday this year, Alice drove him to hospital to have a Doppler scan of his heart. The nurse dimmed the overhead lights, squeezed gel into his hands and asked him to smear it over his chest. She rolled the Doppler around, standing very close behind him, her elbow resting on his hip. Despite the importance of such a scan, the experience felt intimate, almost erotic. 'You probably can't tell me what's in there,' he said to her, 'but it is my birthday today so what do you think about making an exception?'

'I really shouldn't,' she whispered, 'it's up to the cardiologist. But between you and me, I don't see anything.'

'Don't see anything bad…or don't see anything at all?'

It was unfortunate that Jack's birthday coincided with the first date of his cancelled tour. It was to have commenced in Newcastle. Jack stared at the name and date on his last-remaining *Mad Infinitum* poster; his poster head was contorted and split into three or four, as if violently spinning and melting into one, *Matrix* fashion. While Alice was cooking, he ventured onto the lawn at the back of the bungalow. Sitting there in his sunglasses, which he wore most days, even indoors because of increasing photosensitivity, he listened to the neighbour's chickens clucking in their pen and the occasional rumble of trains. *Forty-five today*, he thought, head bowed to the ground; *the Mann with no heart.*

September became a daily thud of mail through the letterbox accompanied by Pandora's stomping and barking. The accumulating junk was to be expected in a property rented out for so many years, but lots of it was for a previous tenant who had unfortunately died, according to the letting agent. Over the previous three months, this dead tenant had risen like Lazarus in Jack's hands. Each time Jack opened the letters he discovered more about the dead man. He had a recurring mental illness, failing eyesight, wore a hearing aid, was interested in model train sets, suffered diabetes and kidney failure, and had oversized feet. And today, with Christmas only four months away, Jack discovered that the dead man had also been a member of the local church choir. The dead man had missed preliminary discussions about a forthcoming production of Handel's *Messiah*. Amongst the dead man's mail, Jack received his own follow-up hospital appointments and an invitation to an introductory meeting with his new GP, Dr. Greaves.

Dr. Greaves

The doctor's surgery was a warm and welcoming environment, just five minutes from the Bunker. Jack had wanted to go alone but Alice insisted on driving. She waited outside the room, staring at Dr. Greaves' name plaque, and worrying. She clutched a plastic envelope containing the results and conclusions about Jack's health. She looked along the line of waiting patients, checking her watch and tapping the plastic envelope. She noticed that the internal walls of the surgery had been made to look like external brickwork, even down to fake pointing, perhaps to create the illusion of solidity and privacy when really they were half-inch chipboard. She was oblivious to the muzak pouring quietly from discreet speakers; well-known hits from the 1960s and 70s.

Dr. Greaves didn't look like her name suggested, thought Jack. Soft, smiley, spectacled, middle-aged, with an open, expressive, if tired face. Eyes mainly glued to her computer screen, she occasionally span around to talk to Jack as a human being rather than an anonymous number. She had an easy-going, jocular bearing, and when she smiled her prominent teeth made her look goofy and harmless.

Jack explained his recent history including the brain tumour theory and the heart monitor, not that he expected the results to have been processed. He told her about his MRIs and the lumbar puncture, without going into the nitty-gritty. He said he was waiting for another MRI, and in the meantime was due another consultation with Dr. Richter who he suspected would sign him off. It was all a bit of a puzzle, he said.

'When was your lumbar puncture?'

'Four or five weeks ago, but I haven't heard anything.'

She span around to face her computer and tapped the keys.

'Would it be on your system?'

'It might be.' She scrolled down. 'Oh, look, here they are. CSF results.'

'From my lumbar?' He thought about getting up and asking Alice to come in.

'Hmm,' she said, looking at the screen for some time. She span back and her friendly open face had folded into one of grave sympathy. Her hands went flat on her lap.

'What is it?'

'I know this was only meant to be your introductory appointment, Mr. Mann, but I'm sorry to inform you the results are not what we might have hoped for.'

'What do you mean *sorry*?'

Dr. Greaves rolled her chair closer to the screen. She removed her glasses, squinting and reading: 'Oligoclonal banding is detected in your CSF, pattern consistent with intrathecal IgG synthesis. But in your serum an abnormality in oligoclonal banding was not detected.'

'And...? My wife's outside, should I bring her in?'

'It usually means you have multiple sclerosis.'

'What?' In his mind's eye, his head split three or four ways just like the image on the Mad Infinitum poster.

'It isn't the end of the world. I've treated lots of MS patients at this surgery and it's possible to manage the condition. You can still be mobile, even if you cannot walk, and in any case that might be years away.'

'Me? MS?'

'There are a number of treatments available depending on which type of MS. Well, you'll need to speak to your consultant about that.'

'Hold on a second.' Jack got up, opened the door and beckoned Alice in. She closed the door behind her and smiled awkwardly at Dr. Greaves. 'Alice, you'd better take a seat. You're not going to believe this.' She sat down looking at him, her face white as paper. 'The doctor says I have multiple sclerosis.'

Her mouth fell open.

'It's not as bad as it sounds, Mrs. Mann. Your husband has protein banding in his spinal fluid but not in his blood, which does point to MS.'

'Doctor Greaves,' she said, 'forgive me, but in the past few weeks Jack's been told he's had a migraine, a stroke, another stroke, neuritis, then he might have a brain tumour and not neuritis. We're still waiting to find out if he has a tumour. Now he has MS? Which one is it?'

'I'm sorry,' said Dr. Greaves, with placatory hands. 'I'm only going by the results. Neurological problems are notoriously difficult. The brain is like a jigsaw puzzle. And you haven't had your nerve conduction tests yet, Mr. Mann. Have you had any sight loss or visual disturbance during all of this?'

Alice shook her head on his behalf. 'You're saying this is definitely MS?'

'They are strong indicators, Mrs. Mann. I'm sorry.'

Dr. Richter

Alice diligently searched the internet for clues to Jack's condition. She did this during her lunch breaks at work or late at night so it didn't worry him. What she discovered further fuelled the mystery. Many things caused oligoclonal banding in a patient's spinal fluid, and not just MS. The key lay in the number of "O" bands. "O" bands indicated inflammation. Alice also noted that Jack had "elevated proteins" in his fluid too, that could indicate an infection. The bottom line was that Jack's body was under attack, or his immune system thought it was.

Jack's burning sensations worsened. He couldn't sleep at night and had taken to wearing padded wine coolers from the freezer. He asked Alice if she could get the folding bed from her dad's garage and he'd try sleeping in the other bedroom because he was forever seeking out cold sections of bed, waking her every half an hour throughout the night.

The spare room was filled with heavy boxes seven feet high. Jack rearranged them against the walls, making just enough room for a camp bed. He turned the radiator off, creating a cooler environment. Any heat made his burning sensations worse. By now, just running his hands under a tepid tap felt like washing them in boiling water.

Alice didn't like the fact he moved out of the marital bed, but understood. Responsibilities at work were mounting and Jack's illness had affected her job. She'd dropped many balls over the past two months and her boss, though understanding, was wondering how long the illness would last. The town's brand new theatre was soon to open and Alice was responsible for its successful delivery and its glittering first night with attendant press coverage and a special royal visit by Prince Edward and his wife, not to mention an entourage of important councillors, local gentry and a long list of funders.

While Jack festered in a room full of boxes that held most of their belongings – a moving metaphor, he thought, for the dream future they'd planned together by the sea – she worked through the night in her room, writing work emails. In a state of pack confusion, Pandora mooched between the two bedrooms, choosing to sleep on the tiles in the hall.

The meeting with Dr. Richter took place on a bright, late September morning. After a long hot summer, leaves were turning blood reds, plum purples and crisp golds, not that either of them noticed. They were thinking only about the words "oligoclonal" and "MS".

The consulting room was on the ground floor of the old part of the hospital, not far from the stroke ward. Dr. Richter specialised in vascular conditions and the healthcare of older people. Her waiting room was full of geriatrics, some with walking sticks and Zimmer frames, others in wheelchairs. The gurney-battered walls were dotted with posters directed at this demographic: early signs of prostate cancer, Alzheimer's, treatments for arthritis, macular degeneration, circulation diseases, and vitamin D deficiency. Jack feared that if he spent too long here he might, by osmosis, age rapidly into a dignified yet musty old gentleman like David Bowie in *The Hunger*.

The meeting took thirty minutes and the outcome was perfunctory. The results of Jack's Doppler heart scan and monitor investigations were all within normal limits. As such, Dr. Richter concluded his illness was not vascular-related. Alice asked about oligoclonal banding but Dr. Richter didn't want to be drawn into a discussion, explaining there were only one or two bands in Jack's CSF. This could mean any number of causes and may not necessarily lead to a diagnosis of multiple sclerosis. She didn't wish to comment on the GP's conclusions, saying the interpretation of blood tests and lumbar punctures should be left to experts. Whatever the cause, she said, the differential diagnosis was still inflammation, as Mr. Swan had originally suggested. As a result she was signing Jack off from her care and referring him to Mr. Swan's outpatient neurology clinic. She made a note of Jack's continuing sensory problems, nerve pain, increasing fatigue and dizziness, but also noted he had a Modified Rankin Score of zero; in other words, no physical disability. She confirmed that nerve conduction tests and an MRI with contrast, commissioned by King's in London, would be completed in the next few weeks. Based on these, Mr. Swan should be able to make a firm diagnosis, she said. 'By the end of October, we should have a much better picture of what is happening.'

A week before seeing Mr. Swan, Jack returned to the hospital for his third MRI. This time he didn't ask for any music, preferring to face the thumping beat of the machine. This time, a nurse slipped a cannula into his right hand ready to feed in the liquid she called gadolinium or "contrast". This would show the consultant any current inflammation of the brain and spinal cord. The machine throbbed and then stopped momentarily. The radiologist's voice came through Jack's headset saying the contrast would now be released and he'd feel it coursing through his veins; ice cold. He didn't bother with his mantra. He saw no protective stone Buddha in his mind either, only a growing tumour. *What will be, will be.*

The Igloo

By mid-October, Jack's dizziness, nausea, brain fog and fatigue had worsened. He woke up each morning feeling as if he'd already completed a marathon. Unable to walk for longer than five minutes or stand for more than ten, he often retired to the camp bed in the little box room he called "the igloo". The igloo inside a bunker.

Some days, the igloo shrank to the size of a coffin, or an MRI scanner. One day, Alice might return from work and find him dead in there; a real Jack in a box.

He could no longer stand the sound or sight of everyday things. The once joyful murmur of children passing by his bedroom window on their way to the primary school had him clapping burning hands over his ears. The TV was unbearable too. He'd developed tinnitus; an unbearable ringing in his ears that heightened at night. He had difficulty keeping up with the narrative content of programmes, though he didn't tell Alice. TV had become a set of incoherent, rolling images with meaningless narrators.

Retreating to his igloo, he listened instead to classical music on the radio. The dulcet tones of the presenters calmed him. Monastic music in particular seemed appropriate for an anchorite cloistered in a Bunker. More often than not, though, when the soft music stopped he felt the lumpen walls of his life closing in, and thought too long about what he'd lost. The world had been a big place once, as large as a globe, then it had shrunk to the size of a hospital, then the size of the Bunker, then the size of a consultant's room, an MRI scanner, and now it was the size of a camp bed in a cold, cold mausoleum.

When Jack wasn't lying corpse-like inside an igloo inside a bunker bemoaning the loss of a past when everything was fine and good, he was at Seagull House sitting stiffly in a chair inside the pinewood office in the garden, where he pondered the loss of a future. A tower of boxes stood in one corner; boxes of hopes, dreams and histories. What could've beens, what should've beens. They'd been taken from the igloo, creating space for the Z-bed.

Jack read the marker pen scrawls on the boxes: *photo albums*, *odds and sods*, *office*, and *Donne*. His eyes were drawn to a shabby box sitting by itself, bearing the word *clippings*. He sat down beside it and took out cuttings from newspapers and magazines. He spread some out in a semi-circle around him. The last full interview he'd given was in 2004 when everything had appeared rosy. It was a full-length feature in the culture section of the *Observer* with his favorite journalist Siobhan Lafferty. He'd never appreciated the comic irony of her last name before:

Stand-up comedian and impressionist Jack Mann shot to fame in the 1980s. His satirical impressions of politicians and celebrities led to voice-overs on *Spitting Image*, earning appearances on TV including *The Royal Variety Show*, *Whose Line is it Anyway?* and *Blankety Blank*. During the 1990s he was a regular contributor to BBC Radio 4, writing and performing sketches, not least the infamous 'Mannologues'. He toured the world, conquering America, where he appeared on *The David Letterman Show*. Success stopped abruptly at the end of the nineties, however, with personal, professional and financial disaster. His wife Alice suffered two miscarriages, Jack split with long-term writing partner John Cockshaw, and in 1999 his accountant did a moonlight flit with most of his life-savings. At the turn of the millennium, at the age of 33, Jack was close to bankruptcy and took an overdose. Weeks later, he was diagnosed with manic depression (bipolar). Now, after a hiatus of four years, Jack is back with a brand new nationwide tour and the release of his first autobiography, both of which are titled *Mann in Black*.

I catch up with Jack at his Fulham maisonette where he's lived with Alice [a freelance project manager] for almost fifteen years. Contrary to his trademark black attire, Jack is sporting blue jogging pants and a grey t-shirt bearing the words "The Fool on the Hill". He is slim and ruddy. After tea and croissants in the kitchen with Alice [seven months pregnant, and also looking the picture of health], Jack leads me up two flights of stairs to an attic room he uses as an office. It's a tight squeeze, crammed with a large oak writing desk that once belonged to his father, bulging bookcases, a tatty leather armchair and a sofa-bed. I ask Jack first about the golden age of the alternative comedy circuit: was it as wild as people say?

'It wasn't so much a circuit as a cauldron, or a cabaret,' he says. 'I used to travel across London in a special outfit my mum made: right side a dress, left side a boiler suit. Half Thatcher/half Scargill? Their voices weren't hard to master. Margaret's had matured and lowered to sound more authoritative, and Arthur's...well, it was practically falsetto.' [Jack's smile is lop-sided, mischievous, disarming]

'So, how did you get from the club scene to *Blankety Blank* of all places?'

'The BBC phoned Gerry last-minute. It was an odd sort of gig. The other panelists weren't rank-and-file anarchists: Cheryl Baker, Philip Schofield, Christopher Biggins and Floella Benjamin. Thank God for Julian Clary in his rubber bondage. [Laughs] I spent most of the show in a gurning competition with Les Dawson. I can't remember much else from the eighties. It was a haze of smoky pubs and stages. I said yes to everything. By that I mean alcohol and drugs as well as gigs. The comedy scene was risk-taking, challenging, and a bit out of control. I was rubbing shoulders with well-known comedians: Alexei, Ben, Tony, Rik. But I wasn't part of the in-crowd. I was too young. Being born in 1966 has proved a disaster. I missed England's World Cup final, and the release of The Beatles' best-ever album, *Revolver*. I was too young for punk in 1977, and I missed the new rock 'n' roll that was genuine alternative comedy circa 1980. By 1986 it was Aids, Third World famine and dole queues. I was a depressed Smiths fan, all dressed up and nowhere to go.' [He does an uncanny Morrissey impression, singing lines from "There is a Light That Never Goes Out"].

'How did you build your career from the eighties into the nineties? You and John Cockshaw were filling big arenas.'

'John and I formed *Cockshaw and Mann* in 1990. It was tough back then. Impressionists were going out of fashion faster than shell suits and mullets. John adapted my absurdist style and subject-matter to changing trends, but we argued about everything. I liked intimate theatres, he loved giant stadia. I liked radio, he loved TV. We became slaves to capitalism, the servants of marketing bods. Despite fame and money, and there was genuinely "loadsa money", I woke up one morning feeling disillusioned, grubby, ashamed. I was going through a depression but didn't recognise it. I phoned John and said: "I can't write over-educated, sixth-form banter anymore", and he said: "Good, I don't think you should either!" And that was that. John went on to bigger, better things, and I...well, I went on to attempted suicide.' [Laughs]

Jack's memoir, *Mann in Black*, is a candid, painful examination of a life filled with love and loss, laugh-out-loud comedy and terrible tragedy. It chronicles his idyllic early childhood in Muswell Hill with West End actress/mother Estella, American journalist/father Jack Mann Snr., and siblings Ernest and Lauren [how their lives were turned upside-down by the sudden death of their father when Jack was fourteen]. Jack went off the rails for a few years, rediscovering himself at Oxford University where he nurtured a love of John Donne, a poet about whom he continues to write occasional papers today; certainly unusual for a stand-up.

'Donne's my guilty pleasure,' he says, pointing to a bookshelf. 'Did you know he was called *Jack* Donne as well as John Donne? We're kindred spirits. I'm fascinated by his merging of comedy and tragedy; his weeping wit. Donne was ill for long periods. Sickness stalked him, but such things made him focus on what mattered. Critics think he was a backward-looking medieval scholar, not a renaissance man, but I'd say Donne was at a crossroads. He was a romantic poet with spiritual obsessions, but had a healthy appreciation of medical and scientific discoveries.'

These happen to be some of the themes explored in Jack's eclectic new stand-up show, which I've seen at preview. I ask him about the title, *Mann in Black*, suggesting people will confuse him with Johnny Cash. After all, he does look a bit like Cash; younger, but similar bone structure, dark hair and brooding good looks. [Jack bursts into song again, doing a fine impression of the Country and Western legend] 'Well, I'd like to wear a raaain-bow every day, to tell the world that every-thing's okay... Cash has a great voice to mimic. Baritone, which suits me now at 37, but his sibilant Ss are the key. In the show, I sing that song in the voice of Tony Blair. What's happened? In less than a decade he's gone from messianic New Labour hope to Bush-loving warmonger. An invasion of Afghanistan? And what are these weapons of mass destruction in Iraq?'

'Your show's polymathic, like your previous *Renaissance Mann* tour: psychoanalysis, philosophy, politics, literature, neuroscience, art history...'

'I'm the proverbial Jack-of-all-trades, master of none. Comedians are cracked philosophers.'

'But it's personal now, more edgy?'

'Well,' he says, 'life without an edge is like a pen without a point, isn't it? Or the Mona Lisa without a mouth.'

'It's interesting. You mention rainbows in your memoir, and in your show...when you talk about the diagnosis of bipolar disorder?'

'Well, Octavian my therapist suggested my ups were sunshine, my downs were rain, and what's created from that combination but a rainbow? It sounds cheesy, but it's a positive view of things. I've taken control of my life again. It's like Carl Jung said: "I'm not what happened to me, I'm what I choose to be". Or, as George Burns put it: "Look to the future because that's where you'll spend the rest of your life".'

The poster for the new tour shows Jack dressed in black, holding a skull and looking incredulously into its hollowed-out eye sockets, Hamlet-style. 'That was my idea,' he says. '*Mann in Black* is about life and death, comedy and tragedy; the Siamese Twins of the soul. The skull that Hamlet holds is that of his father's court jester, Yorick, and the skull is found by a clown; of all people, a clown! There are a few morbid gags and then Hamlet sadly recalls how Yorick was "a fellow of infinite jest". Hamlet understands the light that shines in the dark, but appreciates the darkness that overshadows all mankind.'

If this all sounds like too much melancholy for a stand-up tour, don't be put off. Despite the tragic themes underlying the memoir and tour [sickness, death and decay], Jack Mann is wonderfully adept at turning darkness into light on stage. It's an eclectic, carefully crafted alchemy. Think Kafka with a funny bone. Life [and death] are joyfully anatomised, and it is seriously funny. 'Life has to triumph,' Jack says. 'I have reasons to be optimistic. Alice, the love of my life, is due to have our baby in eight weeks. Third time lucky for us, touch wood [he taps his father's old desk]. I'm fit and healthy [Jack went dry for the whole of 2000, quit smoking, jogs three times a week, and now only drinks at weekends].

I ask him about imminent fatherhood. Will it alter his view of life?

'When I saw him on the ultrasound, this little Mann curled up inside Alice's womb, I was the happiest guy on Earth. I'm calling him Hunter. He'll be the centre of our universe, heralding a new age of Fear and Loathing in Las Fulham.'

'And maybe you'll get new comedy material from your son?'

'Well, I'll take a notepad to the hospital just in case. [Laughs] Alice and I are bringing someone new into the world, even if it's one of war, environmental disaster, global poverty and terrorism. I'll be a good father. I'll deal with the nappies of mass distraction.'

Jack is clearly excited about such a prospect. Before I leave, he shows me a newly-painted room that will be Hunter's. 'I wanted to paint it black,' he quips, 'but Alice fought furiously for pale blue, so we compromised on this Feng Shui-influenced, delicate but still quite manly grey-blue colour.' There's a cot beside the window, and suspended from the ceiling a vintage model of a seagull; something of an heirloom. Jack says he's already thinking about moving to a bigger house, maybe outside London, perhaps closer to Alice's parents in Kent. 'Nearer the sea and clean air...when Hunter gets too big for this maisonette...in a few years? There's no rush...let's see what the future brings. In the meantime, we have everything to look forward to - touch wood.' [He taps the frame of the cot]

And if anyone deserves any sort of luck, it is Jack Mann: the irrepressible *Mann in Black*.

Jack thought: *whatever happened to that seagull?* And then he remembered. He'd torn it from the ceiling of Hunter's room, snapped off the wings, and tossed them into the empty cot. And how had his newborn son died? From a faulty gas line. Just hours old, Hunter had been fed nitrous oxide, instead of oxygen. Laughing gas. Laughing gas. Laughing gas.

Jack phoned Gerry, keeping him up to speed with developments; though really he was clinging onto his best friend. He didn't speak of the possible tumour. Mentioning it would be tempting fate, but he did introduce the possibility of MS.

Gerry wasn't fazed. 'Tell me what it feels like.'

'Imagine you have the worst hangover you've ever had, Gerry, and multiply it by ten. That's where I am now, every conscious minute. I'm so dizzy and sick I can't walk straight or think straight. The brain fog is blinding. My hands and feet are on fire. I'm burning in a living hell.'

'Sorry I asked,' said Gerry, faking laughter. 'I can't imagine it. I don't know what to say, except hang in there, Jack. You're a fighter. You'll survive this.'

'I'm starting to wonder.'

'Blimey, you've overcome terrible things before. Manic depression, my accountant stealing all our money, Alice's miscarriages…and then there was poor little Hunter. You bounced back each time. You'll deal with this, whatever it turns out to be.'

Jack went to the garden office at weekends, avoiding the weekday din of workmen around the house. Cement-mixers, plasterers with buckets, roofers with saws, nail guns and hammers. Once, at the request of Alice, he ventured inside and walked around Seagull House by himself, examining the handiwork and seeing what tasks remained to be done. Alice asked if he could check simple but important things like where the radiators went. Wires and cabling were hanging out of the walls and ceilings ready for fittings and switches. They were, he thought, like his own electrical cabling and wires. He climbed one of the ladders to the first floor and limped around the bedrooms and bathrooms. In the middle of the master, he dropped to the floorboards in a crumpled heap. His dream, he knew, had become a never-ending nightmare.

Jack's father-in-law, Alan, brought him an old walking stick. It was made of hazel, stretched and bent at the top into a wrinkled handle. It was too long, so Jack used a handsaw and chisel to hack an inch off of the bottom, replacing the rubber stopper. When he found the energy to walk Pandora, it was now just a short trip around the bungalows or occasionally to the sea. He could never quite get used to the stick. It was more of a leaning device than an actual walking stick. Without it, though, the world span out of control and his legs buckled beneath him. He asked himself one day, looking out to sea: *How did you get here? How do you get back to where you were?*

Evoked Potentials

Jack and Alice waited in the new wing of the hospital, in the neurology department. A familiar man strode through the security door. He was wearing a mid-blue tweed jacket with leather elbow patches, and carrying a dark briefcase. His neck was long, and his beard was grey. 'Mr. Swan,' Jack whispered. Hoping to be recognised, he tried to catch the consultant's eye, but he strode past with his customary purposeful glide, eyes set forwards, irises like pennies.

'God,' Alice whispered. 'You didn't tell me he looked so scary.'

'He's just back from the Bahamas.'

'Not much of a tan,' said Alice. It was true. Mr. Swan's skin was gaunt, adding to the natural severity of his expression.

Jack was called through, and Alice was asked to stay where she was.

A specialist nurse said she would first conduct the "somato-sensory evoked potential". He rested the walking stick against the wall and removed most of his clothes. She attached electrodes to his head and various parts of his body including his hands and feet, and he imagined he was the central nervous system of Seagull House being tested by an electrician. Small pulses of electricity of carefully graded frequency were run through the cables and around his body. She recorded these on a computer. She said it wouldn't take long, but after a few unsuccessful attempts, during which she grew agitated and the sticky part of the electrodes kept slipping off, she asked him to relax or the test might not work. Finally, she stared at her PC with a surprised expression. She was looking at a series of peaks and troughs on a graph like the seismic shifts of an earthquake. 'Is it abnormal?' he asked. She refused to comment, saying it was her job to record the findings and not to interpret too much from them. That would be for the consultant.

The second test, what she called the "visual evoked potential", involved electrodes being attached all over his scalp. Jack had to look at a chequer board of gyrating squares and lines on a screen; first with the left eye, and then the right, wearing an eyepatch like Jack Sparrow. Again, he asked if it was a normal or abnormal response, and she wouldn't say. All she said at the end, when he was putting his socks and shoes on, was: 'How are you getting home today, Mr. Mann?' When he said his wife was taking him, she replied: 'Good. I don't think you should be driving.'

What it Feels Like to be Dying

The weekend before seeing Mr. Swan, Jack collapsed in the Bunker. The first Alice knew about it was a sudden bang coming from the lounge and Pandora's anxious bark. She ran in and discovered Jack splayed on the tiled floor. 'Alice,' he said, 'I can't walk. My head is exploding. I think I'm dying.' His hands were shaking and his face was as white as a china plate.

Speeding to the hospital, she kept asking, 'How bad is it, Jack?'

'Off the scale.'

'New things?' she said, keeping him talking, gauging the severity.

'I think I'm going to be sick.'

'Migraine sick?'

He shook his head. 'Like nothing on Earth, Alice. Like my mind and body have given in. I'm melting down. I just want it to stop. This must be what it feels like to be dying.'

Seeing Jack hanging onto Alice's shoulder, nurses rushed him to triage. They lay him on a bed and took readings, all within normal range. Alice called her dad and he arrived within minutes, living as he did just behind the hospital.

'Well, what are you doing here, Jack?' Alan said, trying to be funny, but his darting eyes betrayed anxiety.

A junior doctor examined Jack, asking the same old questions. When he heard about the pending consultation with Mr. Swan and the lumbar results, he said, 'Has anyone mentioned MS?'

'Been there, bought the t-shirt,' said Alice. 'And you're premature. Why is everything neurological always MS? There could be a hundred other causes.'

'If this is MS,' said Jack, forgetting he was in the presence of his father-in-law who was always appalled by bad language, 'I'm fucking screwed.' He pretended to need the loo. 'I can't bloody walk,' he said, laughing with embarrassment. 'I left your stick at home, Alan.'

'I'll get a wheelchair,' his father-in-law said, shuffling off.

Alan returned and helped him into the wheelchair. It was, thought Jack, the oddest of his most recent experiences; the role reversal of being pushed along corridors to a disabled toilet by his eighty-something father-in-law. This pensioner who'd mastered the art of decomposing, whose skeleton was held together by metal bolts, whose eyes were murky ponds, whose heart had been operated upon twice (quadruply) and now beat to the artificial rhythm of a pacemaker, whose kidneys had withered away to walnuts, whose lungs had been turned into poppadums because of asbestosis, whose knees creaked like floorboards even when he stood still, whose carpet slippers had been customised to accommodate his arthritic and excessively knuckled toes, whose burgeoning dementia had given him a hand tremor, slurred speech and prescription incontinence pads. This poor man was pushing Jack, who up until three months ago had been a fit forty-four year old who'd run six London marathons, and once climbed Kilimanjaro.

'Thanks for doing this,' said Jack, feeling guilty about all of the jokes he'd ever made on stage about Alan. One gag made him feel guiltier than the rest. *Despite my in-laws' multifarious age-related medical illnesses and obsessions*, he told audiences, *they've been married more than fifty years, and still find time to be "sort of" romantic. You know, unexpected boxes of chocolates, bouquets of flowers, the booking of each other's hospital appointments, the dressing of each other's wounds on Sunday mornings...not so much Fifty Shades of Grey, you understand, as Fifty Shades of Grey's Anatomy...* How they laughed. How he laughed along with them. How the world was laughing at him now.

Alan levered Jack out of the chair and helped him into the disabled cubicle. Jack closed the door on him and clung onto the sink, staring into a cracked mirror. A strange Jack Mann stared back; a hollowed-out Mann. He tried to cool his hands under cold running water and threw some over his face, looking again. He muttered to himself, 'This is nothing this is nothing this is nothing.' In reality, he was the man who was becoming nothing. He clambered into the wheelchair and Alan pushed him back to bed. With nothing more they could do, the hospital discharged him from its care and Alice took him home.

Back at the Bunker, Alice made him lie down on the sofa and placed a blanket over his legs. Jack wasn't talking. She turned the TV on, made him a cup of tea and returned to the kitchen to prepare a chicken casserole. She poured herself a large glass of wine, because, she told herself, that's what you do in a crisis: start cooking, start drinking, then eat; in that order. Whilst the pot simmered, she searched the internet for Mr. Swan. At first there were just bits and pieces, then she found two interesting items: a paper on the future of neurology in East Kent which was based on the findings of a committee chaired by Mr. Swan, and a video posted on YouTube by someone with an unusual interest in parliamentary papers and proceedings. It was an obscure House of Commons Select Committee conducted less than a year ago, and there was Mr. Swan's bearded face and unforgiving penny eyes as scary on screen as the first time she'd seen them in the flesh. He was dressed in a dove grey pinstriped suit and red tie, sitting at a desk beside two other men. They were answering questions about diagnosis and treatment in 2020. The female Chair seemed most interested in the cost of putting changes in place. Mr. Swan provided the answers, saying at one point that research in Kent had shown the importance of prompt diagnosis and correct neurological treatment.

Mr. Swan was lording it a bit, Alice thought, her elbows perched on her farmhouse table, knife in hand, but he had an easy manner that disarmed detractors. Sometimes though, pressing a point too firmly, his easiness strayed into arrogance or flippancy. He waved away questions as if they were annoying horse flies, and then he had a question of his own to ask the esteemed Committee: 'What,' he said, rather rhetorically, folding his arms across his chest, 'what is the worst mistake a consultant can make?' When the panel didn't answer, he said, 'Okay, put it this way, what's the worst thing any medical professional can do when they assess a patient?' After another delay, the Chair said, 'Why don't you tell us, Mr. Swan? You are the consultant neurologist with, I note, more than 40 years' experience.'

'Diagnosis is a compass,' Swan said, 'and a faulty compass is worse than no compass at all. You misdiagnose a patient; let's call him patient X. X is then fruitlessly sent on a journey that costs the primary care trust a fortune. X's illness isn't treated appropriately, X's health deteriorates. Worst case scenario, X dies, and all because of a sloppy diagnosis.' Jesus, thought Alice. It's like listening to Jack's story. Jack might be Mr. X. 'What we are proposing here is an extended research project that will put in place procedures to assist the correct diagnosis of neurological complaints and conditions first time around; this is long overdue if you compare the UK with the rest of Europe. A significant percentage of all patients coming through the doors of our A&Es will have an illness with a neurological basis, but interestingly more than half of these will be sent to the wrong place, like the stroke ward, and seen by the wrong doctors or consultants.'

Despite the magnitude of the fast-approaching consultation (for nearly two months Alice's head had been filled with little more than the "to be or not to be brain tumour" meeting), Alice was no longer apprehensive. Mr. Swan was someone she wanted to meet; an experienced and reliable professional. Someone who'd understand the anguish Jack and she had experienced through misdiagnoses, stroke wards and seeing the wrong doctors.

Languishing on the sofa, watching TV and catching the occasional smell of chicken and herbs, Jack slipped in and out of consciousness. Sick and tired, he thought each programme he watched would be his last, so he hoped it'd be enlightening. Classical music played as the backdrop to a documentary called *Leonardo Da Vinci: The Man Who Wanted to Know Everything.* The Mann who wanted to know anything, Jack thought. The narrator said it was the 500th anniversary of Da Vinci's something…Jack couldn't hear whether it was birth, death or completion of a masterpiece. The screen flickered images and voice-overs. Jack struggled to keep up. There was a chronology, a movement from left to right, but it was a washing machine jumble: Da Vinci as a baby in a crib being set upon by an eagle, birds circling, water flowing, diagrams of flying machines and Vitruvian Man. Da Vinci had had a deep interest in nature, mainly birds and water. He wanted mankind to fly high and dive deep. Pursuit of perfection. Bodies laid out on tables, anatomised. Muscles and bones and innards. Comparisons with Michelangelo: a mural on the wall of the Sistine chapel, *The Last Judgement*, the Second Coming. Christ beardless and virile. People on the left ascending to heaven with angels, those on the right dragged down to hell by demons. A close-up of Saint Bartholomew, the patron saint of butchers, a knife in one hand, skin flayed in one piece from his entire body in the other, hanging white and limp like a ghost's cloak. Upon this deathly frock a face, the face of Michelangelo. A self-portrait of the genius artist; the tortured face of his soul. It almost brought tears to Jack's eyes, thinking about torture, skin, that cloak, that face, as if his own was fading, and the skin of his soul was slipping off beside him on the sofa.

To Be or Not to Be

The consultation with Mr. Swan was scheduled for 11 a.m. Jack and Alice arrived half an hour early. They'd hardly spoken during the car journey, except for a brief conversation about the Select Committee footage. Alice said Jack's case was a perfect illustration of an imperfect system. She said things would be better from now on; they'd see the organ grinder, not his monkeys. Jack thought of flying blue monkeys and Dorothy going to the Emerald City to see the Wizard of Oz. Jack didn't need a heart in his tin chest, a medal pinned to his fur, the IQ of Einstein, a home reachable by balloon, or ruby slippers; his heart and home were sitting right beside him in the form of Alice. What he desperately wanted, needed, was a brain without a tumour.

The waiting area was busy. The double line of seats was already occupied, so Jack and Alice walked down the line into the corridor. They passed the rooms of a Dr. Solomon and a Dr. Rama (consultant neurologists), finding two vacant seats directly outside Mr. Swan's door. Jack rested his father-in-law's cane between his legs, placing both hands on the curved handle.

Nurses, doctors brushed past, going about their duties. Doors opened, doors closed. Patients with gait problems shuffled at strange angles, others hobbled on crutches. A young woman came past in an electric wheelchair. A poster on the wall informed people of what to do when someone had an epileptic fit: numbers to call, survival positions to take. Next to this, a leaflet on the prevalence of depression in MS patients. Beside this, a number for the Samaritans. There was nothing about tumours.

A nurse called out Jack's name, making his heart skitter. False alarm. She only wanted to weigh him and take his blood pressure. She took him to a room close by and sat him in a weighing chair. He'd put on half a stone in two months. His blood pressure was a little high too, but within acceptable limits. He retook his seat in the corridor and Alice knocked her knee against his, smiling to reassure him.

Mr. Swan's door slowly opened. A young man struggled out on crutches. He glanced over his shoulder to thank the consultant before looking down at the floor again, a resigned expression in his eyes.

Jack and Alice stared into the void of Swan's room, seeing two empty chairs in front of a desk, but no consultant. It was 11:20. A senior nurse walked into the room carrying a file. Jack was sure it was his. She put the file on the desk, picked up a different one and left the room, leaving the door wide open. Blood raced in Jack's veins, heart charging in his chest: *to be or not to be...a brain tumour?*

Four young doctors in white coats gathered outside the door. Huddled together, a bank of white, they looked like a bevy of swans chattering excitedly. Jack noticed one of them had bad acne. He looked too young to be a doctor; in fact, they all looked like juveniles. After some indecision, the prettiest and most assured cygnet, one Alice thought might be from Hong Kong or Singapore, took the lead and strode with purpose into Mr. Swan's room, and the other three followed. They stood by the desk, and pulled up four chairs. They placed their briefcases on the floor and sat down. Jack looked quizzically at Alice. He leaned over to check the name on the door. It still said *Mr. Swan.*

'This can't be right,' said Alice, trying to catch the eye of a nurse. 'He must have switched rooms.' The swanling doctors pulled out notebooks and pens, nattering. 'Excuse me, excuse me,' Alice said, finally getting the attention of the senior nurse. 'Can you please tell us what all those doctors are doing in Mr. Swan's room? We have a consultation. Has Mr. Swan changed rooms?'

'No,' the nurse said.

'Oh. So will there be a delay?'

'I don't think so.' The nurse poked her head around the door. 'They're students training to be doctors and will be sitting in on your consultation.'

'What?' Alice got to her feet. She threw a look at Jack. His eyes were rammed shut. 'We're here for an important meeting. We're anxious and don't want students.'

'Madam,' the nurse said, 'students have to learn some time, somewhere, don't they?'

'No,' said Alice. 'Not in our consultation they don't. Please. This meeting is a matter of life and death for my husband. He's about to find out if he's got-'

'It's the students' lives too,' the nurse interjected. 'They have their whole medical lives ahead of them. They're the future.'

Alice's chin nearly hit the floor. Her eyes bulged from their sockets. She drew herself up to her full height.

'If you don't want them to take part today, I'll ask Mr. Swan. It was his idea. I doubt he'll be happy about this.'

'Please do,' said Alice. 'Tell Mr. Swan we don't give our permission.' The nurse walked down the corridor, huffing. Alice sat down again. 'How can these things happen?' she said, shaking her head.

'I'm starting to think I'm jinxed,' he said.

A few minutes later, the four doctors picked up their bags and left the room. Alice smiled at Jack. Mr. Swan appeared, leaning against the frame of the door in his tweed jacket, checked twill shirt and grey trousers. 'Jack Mann?'

The consultant sat behind his desk and leaned back in his chair. He watched Alice close the door and eyed the Manns as they decided who sat where. He noticed Jack's walking stick. 'So, I'm Mr. Swan, consultant neurologist. You are Jack Mann, of course, but you have me at a disadvantage, madam, as I don't know who you are?' Alice introduced herself as Jack's wife and he nodded. He opened a file on his desk, scanned it briefly and stroked his beard. 'You know,' he said, 'about the student thing just now. I understand where you're coming from. I mean, who wants students sitting in on a meeting you've been waiting months for, correct? Actually, who needs students, full stop?' He laughed loudly.

'That's right,' said Alice. 'Though I guess we were all students once upon a time.'

'Exactly,' he said, leaning forward on his leather elbow patches. 'We need students to follow on after us. I wonder if you'll reconsider having them back in, just for the second half of our consultation? They need to learn, and fast. We can teach them a thing or two about neurology, right here in this room. They're next door, waiting. You could help me teach them, and I'd appreciate your help.'

'It depends what we find out,' said Alice.

Swan looked at Jack, noticing the dilated pupils and buttoned-lip. 'Jack, can I call you Jack?' Jack nodded, remembering the first time the consultant had asked that question. 'Jack, you look extremely anxious sitting there. What are you so worried about?'

'I'm worried whether I have a brain tumour or not.'

Mr. Swan shot back in his seat. 'Brain tumour?'

'He had the MRI with contrast last week,' said Alice. 'It was commissioned by King's in London nearly two months ago. We're here to find out the results.'

'Is it a tumour?' asked Jack.

'Who said you might have a tumour?'

'Dr. Richter.'

Mr. Swan's face went pink. 'Oh dear.'

'Dr. Richter phoned us at home and said you had a meeting and there was a show of hands, and Jack's second MRI showed a possible tumour.'

He shook his head in frustration. 'A show of hands? God. Jack, I've had a good look at the MRI and can say categorically that you *do not* have a brain tumour.'

'One hundred percent?'

'No brain tumour, one hundred percent.'

'So what is it then?' asked Alice, sighing.

His penny eyes rolled over to Jack. 'That's what I'd like to ask *you.*'

'Me?'

'Yes. You came in here, shoulders touching your ears, eyes down to the ground. You were naturally anxious, and you're still anxious. I mean, your shoulders are lower and you're looking me straight in the eye which is progress, but I sense fear. You're thinking, if this isn't a brain tumour, which it isn't, what else could it be?'

Jack hesitated.

'You see, I think you know what it is but are too afraid to say. In my experience patients are their own best diagnosticians. What else are you most afraid of, Jack?'

'Multiple sclerosis.'

Mr. Swan nodded. 'I concur with your diagnosis. It's hard to take, I know, but I've looked at your MRI and the large white matter lesion in the right cerebral hemisphere is clearly enhancing. This is causing your left-sided symptoms.'

Alice didn't like the word "enhancing". On the internet she'd read enhancing lesions were bad news. 'If that's the case, why are Jack's symptoms on *both* sides of his body?'

'Yes,' said Jack, holding up his hands. 'And the left side of my face but the right side of the back of my head.'

The consultant seemed perplexed.

Alice asked: 'What did the nerve conduction tests show, Mr. Swan?'

'You've had evoked potentials?'

'You ordered them,' said Jack.

Alice got the impression Mr. Swan hadn't read Jack's notes. She watched him skim them. He was winging it, and her heart sank. This paragon, this advisor to government, this highly respected consultant with more than forty years' experience was flying by the seat of his pants. While she'd been out of her mind with worry, waiting for the results from tests and scans, Mr. Swan hadn't given them a second thought. 'Ah, yes,' he said, 'positive for sensory, negative for visual. I see your lumbar has come back with O-bands.' It was as if this was the first time he'd clapped eyes on the results.

He looked up from his notes and saw Alice's arms locked over her breasts in a defensive posture. She was frowning. He noticed too that Jack's eyes had glazed over; no doubt still reeling from the revelation he really did have MS. It was always difficult knowing which way a patient would go straight after being told, from telling his first-ever MS patient in the 1980s to now, telling his last-ever NHS patient. Stupefaction was the norm, but blind denial and anger wasn't uncommon. Soon the poor chap would start the grieving process, every stage a necessary hurdle to acceptance. He wanted to tell Jack Mann the truth; that yes, MS was an incurable neurodegenerative disease which acted like a weeping wound that eventually killed, but it needn't feel like a prison sentence, not with appropriate care, support and treatment. Some of the happiest people he'd ever known had multiple sclerosis. He'd once met the world famous cellist Jaqueline Du Pre and she had one of the most aggressive sorts of MS. But did this stop her playing? Well, yes, eventually it did, but she continued with her art for as long as she could, and bravely so.

Mr. Swan knew he'd spent far too long that morning talking to his students instead of reading patient files, but there was precious little he could do about that now. These kids would take his place, eventually. Today was the day of his official retirement; his Swan Song. He was hoping it might be his Swan Song D'amour too, as one of his gang of four students - the sexy, hardworking 22-year-old, from rich Singapore stock - had cheekily asked if she could come along to his farewell lunch. He'd said no, but casually invited her to the post-lunch drinks, and the thought of such an opportunity had preoccupied him ever since. He was bailing out of the NHS today, collecting an early pension, sailing around the Caribbean for six months, then continuing a lucrative part-time private practice just around the corner from the hospital. He was also looking forward to getting back to his favourite pastime, tennis. He deserved some rewards for his long, diligent service to the public, helping thousands of patients, sitting through countless meetings and helping to transform neurological services in Kent, if not the whole of the UK. Recently, of course, he'd been winging it a bit; a clear sign of demob happiness. He was winging it now, but the patient's wife, unblinking across the desk, was onto him and there was only one thing he could do in such a situation. He'd deployed his secret weapon a few times over the years; a break in the consultation allowing time to read the full patient history, and giving the patient time to absorb the horrid news. It was a win-win, if his acting skills were still up to scratch.

'Excuse me,' he said, raising a finger as if to hush a noisy crowd. 'I've been expecting this call.' Alice watched him pick up the clunky receiver of the telephone on the desk. It hadn't rung out and she wasn't sure if it had flashed either. 'Yes, speaking,' he said, with a serious tone. 'I see. I see. Yes. One moment please.' He looked up, saying, 'I'm sorry but I really must take this urgent call.' When they didn't seem to get the message, he covered the mouth piece with his palm and said to them, 'It's someone with a *real* brain tumour? If you can please wait outside and give me ten minutes, I'll be right with you.'

They sat in the corridor and watched the door close. Alice squeezed Jack's hand. 'I'm so sorry.'

'Well, now we know,' he sighed. 'Guess our new GP was on the money.'

'Do you think Swan's read your file? I bet he's speed-reading it right now. If that phone call's genuine I'll eat my handbag.'

'That's what I thought,' he said. 'When you asked him about the nerve conduction tests it was like Toto pulling the curtain back on the Wizard of Oz, revealing him not to be God but an ordinary man.'

'What?' she said. 'Anyway, at least he looked at your MRI, Jack. You don't have a tumour.'

'I should be leaping up and down, so why does it feel like I've won the lottery but lost the ticket?'

As promised, ten minutes later the door opened and they retook their seats. This time Mr. Swan seemed well-organised. He turned his computer screen around and showed them Jack's scan, pointing out the area of inflammation. Jack thought it looked like an innocent cloud. Mr. Swan explained "demyelination", "white matter lesions" and MS. There were different types, the most common being "relapsing-remitting"; the sort he believed Jack had. There were worse kinds, he said, like "primary progressive". There was even a rampant form of malignant MS when a patient might be dead inside a year, but those cases were very rare. He told Jack that all things being equal, presentation in men was worse than in women. He said Jack was unlucky to show the first signs in his mid-40s, but it did happen.

Regarding treatment, he'd initiate methylprednisolone, 500mg/daily for five days, to calm the current inflammation. It was a steroid and Jack might find sleeping difficult, acting as it did like speed. 'More medium-term, you may well be a candidate for Beta-interferon, and I'm referring you to an MS consultant.' He told them he'd also contact one of the MS nurses, and he said there was a great therapy centre just up the road; a charity-based organisation that supported patients and treated their symptoms. 'You must never think you're alone,' he said. 'The nurse can put you in touch with them, and she'll no doubt give you lots of leaflets and information when you meet. Now,' he said, clapping his hands together, 'are we okay to have the trainee doctors back in?' After some hesitation, he said, 'It says in your file you're a professional entertainer, Jack. Is that singing or dancing?'

'Neither,' said Jack.

'He's a stand-up comedian.'

Well, who'd have thought it? thought Mr. Swan, *my very last case in this hospital, and it's the tragedy of a comedian. There's something apposite about that. Although he looks nothing like a comedian.* 'Well, shall we put on a short performance for the students, Jack? You won't have to crack any jokes, and it would be good for them to see a physical examination first hand and ask a few questions?'

The four young wannabe doctors trooped in and retook their seats. The oriental beauty with long black hair had removed her white medical coat, setting her apart from her cohort, but her natural beauty separated her from them anyway, and she was fully aware of this. She was wearing a thin silk blouse and dark knee-length skirt, and sat closest to Mr. Swan, crossing her shapely legs. From the flash of her red soles Alice knew the smart shoes were Louboutins. She took out a notebook and clicked the top of a silver pen. The others, all men armed with cheap biros, smiled at Jack with keen, half-embarrassed faces.

Mr. Swan explained the physical examination was a way of assessing the level of disability. He asked Jack to undo his laces and remove his shoes and socks, as well as his jacket. He could leave his t-shirt on. 'First question,' he said. 'Is Jack left or right-handed?'

The young men hadn't been paying attention, and the oriental woman said, 'Right-handed, Mr. Swan.'

'Good spot. You can tell a lot about a patient by watching them undo their shoelaces. Did you notice, for instance, that Jack had no difficulty untying his, and they were double-tied? He's quite dexterous. Now, Jack, can you repeat after me…British Constitution.'

'British Constitution.'

'Good, good.' Mr. Swan then asked Jack to walk in a straight line across the room, heel to toe. 'That's it, as if you're walking a tightrope.' Then he asked Jack to stand still for thirty seconds in the centre of the room with his eyes closed. He nodded at his students.

'Negative Romberg,' said the doctor with acne.

Whilst Jack's eyes were still closed, Mr. Swan asked, 'Can you touch the tip of your nose, first with your left index finger and then with your right. And…?'

'Again, negative,' said a student.

Jack was asked to get on to the bed where he was examined, just as he had been on the stroke ward, though without being asked to drop his trousers. Mr. Swan spared him this ignominy. Instruments were dragged down the soles of his feet. 'Plantars…?'

'Down, Mr. Swan,' said the woman.

'Which is a normal reflex, Jack,' he said, patting him on the shoulder.

He shone a light in each of Jack's eyes saying that these were normal too. 'Okay, you can get dressed again,' he said, retaking his seat and turning towards the four trainees. 'What else could be causing Jack's other symptoms: the tinnitus, brain fog, unsteadiness and nausea that he has reported? He uses a walking stick. There it is in the corner.'

'Anaemia?' said the doctor with acne.

'Look at the patient. Does he look anaemic?'

Jack was beetroot.

'B-12 deficiency,' said the oriental doctor.

'Yes, good answer, but does B-12 give you oligoclonal banding in your CSF or make you think you've just stepped off a liner from Tahiti?'

She shook her head.

'Guillain Barre Syndrome?' blurted a doctor who hadn't said anything up until this point. Jack remembered what the Time Lord had mentioned weeks ago. "Gillian Barry" syndrome he'd called it.

'How paralysed is Jack? What Modified Rankin score do you think I'm going to record?'

'One,' said the doctor with acne.

'Almost zero?'

'It was a rhetorical question. Of course it's zero. This isn't GBS or any other rare neurological disease, it's MS, but there doesn't appear to be any muscle stiffness or cramping, and no visual affect. It's wise to think about differentials when first diagnosing a patient. Do you have any questions you'd like to ask Jack?'

The oriental woman raised her hand. 'How long have you had a tremor?'

'What?' said Jack.

'Jack doesn't have a tremor,' said Mr. Swan.

'I noticed one,' she said.

'Okay, let's go with it, Jack.' He took a sheet of paper from the file and asked Jack to stretch out his arm and turn his right hand over, palm down. He carefully balanced the paper on top and stood back as if he'd just lit the taper of a Jumping Jack firework. Everyone in the room stared at the trembling sheet. 'Okay, there's mild tremor. Well spotted, but it's mild, and what do you expect when you've just been told you have MS?'

'He's...' said the oriental doctor, hesitating.

'Yes, he's...?'

Jack noticed she was looking at the small hoops of sweat that had developed under his armpits.

'Nothing,' she said.

'He's nothing?' said Mr. Swan, long neck extending. 'Excuse my trainee neurologist, Jack. I've heard of poor observation before but you're more than nothing to me.'

'He's sweating,' she said.

'Good lord. He's anxious. Look, his pupils are dilated like eight balls, even in this bright light. And it's hot in here. None of these are signs of a differential. However,' he said, 'you've hit the nail on the proverbial head regarding Jack's symptoms that are *not* MS-related.' The oriental doctor smiled for the first time, making her, so the consultant thought, probably the most attractive woman in the hospital, if not the whole world. 'Jack, your unsteadiness and nausea are a by-product of your anxiety. There are no abnormal brain stem signs. There's a relative paucity of signs on your MRI. You have zero disability. On the MS scale of things the prognosis isn't as bleak as you think.'

Having first reassured them, he thought he'd better fill them in on other possibilities. He placed both hands on the table. 'Now, I should tell you before this consultation is ended that there's a small chance I've got everything completely wrong.'

Jack and Alice's mouths dropped open.

'Yep. Sometimes the human body and diseases of the central nervous system in particular, move in mysterious ways. But I want you to know that I have a pretty good record for diagnosis.' Alice could see Mr. Swan was playing to his gallery of keen students, showboating like a QC to a jury, but she didn't mind. 'I'm quite proud of the fact that over many years I've managed to diagnose 90 percent of my patients correctly. True, it's not a perfect score, but you'll find it's relatively high in the field of neurology, or any other field for that matter. That's to say, one in every ten patients who walks through my door walks out of it to develop something else entirely, or their MS is worse than I've predicted, or not anything like as bad as my prognosis. But 90 percent is a good statistic. I'd have confidence in that fact if I were you.'

Before concluding the meeting he asked Jack and Alice if they had any questions. Jack asked how fast his decline into disability might be. The acned doctor said, 'That depends on the type of MS and the distribution of white matter lesions through space and time.'

Mr. Swan concurred. 'MS is unpredictable, but at the moment things are not looking too bad, Jack. I know that isn't the answer you want, but it's all we've got to go on. You'll know more after seeing your MS consultant. '

'Can I have more amitriptyline for the pain? It's getting worse.'

'Of course, I'll write a prescription.' As he was writing it, he stopped and asked, 'You don't have any other medications or illnesses that I should know about?'

'I have manic depression.'

'MS *and* bipolar? That's a bit of a double whammy. Well, here you go, Jack. Ten milligram tablets. Up the dose if necessary, but don't take more than five or six spread out over the course of a day. Consult your GP or your MS consultant if that doesn't help.'

He told the students to leave, and then he shook the Manns' hands. Jack asked Alice if she'd mind waiting outside as he had a couple of private questions. Jack closed the door and leaned on his walking stick. 'I know I have MS, Mr. Swan, and you've explained things very clearly, but man to man, what are my chances of staying out of a wheelchair?'

Mr. Swan stroked his beard. *How long's a piece of string?* 'The brain can only do one of two things. It can re-route, or it can shut down. As a man in his forties, the deterioration might arguably be sharper than say a young woman in her twenties with relapsing-remitting, but I doubt it will be the case. You've not leapt straight into primary progressive. I hate the words "mild MS", because I know the havoc it causes, but I'd say your chances are reasonably good. I can't specify if or when you'll need a wheelchair, but you know eventually this disease will take a certain toll.'

'If there's one piece of advice you can give me in the meantime, you know, about changes I can make to my life that might help me with my MS, what would it be?'

Mr. Swan stroked his beard again, thinking just how amazing the human capacity to survive was. This Jack Mann, his last ever NHS patient, who'd been told he had MS and who gave a fine impression of someone steamrollered, was now, forty-five minutes later, taking possession of his disease and control of his new situation. There was hope for this patient. 'Yes. Eat plenty of oranges and bananas,' he said. Mr. Swan couldn't believe his own ears; his very last words to his very last NHS patient: *oranges and bananas*.

The Grief Journey

Mr. Swan had been right; the steroids kept Jack wide-eyed for five nights straight, as if he'd swallowed a bucket of uppers, though it made no impression at all on his symptoms. Unbearable pain in his hands and feet continued. A higher dose of amitriptyline eased the burning sensations during the day, but each morning Jack awoke with intense pins and needles, and now his lips seemed glued together as a side-effect of the medication. Stepping barefoot on smooth tiles was like walking on broken glass, and every night he lay on the camp bed in his igloo room, ice-cold wine coolers encasing sizzling hands.

During this time Alice and Jack discussed what to do next. First, should they tell friends and family about the MS? For too long they'd contained the threat of a possible brain tumour and it had nearly caused implosion. They were not going to make the same mistake now that he had a definite MS diagnosis.

Alice's parents were the first to be told. Pat and Alan were full of sympathy, and said they'd help any way they could. Gerry, although surprised, was not as shocked. He knew a little about MS already from Fran, who'd had an auntie with the disease. Ernie, likewise, had had his suspicions.

News quickly spread along the grapevine, and Jack realised during the following week that reaction to his illness split into two schools: some old friends he'd not contacted for years telephoned support, rekindling distant memories from the comedy circuit as far back as the 1980s. Names and faces that hadn't crossed his mind since that time were once again fresh, and he was grateful. On the other hand, some people he'd regarded as fairly close seemed to evaporate into the ether.

There was a downside to so many phone calls. Naturally telephobic for most of his life, the recent calls from Dr. Richter had escalated Jack's fear and set it in granite. He wouldn't say the Bunker was deluged, but by the third week the phone would ring three or four times a day and he'd nearly always leave the calls to the answer machine. John Cockshaw, his old comedian friend and writing partner, left a long message saying he was sorry to hear the sad news, and that if Jack needed to talk, he was there for him.

The truth was, Jack no longer wanted to talk about MS. He wished he hadn't agreed to tell anyone. But it was too late. The box of frogs had been opened and they were springing every which way. He was labelled "damaged goods". Gerry wanted to use the news as a different kind of springboard. It could be good for exposure.

Jack was in a tail-spin. He read in a leaflet given by his newly appointed MS nurse that he'd go through a journey of grief in several stages: shock, disbelief, denial, anger, fear, self-blame, loss, and finally, realisation and accommodation. From there, the leaflet said, he could move on. He was stuck between denial and anger, and just wanted to be left alone. He didn't even want to talk about it with Alice, who spent hours each evening researching the different treatments available for MS, including revolutionary research trials using chemotherapy. There was an excellent online forum too, she said, and he could even register anonymously.

Instead, he wanted to fill his ears up with sand, trudging around the Bunker wearing headphones, listening to the hardest rock music he could muster. He wanted it all to go away. He wanted to be normal, and feared he couldn't ever be normal again. Was this stage five: fear?

He was invited to the MS therapy centre by his nurse, and he didn't want to go, but go he did, because Alice insisted and she'd taken valuable time off work. The building was on the edge of the city, less than a mile from the hospital. Nestled beside a rugby field, it was little more than two old portacabins wrapped around a large, hyperbaric oxygen chamber. Jack hobbled in with his walking stick. He could see people through the portholes of the oxygen chamber, masks over their faces. They all gave him the thumbs up. The young woman responsible for checking the gauges, herself an MS patient, said it was necessary to sit in the pressurised chamber for hours, day after day at the beginning of a course of treatment, but the process of oxygenation really helped with symptoms, especially fatigue and brain fog.

Jack met the manager, a charming woman, and then he was a member, and so too was Alice as his nominated carer. Just the sound of it was wrong to his ears; Alice, his "carer". They were given tea, and sat down at a table listening to the conversations passing between other MS patients. Despite cold beating at the single-glazed windows, steaming them up, the atmosphere inside was warm, friendly and supportive. The manager explained that besides the oxygen chamber, the centre offered acupuncture, massage, physiotherapy and counselling. 'Some people just pop in for a chat and to meet friends,' she said, smiling. Alice was keen to hear more, discovering that the portacabins had been in situ for over thirty years and were no longer fit for purpose. A new centre needed to be built. It'd be state-of-the-art, with a hydrotherapy pool. The project needed funding, and Alice offered to help with publicity for sponsored marathons, scooter rides, jumble sales, coffee mornings and quiz nights.

Jack had zoned out, and was only partially aware of conversations. His dizziness, usually worse when standing, was spinning him about even though he was sitting down. He looked around, paralysed inside by the sight of so many wheelchairs and hospital crutches. One woman couldn't speak or control her head. She was practically dead from the chin down; yet she seemed happy with her carer by her side, feeding her cake. An elderly man sitting at another table waved, reminding Jack of Wilfred from the stroke ward; he had the same far-away look in his eyes. Jack went across to him, and they discussed shared symptoms of sensitivity to light and temperature. Alice, engaged in a conversation elsewhere, watched her husband at a distance, viewing his action as a sign of progress.

The MS nurse gave members a refresher course on pain and fatigue, but Jack hobbled outside for air. It wasn't just dizziness; it was seeing the stages of a certain future set out before him. On his way out, he noticed a man in a wheelchair smoking a cigarette. His arms looked stiff in the cold and he was lost in thought, staring up at a tree in the middle of the car park.

The man, in his thirties, looked up at Jack's face and down again at his feet, spying the walking stick. 'They're after choppin' this tree down,' he said, in a Glaswegian accent. 'The rugby club is.' The trunk of the tree was two feet thick, the branches sweeping left and right in a bracing November wind. The streetlamp behind it transformed the canopy into a magical, intricate spider's web of wood. It reminded Jack of the old cherry tree at the end of Marine Walk, not far from Seagull House, though that had suffered from gales and leaned away from the sea.

'Drivers havin' trouble gettin' in and out on match days.'

'Why chop it down now?' asked Jack.

'Och, over my did body. The tree's stayin', even if I have te chain my wheelchair to it.'

There came an awkward moment when the man offered Jack a cigarette and he turned it down. He understood the camaraderie that came from such an exchange. A cigarette could kill but it could also bond strangers briefly together. 'Ye have MS?'

Jack nodded. 'Just diagnosed.'

'Aye,' he said. 'I remember that day.' He lit his cigarette with a brass zippo. 'I wes standing right where you're standing, not two years since.'

Jack found himself staring at the muddy ground beneath his feet.

'I had a stick just like ye too, then six months it's crutches, then three months ago I couldne get outta bed. The legs...' he banged them with his hand, '...packed up they did. I'm in this machine now.'

'I'm sorry,' said Jack.

'I wes in the army, fought all over Europe, Kosovo and that. I lost me best mate o'er there. It was hell o'er there, but nothin' like this hell. At least you could walk away frem it.'

'What happened when you got back?'

'The day I get oot, same day mind, the world at me feet, I get pins and needles up and down me legs. Sem bloody day. Everything's gone te shit ever since. Primary fuckin' progressive.'

'I'm so sorry.'

'Aye, so'm I.' He dragged on his cigarette and stared at the tree. 'Thirty-six next month and a happy birthday it'll be alright; me and me mate MS for company.' When Jack didn't say anything, he said, 'So, wet type ye get?'

'They don't know yet.'

'Aye. It teks time te work it out. Maybe you'll get lucky.'

'I hope so,' said Jack. 'Do you have family or friends who help?'

'Na, they all live in Glasgow. Not one of them wants te know. Thank God for the centre.'

'And have you been back up to Scotland…since you found out about the MS?'

He shook his head, and stared at the tree. 'Ye find out who the good people really are when this atom bomb drops on ye hid.'

Alice appeared at the door of the portacabin. The manager waved at Jack and he returned the compliment. He turned again to the soldier. 'Are you going to be okay?'

'Aye, ye have te be.'

'Well…you take care.'

'Youse too,' he said, eyes locked on the tree.

King Edward

Alice's parents visited the following afternoon. Pat needed help lifting her swollen feet over the threshold. Eighty-one years old and crippled with arthritis, she moved gingerly into the lounge with the aid of two walking sticks; tiny steps punctuated by 'Ooh,' and 'Agh'. There was no synovial fluid in her knee joints, bone ground against bone, and the pain was sent from hell, she said. She didn't get out of the flat much, preferring to stay in and watch TV, although "watching" TV was difficult as she had macular degeneration in both eyes. Alan called her a "home bird". He had to do all of the shopping.

Yet, somehow, the traditional gender roles of their wartime generation had not been affected by their disabilities. Pat still cooked and Alan rarely went into the kitchen, except for a glass of sugar-free lemonade last thing at night. Everything Pat cooked was out of a tin, a packet or the freezer. Nothing was fresh except milk and salad. It was hard, but she tried at least three times a week to prepare and cook a piece of pre-packed meat, usually pork, and always in the same sauce made from a tub of gravy granules. This involved defrosting a joint in the microwave, then cooking it slowly in a hot oven and reheating it again in the microwave just before serving it two hours later. Alan once confided in Jack that the meat, no matter what it had previously been, always had the texture of slipper insoles, though he'd never tell his wife this. Jack had volunteered to make them a meal at least once a week; a vegetable chilli or chicken broth. Occasionally, as a surprise on a Sunday, he'd cook a whole chicken with steamed vegetables and roast potatoes, bringing it to them like meals on wheels. These meals had stopped the day Jack fell ill. He no longer did much in the kitchen except feed Pandora and make cups of tea. Even these everyday activities had become onerous. A kettle full of water was a dumbbell. Lifting a ceramic dog bowl full of food was like doing a bench press.

Alan asked Pat not to go on about her painful knees, given Jack's obvious discomfort. Alan never went on about the pain he had in his head, chest, arms, knees, ankles and eardrums, did he? No, he just got on with it.

'That's what men do, isn't it?' Pat replied. 'They keep it in, but I see it in your face, Al. Sometimes you let it out.' She was referring to his ability to store up negative kinetic energy from the pain until it all got too much and he'd blow his top like Krakatoa.

Jack didn't talk about his pain either. Wretched though it was, talking about it just made it worse. It was the kind of pain that could tip the balance in someone's mind and make them do something stupid. The thought of living with it for the rest of his life forced him to the precipice of depression every night and each morning, but such thoughts he kept to himself. His only hope was that the pain would one day go as quickly as it had arrived.

'How's my favourite son-in-law?' Pat said, making light in the dark.

Jack kissed her powdery cheek and eased her down onto the highest chair in the lounge. Trying to get up again later would be a big problem. They'd need a crane and a harness, she said. That was a reference to her weight as much as her knees. She wasn't shy about talking about the weight she'd struggled with since her thirties. 'Don't ever get old,' she said.

They had mugs of tea with chocolate biscuits and talked about Jack's MS; the real reason for their visit. 'You've got to fight this,' Pat said.

Alice pointed out that this wasn't influenza, it wasn't even like cancer. There were no cures, but there was hope that chemotherapy might help some types of MS.

Pat started to well-up. 'Chemotherapy? Will Jack go bald?'

'We'll see what the consultant says.'

'How you bearing up, Jack?' asked his father-in-law. 'You look tired.'

'Surviving, but I don't really want to talk about it.'

'There you go,' said Pat. 'He's just like you Al, bottling it up.'

'Pain is good,' said Alan. 'It's your body reminding you you're still alive.'

Alice heard Jack's sigh, and frowned. She loved her father but knew him only too well. Having experienced and survived so many illnesses and health scares during the course of his lifetime, and having outlived most of his contemporaries, Alan had grown accustomed to telling people what they should do about their ailments, pains and prescriptions. His intentions were only ever good, but he sometimes came across as a self-appointed guru.

'Dad, it's neuropathic. It's not like your shoulder pain. It's to do with the messages sent along the nerves from the brain around the body.'

'Still,' he said, 'pain is good. It means you're alive.'

'Or it means you're going to die,' said Jack, killing the atmosphere. 'Like I say, I'd prefer not to talk about it.'

'Of course, Jack,' said Pat, glaring at her husband.

'You just hang in there,' said Alan. 'There are all sorts of painkillers. I can't take morphine myself as it makes me throw up.'

'I'm okay on patches,' said Pat, lifting the sleeve of her blouse to show Jack.

He didn't love his in-laws the same way Alice loved them, but he did respect and admire them, and most times enjoyed their company. One giddy Christmas morning not that long ago, he actually wrote in a card that he felt like their son as much as their only son-in-law, which, when he came to think about it later, was a bit weird. They kept the card and put it up on their mantelpiece every Christmas. They sometimes went off-piste leading Jack down various memory lanes about people he didn't know and never would; but a lot of these family stories tended to revolve around Alice. They had made her who she was, and he loved all of her. When he thought about it, she had inherited a lot of their resilience, backbone and feistiness. When he looked at his kind in-laws, he saw Alice, and in Alice he saw a natural reflection of them.

The conversation shifted towards the future, and Alice said she'd look into stairlifts.

'The NHS should pay for that,' said Pat.

'It's good to future-proof a building,' Alice's father said, ever the retired engineer. 'Are your stairs wide enough in the new house? Are the walls strong enough for bolting? You'll need a good turning circle at the top.'

'I'll speak to the builder,' said Alice.

'And you might want to think about having a bedroom downstairs,' said Pat.

Pat and Alan had been sleeping in separate rooms for thirty years. Their various medical issues and trips to the toilet during the night made it essential if they were to get any meaningful sleep, but they hadn't been forced into this situation until well into their fifties; Jack was already forced by painful circumstance to sleep alone in his igloo at the age of forty-five.

'It was going to be open-plan downstairs,' said Alice, 'but there's space for a single bedroom if we shave something from the hall and the dining area beside the cloakroom. I'm going to talk to the builder. What do you think, Jack?'

'I don't know,' he said. He was a passenger to their conversation. In fact, he was having trouble following sentences, full stop.

'You should qualify to get a disabled parking badge and disability pay,' Alan said.

'I've already ordered the forms online, Dad.'

After her parents had gone, Alice remarked that Jack needn't have been so sharp with her father on the subject of pain. Jack snapped. He didn't want to talk about it with her father or with her for that matter. He trudged to the camp bed in his little igloo room and pretended to go to sleep.

In the morning, the air between them hadn't cleared. Jack said he wanted to see his mother in London and was prepared to drive rather than get trains. Alice protested saying she'd drive, but it'd have to be another day as she had wall-to-wall meetings. There'd been a few security glitches with Prince Edward and his entourage, but a rearranged timetable had been sorted out.

Jack said flippantly, 'All that security for a King Edward?'

It was an innocent enough pun on Prince Edward, who would never become a King because of older siblings, but Alice didn't enjoy or understand the potato reference. Neither did she appreciate Jack mocking her work, especially after so much blood, sweat and tears had been spent on the theatre project. As she pointed out, she currently had five flipping jobs and was close to exhaustion: working full-time on the theatre, being a housewife, a carer, a chauffeur, and a project manager for Seagull House.

'Chauffeur?'

'Your jokes are starting to misfire,' she said.

'That will be the MS, the brain damage.'

She ignored this, hoping it wasn't going to be Jack's last resort whenever they disagreed about anything. She calmly repeated that she'd drive him to see his mother another day.

'I'm driving over this morning and there's nothing you can do about it.'

'Jack,' she said, folding her arms. 'Look at yourself. You can barely stand without a stick, let alone walk...how are you going to drive for two hours there, and two hours back?'

'I don't drive standing up,' he said. 'Your mum and dad are almost parked on our doorstep. You see them three or four times a week. I haven't seen my mum since we moved down here. Four months. She's probably forgotten I exist.'

'I'm their only child, Jack. My parents depend on me.'

'I can't leave everything to Lauren.'

'I know, but can't it wait a few more days?'

'No, it's today or never!'

'Right,' she said. On her way out she looked for his car keys; hiding them had been her plan from the very moment he mentioned driving, but they weren't hanging up in the key cabinet. They were already nestled in the pocket of Jack's jeans. She slammed the front door so hard that Pandora flew into the kitchen and hid behind her master's legs.

Five minutes later, she was on the car speakerphone pleading with him to change his mind. He said how sorry he was for making a silly joke about Prince Edward, and she said she couldn't give a fig about him. She only wanted Jack to promise he wouldn't drive.

For a moment, he acquiesced, and then he had a flash of inspiration. 'Okay, you win. We can drive over another time.' She'd never know he'd driven to Muswell Hill and back. If she phoned when he was driving, he needn't answer because he had a battery of excuses for not picking up: sleeping (she'd apologise for waking him), walking Pan (he shouldn't have, but thanks for saving her the job), checking on Seagull House (he shouldn't have, but grateful to him for keeping an eye on things). When really he'd be well on his way to the nursing home in North London. He hoped he'd have enough strength to get there without killing himself on the motorways. It had been more than twelve weeks since he last sat in a driving seat.

Family is All You Have in the End

Within twenty minutes of getting in the car Jack was questioning his sanity. It wasn't just fatigue, nor the fact he couldn't feel the pedals with his feet or the steering wheel with his hands; it was the mental fog clouding his judgement at roundabouts and changing lanes on the motorway. Cars, motorbikes and lorries skated across his field of vision as blobs and blurs. In the end, to the fury of other drivers, he stuck to the middle lane. He stopped twice en route, to steady himself as much as to buy flowers and chocolates for his mother. He hobbled in and out of the service station wondering if he should just give up the ghost. The night would fall like a curtain at four o'clock and he wouldn't be able to drive back in the dark with all the flashing lights morphing into scratchy lines in his eyes.

He arrived at mid-day. The nursing home was red-bricked, modern with clean lines and ample parking. It always scored highly in official inspections, being efficiently run by its eastern European manager, Magda; a polite and fastidious woman. In the past, he'd always booked ahead and included an appointment with her to discuss his mother's care. This time, it would have to be ad hoc. Perhaps, he thought, he might see what the home was really like, day in, day out. His mother's vascular dementia had worsened, even the last time he'd visited in July. She'd had a vascular "event" back then, similar to a small stroke, during which she'd lost all memory, including her own name. Lauren had broken down in tears. But within a couple of days Estella regained most of her memory, even if only retained for short periods.

As luck would have it, Magda buzzed Jack through the main door, greeting him in the hallway. Her hair was the usual jet black, even though she was in her late fifties. The colour turned her face to milk. 'What a surprise,' she said, shaking his hand and spotting the stick. 'Something happens to your leg, Mr. Mann?'

'Oh this,' he said, thinking on his feet. 'I twisted some ligaments. Sorry I haven't been in for a while...'

'That is fine,' she said. 'Your mother has had lunch already and is sitting in the small lounge watching TV.' That was one thing Jack always regarded as odd; the rigid timetable: breakfast at six, lunch at eleven-thirty and dinner at five. Residents were tucked up in bed before eight, like toddlers. He'd forgotten this routine and was disappointed in himself. His mother would be sleepy after her lunch and he wouldn't have much quality time before her eyelids started drooping.

'How's Mum been?' he asked, walking with Magda along the corridor.

'You know she has had a fall last week?'

'No one told me.'

'Your mother gets out of bed in the middle of night for to use the toilet. She climbs over the bed bars and stumbles into the bathroom door, hitting head in the dark. A nurse and doctor have seen her. She has a small bruise. I thought Lauren was telling you this?'

'Doesn't Mum wear incontinence pads?'

'She pulls them off.'

'Isn't there an emergency cord by the bed?'

'There is, but she forgets it.'

Jack's mum had been doubly incontinent for some time. It was one of the reasons he'd transferred her. Estella needed round-the-clock attention. A fierce advocate for public services, she'd insisted on staying in a council-run home at first. There, she'd shared a room with a much older patient whose advanced dementia had made night times a miserable adventure. Each time Jack and Lauren had visited, their mother was wearing other patients' clothes, some with ancient stains down the front. The rooms and corridors were a heady mixture of chlorine, body odour and urine. The residents spent most of their time sitting in rows in an enormous lounge, staring into the middle distance. They were not offered mental stimulation, except for the occasional game of bingo. The staff seemed to be different each time they'd visited. In this new, smaller nursing home, it was always the same staff.

Lorraine, the Irish nurse responsible for looking after Estella, waved across the lounge. Jack spotted his mother in front of the TV, sitting beside another old lady in a winged, high-backed chair. 'I leave you to it,' said Magda, smiling.

Jack leaned his walking stick against the back of his mother's chair. A re-run of *The Antiques Roadshow* was on TV. His mother's face was tipped upwards as if she was staring at the screen, but when he knelt down beside her he realised her eyes were lightly closed and her mouth was slightly agape. The lady beside her grinned, her spotted hands tapping the arms of the chair. Jack placed a finger to his lips and winked at the other lady. Estella's breathing was slow and steady and it was clear she was sleeping. He was happy just to be by her side a while.

Estella Ward, that was the name she kept even after marrying. Estella Ward, London-born actress, wife of Jack Mann Snr., American travel writer, journalist and sometimes science-fiction writer. They cut quite a fashionable couple back in the sixties and seventies. Though she hadn't acted in nearly two decades, and time had lined her forehead, she'd maintained the striking elf-like features that had got her plenty of theatre work. Though she no longer wore make-up, unless Lauren prettied her up before taking her out on jaunts, she had good bone structure, natural colour in her cheeks, and her lips were not as grey as those of her neighbour. Her thick silvery hair had been swept back from her face, folded and held in place near the nape of her neck with a tortoiseshell clasp. The bruise was purple and yellow at the hairline near her temple.

Gently, he squeezed her arm. 'Hello, Mum, it's me.'

She opened her eyes. 'Well, I wondered when you'd get here.' He kissed her on the cheek and showed her the flowers and chocolates. 'Lovely,' she said. 'What are they for?'

'For your birthday. I missed it.'

'My birthday?' she said. 'What time do you call this? We've already had lunch, haven't we, Eileen?' The old lady grinned at Jack.

'What was it?' he asked, taking a seat beside his mother.

'Chicken and something,' his mother answered. 'Eileen, it was chicken…and what was it?'

'Chicken,' said Eileen.

'No. Something else, Eileen. Not chicken *and* chicken.'

'Jam roly-poly.'

His mother laughed. 'Not chicken and roly-poly was it? Eileen's a bit touched.' She pointed to her temple, saying 'ouch' when she hit the bruise.

'I've heard you've been falling over, Mum.'

'My legs are no good.'

'You should press the buzzer or pull the cord beside the bed, Mum.'

'Oh yes,' she said, 'the buzzer.'

'I wouldn't mind a roly-poly with him,' said Eileen, pointing at a well-dressed man on TV. He had a dark moustache and a pink handkerchief poked out of his top pocket. 'Some are born to stocks and shares, others to mops and stairs.'

'What are you going on about now, Eileen? Are you a Bolshevik already?'

Jack was happy to see his mother so lively and pleased she'd found another friend, since her last one hadn't come back from hospital. 'Eileen's recovering from an operation, aren't you, Eileen?' his mother said.

'Sorry to hear that,' said Jack, looking over.

'Yes, they've sewn up Eileen's anus.'

'They did,' she said. 'Sewed it up. No more *poop-poop*.'

'And as if that wasn't bad enough,' his mother said, 'Eileen's just found out her daughter has cancer.'

'That's just awful,' said Jack.

'It's all in her nymph loads,' said Eileen, and Jack had to stifle a smile conjured by the malapropism. 'She only just got back from one of those all-exclusive holidays, where you're not allowed to eat or drink anything? You know…a health spa.'

'Listen, Mum, are we okay to go back to your room and have a good chat? If it's alright with you, Eileen?'

'Oh yes,' she said. 'I'm not going anywhere.'

Lorraine offered to put a kettle on. 'I'll get the walker, and put these lovely flowers in a vase.'

Jack helped his mother to her feet. She held onto his arm while the walker was brought across. He left his stick at the back of the chair, holding onto the chocolates and concentrating now on his mother's little steps. Her ability to walk had seriously deteriorated. It took fifteen minutes walking from the lounge to her room, no more than thirty yards, and they had to stop every few paces while she gathered the strength and courage to carry on. At one point, during a break in walking, she asked how long Jack had been in the jazz band. 'Which jazz band would that be, Mum?' She didn't elucidate. He asked when she'd last seen Lauren.

'I haven't seen Lauren for…since she took me to that exhibition.'

'What exhibition was that, Mum?'

'The Perry Mason exhibition, at the Tate.'

'Perry Mason? The fictional private eye Perry Mason? What could possibly have been in the exhibition?'

'It was all cups and teapots with penis handles,' she said.

It took Jack a while figuring it out; malapropisms being contagious within the confines of the nursing home. 'You mean the *Grayson Perry* exhibition?'

'Yes, that's what I said, didn't I? Lauren's got a new car,' she said, as they approached the door to her room.

'Oh, she got rid of the old one?'

'Sold it for scrap. Squished down to an Oxo cube.'

'What's her new one like? What's the make?'

His mother couldn't remember. 'It's large, square, blue, and has everything on the inside.'

'What…like a Tardis?'

'No, Lauren said it was a Yaris.'

Jack smiled and helped his mother into an armchair beside the single bed. He looked around the room. Two of the walls were still crammed with framed family photographs that Lauren and Ernie had provided. Some were of Estella during West End productions like Lionel Bart's *Oliver!* She'd sung the part of Nancy. She was wide-eyed and glowing after a final night party. Some were of Jack Snr. and

Estella on their wedding day, others of Estella holding Lauren as a baby, some of Ernie, his wife Ariel and their two boys, Ryan and Gus standing on the Golden Gate Bridge. There was only one of Jack and Alice, taken on a relaxing holiday to Lisbon. Why had he allowed Ernie and Lauren to colonise the walls and not thought to have brought more of his own photographs?

Jack's eyes were drawn, as always, to one photograph in particular, sitting by itself on the windowsill. It was sepia and had been taken by Jack Snr.: a proud mother sitting in the middle of a sofa, Jack on one side, head resting on her shoulder, Lauren on the other sticking her pointy tongue out, and Ernie standing behind them, arms outstretched, a smile as broad as his face. Jack remembered the occasion; his mother's birthday. A year and a half before Jack Snr. blew his head off with a shotgun. Jack stared at the photograph wondering if his father had known about the lung cancer when he pressed that camera button.

Estella noticed the lingering look and said, 'Family is all you have in the end.'

Lorraine knocked and came in with a tray of tea and Battenberg slices. She left the room, returning seconds later with a vase full of his flowers. 'There you go now, Estella,' she said, with her soft Irish accent. She put the vase on the windowsill beside the sepia photograph.

'Thank you, darling,' said Estella. 'They're lovely they are.'

They talked for a while. Jack was going to tell her about his awful summer, the misdiagnoses and multiple sclerosis, but stopped himself. How could such knowledge help his frail old mother? He enquired instead about her daily routine, how often she was washed, who cut her toenails, how often she had her hair cut. He said her hair looked nice. He told her Alice was still building a theatre and that Prince Edward and Countess Sophie were going to cut the ribbon, and he'd try to get a photograph for her wall. 'That would be nice,' she said, her concentration beginning to fail. Jack checked her bathroom, making sure it was clean, which it was. The conversation tailed off and she dozed in the chair, waking a few minutes later, staring at him curiously and pointing at the wall. 'Ernest lives in America.'

'I know,' he said.

'My Jack does too.'

He resisted the urge to say Jack Snr. couldn't be living in America because his ashes had been scattered in the back garden of their old house in Fortis Green, Muswell Hill.

They finished their tea, neither eating the cake. 'Well, I should be going now,' said Jack, getting up. He wrapped his arms around his mother who remained seated. He kissed her warm cheek. 'You're tired. You always have a nap after lunch, don't you?'

'How would you know?' she said. Jack started to pull his coat on. 'Are you going already?'

'It's time to go,' he said.

'And will you come back?'

'Of course I will,' he said, feeling unsteady on his feet. 'So, what have you got planned for the rest of the day?' He thought Magda might have organised something better than bingo for the afternoon. Perhaps a jazz band and a singalong.

'Oh,' she said, glowing with pride, 'my son is coming in to see me.'

'Who's coming in?'

'Jack, my youngest,' she said. 'He's a famous comedian you know, but thank you for the flowers.'

Jack sat in his car trying to pull himself together. This is what dementia can do, he told himself. She's still your mother. Only it felt like he was losing her to the void. She hadn't recognised him even though he'd repeatedly called her "Mum" to shore up her memory and avoid embarrassing misunderstandings. But there it was upon parting. She knew she had a son called Jack, only it wasn't him today. She thought her dead husband was alive and well in America. When he'd gone back to the TV lounge to collect his stick and seen the empty space his mother had left, and the barest impression of her elbow on a cushion, he'd wanted to weep. He telephoned Lauren but she wasn't answering. Ernie said she had some supply teaching, so perhaps his sister was working.

When he pulled up beside a blue Yaris in Lauren's allotted parking space, Jack thought his luck was in. He peered through the car window and saw one of her scarves on the back seat and a scrunched-up cigarette packet. He walked around the side of the large, subdivided Edwardian villa. He looked up and noticed that one of her windows was open. He pressed the buzzer and waited. He pressed it again and waited another few minutes. He stepped back and shouted up at the window. He called her again on her mobile, imagining he heard a ringtone coming from the window. The ringing stopped and went to voice mail. He left a message: 'Lauren, where are you? I'm standing outside your flat.' He sent a text message saying the same thing. He returned to his car and waited inside thinking she may have nipped out to the shops.

After ten minutes, he scribbled a note on the back of an envelope; if nothing else, to prove he'd driven up to London to see their mother. He posted the note through her letterbox, shouting up at the open window again. He walked around the building to where the wheelie bins were stored. Lauren's general waste and recycling bins were marked with her flat number, 2B. For some reason he felt compelled to look inside and for one horrible moment thought he'd flip open a lid and find his sister's corpse squashed inside. What he found instead was a bin crammed with empty wine bottles and lager cans. It looked like the residue from one hell of a party. He looked inside the other bins, 1A and 1B, 2A, 3A and 3B. They were almost empty, as if the rubbish had been collected recently. He stood there, thinking: *is my sister a raging alcoholic? Is she stocking up at the local off-license right now?*

He waited inside his car again, having a sudden flashback to a party his mother once had at the family home. Jack and Ernie had been charged with serving champagne to their mother's Fabian Society friends. The guests got drunk, and one of them told Jack his mother's absences from Society meetings were becoming legendary. 'Estella's a fine actress, no question,' this man said. 'But she keeps offering the same excuse. She's at the doctor's with Lauren, or she's at the hospital with Lauren. Lauren's got this, or Lauren's got that, when all along your mother's been attending Socialist Worker Party meetings instead of ours.' The Fabian laughed his head off. 'Jack, everyone knows, everyone says, everyone says your mother has Munchausen's by Trotsky!'

Jack marched over to his sister's front door again, looked up and shouted, but she didn't respond. Then his phone vibrated with a text message: *Hi Jack sorry in Amsterdam with friends, will call when I'm back! L xxx* It was entirely possible she'd left her window open by mistake and flown to Amsterdam with friends. No reason why she'd have told him in advance. After all, they were not as close as before.

As he drove south and east on his way back to the Bunker, and the sun was beginning to fade and drop in his wing mirrors, he thought about that sepia photograph on the window sill and what his mother had said: *family is all you have in the end.* But in just one day he'd managed to lose his mother and his sister, and his only brother lived on the other side of the world. Of course, these things hadn't happened in just one day, they'd taken years; but those years had rushed by as quickly as the white lines rolling under the wheels of his car.

He returned to the Bunker in good time, parking in the same spot as before. Just as well, because Alice had decided to finish earlier than usual, arriving home minutes after his return. She asked what he'd been doing, and he said sleeping. 'Then why do you look so tired?' It was true. The drive to Muswell Hill had drained him, and he spent the rest of the evening slumped on the sofa. If he ever had to make that trip again, he realised, Alice would have to be his chauffeur.

After dinner, Alice had a surprise for him. There'd been a delay with the completion of Seagull House, she said, something to do with the kitchen-fitter or the plasterers, or the men fitting the cedar weatherboarding. Jack and Alice wouldn't be moving in until after Christmas now. This provided time, she said, to choose things like carpets without any rush. She laid samples out on the floor in front of him, stepping back to have a good look. 'Of course,' she said, 'we'll have to see them in natural light, but what do you think?'

All of the samples were pale and called things like 'clear sand', 'coral reef', 'sea stone' and 'mineral'. Alice liked the sisal weave. It would look good in the hall. She flipped through striped carpet samples, ones to run up the stairs. They were very "beachy", she said. Jack could only think of stairlifts whenever she mentioned stairs. She showed him some 'housewarming gifts' she'd bought for Seagull

House, including a model sailing boat, strings of seashells and vintage signs that could be hung up: a small metal one saying *Life is Good, Relax*, and a larger driftwood one, *May the World be Your Oyster*.

Alice's optimism in the face of Jack's illness was phenomenal, to such an extent he wondered if it was masked denial, or the 'make do and mend' outlook inherited from her parents. Either way, he went along with her, staring down at the samples, nodding to please her. Next were light fittings. She had a clutch of folders from a shop in town. She fancied stainless steel lanterns for the ceiling in the dining area. Dimmer switches throughout downstairs. No brass. All clean stainless steel. There was a lovely crystal chandelier they might want to consider for the lounge, too. It was artist-designed in Whitstable. They could have a look at the weekend, she said. Then there were bathroom fittings and blinds and curtains. She was thinking they could have plantation shutters for all of the bedrooms; an off-white, maybe. And now, because of his MS, she was thinking of having a wet room downstairs instead of a cloakroom.

Jack's brain was melting. His hands and feet were scorching. He asked if they could talk about these things later. It should have been a joyful time, choosing fixtures and fittings, carpets and blinds, and Alice had a Christmas excitement in her voice. But Jack knew he might never live to live in Seagull House. His mind was already half-decided. The conversation with the soldier had convinced him he'd end up just like him, with primary progressive MS. And like the soldier, he'd be in a wheelchair inside two years. Alice deserved a better life than the one he could now offer. *If you genuinely love her*, he told himself, *you'll let yourself go, not slowly fade away*. What was it his Dad once said, that the writer Jack London once wrote? The proper function of man is to **live, *not to exist***? *Be ashes, **not** dust*? *Be a meteor, **not** a sleepy and permanent planet*?

The Fox and the Blankie

It was thoughts of his dad that turned over in his mind; 2:15 a.m. by the light of the small alarm clock. The night had been interspersed with the sound and vibration of the occasional train, broken unexpectedly by the cackling of foxes nosing around the garden. Ordinarily, it would have sounded eerie, their throaty yelps circling the neighbour's chicken pen. But Jack was transported backwards, hurtling nearly forty years in seconds.

He was standing beside his dad at the side of a country road in Devon. They were renting a cottage that summer. The weather was inclement and cold at night. Estella had sent Jack Snr. out to buy firewood from a farm shop, and Jack Jnr. had jumped in beside him, set for a short adventure. They'd taken a tight corner narrowly avoiding something on the road. His dad pulled up and put his hazards on. 'Stay here, kid,' he'd said. Jack watched his father kneel down to look at something in the road. His father shook his head and walked to the verge, poking around a ditch, and young Jack climbed out to investigate.

A small fox was stretched out on its side, a long string of sausages spreading out from its stomach. Its underbelly had been ripped open. 'Get back inside!' Jack Snr. shouted, emerging from tall bushes with what looked like a tree stump. 'Dad, it's still breathing,' said Jack, seeing the glassy eyes move, and the red-grey fur heave. 'What'll we do? Get a vet?'

'There's only one right thing to do,' he said. 'If you're not getting in the car, turn around.'

'I want to see,' Jack said.

'Close your eyes, kid.' He raised the stump above his head and whispered, 'I commend your spirit to the sky.' Down came the stump making a deadly mash of the fox's head, and there was silence. 'Now if you wanna help, fetch me your mom's blanket from the back seat.'

'Mum's best blankie? Her blankie of love?'

'Yes her blankie of love. We need to put this somewhere safe.' He pointed at the ditch.

Jack handed over his mother's travel blanket and his father scooped up the fox. 'It won't have felt anything,' he said, placing it in the undergrowth. 'Better than leaving the poor thing in the road to die slowly and trampled to nothing.'

'What about mum's best blankie?'

Jack Snr. ruffled his son's hair. 'The fox needs it much more than your mom.'

Frangate

Alice brought a bowl of cereal and a mug of tea into the igloo at about 7:45 a.m. shivering with the cold in there. She said chirpily that the sea stone sisal sample was looking good in the daylight. She then dropped the bombshell that Fran was coming to visit later in the morning. Alice had been having lots of conversations with her, taking calls at work. The contact had been increasing after the news of Jack's MS. Alice sat down on the edge of the camp bed, nearly tipping it up in the air. She told him that Fran's auntie had had MS so she knew a lot about the disease and had some books to give him.

'I don't want books, Alice. I don't want visitors either. Look at me.'

She stood up and the metal legs of the camp bed banged on the floor. 'Fran's doing this out of the goodness of her heart. Gerry thinks it might be good for you to see people instead of becoming…what did he call it…? Inspector Recluseau.'

Jack groaned.

'You have to let people in, Jack.'

'Now I'm Jack the doorman. Listen, I don't want to be a black hole my friends disappear into.'

'It's not all about *you*. Fran's coming over for a chat, that's all. She's lovely. She wants to support *us*. That's what friends do, in case you've forgotten.'

'Alice, I hardly know her. She's nice, but we only met once at Glyndebourne.'

'She and I have become friends,' said Alice, 'and to be honest, I needed someone to talk to. I can't talk to anyone at work.'

'Fine, but why come and see *me* if she's *your* friend?'

'Isn't it obvious?'

He shook his head.

'Because she's Gerry's girlfriend and Gerry's your only proper friend.' That shut him up. 'Now, Fran's going to be here about eleven. She's driving over from Brighton. She said it would only be for an hour or two and not to bother with lunch, but I've made some sandwiches and put them in the fridge. There are biscuits in the cupboard. All you have to do is serve them, make tea or coffee…and not be a complete arse-hole.'

'How do I explain the mess?'

'Fran knows we're renting. Anyway, I've tidied. I've been up since a quarter to six. I've given Pan a short walk, so you don't even have to worry about that.'

'Okay,' he said, sighing. 'It's just…you know…look at the state of me.'

'Have a shower and a shave. You'll feel better about yourself, I promise.' She opened a window to let in some fresh air, bringing back memories of his mother doing the same thing when he was a teenager. In fact, thought Jack, his illness had a made a little too much of a mother out of his wife.

Alice left for work and Jack lingered in bed. Pandora jumped up and curled into a big hairy ball on top of his feet. He heard and felt regular commuter trains travelling on the tracks to London via Faversham. Seagulls screeched in the sky and children shouted on their way to school. Yummy mummies gathered, chattering.

Once upon a time, Jack and Alice were going to have children. Careers had always come first, but they'd tried a number of times in their thirties. After two miscarriages, they thought about IVF, surrogacy, even adoption, but focused instead on each other and work. And then, just when they were thinking of giving up, Alice fell pregnant with little Hunter. But their new-born son died just hours after birth, didn't he, and then, not long after, Alice became ill. Painful periods became continual tummy aches which led to investigations and the discovery of pomegranate-sized cysts. And children became history.

Post plopped through the letterbox and Pan raced into the hall, barking. It forced Jack out of bed. An envelope was lying on the coir mat, a blue NHS logo in the corner; an appointment to see MS consultant Dr. Rama in three weeks' time.

He took a shower, wobbling on his legs, hanging onto the plastic screen for balance; just lifting a leg over the rim of the bath felt like attempting a high jump. He washed with difficulty using one hand. He shaved, and then he brushed his teeth. He couldn't feel the roof of his mouth or his lower lip with his tongue. He stood naked before the full length mirror and didn't like the insult that stared back; a dark-eyed, flabby ghost. His shoulders had rolled forwards and his spine was slightly bent as if he was turning into Quasimodo. He looked eighty-five, not forty-five. He thought: *why is this happening? Why didn't the steroids help? Why is this still going on? Why is it getting worse? This isn't relapsing-remitting. There is no remitting. This is primary progressive MS.*

An hour before Fran knocked on the door, a free newspaper was thrust through the letterbox, sending Pandora into a frenzy. Jack slumped in his tatty leather armchair and read the front page. A woman, an artist in her fifties, had walked onto a local level crossing at night and thrown herself under one of the fast trains to London. Her marriage had been in tatters, the paper said. She'd been having an affair that ended abruptly. She was on anti-depressants. The paper said that in the last year across the UK over 250 people had thrown themselves in front of trains. In just three years, six people had killed themselves at the exact same spot on the local railway line. Samaritans had put up posters to discourage others doing the same. There was a campaign to close the crossing.

Fran knocked at the door. Jack took a deep breath and checked himself in the hallway mirror before opening. 'Hello there,' Fran said, kissing him on both cheeks. She was heavily perfumed: cinnamon, cloves and patchouli. 'How are you, my poor Jack?'

'Okay,' he said, because that's what you say when you don't want to ruin a conversation from the word go. Really, he was so dizzy he could vomit, so weak his legs might buckle, and his hands were hellfire.

There was an awkward moment, standing together in the tightest of hallways, when Fran looked as if this was a mistake and Jack recognised it in her eyes. She was as pretty as he remembered; perhaps not quite as petite, a bit rounder in the face maybe, possibly more voluptuous. Perhaps it was the artfully Boho faux fur coat. She'd let her hair grow longer. Thick, shiny strands spilled over her furry collar and down her shoulders. She placed a rucksack on the tiles and unslung a vintage handbag from her shoulder. She unbuttoned her coat, slipping out of it with ease. Jack hung it on a peg. She looked like a beautiful beatnik from the 1950s; black roll neck and moss green skirt.

Pandora, for once, didn't jump up at the stranger. She just circled the knee-high boots. Fran bent down to say hello and her corduroy skirt rose up past her knee caps that beamed through her tights like two faces in fog. Pan went straight for Fran's mouth with her lapping tongue, and Fran's head darted back. 'Agh!'

'Sorry,' said Jack, getting hold of Pan by the ruff. 'She loves licking people.'

'Friendliness is nothing to apologise for,' she said, wiping her lips with the back of her hand and smiling. Her eyes were heavily made up, but the natural green of the irises shone brightly and intelligently as they had done at the opera. She stood up straight and he noticed the red necklace hanging around the black roll neck. Alice had one similar she wore in the winter months; bold beads like giant holly berries.

'Not everyone loves our adorable, mad Pandora.'

'I can't imagine why,' she said, patting her. 'She's beautiful, aren't you Pandora?'

'You're looking well,' he said, making conversation.

'Thank you,' she said, making a shivering sound. 'It's lovely and cosy in here. I think my heater's on the blink.'

'How was the drive over?' This was how he was going to play it; short, sweet, meaningless conversation. 'Please, come into the kitchen.' He only had to do this for an hour or so for Alice's sake. 'Take a seat. Sorry for the mess.' He looked hopelessly about, spotting breakfast dishes piled in the sink.

'It's very bijoux,' said Fran. She put her rucksack down, pulled up a pine chair and sat at Alice's farmhouse table. 'You'll be moving into Seagull House soon, won't you?'

Jack nodded. He switched the kettle on and got Alice's sandwiches out of the fridge. He removed the cellophane and put them on the table alongside two side plates. Then he poured some chocolate biscuits onto another side plate. It was beginning to resemble a children's picnic.

'You didn't have to go to all this trouble.'

'I didn't,' he said, 'Alice did.' Realising this sounded unfriendly, he added, 'I've been a bit…sick.'

'Oh, Jack, I know. How are you coping?'

He sat down opposite her and slipped a mug of tea across. 'To be honest, it's been hell.'

'But at least they know what it is now.'

'Yes.'

'Do you want to talk about it?' When he hesitated, she said. 'Alice probably told you I had a relative with MS?' She bent down, unzipped the rucksack and pulled out a trendy box of chocolates and some books. She stacked the books up in a tower on the table, spines facing out: *All You Need to Know about MS, Me My Self and MS, Coping with MS, Living with MS.*

'Thanks, Fran. You shouldn't have, really.'

'One of the things Auntie Jane told me, the most important thing that kept her going when things got tough, was *talking* about it.'

'Here, take a sandwich. Looks like there's egg and cress, mozzarella and tomato and houmous, I don't know what this one is.'

'Alice was in tears, Jack, tears down the phone.'

'I forgot to ask, do you take sugar, Fran?'

She shook her head. 'Alice needed to talk. She was in pieces. She doesn't see why you can't talk about it.'

He could see where this was going, which was one of the main reasons he hadn't wanted visitors. 'With respect, Fran, that's up to me, isn't it? If I want to talk, I will. If I don't, I won't. Sorry.'

There was an awkward silence. Fran's face flashed crimson. 'I shouldn't have come,' she said, making to get up.

'Don't go, you've only just arrived,' he said, panicking that Alice would kill him if it went wrong.

'Tell me if I've made a mistake, Jack. Just tell me to go if you want.' She got to her feet, and turned. 'I've overstepped the mark…'

'Don't go, please. I didn't know Alice was in pieces. It's my fault. Sit down, please.'

Fran turned back. 'Shall we start over?' she said, settling again in the chair. 'I've not come to exchange pleasantries. I'm just making myself available as a friend. I know by that look in your eyes you're thinking, "Friends? We don't know the first thing about each other". Well, maybe we can start to understand and know each other now, as friends?'

'Friends,' he said, astonished by her frankness. 'Does Gerry know what he's let himself in for with you, Fran?'

'That's what he likes about me; my directness, no faffing about.'

'I feel as if you, Alice and Gerry have got me in a pincer movement.'

'Now that's better, you're talking about how you're actually *feeling*? Alice said you'd locked yourself away. MS isn't the end of the line, Jack. Auntie Jane had it for a long time before she died of something else entirely, at eighty. She made the best of things, led a relatively normal life and thoroughly enjoyed it. She battled through. These are some of the books she left behind.'

Jack stared at the odd-angled, dusty tower. 'I'm guessing from what you're saying that your auntie had relapsing-remitting?'

'Yes.'

'I might not have the same, Fran. It could be more aggressive because of my age and gender. They're not sure. I could be in a wheelchair inside two years, maybe in months.'

'And maybe you won't, Jack. Not everyone ends up paralysed. You need to take control of this before it controls you. You don't want to become a passenger to illness.'

Need? Want? 'Pardon me, Fran, but only one person sitting at this table actually *has* MS. Only one of us is frightened of going blind and losing control of his bladder and bowels before the age of fifty. I know you mean well, and I'm grateful, and I'm sure your Auntie Jane was a strong, wonderful woman and you probably learnt a great deal about the illness because of her, but simply *knowing* about MS is not the same as *having* it.'

'Go on,' she said, wounded.

'Fran, I've only just discovered that I have MS, okay. It's been a few weeks, that's all, after months and months of blunders and false alarms that would make your hair turn white. I need time to adjust. Everyone's rushing me. MS consultants, MS centres, MS nurses, MS forums, MS, MS, MS. MS ad infinitum.'

'Tell me about the blunders.'

He warned her: 'You're in for a helluva ride.' He started his story from the very beginning. That night at Glyndebourne, pretending nothing was wrong for the sake of politeness, wandering through the calamitous maze of A&E, then his worst experiences of what he called the "National Hell Service". He couldn't stop the sense of Bedlam pouring out: needles, screams, chaplains, stroke victims, flat-liners, old ladies dying in front of him, Greek tragedies, brain tumours, waiting, waiting, waiting, mistakes, let the hounds see the hare, spoons and balloons, everything, everything. And he didn't hold back on the detail, not embellishing a thing, no exaggerations for comedic effect. 'A nightmare Kafka couldn't dream up.'

Then he went on and on about a young soldier in a wheelchair and a tree in a car park. Fran couldn't stem the flow of woe; couldn't get a single word in. She stroked Jack's dog, and listened. It was as if she'd unwittingly turned into Pandora, the mythical girl who opened a mysterious box, unleashing all manner of ills and malevolencies upon the world. He went on interminably, and the more he went on, the redder his face became.

'Can I stop you there a moment?' she said.

'Sure, but I haven't told you about the bloody students and the consultant yet. "Well, it's the students' lives too" the nurse said, and Alice said-'

'Do you realise,' said Fran, looking at her wrist watch to reinforce the point, 'I've been here for over an hour, and you haven't stopped for breath in half that time, and you haven't once asked how I am, or how Gerry is?'

Jack had to consciously prise his eyebrows down his forehead. 'Oh, I am sorry. Have my near-death experiences been boring you?' She prickled, but it was too late to take it back. He replayed her last words in his head, thinking: *you don't have MS. I don't know you. You don't know me. What could be more important than the disaster of my last three months? A cancelled tour, dead-end career and death lurking around every hospital corner.*

'Because if you had've asked, I'd have told you I'm pregnant.'

'Good God,' he said, as if he'd been shot in the chest.

'I'd have told you that Gerry is over-the-moon and that we're going to have the baby next summer.'

'Why didn't Gerry say something?'

'You see, life goes on whether you have MS or not, Jack, with or without you, and your life must go on too.'

'Did you tell Alice?'

'Of course.'

'And how was she?'

'Very happy for us.'

'You know we lost a child?'

'Gerry told me. I'm sorry.'

'Didn't you think Alice might have mixed feelings about your good news?'

'She was happy for us, Jack. It's you she was worried about.'

Jack paused for a few seconds, digesting the information. 'Fran, Alice couldn't bring herself to tell me this news. Why do you think that was?'

'Maybe she thought you had too much on your plate?'

'Well, maybe that's why Gerry didn't tell me when we spoke just three days ago…because I had too much on my plate. But *you* couldn't wait to tell me, even if my plate was piled to the ceiling.'

'What?'

'Fran, the woman I love can't have children. Our only son died, from of all things laughing gas! You and Gerry are together less than six months and bang there's a baby. Anyway, I'm very pleased for you. Congratulations.'

Fran looked baffled and uncomfortable and tried to shift the focus. 'We think we conceived that magical night at Glyndebourne.'

'Magical? Oh thanks. It was magic for me too. Do you know what the star configuration was that night? Mars with Leo rising?' Francesca made as if to get up, and he didn't stop her this time. 'Did you come here to tell me you were pregnant, masquerading as a Samaritan for the MS hangers-on alliance?'

'I obviously made a mistake,' she said, walking into the hall, looking for her coat in the dim light.

He followed her. 'You want honesty, Fran, you want feelings? I can't stand opera. Neither can Gerry. He doesn't know his arias from his elbows. I've known him more than twenty-five years. The more I think about Glyndebourne the more I know it was some sort of twisted fate. It could be the death of me; an opera about dead people and ghosts. It's haunted me ever since, but now it represents a new beginning for you. How's that for irony?'

She pulled her coat from the peg, dropping it on to the floor.

'I'm really pleased for you and Gerry. I am, truly. But for me this whole situation is beyond a joke. You were coming over to support me, Alice said. You sit down and ask me to talk, to show my feelings, and when I let my guard down and tell you how terrible it has been, that my future, and Alice's, is a lot bleaker than yours, you say, hey, what about me? I'm pregnant, life goes on. Oh, that MS thing? Get over it, like it's a fucking headache. Well, I've got a newsflash for you. Life goes on for some people, but not for others. It doesn't go on for me, Francesca. Not for me.'

She fumbled with the door lock and Pandora barked. Jack opened the door and ushered her onto the drive. She threw her fake fur onto the back seat of the car and slammed the door. She looked once more over her shoulder before getting into the driver's side. He watched her pull out of the drive and disappear down the road. His heart was thumping. He went indoors and closed the world behind him.

He bent down to his tail-thumping Pandora. 'I think that went pretty well,' he said to her. 'What do you think?'

Jack stood at the kitchen sink looking out across the garden to the distant railway track. He had a pen and paper in his hands, and when the trains passed he made a note of the times. He double-checked them on the internet. There were three trains an hour and they came in both directions at a good speed just before slowing at a nearby station. He poured himself a drink and sat in the conservatory, still trainspotting. If he was going to throw himself under the wheels of a train there was no greater opportunity than the one afforded him at the Bunker. He assessed the garden. Although the canopy of leaves had already fallen, partially revealing the sidings, the trunks were massed thickly. The garden to the left was hidden by mature conifers and the neighbours on the right also had evergreens. These would provide excellent camouflage. All he had to negotiate was a barbed wire fence. He could use an old rug stored in the shed, hang it over the top and climb over. He made his mind up. He'd do it tomorrow, after Alice had gone to work, after he'd written his last letters.

But first he'd have to pacify Alice, who was sure to return from work in a terrible mood. The landline and his mobile had been ringing incessantly since 3:30. Alice had already spoken to Fran and Gerry. The message she left on his answer machine was simply: *I don't believe you have done this to your best friend*. But there were at least two sides to every story, he thought, already drinking wine for the courage to tell his.

If I Had a Gun

Alice was angry, but wedded to her growling temper was an expression of resignation and sadness. Francesca had told her everything, describing Jack's meltdown at the kitchen table; that he'd shouted at her. He didn't remember shouting, but agreed, he'd blown a fuse, and so what?

'You've burnt all your bridges now,' said Alice. 'You've lost the trust of your oldest and best friend. You've ostracised yourself.' When he made no comment, she said, 'No man is an island, remember? Except Jack Mann!'

'Why didn't you tell me about their baby?' She didn't have an answer, which he thought was an answer in itself. Rain was falling heavily and he couldn't take his eyes off it. 'If I had a gun right now,' he said, 'I'd blow my bloody head off.' As soon as he'd said it he realised the resonance with his father's suicide.

Alice glared. 'If I had a gun right now I'd blow your bloody head off myself.'

Ordinarily, this type of ludicrous, escalating exchange heralded a truce, smile, laugh, hug, maybe tears, sometimes sex, but he had genuinely meant it, and so, he thought, had she. 'Fran shouldn't have come. I don't want spectators. I'm sick to the back teeth of all this talk. It just goes around and around and around in my head until I fall over with it.'

'I don't know if you're in denial or just plain mad,' she said, exhaustion in her voice. 'You've thrown away everyone who wanted to help.'

He caught her eye. 'Does that include you, Alice?'

She got up from the table and took something from her shoulder bag. 'A present,' she said, placing a paper bag in front of him. 'Something for the house. I saw it in a window and thought of us.'

'Where are you going?'

'To see mum and dad.'

'In this rain?'

'What's rain got to do with it?' she said.

He heard her car door closing, the engine firing, the wheels sloshing through surface water. He peeked inside the paper bag and saw an object wrapped up in special, crinkly paper, sky blue with sailing boats and beach huts on. He took the object out. It was about eight inches high, a few inches wide. He unwrapped it slowly, seeing the wooden beak emerge, a red spot on the underside of the bill, then its head, the eyes hooded and all-seeing, all-knowing, then the clean grey wings, proud white chest and black tail feathers, spotted white. The legs were a single red post, attached to a dark blue wooden block. There was a little card too, and words: *A seagull for Seagull House! xx Alice* He stood it in the centre of the table, thinking about that night, so long ago now it seemed, when he, Alice and Gerry had each stood up declaring themselves to be the real seagull.

The seagull always dies. Isn't that what Gerry had said?

Alice drove to the local supermarket. She hadn't known where else to go. At first, she'd driven up and down the seafront aimlessly, then she remembered they needed wine. God, she needed wine and to hell with her liver. Her day at work had been awful, punctuated as it had been by unsettling conversations with Fran and Gerry. She'd had to push these to one side, to cope with her growing workload. The theatre was due to open in a few days and panic had set in among staff. Everyone wanted to be in line to shake the Prince's hand. Pressure was mounting. On her way home from work she'd called her parents on the hands-free. Once again, as she'd heard so often, they'd talked about fresh ailments and illnesses, hinting that they could do with some help getting to upcoming hospital appointments. Once again, she'd told them it depended on how ill Jack was, how her timetable was, but she'd do her best to help. She'd brought Jack a seagull, and was crying now with the irony. She'd become a mother bird, constantly feeding the screaming needs of her parents, her husband, her bosses and her team. But who would feed her needs?

Tap-tap-tap came at the glass on the passenger side. Alice wiped the tears from her cheeks and let the window down half way. She saw the handsome face of a boy dressed in a red anorak, hood up. He would've been about Hunter's age. 'Can I help you?' she said, leaning across and smiling.

'Mummy says you can't park in a child-only bay,' he said angrily, turning and pointing to a nearby people-carrier. Alice peered over his shoulder, glimpsing the pious-looking face of a woman in the driver's seat.

In such a state, and in heavy rain, Alice hadn't realised where she'd parked. Anywhere would've done. And what did it matter? The car park was practically empty. She could see, even through the rain, that most of the child-only bays were unoccupied. 'Please tell mummy this,' she said to the boy. 'It's not against the law to park here. Tell mummy, I'm feeding my inner-child.'

The boy looked confused, and ran back to his mother's car. He repeated loudly what Alice had said, and the woman tutted, scowling through her open window. 'Get in poppit,' she said, and the boy jumped into the rear seat, slamming the door. The people-carrier passed slowly by. The woman stopped briefly, and shouted out of her window, 'You selfish cow!', then she sped away.

Alone again, mother bird draped her tired wings over the steering wheel. *If I had a gun*, she thought. *Thank God I don't have a gun.*

A Day in the Life

The next morning, Jack decided today was the day. Neuropathic pain had kept him awake until three o'clock. He'd listened to trains rumbling past every hour and imagined what his body might look like cut in half. He'd concocted a plan in his head: atone with Alice, get dressed, take Pandora on one last walk along the Slopes, say goodbye to Seagull House, write last letters to Alice and Gerry, get rug from shed, place it over barbed wire fence at bottom of garden, lock Pan in Bunker, 3:15 p.m. make way to foot of garden, hide behind thickest trees, at 3:27 precisely hurl himself under oncoming wheels of London-bound train; the termination of a life well-travelled.

The plan was already badly executed. *The best laid plans of mice and Mann,* he thought. He wasn't awake in time to kiss Alice goodbye. She'd sneaked off to work early. Normally, he'd hear the kettle popping, smell toast burning or hear Pan yelping to go out. But this morning he'd slept through all of the above. He hadn't wanted things to end on an argument, but rather than put him off, this further fuelled his motivation to do what he planned. The normal Alice wouldn't have crept away leaving a curt note for him in the kitchen. The normal Jack would have made sure the argument was settled last night. He would never have let it fester. The normal Jack would not have behaved the way he had, sitting at the table with his best friend's girlfriend. But nothing was normal anymore.

Alice's note suggested counselling; someone to help him overcome his anger and denial. What she didn't know was that Jack was no longer angry or in denial; not as he saw things. On the path of grief he thought he'd already passed the landmark stages of shock, disbelief, anger, denial and self-blame, and was now consoling himself with the milestones of realisation, acceptance and accommodation. He'd realised that this was how it would be for the rest of his life; all he had to do was accept the tragedy and accommodate the fact he could prevent a miserable future. By ending his wretched life he would be handing a normal life back to Alice, and he was doing it before they moved into their new house, so all bad memories could be locked inside the Bunker forever and Alice might live more peacefully with the memory of him.

Her note said: *We need to talk.*

All of his talking was done.

Fetching Pan's lead, he agreed with himself that a man's life was as long as a piece of string and his own had just snapped. The only people he felt sorry for were the train driver and passengers. The driver was the one who'd need counselling, and the passengers would be late getting to their stations. Jack would be a front-page headline in the free local newspaper just as the poor artist had been. His life had boiled down to one of two things: pleasure and pain. These were the principle drivers in human life, weren't they? An unconscious oscillation between these two points dictated or determined courses of human action. Apart from masochists, sadists and the mentally unstable, life was simply a matter of limiting the pain and extending the pleasure. By killing himself he was being altruistic; he was ending his own pain and simultaneously contributing to Alice's future happiness. In other words, he was doing the world a favour.

With his loyal dog and walking stick by his side, he hobbled to the sea. The water was brown and sludgy, churning and rolling in like mud. Jack took pleasure releasing Pandora and watching her run to the shore. She wanted him to throw stones, but he couldn't make it across the pebbles. Instead, he walked her along the concrete promenade, past rows of colourful beach huts, one of which he'd planned to buy in the summer. The sky was darkening, perhaps carrying snow. The air was cold enough for it to fall.

After climbing the steps back up to the Slopes, Jack's legs gave way, so he rested on a bench; his favourite bench because of an inscription, a dedication to a retired ship captain who'd "loved this view". He wrapped himself up in his long, black coat, and Pandora jumped up beside him, licking his face with her warm tongue. She looked where he was looking; far out to sea where the wind turbines stood in a line, their bare white arms turning. His head was as light as a bubble. It might ease off his shoulders and float away like a helium-filled balloon on a freezing thermal. Everything was cold, except his hands; those useless burning hands, sitting in his pockets like hot coals in a fire basket.

The ground rumbled beneath his feet, as it sometimes did in this part of Kent. When he'd first felt the earth tremble he thought it was an earthquake, but neighbours put him straight. It was either the shuddering vibrations from the Ministry of Defence testing explosives at Shoeburyness, in Essex, or it was pile-driving for new wind turbines far out at sea.

He whispered goodbye to the captain's bench, to the beach huts and to the wind turbines, returning to the Bunker via Marine Walk. He wanted to have one last look at Seagull House. As he turned the corner, he moved past the stump of a tree, not realising at first that it had once been the old leaning cherry tree he'd admired. Someone had chopped it down. It had been the last one on the road, and he thought of the young soldier and his magical tree in the rugby club car park. No soft pink blossom would bloom next spring or drift down the road in early summer. No cherry plums would hang in clusters from branches in autumn. No shadow would fall onto the road from the street lamps in winter. No lines of snow would pile up on its bare, branching shoulders and lie in its creases. All that was left now was a flat, pale stump and unruly roots.

Keith the builder was barking orders at men inside Seagull House. Jack hadn't seen him in weeks; a tall, comedic man always full of banter. Almost a year ago now, Keith had told him about the number of terrible accidents that had befallen men in the building trade. Some of these Keith had seen with his own eyes (lost fingers and crushed toes), others were second-hand stories. He'd told Jack about a carpenter from the 1930s who couldn't find employment and travelled as far as Canada to work for a logging company. The firm had a side-line in veneers. The man's job was to shave rough tree trunks down into thick planks, and then, with the finest cuts of oak, make veneers. It was the latest fashion in furniture. The man regarded it as menial, for he was a highly qualified English carpenter, but at the end of the day it was simple and he was earning good money. His job was to feed wood into a saw that cut it finer than a sheet of glass. But you had to feed the planks in gently and at the right angle or they'd buckle and snap. This could be dangerous, as the wood was not only as thin as glass, it was just as sharp. You were supposed to switch off the machine whenever there was a jam. One day, in a hurry to finish his last lot of the day, the carpenter forced a sheet through so hard it snapped in two, one half whistling straight up past his eyes. Others in the warehouse heard the yelp, even above the machinery, and then the awful groan. The English carpenter turned around to face everyone, arms outstretched, eyes swimming in bright running blood. He staggered a few yards and fell to the floor; no nose, no eyebrows, no chin and no forehead, his face as flat as a table. Men mopped with their own shirts but the poor creature died seconds after; not from blood loss, Keith said, but sheer shock. Ever since then, Jack could see the flattened face and blood-filled eyes whenever he spoke to the builder, and it was no different today.

Keith was surprised to see him, having heard from Alice of his flaring MS. He walked Jack around the house, proud of his handiwork and explaining how close they were to completion. The kitchen-fitters were starting next week. The roof was finished and the double glazed windows were in. He was most pleased with the staircase he'd had specially made, built extra wide with a large turning circle at the top to easily accommodate a stairlift. He showed Jack the revised floor plans including a small bedroom downstairs and a wet room right next door. Bathroom fixtures and fittings were in and they were only waiting for the tiler to finish the job. Every wall had been plastered and was drying out under special heaters. The builder was waiting for the walls and ceilings to go off before the decorators arrived. He apologised for the six-week delay, blaming it on difficulties with the supply of steels and last-minute changes that Alice had requested. All in all, he said, everything had worked like clockwork and he'd soon be starting two new attic conversions. His voice echoed around the hard surfaces of the empty building. 'The solid oak flooring's going in on Wednesday,' he said. 'You wanted the herringbone pattern?' Jack nodded, but wasn't taking much in. 'The gas and electricity will be properly reconnected when the kitchen's in. You wanted your island in galaxy granite?' Jack nodded. 'The rads are all sorted. You have a high capacity combi boiler. Alice has probably told you all this.' Jack nodded, though Alice hadn't mentioned so much. This, he thought, will be my last ever conversation with another human being and it's with a builder about a combi boiler.

He fed Pandora when he got back. For a moment, staring out of the Bunker's kitchen window, he resented the old Buddha. The sculpture of solid stone would outlive him. The Protective Buddha was in the far corner of the garden half-facing the bungalow. Just over its right shoulder, the wire fence.

The phone rang out. He let the answer-machine kick in. It was Alice saying she'd be back from work at six. His head was spinning. He took some paper and envelopes from a drawer in the kitchen, walked through the lounge into the conservatory and sat down to compose his final letters. Pan lay down by his feet, under the dining table. He wrote Alice's letter first, asking her to forgive him and to please understand his reasons. He wanted her future to be full of joy and freedom, not shackles and burdens. He asked that whenever she felt loss to remember the first time he'd ever made her laugh, and to hold that thought in her head for as long as humanly possible. *Twenty years of hand-in-hand happiness is worth much more than a handful of sadness.* It was all terrible, he thought; his useless grappling with English and maths. It was twenty-five years, not twenty. He asked that his ashes be scattered at the bottom of the garden at Seagull House. It was secluded down there by the tamarisk. If she wanted, she could plant a Japanese maple and mix his ashes in with the soil, so the bones of him could feed a young tree. *Enjoy Seagull House*, he wrote, *but maybe you'd like to choose another name.* To Gerry, he offered thanks for a quarter of a century friendship, and for shepherding him all those years. He wished him well with fatherhood. He asked him to keep a watchful eye on Alice.

A train passed by the end of the garden just as he was signing off with kisses. He sealed the envelopes at 2 p.m. He knew with complete conviction that at 3:15 he'd make his way down the garden and at 3:27 it would all be over.

First things first. He retrieved a rug from the shed, walked past Buddha and placed it heavily on top of the barbed wire fence, making it sag low enough to hook his legs over. Everything was in order. On his way back to the conservatory, he stopped at the Buddha and asked him for the strength to go through with his plan. He was greeted with the Buddha's customary silence. In the time he had left he decided to play some CDs including the Beatles' compilation album *Love*, mixed by George Martin; the album he'd heard during his first MRI scan. He no longer associated it with the scanner, only with his father. He thought how sad it was that he was going to make the grade in the same way as his dad; suicide in his mid-forties.

At 2:45 p.m., he started to get the kind of jitters soldiers probably got before going over the top in the trenches, waiting for the whistle. His hands trembled. He poured whisky, knocking two glasses back in quick succession. In less than half an hour he'd be on the other side of the barbed wire, with no war to win. Another train passed and he knew it would be the last to get through today. He thought about so many things, so many people, and Alice so many times. He remembered how he'd tried his early *Mad Infinitum* routine out on her. She was good at fine-tuning the punchlines. *Mad Infinitum*, he thought; *the irony*. Over the course of a few months the title of his tour had become the title of a different kind of journey. Not one made on roads and railway lines to cities on the comedy circuit, but a journey through corridors, wards and consultation rooms along the maze of the NHS. Don't become a passenger to your illness Fran had told him, and he wasn't going to.

Jack sensed anxiety in Pandora, or was it the other way around? She was sitting plum centre on his feet, looking into his eyes. He stroked her. 'Now, Pan,' he said, 'you've been my companion for a long time, and now your job is to look after Alice.' Hearing her name, Pandora's ears pricked. She glanced over her shoulder towards the hallway thinking she heard Alice's keys in the door. Her hazelnut eyes flicked left and right and her bushy tail thumped the tiles. When Jack stood up she knew he was going somewhere important and started to bark; she was so loud she blocked out the Beatles, so he turned the music up.

The *Love* album was nearly half way through and he realised, looking at his watch, that he'd probably never hear the end of it today.

Though, if he was lucky, and the train was running a few minutes late, he might hear one of his father's favourite tracks: "A Day in the Life". About a man who made the grade.

'Well, goodbye my faithful friend,' he said, giving Pan a final squeeze. 'My time's come.' She barked when he closed the conservatory door.

When he reached the Buddha he stopped and rested his walking stick against its shoulder. He leaned over and kissed the top of its mossy head, smiling: 'Where were you when I needed you?' A robin flew down from a tree, landing on the place he'd kissed, its chest puffed, round and as red as a clown's nose. It chirped, twitching twiggy legs, and Jack heard a tiny voice in his head say: *this isn't nothing, Jack, this is really something.* The earth shuddered under his feet.

3:19 p.m. He stepped over the rug and barbed wire. The barking continued in the conservatory, and Jack realised he'd left a top window ajar. The barking and the Beatles were funneling through the aperture. He made his way between tree trunks, heart beginning to race. He stopped in No Mann's Land, a couple of yards from the tracks. Pandora had stopped barking. She was trying to work out the puzzle of his sudden disappearance. Only the sound of the Beatles leaked through the open window. His hands began to shake again. He peeked around a tree and saw Pandora sitting bolt upright at the door, eyes glued to him. Small birds chattered and flew from tree to tree and branch to branch; the robin was noisiest, no doubt drawn to the earth disturbed by his feet. Jack's presence had caused quite a stir. *The birds are my final hecklers,* he thought.

3:23. He climbed the moist, muddy bank onto the sidings, hiding behind the thickest of tree trunks. He stuck his neck out and glanced up the track. The air was fresh and peaty in his nostrils. He checked his watch three times. The earth shuddered again. He thought about saying a prayer, like the nice chaplain had done at his bedside after the lumbar puncture, but words failed him. He could think only of Alice, and the love he was throwing away. She'd be chairing an important meeting now, or perhaps casting her thoughts to dinner tonight.

A voice drifted over the hedge of a neighbour's garden and his heart knocked at his ribs. 'There you go,' the woman said, tenderly. 'You're free again.' His neighbour was standing in the centre of her chicken pen, throwing seeds onto the ground for her hens. 'I'll be back in ten minutes,' she said.

By which time I will be dead.

3:26. The train was due any minute, but there was no sound or vibration on the track. The Beatles were still audible. "While My Guitar Gently Weeps" bled into "A Day in the Life". Pandora was silent. Jack waited, listening to the song, ready to pounce onto the railway track. He heard some news that was rather sad, and could only laugh. Someone blew their mind out in a car, and a crowd of people stood and stared.

Again, the earth shuddered. 3:29.

It was getting gloomy. A thin fog was descending. Jack shivered against a tree. John Lennon had nearly finished singing; the ending, a beautiful cacophony, vibrating through the air, fizzing to nothing. There was a natural pause and "Hey Jude" started. Paul McCartney's turn.

No train, by Jack's watch two minutes late. He stood with his back against a tree. St. Jude, the patron saint of lost causes and desperate cases, pleaded with him to take a sad song and make it better.

Jack heard a sound and felt a vibration through his feet that wasn't an MoD bomb or windfarm pile-driver. Two bright lights thundered through the distant mist, and the track hummed. He scrambled up the gravel on hands and feet, crouching close to the line. 'I commend my spirit to the sky,' he said, and counted, 'one…two…three,' before jumping, arms out in front as if diving into a secret sea. Just before landing, he saw Alice one last time, on their Jamaican honeymoon, in a gazebo garnished with exotic flowers.

He landed with a crunch, eyes closed, chest ramming the hard metal rails. *I'll be cut clean in half.*

The wheels of the carriages juddered and screeched on the steel, unable to stop for a hundred metres, by which time the passengers gawped out of their windows at the embarrassed wreckage that was poor old comedian and fool, Jack Mann. The robin, unafraid of the commotion, flitted down to the freshly-turned earth, and drew out a startled, purple worm.

-PART FOUR-

Hope is the thing with feathers-
That perches in the soul-
And sings the tune without the words-
And never stops - at all -

Emily Dickinson

In reality, hope is the worst of all evils, because it prolongs man's
torment.

F. Nietzsche, *Human, All Too Human*

Looking Forward, Looking Back

When Jack was a boy, no more than 12 years old, his father was called into school to see the headmaster. Jack was in heaps of trouble. He'd "insulted" and "humiliated" his maths teacher Mr. Cobb. Up until this point in his tender life he'd never done anything confrontational. He'd been a polite, funny kid, as his father could attest.

Jack was no good with sums and numbers. At secondary school this difficulty increased tenfold. The school had a policy of streaming and, as Jack excelled in languages, he was in the top sets for English, French and German, but also in the top group for maths; a skill that confounded him. Whilst other pupils swam freely in the sea of algebra and long division, Jack flapped about helplessly like a stranded fish gasping on the deck of a boat. When asked by Mr. Cobb to solve a specific mathematical equation, Jack's friend used to slide the answer across on a sheet of paper. Jack worked out how to get his homework right too. He'd take records in from home and exchange them for a copy of his friend's homework. To all intents and purposes, Jack was as good at maths as he was at speaking German or deconstructing Shakespeare, but this process had turned him into a liar and a thief, as some of the records he took from home were Ernie's.

Half way through the school year there'd been an examination and Jack's reliable friend wasn't sitting beside him. He'd come bottom of the class and Mr. Cobb decided to make an example. When he handed back everyone's papers he made fun of Jack's inability to do the most basic problem-solving, saying that in more than twenty years of teaching he'd never seen such a poor show, adding that his pet cat Pythagoras might have scored higher. Jack was used to laughter. He'd become a bit of a clown already, doing impressions for his friends. He could do Laurel and Hardy standing on his head. He could do Mr. Cobb too, and frequently had his mates in stitches doing other teachers. But up until this point in life, the laughter had always been *with* Jack, not *against* him. Roars, backslaps, hoots, howls and claps were now replaced by metaphorical punches. He was a laughing stock.

'Mann is a bit of a mystery,' Mr. Cobb told the class. 'Mann lives with his head in the clouds! Mann didn't make the grade. Why such a miserly result unless he's been cheating during the past two terms?' The colour of Jack's face produced the rhetorical answer making the pupils laugh even more. Instead of taking it on the chin, Jack stood up, put his thumbs inside an imaginary waistcoat, just like Mr. Cobb's real one, and said in his finest Cobb voice that sounded like W.C. Fields: 'Mr. Cobb, you have the brain the size of a planet.' The maths teacher beamed with the compliment, until Jack added, with perfect timing, 'In fact, it's as big as your anus.' It was enough to land him in lunchtime detention. Worse, he'd been asked to stay back after final bell, as his father had been called in to see the headmaster.

The other schoolchildren had left by the time Jack Snr. arrived in a bad mood. He'd had to cut short an important meeting with a national newspaper. 'What's this all about, kid?' he asked, standing outside the headmaster's office. 'Your mother's in rehearsals. I had to come.'

Before Jack had time to answer, the door opened and they were invited into the office. Mr. Cobb was sitting in the corner, his long face bathed in light from the window. He'd put on a long, black academic gown over his suit and waistcoat. The headmaster asked Mr. Cobb to explain events. When Mr. Cobb repeated the words "as big as your anus", Jack Snr. had to restrain his facial muscles from fitting. His face, Jack remembered, was fixed in a watery grimace; just how a person laughs without laughing.

Jack was sent outside while the three adults discussed the subject of his punishment. He stood close to the door and heard his father say to the headmaster, 'Now, I'm a very busy man, and if you ever, ever call me in for such a minor thing again, I'll bill you for wasting my time. The kid's been punished already, hasn't he? And you,' he said to Mr. Cobb, 'you need to grow a sense of humour.'

A few minutes later, he appeared at the door and placed an arm around Jack's shoulders walking him straight out into the car park. Inside the car, he turned and said, 'Listen kid, you may not be smart with math, but you sure have a way with words.' Jack remembered, his father's eyes creased, the corners of his mouth curled and he broke into a deep, bear-like laugh. 'As big as your anus! Wait 'til I tell the guys in the office!'

Looking back, that may have been the moment young Jack Mann discovered what he most wanted to do in life; not to make everyone laugh, only his dad. His father's laughter was more precious than gold. Sometimes, standing on a stage before hundreds of punters, his father long since dead, Jack would tell jokes as if Jack Snr. made up the entire audience. 'Whatever you do in life, kid,' his father had said in the car, 'don't ever stop being a kid. Remember that for me, will ya?'

'But what about when I'm grown up and have my own kids?'

'Especially then, kiddo, especially then,' his father said.

And this memory took Jack back even further, to when he was at primary school, and the teacher Mrs. Gill went around asking each pupil in turn what they'd like to be when they grew up. One wanted to be a dancer, another a painter, another a gardener; others wanted to be nurses, doctors, pilots, astronauts, footballers or soldiers. When Mrs. Gill reached Jack, he wanted to be different, saying, 'A seagull.' And everyone laughed. He was ribbed about that for the rest of his time at school, even by close friends: 'Here's Jack Seagull.' 'There's Mann-Gull.' Above his bed, in his old Muswell Hill home, there was a model seagull suspended from the ceiling by wires; something his father had bought back from San Francisco. When Jack went to sleep each night, he dreamed of being that bird, flying over land and far out to sea.

How time had flown, Jack thought, like a seagull flies, going away and coming back with the tide.

These were the first things that sprung to Jack's mind as he picked himself up from the railway tracks and rushed down the bank to the trees. Somehow he'd cheated death, like he'd cheated maths. The seagull hadn't died. If he'd been any good with maths, or if he'd flown over the railway lines in advance, he'd have noticed there were two pairs of tracks, not one. The train he'd try to throw himself under had glided silkily by on the distant pair and stopped a little further down the line.

He scrambled over the barbed wire fence and dragged the rug back to the shed. His breathing was ragged and shallow; each breath painful against his ribs, as if he'd fractured them. His hands were bloodied and pitted with gravel from the sidings. He returned to the conservatory and Pandora leapt up to his face, licking. He didn't know whether to laugh or cry, kneeling down and burying his face in her fur.

Twice he'd tried to kill himself. That first time had been a cry for help, but this second was truly intended. Yet somehow, not just through stupidity or lack of preparation, he'd been granted another pardon. He cleaned his hands, paced the tiles and looked back at the garden. His walking stick was still standing against Buddha's shoulder. He thought about what he'd said to the statue: *Where were you when I needed you?*

He retrieved the stick, returned to the Bunker and hid his goodbye letters at the bottom of a pine drawer in the igloo room. Sitting in the lounge in his tatty leather armchair, he felt such sadness. Nothing had changed. He should have been gone. It should have been over. He stared at his grazed hands; he should have been in bloody pieces.

Alice came back from work just after 6 p.m. Within minutes of her arrival, a knock came at the door. She opened it to find two serious-looking men in high-visibility jackets. They said they were transport police, and asked if she had seen anyone loitering at the rear of the property, as a train driver and a few passengers had seen a man mucking about on the railway line. She explained she'd been at work and called for Jack who she said was ill with MS. 'Is it a prowler?'

'We don't think so, madam,' one of the officers reassured her. 'Sometimes cranks and drunks wander along the railway lines, but we've had a spate of suicides the past year or two at the crossing about a mile away. We thought it might be another. He's probably wandered off by now but we need to check.' He waved a torch in the air.

Jack and Alice opened the side gate and stood on the patio watching the glow of the torch beam as it swept left and right over the foot of the garden and the barbed wire fence. Seeing a dip in the wires, one of the officers hooked a leg over, jumping across; the other man stayed put, calling out to his colleague. 'Anything?'

'Some disturbance, but a fox could've done it. There's a chicken run next door.'

Alice linked arms with Jack, noticing the grazes on his palms. He said Pandora had pulled him over in the road, and he'd bruised a couple of ribs too.

'You've got nothing to worry about, madam, sir. Sorry for disturbing you.' The police walked up the drive. Within an hour, trains were running freely again as if nothing had happened.

The next day Jack put on a brave face and, without prompting, telephoned Gerry. He offered congratulations on the pregnancy. Gerry was a little cool, and suggested an apology to Francesca was in order. That was the trickiest of all. Fran was gracious in victory, saying she understood his anger, no doubt brought on by depression which was part and parcel of coming to terms with multiple sclerosis.

Jack returned to the MS centre, meeting with the manager, Sarah, with whom he discussed counselling. She said it was his lucky day because the counsellor was available that afternoon, if he could wait an hour and a half. The old Jack would have made a feeble excuse and slipped away, but the post-suicidal Jack said he would stay on. Sarah also told him he'd missed an introduction to traditional acupuncture and the acupuncturist, Jin-jing Li, was taking bookings. 'This isn't the acupuncture you get on the NHS you understand, something that treats the symptom not the cause. This is holistic, treating the whole body and mind, the chakras and meridians.'

Waiting in the lounge area, still struggling to make meaningful eye contact with other patients, Jack noticed a whiteboard with names on. His own and Alice's were near the top as newly paid-up members, and Alice had also donated an extra £100. Other names had raised various monies from sponsored marathons, bike rides, boot fairs, raffles and mobility scooter jaunts.

Jack looked about him and for the first time appreciated a community at work. Volunteers making tea and coffee, bringing biscuits and cakes out on plates, doing the washing up, cleaning the toilets, managing the oxygen chamber, staffing the reception desk.

People in wheelchairs or standing with crutches were laughing. Sun shone through the portacabin windows, lighting up their faces. The Scottish soldier introduced himself as Stevie. Jack said to him, 'I see your tree is still in the car park.'

Stevie replied, 'They've had a change o' heart. The tree's got a reprieve.'

They chatted about ordinary things like football, rugby, the weather and the Christmas muzak that was playing. Jack looked up at the bright red and green decorations hanging from the ceiling running from corner to corner in paper chains. A nicely decorated fir tree was standing at the main entrance, Christmas lights twinkling.

A young Chinese woman came out of Sarah's office, her face as pretty as a moon. 'Our new acupuncturist,' Stevie said. 'Jin-jing Li. I've booked four sessions.'

Jack approached awkwardly with his stick and introduced himself. Her smile was soft and open, her eyes narrow, dark and cool. He asked if it was the right time to book an appointment. She took a small black notebook from her bag and offered him four dates in the New Year. 'You want to meet here or main practice in Pilgrims Road, near bus station?' She gave him a business card with her name, qualifications and an elegant blue dragon on.

'Near the station is perfect.'

She picked her bag up from the floor. 'I must go now.'

Alice appeared in time to meet her. 'Please to meet you,' Jin-jing said, shaking Alice's hand. 'See you January, Jack.' She waved to everyone as she walked through the portacabins and out of the main door.

'I see a counsellor in about twenty minutes, Alice.'

'No you won't,' she said. 'I've been told the counsellor's car broke down.'

'It doesn't matter,' he said. 'I feel like I've had all the counselling I need.'

Orville, Jack, and the Beanstalk

Two nights before their meeting with MS specialist Dr. Rama, Jack and Alice attended the opening of the town's impressive new theatre. Alice had bought an elegant evening gown with sparkling sequins. She wore the necklace and earrings Jack had given her as a birthday gift two years before. She'd been to her hair stylist who'd given her a brave new look. Instead of her usual sleek brown bob, he'd manufactured a masterpiece of warm browns and subtle highlights of gold and amber. Jack forced himself out of bed and into a suit and tie. He was close-shaven, clean and smart, but when he posed in the full-length mirror it appeared as if the suit was doing all the work.

En route to the theatre, Alice took a detour to her parents' flat. She wanted to show her mum and dad how glamorous they both looked. 'Make sure there's a photograph of you meeting Prince Edward,' her father said. 'We can put it on the wall.'

'Have you practiced your curtsey?' her mother added, and Alice curtseyed beautifully.

For a moment, standing there, Jack thought he would faint, his head was so light, his body temperature so unfathomably high. His hands were like firebrands. He wanted nothing more than to pour amitriptyline down his throat, lie down in one of his in-laws' beds and sleep until morning, or longer.

The evening passed without incident or drama, other than the pre-arranged performances on stage. Alice flitted around her new theatre alongside the chief executive, introducing Prince Edward to the great and the good: the mayor, his wife, leader of the council, theatre manager and many funders. She worked the room effectively. This new cultural landmark, visible from miles around, had been conceived in a time of plenty but built in a time of austerity to deliver the public artistic entertainment and youth education. It'd been Alice's labour of love for five years. Any awkwardness felt by Jack occurred only when Alice wandered off to speak to people and he stood rooted like Stevie's tree in the MS centre car park.

During the long first interval, when the royal party was assembled in the smaller studio theatre for refreshments, Alice introduced Jack to the prince, saying that her husband had once performed at the London Palladium in the Royal Variety Show and had met the Queen. 'Gosh, your hands are delightfully warm, Mr. Mann,' the prince said. 'You met my mother, you say? And what were you performing at the Palladium?'

It was more than embarrassing in Jack's memory. He'd been in his early twenties, just breaking into TV. Gerry had wangled him a slot through theatrical skullduggery; blackmailing another agent over an affair with a dancing girl. Having prearranged subject matter acceptable to the royal press secretary, Jack had veered off course on that vast empty stage because of nerves, naivety and oodles of cocaine, forgetting half of his set. He was supposed to be sending up politicians and celebrities with impressions, but rambled aimlessly, finishing with a fine impression of the Duke of Edinburgh, and a word-for-word imitation of the "slitty eyes" remark the royal dignitary had made when visiting China. In fact, Jack's ten-minute routine had been so disjointed and edgy it was edited down to less than three for TV. When he met the Queen and the Duke after the show, she nodded and the Duke said, 'Really rather good, young man.' The highlight for Jack, however, had been the twenty minutes *before* his disastrous performance. Low down the bill, Jack had been foisted on ventriloquist Keith Harris who wasn't too happy about sharing a room. His ten-minute slot approaching, Jack paced back and forth, sweating. He went to the bathroom three times, twice snorting cocaine. Harris said: 'If you don't sit down, chuck, you're going to wear a hole in the Axminster and give my Orville a heart attack.'

So Jack sat on a chair staring at Orville the Duck and Cuddles the Monkey. The puppets were sitting on a make-up table, eyes peeled. Jack was greener around the gills than the fluorescent duck. He got up and started pacing again. Harris took Orville down and rested him on his lap. He rearranged the duck's oversized nappy and safety pin, and as Jack paced the length of the room Orville's funny face turned and followed him. Orville said in the ventriloquist's trademark falsetto: 'Do you need to borrow my nappy?' And Jack replied: 'I don't think it's big enough.' This made good material for later stand-up shows, even if he was never invited back to the Palladium. It was on Jack's CV and Gerry milked it mercilessly for the next ten years: "As seen at the London Palladium".

Jack left the new theatre celebrations soon after Prince Edward had departed. He'd grown fatigued, and took a cab back to the Bunker. Alice stayed on for the post-performance party. When she returned in the small hours, a little tipsy, she came into the igloo and fell onto Jack's camp bed gushing about how wonderfully handsome he was, and how proud she was to have him on her arm. He held her tight and kissed her. 'Forget me, and all the princes, princesses, OBEs, sirs, dames, and royal hangers-on,' he said. 'You were the star of the show, Alice.'

Panto season began in earnest. Jack and the Beanstalk was playing that winter, of course, and Jack forced himself again to the theatre. Although they didn't have children to take (perhaps they took their inner children), panto had always been part of their ritual run-up to Christmas. Alice relished the sound of the excitable families screaming with pleasure, and Jack revelled in Alice's booing of the baddies. She always lent a part of herself to the childish melodrama, and tonight even Jack participated. He couldn't help thinking that he had his own beanstalk to climb, though; the forthcoming consultation with Dr. Rama when he'd discover what type of MS he had and what treatment he should start. He looked around the noisy auditorium knowing that in a venue this large, with a capacity of more than a thousand seats, that statistically one person there would have MS, and that particular night Jack was sitting in his seat.

'Oh no he isn't!' the children roared at the frightening giant.

Oh yes he is, thought Jack.

The Mann With Two Brains

The next morning, the telephone rang and Jack saw number "unrecognised". He answered, thinking it would be Ernie. His heart sank when a woman said she was calling from the hospital. She introduced herself as a physio from the stroke rehabilitation unit asking if he was coping with residual symptoms, and if he had had enough support since his stroke in August. He told her there'd been a mix up. 'If you check my records you'll see I never had a stroke in August. I have multiple sclerosis.'

'Oh,' she said, 'it doesn't say on the system. Sorry to bother you.'

Jack hung up the phone, thinking how disconnected the NHS was; its heart was in the right position, but its head was all over the place. In fact, the NHS had too many heads in general, none of which talked to each other. Joke, he thought: how many consultants does it take to change a lightbulb? Answer:five. Two to determine what type of bulb is required, one to find the money to buy it, another one to screw it into the ceiling, and the last to realise it still wasn't working when you flicked the switch.

Jack and Alice were sitting directly opposite Dr. Rama's room, watching patients come and go. They were invited in by a nurse and sat down in front of the MS consultant; a short Indian gentleman with a square face, neat and glossy dark hair, and a thin pencil moustache. He had a friendly, courteous manner.

At first, it was hard understanding him because he was so softly spoken. He asked Jack to recount his history, then he asked him to take off his shoes, socks and jacket and gave him a full clinical examination, just as Mr. Swan had done. He spoke into a small Dictaphone as a reminder to himself: patient, right-handed comedian entered room with help of one stick saying legs were wobbly. Visual acuity 6/5 bilaterally, colour vision 14/14 bilaterally, optic fundi normal, visual fields normal, extraocular movements normal, cranial nerves within normal limits, bulk, tone and power of all muscle groups normal, reflexes normal, plantars downgoing, can walk on toes and heels and can tandem-walk, can hop on either leg. Romberg's sign negative. All sensations including pinprick, touch, vibration and temperature were within normal limits. No cerebellar signs.

'I can say to you, Mr. Mann, that all of your clinical signs are within normal limits.'

'What type of MS have I got?' said Jack, pulling his socks on.

'Well,' the doctor said, 'combined with your MRI results that show only one area of abnormal signal next to the right ventricle, it means there is insufficient evidence to diagnose multiple sclerosis.'

'What?' Alice said. 'Mr. Swan said the MRI showed inflammation or enhancement, and prescribed steroids.'

'No,' said Rama, looking at his computer screen. 'There is no enhancement.'

'So Mr. Swan made the wrong diagnosis?' asked Jack.

Dr. Rama didn't wish to comment on his predecessor, only to say Mr. Swan had retired from the hospital. He turned his computer screen half around. 'You see here?' He pointed to a graph. 'On the scale of disability running from zero to one hundred where one hundred is death by multiple sclerosis and zero is no affect from multiple sclerosis, you are at zero.'

'I don't understand,' said Alice. 'How could Mr. Swan diagnose MS if there was no enhancement? He either read the wrong scan or read the right scan incorrectly. They are the only two explanations.'

'Unless I'm the man with two brains,' said Jack.

Dr. Rama scratched his head. 'Surely, this is good news?'

Alice cleared her throat. 'We just want to know what this *is*, not what it *isn't*.' She shook her head. 'Mr. Swan advocated beta-interferon.'

'You're not a candidate for disease-modifying treatment. Believe me, you don't want to be injecting yourself with poison unnecessarily.'

'It's unbelievable,' said Alice, folding her arms. 'Is there anyone else we can discuss this with, Dr. Rama?'

He stood up. 'Wait a moment. I'll consult with my colleague Dr. Solomon, the lead MS consultant.' He left the room, taking Jack's file with him.

He was gone five or six minutes. In that time, Alice scanned the room as if for answers. 'Deep in my gut I knew it wasn't MS.'

'You never said, Alice.'

'I didn't want to give you false hope. It could be one of a hundred things.'

The walls were paper thin. Voices mumbled through an adjoining room. None of them belonged to Dr. Rama. They were the voices of a different consultant asking a patient if she'd experienced headaches or nausea in the mornings, and a fearful woman replied, 'Bad ones four or five times a week, worse in the mornings, making me throw up.' Her accent, Jack thought, was Cornish. Then another similar accent came, deeper and more mature; probably the patient's mother or older sister. 'Have you looked at the new scan?' There was an awful silence and the consultant said: 'I'm sorry, but you definitely have a tumour and it has grown substantially since our last meeting.' Jack looked at Alice, thinking about the fake telephone call Mr. Swan had made during their consultation. The young woman didn't say anything; the older woman asked further questions on her behalf: How bad is it? How large? Would it require an operation? Was there any treatment instead of an operation? Would there be a biopsy? 'How long do I have to live?' the patient said finally.

The door opened and Dr. Rama marched back behind his desk. 'Well, Dr. Solomon agrees. We'll send your MRI scan back to King's College Hospital in London for further opinion from their chief neuroradiologist, Mr. Knox.'

'But *he* was the one who ordered the scan with gadolinium in the first place,' said Alice. 'He's seen it already.'

'I don't think so,' said Rama. 'Who ordered it did you say?'

'It's like déjà vu all over again,' said Jack.

Alice sighed. 'This is turning into a comedy of terrors. Dr. Richter the vascular consultant asked King's in September to look at the scans done in August. King's asked for a new MRI scan with gadolinium.

That was done in October. From that scan Mr. Swan misdiagnosed MS, only last month. All of this should be on file.'

'It's safer to send everything to Mr. Knox. Belt and braces.'

'How long will it take?' said Alice. 'Because it's been four months since the onset of symptoms, symptoms that are worsening, and we're no nearer an answer. Whatever's causing my husband's illness seems harder to discover than Rumpelstiltskin.'

'A few weeks,' said Dr. Rama. 'I shall write to you when they get back with their report. And remember, Rumpelstiltskin's name was eventually discovered, was it not?'

'What am I suffering from if it's not MS?' asked Jack.

'Inflammation, probably caused by a demyelinating process. It's called CIS or Clinically Isolated Syndrome. In other words, something has caused your own cells to attack the myelin sheath around your nerves, like MS.' He took up a pen and drew a diagram on a scrap of paper. 'It's like the insulating cable on electrical wires. But there hasn't been a definite second event in time, and neither is there evidence in space, in other words, the lesions in your brain are too few.'

'So is there a chance this CIS can turn into multiple sclerosis?' said Alice.

'Good question. Statistics vary, but with abnormal MRI results and oligoclonal banding in Jack's spinal fluid, I'd say there is a stronger chance of turning into clinically definite multiple sclerosis. You have a 50/50 chance of developing it during the course of the next five years.'

'But it might never convert?' asked Jack.

'Let's see what Mr. Knox says at King's.'

'One thing I don't understand,' said Alice, 'is the fact that Jack's symptoms never go into remission. He's fatigued non-stop. The pain is never ending. Could the inflammation have been caused by something other than MS, like migraine...or lupus...or vitamin B12-deficiency?'

'Migraines and lupus don't give you brain lesions,' Dr. Rama said, dismissively. 'And you've been tested for B12.'

They shook their heads. He flicked through Jack's file. 'I apologise. B12 and vitamin D3 should have been checked at the very beginning.

I'll request these now. Go straight to phlebotomy after this consultation. Give them this.'

Dr. Rama understood this to be the end of the meeting until Jack asked, 'What about the pain? I can barely sleep. It's as if my hands have been dipped in molten lava and the skin has been flayed from the soles of my feet. It's soul-destroying.'

'There is no such thing as pain,' said Dr. Rama, folding his arms.

Jack's body tensed. He had to stop himself from grabbing Rama by the throat. He took a deep breath and said: 'If you knew what it's like to burn alive every day and night for months without relief you wouldn't say there's no such thing as pain, doctor. It's enough to make a sensible man throw himself under a train.'

'No, what I meant was you are experiencing the *sensation* of pain, but *clinically* it is only the *subjective* miscommunication between the brain and the peripheral nervous system. Like a trunk call?'

After Dr. Rama had picked himself up from the floor feeling the bridge of his broken nose, Jack said, 'What you are experiencing right now, doctor, is the subjective miscommunication between a patient and his consultant.' At least, that was what Jack imagined doing and saying. In reality, he remained stock still in his chair, grinding his teeth.

'The wrong messages are being sent or the correct messages are being wrongly interpreted or a combination of both,' Dr. Rama said. 'We can give you Gabapentin, 300mg daily, increased in 300mg steps every three to five days, up to a treatment dose of 1.8gm per day.' He wrote out a prescription. 'And if that doesn't help, we can try Pregabalin. And if that doesn't work, we can try opioids. We can manage your pain in steps, Mr. Mann.'

During the car journey back to the Bunker, Alice couldn't brush from her mind the image of Mr. Swan. The man who thought he was God, who was so proud of his 90% diagnostic success rate, who had strutted before his mesmerised students like a cockerel, who'd faked a telephone call about a brain tumour, who'd advised government on neurology, who'd said the most damaging mistake a doctor can make is misdiagnosis, the man who'd made such a mistake with Jack. If Swan was the God of consultants, she thought, what hope was there..?

Major Tom, Dr. Google and Eureka

Jack ransacked the internet for "Clinically Isolated Syndrome" and discovered Dr. Rama was out of touch with current research. Rather than having a 50/50 chance, the actual likelihood of developing MS in the next five years was closer to 80%. Patients with abnormal MRIs and spinal fluid were at higher risk of conversion, and the chances of converting after this period increased year on year. In America, CIS patients often started treatment for MS because it *delayed* conversion.

Trying to remain positive, he trawled the internet further looking for other possible causes of his illness. He consulted academic papers, patient forums and media articles. Perhaps this was the wrong thing to do; discovering the full range of neurological calamities that can befall a human being, including motor neurone disease, sarcoidosis and HIV. Using his PC as a medical encyclopedia and virtual G.P. was a minefield. Jack shared symptoms with countless other diseases, the commonest of which was still MS, and most were similarly incurable and degenerative. "Dr. Google" was self-contradictory too. He'd say one thing one minute, something else the next. Most forums were based on patients' subjective experiences, predominantly in America. Stories were anecdotal and nightmarish. Members of discussion groups with no apparent medical training were diagnosing new members with all sorts of illnesses. Although the forums were supportive, twenty people could have wildly different opinions on the same person's symptoms.

When Alice returned home Jack was already in bed, feeling as though his brain was oozing from his ears. His hands hibernated in wine coolers and he struggled to sleep, listening to trains passing, and the yelping of foxes. He must have drifted off eventually, because he awoke at four in the morning startled by the rare glimpse of a dream. He was grateful for the nocturnal driftwood churned up by the sea of his unconscious. For months now, he'd lost all sense of dreaming or all memory of dreams. He didn't know if this was his mind melting down or the side-effect of painkillers, but whatever arrived in the summer, this affliction, this unwanted guest, it had acted like a thief in the night stealing all of his dreams in its swag bag.

But this night there remained a bold image of his old collie, Major Tom, the white ruff of his neck flashing in the moonlight as he charged through woodland. Jack had been hot in pursuit. Tom picked up the scent of something and was hunting it down, barking as he ran. On the brow of a hill, in a frosty clearing, Major Tom stopped abruptly, sniffing the ground, then arching his back in silhouette. He threw back his head and howled like a wolf. In the undergrowth beside him was a moving bundle; the old blanket that had belonged to Jack's mother. Her blankie of love. Jack knelt down, unfolded it and discovered a fox cub that looked up into his eyes. Jack threw his own head back and howled at the stars as if he too was a wolf. And when he looked down again, the cub was no longer there, replaced by a baby. All the things he'd seen die in real life had come back to life that night: poor little Hunter, poor Major Tom, poor fox cub.

It had been a long time since he'd reconnected with Major Tom. Alice had brought him home as a Christmas present; a small puppy of black and white, twelve inches tall, twelve weeks old. They'd trained him, pampered him, fawned over him and loved him for thirteen years, never failing to marvel at his howling at sirens. Every howl was tailored to suit different sirens. And here he was, this night, almost alive, howling in Jack's head like a supercharged alarm bell. *Howling,* Jack thought. *Woodland. A hiking holiday in Wales. 18 months ago? Sandals and shorts. Horses and sheep. Field upon field of livestock. Pulling ticks out of Major Tom's skin. Disgusting, swollen parasites engorged with blood. Major Tom died three months later and I,* Jack thought, *I started to feel unwell too.*

Pandora heard Jack shuffle into the kitchen. She sat by the cupboard where her treats were stored. When he looked at her, she wagged her tail. How different Pan was to Major Tom. Just like children, each dog has its own personality. Pan couldn't or wouldn't howl; it was more of a half-hearted gargle.

As the PC took time booting, Jack recalled other medical ailments that followed his hiking holiday; mysterious bouts of flu, and colds he couldn't shake for weeks that stretched into months. He'd been forced to cancel social engagements and one-off charity nights. Aches, chills and a crushing fatigue happened without physical exertion. Even odder, a stiff neck that was *just there* one morning and stayed for two months, so painful he couldn't turn his head despite physiotherapy or strong prescription painkillers. And all of these things he'd forgotten about until now, after the Major Tom dream. And hadn't these non-specific illnesses originated with an unusual rash on his leg? Yes, pale in the centre with an outer border of red that spread outwards in an oval shape at least a foot in diameter.

All of these symptoms *after that rash* that was so extraordinary he'd gone to hospital and they diagnosed cellulitis, giving him five days of antibiotics. It was as if he'd come back from Wales with a curse. Tom died, then his own series of unexplained health scares that Dr. Munch put down to the stresses of everyday life and Jack's anxious over-thinking. But does anxiety give you remarkable rashes and a stiff neck lasting weeks? How many times had he broken into a cold sweat and dizziness, almost fainting? And then there were other unexplained things: testicular and bladder pain requiring more hospital visits, scans, blood tests, prescribed drugs. *Were these things connected?* Weight loss; a stone and a half in three months *after Wales.* Sleeplessness. Nightmares. Photosensitivity, tinnitus, the list went on. And one night, he remembered, he was sitting in the kitchen of the Fulham maisonette, and he'd said to Alice: 'Something terrible's happening to me. Something's inside me.' And she was worried he was falling into a depression, which was one of the reasons they decided to sell up and start again by the sea, hoping to leave illness behind.

Sitting now at the farmhouse table in the Bunker, he typed in all of his non-specific illnesses along with the word "tick". For half an hour he came across the same single answer: *Lyme disease*. A bacterial infection carried by ticks transmitted to mammals from a bite. Undiagnosed and untreated, it could lead to life-changing illness including damage to the central and peripheral nervous systems. Pins and needles, numbness, brain lesions. *Commonly mistaken for MS*. His heart raced with recognition. European strains of the disease were more likely to be neurological. *Tick, tick, tick, tick, boom!*

He researched for hours, coming across American websites. One of these belonged to a "Lyme-literate MD" who preferred to call Lyme "Multi-Systemic Infectious Disease Syndrome". Having treated thousands of patients from across the world, the doctor had formulated a questionnaire or checklist for Lyme. If a patient scored 46 or more there was a *high probability* he had a tick-borne disorder. A score between 21 and 45 and the patient had a *possibility* of Lyme. A score of less than 21 and the patient was *very unlikely* to have Lyme disease.

Jack got a pen and paper and completed the 55 questions as honestly as he could, underscoring himself in places to counterbalance any unconscious exaggeration born out of a need to name his illness. He scored highly on fatigue, motion sickness, vertigo, tinnitus, burning pains, depression, difficulty reading and writing, sleeplessness, the initial rash, a visit to an endemic region for ticks, testicular and bladder pain, stiff neck, and misdiagnosis of multiple sclerosis. He added up his scores from the four different sections and was astounded by his final result: 94. Lyme, according to this questionnaire, was certain.

Lyme disease.

He'd seen the name before, but thought it too rare, too "American". The more he researched, however, the more likely it became. The bite from a tick and transmission of a vile, parasitical bacterium called "Borrelia" that if left untreated could affect the entire human body, most notably the nervous system, including the brain. Late-stage Lyme could cause white matter lesions and neuropathies, tingling, numbness and extreme fatigue, just like MS or syphilis. In fact, around the world experts were calling it "the great imitator".

Could he have been bitten in Wales? Could he have been bitten in London? Could his beloved dog have brought ticks home in his fur? And Jack remembered how he'd slept in the lounge with his dying Major Tom. How he'd slept on the sofa where Tom sometimes slept. And soon after came the expanding Lyme rash, *erythema migrans*.

Now Jack was pacing, wanting to wake Alice. His head was full of questions: why didn't anyone ever suggest Lyme disease? Was it just too rare in the UK? He looked again at photographs of Lyme rashes. Most were identical to the one he had. Yes, everything added up: not stroke, not tumour, not MS, but Lyme, Lyme, Lyme. A bomb seemed to go off in his head. Lyme was a name for his illness, a cause, and it was also a light at the end of a tunnel; a light that was no longer a train. It was a way out into daylight.

The excitement grew too much and he woke Alice. He sat on the edge of her bed telling her things before she was fully conscious. She asked him to slow down. She pushed herself up the bed. 'You've never been right since that trip to Wales.'

He told her about what happened when an infected tick passed nasty bugs into the blood stream. How bacteria sought out hiding places to breed and prosper, like terrorist sleeper cells. 'The terrorists have infiltrated the building of me,' he said. 'They got in at the ground floor (foot), spread to the next floor (leg), evaded all security (immune system) by disguising themselves. They took the express elevator (spinal cord) straight to the command centre (brain), holding my whole body to ransom. Now they are hiding out in all of my vital organs.' He rambled, how Borrelia can be killed off with antibiotics if caught early, but how hard they are to kill if they've had time to spread and hide in the brain, the heart, the liver, and the lymph nodes. 'In fact,' he said, 'the little bastards can live almost anywhere in the body. They're living in my brain, Alice.'

'My God, Jack. Could you have Lyme disease?'

'Everything fits. We just need to prove it.'

Dr. Oiseau

Being so close to Christmas it was impossible to make an appointment with Dr. Greaves. If he wished, the administrator said, Jack could see the locum, Dr. Oiseau, who was acting as temporary cover. In her mid-twenties, she was probably from France or Belgium, judging by her accented English. Jack had always been very good at locating the provenance of accents, particularly European, but his ear had become muddied with illness; hampered by a growing mental fog and tinnitus.

He explained his medical history and Dr. Oiseau skimmed the evidence on the computer screen. He told her Dr. Rama was exploring other differentials such as B12 deficiency, but had discounted migraines as they didn't cause brain lesions.

'Non,' she said. 'Migraine can cause white matter lesion. I saw a patient with a long 'istory of migraine, and after autopsy many small lesions were discovered in 'is brain that were not accounted for by age, dementia or Alzheimer's.'

'Oh. I don't know who or what to believe anymore,' said Jack. 'I just want to find out what's wrong with me.'

'Bien,' she said, looking at her screen, 'we can discount vitamin deficiency. B12 result is within normal limits.'

'What about vitamin D3?'

'That doesn't appear…attendez…there's a note on your file.' She peered at the screen. 'Your blood sample for D3 'as been lost, Mr. Mann. This sometimes 'appens. I shall reinstate it. You can either give blood 'ere at the surgery or directly at the 'ospital. I think the phlebotomist is in today.'

'I wanted to talk to you about blood tests,' he said, telling her about his array of neurological symptoms that had confounded most of the doctors.

She turned away from the computer to face him. 'It's like a great mystery, isn't it? Like a crime novelle. You say the worst pain is in your 'ands?' She leaned forward in her chair. She took both of his hands in hers. Dr. Oiseau pressed his fingertips saying the circulation was good. 'Regardez,' she said, 'ow the blood return? But they feel cold, not 'ot as you describe.'

'Normally they're on fire. I could boil eggs in my palms in less than six minutes.' He told her about his suspicions of Lyme disease and his many symptoms from eighteen months ago. No one had joined up the non-specific dots. 'It all started a few weeks after the Brecon Beacons.'

'Interesting,' said Dr. Oiseau. 'And no one 'as tested you for it before?' She typed *Lyme disease* into her search engine and read for a few minutes. 'Bien,' she said. 'I'm ordering a blood test. You can do it today.'

Jack Mann Syndrome

Two days later, Jack and Alice were back at the hospital for a meeting with the MS nurse. Jack had met her once before at the centre, but this meeting had been arranged to discuss pain management. Gabapentin was having no effect. Worse still, the drug was presenting side effects including mouth ulcers, and, if anything, Jack's neuropathy was worsening. On top of the burning, newer symptoms had arisen. Half of his tongue and pallet had gone numb, and his nose was tingling as if the top layer of skin had been grazed off. Also, lying awake at night, he got the strangest feeling that his legs weren't part of him. He could feel them all right, but in his mind they weren't connected to his body; like they belonged to somebody else. 'Is this normal?' Jack asked.

The nurse shook her head. 'The most important thing is to get the pain under control. I suggest switching to Pregabalin. It's more effective. Dr. Rama is away today, so I'll ask Dr. Solomon for a prescription. In fact,' she said, getting up, 'I'm going to ask Dr. Solomon to come and take a look at you right now. It's fortuitous, he's just next door.'

Dr. Solomon, the lead MS consultant, was in his fifties, medium build, clean-shaven. He was wearing a pink, pin-striped shirt. A distinct woody aftershave wafted through the room when the door closed behind him. He sat down at the desk and the nurse stood beside him. Once again, Jack gave a brief account of his illness and Dr. Solomon said he was aware of the diagnosis of Clinically Isolated Syndrome, having already discussed it with Dr. Rama.

'Tell Dr. Solomon about your nose, Jack; your nose, and your mouth,' said the nurse. 'Tell him about your legs.'

Jack told him and Dr. Solomon had a hard time explaining.

'Is it a normal sign of MS?' asked Alice.

Solomon shook his head.

'Have King's got back about my MRI scans?' asked Jack.

Dr. Solomon had the look of someone who'd been roped in to do someone else's work. He switched on the PC, got Jack's information up on screen and said King's had not yet reported back to Dr. Rama about the MRIs. They would be back in the New Year.

Given that she had the lead MS consultant in front of her, Alice took the opportunity to ask further questions: Why did so many of Jack's symptoms not correlate with MS? Why were his symptoms bilateral when the lesion was only on one side of his brain? Why, if this might be relapsing-remitting MS, had none of his symptoms dissipated in four months?

Dr. Solomon couldn't explain. 'The effects of demyelination are particular to the individual. You could have "Jack Mann Syndrome" for all I know.' He re-examined Jack's MRI scans, saying he was honestly baffled.

'Was the initial diagnosis of MS dependent on the abnormal MRI scans, the protein banding in Jack's spinal fluid, or the evoked potentials?' Alice asked.

'I don't know,' he said, surprised by her medical acumen.

'Mr. Swan misdiagnosed Jack with MS,' she said.

'I can't comment on that.'

Jack piped up: 'What are the chances of this being Lyme disease?'

'What?'

Jack explained he was waiting for blood results for Lyme disease, and Dr. Solomon frowned. 'Lyme's disease is incredibly rare.'

'Yes,' said Alice, 'but rare doesn't make it impossible. You said you can't explain Jack's symptoms, but Lyme does.'

'Officially we get maybe two cases of Lyme's every year at this hospital. You'll need to discuss this with Dr. Rama. There's a raft of differentials more likely than Lyme's disease.'

First of all, Alice was thinking, *it's not "Lyme's disease", it's "**Lyme** disease". Secondly, what other differentials?*

Christmas at the Bunker

This must go down as the worst Christmas Day to date, thought Jack, celebrating the festival in a charmless bungalow, exhausted through lack of sleep and drowsy on the new painkiller Pregabalin, the chemical properties of which meant he shouldn't drink alcohol. Charged with doing the roast potatoes, still dressed in his pyjamas and slippers, he forced himself to peel King Edwards at the kitchen sink. He stared momentarily out of the window towards the Buddha and the railway track. For once, there were no trains. Alice flitted from fridge to cupboard to oven, fussing over the turkey and trimmings. Thoughtfully, she sipped her champagne and orange juice behind his back, not right in front of him, though he noticed. That's what they always used to do on Christmas morning; drink bucks fizz first thing, eat smoked salmon blinis, and play alternative indie Christmas songs.

Traditional carols bounced around the hard surfaces of the Bunker this year, to please his in-laws. Pat and Alan were due in an hour, but Alice had prepped the turkey a little late in the morning so they wouldn't be eating until three o'clock. As usual, Alice's parents would get grumpy waiting and Jack would have to amuse them. Not that Jack was in the mood for amusement or even had the energy to pull crackers. Just standing at the sink took all of his willpower. Peeling and quartering a bag of spuds, a process that normally took twenty minutes, had already taken an hour.

'When are you getting dressed?' Alice asked, sensitively hiding her glass behind a stalk of Brussel's sprouts.

'Now,' he said, leaving the potatoes in a saucepan of water.

Half an hour later, he emerged to find that Alice had nipped out with Pandora. He opened the fridge, picked out the bottle of champagne and drank straight from the neck. If he was going to do Christmas at all he was going to do it merry, and to hell with painkillers. Though he loved his in-laws, he'd never been locked in the same room as them for five hours stone-cold sober. In Alice's absence, he shifted a fresh bottle of champagne from the wine rack out into the freezing cold. He rested it beside a glass, behind a downpipe outside the kitchen door. Whenever he wanted a drink, he'd say he needed some air.

By the time Pat and Alan arrived, he'd drunk two thirds of a bottle and was giddy. He helped his mother-in-law inside with her walking sticks, led her slowly to the conservatory and sat her down at the dining table overlooking the garden. He poured her a sherry and his father-in-law a whisky. Alan said he was going to enjoy himself - not too much mind, he wasn't one for excesses, but this Christmas he was more chipper than normal, as if his ancient aches and pains were less bothersome, or he was trying hard to be happy, making up for Jack's quietness.

Pat downed her glass of sherry. Jack re-filled it, and that was when the strangeness swept over his body, starting in his stomach and rushing to his head. The conservatory revolved, its windows spinning as if he was on a magic roundabout. He grabbed hold of the table cloth thinking he'd be sick over the beautiful arrangement of wine glasses, napkins, cutlery, candles and decorations.

'Are you alright?' his father-in-law said, grabbing his elbow, but Jack couldn't hear the words. He felt his face reddening and then burning, and he rushed to the bathroom. He dropped to his knees and hugged the toilet bowl with both hands, though nothing came up. He stood again, looked in the mirror, and a ripe strawberry stared back. Pearls of sweat had formed at his brow, and his eyes span like cartoon wheels. He grabbed hold of the sink for ballast.

'Jack?' called Alice from the hallway.

After he'd thrown cold water over his face and dried it on a towel, he opened the door.

'My God, it's Mr. Tomato Head,' she said. 'You look like you've spent two days under a sun lamp.'

'I need to lie down,' he said, moving gingerly to the bedroom.

'Do you need an ambulance?'

'I'm not going to hospital on Christmas Day. I'd rather die.'

'You've been drinking!'

'Only a couple.'

'Oh, Jack, I told you what would happen.'

'Happy Christmas, Alice.'

She brought him a glass of water, asking if he wanted to see a doctor. 'No,' he said. 'I'm sick of doctors. Sick, sick, sick.'

He stayed in bed while the others ate Christmas dinner. He listened to their knives and forks scraping on the plates. By the time they started on the trifle, his face had cooled, the room was no longer spinning and the nausea had passed. He joined them, and Alice brought out a plate of food she'd left in the warm oven. He picked at it, drinking water.

By now it was already dark and Alan was holding court. For someone who didn't believe in seasonal decoration or buying a Christmas tree, or even answering the door to carol-singing children, Jack's father-in-law had turned into a reformed, exceedingly happy Ebenezer Scrooge. Two whiskeys and two glasses of red wine down, an unheard of quantity before today, he was the first to pull his cracker and don his paper crown. He was the one telling the jokes, reading the trivia and roaring with laughter. 'What do you call a man with a cliff on his head? Hold on, got that wrong. What do you call a man with a seagull on his head? Cliff.' It was a remarkable role-reversal. Not known for excess, Alan managed not just a second but a third helping of trifle. He was the one topping up Alice's wine glass when normally he'd be the first to question how many units an average woman should healthily consume. When they retired to the lounge, Alan hummed along to the carols, tapping his finger on the arms of Jack's tatty leather armchair. Making a toast near the end of the evening, Alan stood up, raised his glass and said: 'Here's to the future! Happy Christmas, one and all!'

On Boxing Day, Alice and Jack took Pandora for a walk along the Slopes. A brisk wind beat against their faces, reddening their noses and watering their eyes. Jack hadn't needed his stick, his legs a little stronger than usual. He wasn't up to walking on the stony beach, though, but did agree to visit Seagull House. The sky was turning grey by the time they turned the corner of Marine Walk. A whisper of snowflakes blew above their heads as they let themselves in.

The power wasn't on; there were last minute changes to light fittings and the position of the new range cooker. Everything smelled new. The wooden floors, woollen carpets and freshly-painted walls, seaside shades of cool blues, dove greys and stony whites. They walked from room to room, spending time in each one, suggesting where their furniture might go and what new pieces they should buy in the sales. Standing in the lounge, Jack said: 'I want to get rid of our sofa.' When she pointed out it had only just been reupholstered, he said, 'It reminds me of all the horrible things that happened to me.'

In the master bedroom, Alice took hold of his hand and led him towards the floor-to-ceiling windows harbouring views out to sea. She slid a door open and pulled him onto the glass-brimmed balcony. Snow was falling heavily now and landed on the shoulders of their trench coats. Alice kissed him and he tasted her lipstick. She said that this would be their new start; not the Bunker, not illness, not sadness. 'No looking back,' she said. She stepped into the room again and pulled a present from her large handbag. 'Here,' she said, smiling. 'I kept it secret until now.'

He started to unwrap the paper. 'What is it?'

'It's the final piece in the puzzle of our dream.'

Inside the wrapping paper was a stylish Perspex name plate in silver and black: *Seagull House*. 'It can go beside the new oak door,' she said. 'I got the electrician to wire in a fitting, but we haven't chosen a light yet. I was thinking brushed steel.'

'It's lovely, Alice.'

She hugged him. 'One more thing.' She took something else from her bag. 'You should always bring something symbolic into a new home.' She handed him the wooden seagull she'd bought weeks before. 'Why don't we put him on the window sill at the top of the stairs, or on the landing?'

'Yes,' he said. He placed it on the sill and turned the beak towards the glass. 'Now it faces where it should. Not onto a railway line, but out to sea.'

-PART FIVE-

The further society drifts from the truth, the more it will hate those who speak it.

George Orwell

Extreme remedies are very appropriate for extreme diseases.

Hippocrates

Sudden Life Syndrome

Mid-January. Everything was on the removal van outside the Bunker; all except the old sofa and Jack's large stone Buddha, which was sitting serenely on top of a wooden pallet in the drive. One of the removal men leaned on the hand-pallet truck explaining that the statue would have to be moved separately. He'd requested another van that had a platform lift.

Jack stayed at the rented bungalow with Pandora and Buddha while Alice went on ahead with the rest of their possessions. Jack was left holding Pandora's leash, standing beside Buddha. 'Well, old friend,' he said to the statue, 'it's time for a new home.' The Buddha remained silent. Half way through winter, moss had grown around his neck and shoulders, covering him like a cloak trapped under a thin film of ice. Behind Buddha sat the long sofa that was earmarked for a local charity shop. A truck turned up and one of the charity men asked if Jack was sure about letting it go as it was in fine condition. 'No man could ever be more certain,' he said.

He watched them carry it onto their truck and felt a load lifting from his shoulders. He returned indoors, found an empty cardboard box and started to fill it with the remains of their lives in the Bunker; bits and bobs left on window sills and in the far corners of cupboards and drawers. At the bottom of a built-in wardrobe he discovered a shoe-horn he'd never seen before. It didn't belong to Alice, so he assumed it belonged to the previous resident who'd died; the man with oversized feet. Jack replaced it and moved from room to room, stopping in each one to offer quiet goodbyes. He stood for a long time in the centre of the small second bedroom, now entirely empty of boxes; the "igloo" he'd spent five of the last six months buried inside.

The only things left now were cobwebs in the corners of the windows, limp net curtains, the paper carcasses of dead spiders, and loose balls of dog hair blowing around the tiles. This was the room he'd thought he'd die in; the place he'd deliberately made cold to stave off the burning. This was the place that became a coffin. Jack stared down at the exact place the Z-bed had been and saw himself writhing in agony, hands pressed to the walls. But this cell had also been a cocoon, a cold sanctuary, hadn't it? It occurred to him as he closed the door on this other world, that a small part of him would remain trapped inside the igloo forever, like a ghost, and a tiny part of the igloo would remain inside him too.

He closed the front door and a large white van pulled up. Two men got out. They opened the rear doors, pressed a button and lowered the lift platform to the ground. One stood behind the stone statue, placing his hands on its back. The other grabbed hold of the truck and levered the pallet high off the drive. 'One, two, three,' he said, pulling hard. The other man pushed and they managed to drag it onto the platform. 'Heavier than a piano,' one of them puffed. They pressed a button and the platform rose up. Buddha looked out from a great height, though his eyelids were always closed in contemplation. Perhaps he saw with his third eye. The men pulled and pushed him from the platform into the back of the van, clicked the lift back into position and closed the rear doors. 'Buddha gets a van all to himself,' one of the men laughed.

When they arrived at their new home, three vans were parked outside. One contained most of the furniture and kitchen appliances from their flat in Fulham that had been in a storage facility; the second had everything from the Bunker, and the third had only Buddha. Three removal men were already working their way through one van, carrying the heaviest things first: tall, stainless steel fridge, kitchen dresser, sets of drawers, wardrobes, beds. Alice stood in the hallway issuing instructions. Boxes were marked up for specific rooms and those that weren't were stacked up against a wall in the garage. Jack took Pandora down to the office at the foot of the garden and stayed there for the next three hours, communicating with Alice via his mobile phone.

A removal man walked down the garden carrying a box of books. 'Your wife said these are for your office?' Another man arrived with more books, and another box. Before too long, the wooden office had standing room only, boxes reaching the ceiling. One of the men said, 'We only have the Buddha left now, and the arbour. Where are they going?'

Jack walked him behind the office into a large, secluded, gravelled area, beyond an old tamarisk tree. He pointed to one corner, close to an overhanging bamboo plant. 'He's to face east,' said Jack. 'And if you could put the arbour in the other corner facing the Buddha, thank you.'

Jack watched three men carefully lift the statue off of the pallet and place him on the stones. 'Nice spot for Buddha,' said one of the men, standing back and appreciating the statue in his new surroundings.

'The weight of three men,' said another, wiping sweat from his brow.

Alice tipped them generously for their fast, efficient work. 'Good luck in your new home,' the foreman said. Jack and Alice stood on the drive watching the three vans disappear at the far end of Marine Walk.

'Thank God for the garage,' said Alice.

Jack looked through the open door. Boxes lined one entire length of the space, three feet deep, floor to ceiling. A large gilded mirror covered in bubble wrap was propped against them, and he asked why it wasn't put in the house. 'Because gold isn't really a seaside colour,' she said. 'I'm going to paint it chalky shades of grey, blue and green. It should reflect the sky and the sea. Gold leaf is too baroque.'

'Baroque was alright in our Victorian flat,' he said, smiling.

'Now we're living next to the sea in our brand new house,' she said, 'it's time for a change.' A seagull landed on the roof, squawking, and tidying its wings. 'Looks like we've got company,' said Alice, looking up. Another seagull swung in from the sea, dropping out of the sky onto the roof tiles, landing with skill right beside the other bird. 'Maybe they're a mating pair and we'll have baby gulls.'

'Maybe,' he said, placing his arm around her.

The Stomach

Jack's appointment with Jin-jing Li was booked for mid-day. Despite Alice's offer of a lift, he wanted to make his own way to the clinic in town. He'd lost many things over the last few months, not least his core strength, and now he clung to the final vestiges of independence. Showering and shaving had taken him an hour, bleary-eyed and trembling. When he'd looked in the mirror, dark expanding rings peered back from his sockets and an extra stone of flab hung loose around his waist. Another symptom of his illness, or side-effect from medication, was extreme photosensitivity. Even on the dullest winter day, light pierced his eyeballs like a fire-flash from an explosion. Most days this forced him to wear sunglasses, inside and outside Seagull House. Only that morning, Alice had brought him tea in bed and stood in front of the large bedroom window for a few minutes, talking. The light surrounding her was blinding, making him squint. After she left the room, a perfect silhouetted image of her head and shoulders remained where she'd stood, as if a photograph negative was standing in front of the window, and this image had lasted thirty seconds before dissolving from his retina.

Dressed in his long black overcoat and sunglasses, he waited at the bus stop. Sleet started to fall. If anyone paid close attention they'd have noticed him swaying back and forth in the buffeting wind. He stepped on to the bus unaware of the strange glances from other passengers.

Tankerton's main street was busy. The bus crawled at a snail's pace, slowing at double-parked cars. The brakes screeched at pedestrian crossings and squeezed through bottlenecks. With the sleeve of his overcoat, Jack wiped a porthole in the condensation and gazed out of his window, imagining he was inside a submarine passing through a sea of deep-water cars and random fish-people. As the bus drew slowly down the main street, Jack noticed for the first time how peculiar the assemblage of shops; more especially, how each one seemed curiously linked not by bricks and render but by the invisible chains of a theme: turf accountant, a shop for baby clothes, prams and accessories joined to one selling toys and games, leading to another called "Tankertunes" selling old records, to another shop selling sportswear and snorkel gear, to a wedding shop with rails bowed down with ivory gowns, to a microbrewery, grocery store, chip shop, Chinese takeaway called "Wok-a-Noodle-Doo", Indian restaurant, butcher's, wine merchant's, hair stylist, pharmacy, a gym called "Fit Club", a mobility scooter shop, a charity furniture store, a second-hand clothes shop, the chain ending abruptly with a funeral directors at a roundabout that the locals called "the circus". There was something here for everyone at any stage of life, all in the correct chronological order; toddler to teenager to middle age, to death shall we part. As the bus trundled by, the shops seemed to act like spokes in a human wheel of fortune.

Perhaps it was just Jack's current frame of mind to think bleak thoughts, but he'd walked the length of this road a number of times without noticing how *short* the distance from one end to the other, topped and tailed by a gambling den and men dressed in black. You could saunter down it in less time than it took to smoke a cigarette; babies, Bombay potatoes and burial in barely fifteen puffs. Ordinarily, in any case before the mysterious illness had struck, Jack could've pictured himself standing half way along its length, perhaps outside the grocery store looking at oranges in wooden crates, or at the small bar of the microbrewery drinking a local draught, or inside the wine merchant's choosing a bottle or two for "Fizz Friday". But now, from the snail bus, he envisioned himself limping mid-point between pharmacy and undertaker; an image hard to shake off.

The bus juddered to a halt at the roundabout; the circus. Everyone at the kerbside windows stared soberly out at the family undertakers. The Berrys. *You couldn't make that up*, thought Jack. The window display involved a marble headstone, a wreath and a sign saying the proprietor worked with experienced monumental masons. At the other end of the window, a black tie hung limp on a board: *Black ties, £5*. Alongside this, a small model of a black, horse-drawn carriage complete with a top-hatted figurine holding the reins; a macabre addition to a Dickensian doll's house.

As the bus took the roundabout, a driverless hearse could be seen parked on a side-road, engine running, plumes of smoke belching from the exhaust, a coffin wedged above, behind glass, nestled in fresh flowers that said: *DAD*. Once upon a time, Jack regarded the sight of a coffin philosophically as a timely reminder to those whose minds still ticked with thoughts, whose hearts still pumped with passions, whose loins still yearned for pleasure, to get on with their lives and be quick about it. But today, the vision pressed down on his head like a lid made of lead. Life had become a stranger, a stranger with suffocating hands.

By the time he reached the central bus station Jack had banished his darkest thoughts. He walked a short distance to a row of Georgian terraces on Pilgrims Road and stood by the wrought iron railings of the acupuncture clinic. Jin-jing Li's name was visible on a silver sign along with the names of four other practitioners, homeopathic and otherwise. Acupuncture was not something Jack had ever tried before. Alice had received treatments in London for lower back pain and to balance her chakras. Jack's father had tried it to help him quit smoking, without success, though he always appeared happier and more relaxed after sessions. MS patients at the therapy centre lauded the benefits of traditional acupuncture, so maybe this could be the beginning of something, he told himself.

Jack made his way into a plain, narrow hallway stopping at the foot of stairs. He entered an ochre-coloured waiting room that smelled of a delicate, calming aroma; rose petals, maybe. Chairs lined two walls and a sash window looked out upon a garden at the end of which stood a mature silver birch, its bare winter branches waving.

Jack removed his sunglasses and coat, and sat down. A fig tree overhung the room from an alcove, its leaves a deep, healthy green, and on the window sill was a twin-stemmed orchid about to come into flower. One of the walls was being used as a noticeboard, covered with printouts and articles on healthy living, meditation, yoga classes, "Healing Wells", the perils of vaccines and flu-jabs, modern-day farming practices, all overseen by a prominent poster of the Dalai Lama. A handwritten side of A4 said: *Please take articles to read, but remember to replace. Thank you.* Beside this, another hand-written note: *Please turn off your mobile.* Opposite, on a redundant chimney breast, were leaflets and calling cards advertising a range of treatments; traditional acupuncture from Jin-jing Li who specialised in the "School of Five Elements", and other professionals with added experience in Scenar Therapy, Cosmodic Technology, the Low Level Laser and the Russian Treatment Blanket. Copies of National Geographic magazines were stacked in neat piles on the coffee table alongside recent online articles, one of which concerned the worldwide overuse of antibiotics, not only in farming but in doctors' surgeries. Jack flicked through one of the magazines marvelling at the deep-sea photography; strangely beautiful monsters that lurked way beneath the surface of the oceans.

Footsteps travelled down the stairs and a tall, shaven-headed man poked his head around the doorjamb. 'Hello,' he said. 'And you are..?' Jack introduced himself. 'Ah. You're here to see Jin-jing.' He strode into the centre of the room and Jack stood up to shake hands. 'Welcome to my clinic. I'm Michael Wasser.' His handshake was firm, his eyes denim blue, wide-open, excitable, intense and penetrating.

They spoke briefly about the MS therapy centre where Michael Wasser had worked as an acupuncturist. His English was near perfect, but Jack noted a hint of the Low Countries; possibly Holland. Michael saw the magazine in Jack's hand and mentioned an article about the power of micro-algae discovered by some clever Russians. 'Powerful enough to heal cancer.' Footfalls could be heard on the stairs. Jing-jing shook hands with a departing client in the hallway and came in to the waiting room.

'Isn't it, Jin-jing?'

'Isn't what?' she replied, smiling up at Michael.

'I'm telling Jack about the wonders of F1, F2 and F3 algae.'

'Oh,' she said. 'They wonderful superfood. Full of antioxidant.'

'Jin-jing's taking F1 for maintenance, but she started on F2.'

'Who takes F3?' said Jack, feeling as if he should join in.

'That's the strongest concentration of algae,' said Michael, 'for those who really need to kick-start their immune systems.'

'We maybe talk about this in our session,' said Jin-jing.

'Good idea,' said Michael, clapping his hands together. 'I'm going to make tea.'

'Would you like some?' asked Jin-jing. 'We only have herbal.'

'Whatever you're having, thanks.'

'Chamomile, I think. Mike, could you make it? I must re-set room.'

'You see?' he said, beaming with positivity. 'A clinic that makes you tea as well as makes you better.'

Jin-jing trotted up the stairs and Mike disappeared through a basement door.

A few minutes later, Jin-jing reappeared, asking Jack to go up and through the first door on the right. The stairs were steep, and he hauled himself up using the bannister rail. He sat down in a chair beside a desk tucked in one corner, near a large sash window. The room was small, dominated by a long treatment table covered with thick strips of oat-coloured tissue paper. On the window sill was a freshly-lit joss stick sitting in a ceramic holder. Tapers of scented grey smoke swirled across the room.

A moment later, Jin-jing arrived. She placed two mugs of tea on the desk, sat down and opened a fresh file. Her long black hair was drawn from her face, tied at the back with a scrunchie, exaggerating the roundness of her pretty, moon face. They talked for a while about Jack's illness and recent diagnoses, including multiple sclerosis and the current one of Clinically Isolated Syndrome. Jin-jing wrote notes, looking up now and then, making small comments to encourage him.

'Really, they don't know what's wrong except the symptoms mimic MS, but it turns out lots of things mimic MS, including Lyme disease.'

Jin-jing placed her pen on the table. 'Interesting. I treat patient with Lyme about one year ago. She's living with it so long, but NHS coulden find anything in her blood.'

'Then how did she know she had Lyme?'

'Private tests positive.'

'Did they treat?'

Jin-jing shook her head.

'I might have Lyme. So many mistakes, so many missed opportunities.'

'They never admit mistake. You start askin question and shoulders come together. Doors close. I train to be nurse and saw it happen. They are expert. No one question. You have tightness in muscles?'

Jack shook his head. 'I have burning hands and feet, some numbness down my left leg and left arm. I'm exhausted most days, and I'm dizzy like I'm drunk. But it's not to do with muscle weakness. I don't think I have MS. Technically, I don't. Things don't add up. Whereas with Lyme everything adds up. The facial numbness I got on one side that they thought was a stroke? It was more likely to be Bell's palsy brought on by nerve inflammation.'

'Doctors look for easy answer, take path of least resistance. Not whole body, only differen part. Human body complex. All connected. Traditional acupuncture look at whole organism, not separate organ. It's why I left the training course for nurse. I see too many things go wrong. Everyone expert in one field only. For generations my family in China use acupuncture alongside conventional doctor.'

He asked her about her childhood and she told him about a small town in China and how her father moved to London to work for a computer firm, taking his family with him. 'Now he retired businessman back in China, living in same town he was born in with my mother and sister. I have an auntie, an acupuncturist for thirty years. I don't know why I don't study acupuncture earlier than now.' She smiled. 'Better later than never.'

'Jin-jing is a lovely name.'

'Thank you,' she said, blushing. 'People say it mean clear or bright, or crystal. Others say it mean gold mirror.'

Jack thought of the large gold mirror that used to belong to his mother, that hung on the chimney breast of his Fulham flat but was now covered in bubble wrap in the garage of Seagull House.

Jin-jing explained the principles of the school of five elements: wood, earth, metal, fire and water. She said everyone had features of all five but usually one predominated. She spoke of yin and yang, chakras and movement of energy around the body. She said she wouldn't treat symptoms but systemic causes, although many of the symptoms might go as a result. Ideally, she said, your mind, body and soul should improve. The natural flow of energy should get better, but it might take many sessions. 'Body is temple,' she said, and he thought, *my temple has been ransacked by Godless creatures, turning it into one large torture chamber.* She said her family were Buddhist; a hard thing to practice in communist China, especially after The Cultural Revolution. She asked if Jack was a spiritual man, if he believed in the soul, then apologised for asking as he seemed uncomfortable.

'The soul's gone out of fashion in the west,' he said. 'My father was *kind of* Buddhist. I've got his old Buddha statue. I'm making a Zen garden. Buddha sits in one corner, but he's not one for communicating.'

'You talk to him?'

'Yeah, but he's taken a vow of silence.'

'Buddha not always communicating in words, but feeling or action. You give him gifts? I find a flower from the garden work. Show him you believe and he will communicate. But he might not speak as you understan.' She paused a moment, looking for her needles. 'You say your father Buddhist?'

'He was from California and believed in all kinds of new age stuff; the power of the third eye, and the power of psychedelic drugs too, of course. He believed in reincarnation. He died when I was a boy. Cancer. Well, cancer was the cause.'

'I'm sorry, that must have been difficul.'

'It hit Mum hardest. She never re-married.'

'Your mother still living?'

'In a nursing home. She was a glamorous actress once. Stage mainly, though she had small TV roles. She was in Roald Dahl's *Tales of the Unexpected*. She had a walk-on part in *Dr. Who*.'

'Wow!'

'Mum's only line was: "Doctor, why is it always the daleks?"'

'And what your father do?'

'Apart from drinking and smoking himself to death, he worked as a freelance journalist. Sports and travel pages. He loved to travel. He came over to the UK in the sixties.'

'Maybe, as Buddhist, he travel even now,' said Jin-jing, smiling. 'And your mother, she spiritual?'

'Mum said religion was the opium of the masses.'

'But open mind is good thing, no?'

Jack nodded. 'I took after my father. I *kind of* believe in the soul, but not a God or collector of souls? When I was at university my favourite writer was John Donne, the metaphysical poet?'

'Why him?'

'I studied Donne at school, and something clicked. The more I read, the more I understood, as if…it sounds daft now…as if I was somehow a part of who he was?'

'Or he part of you.'

'I read loads of writers at university; Poe, Kafka, Wilde, Kerouac, Dickinson, Eliot, Lewis, but I wrote my final dissertation on Donne and metaphysics. I foolishly took a Jungian approach to Donne's dream-like poetry, his unconscious? Anyway, it was a long time ago. Donne believed in the transmigration of souls. I oscillate. Like science, my head says *no*, but like art my heart says *maybe*. So, do you believe in life after death?'

She laughed. 'Jack, I believe in life after life.'

'Of course, as a Buddhist.'

'Soul live in entire body but hang out in heart and mind. Lives are row of candles. Each new candle is lit by flame of dying candle that come before. Each candle is of itself, only energy come from dying candle, not continuous, single soul? Science not prove if soul exist, but don't mean it not there.'

Jack was reminded of Charlie Chaplin in *The Great Dictator. There are no experts in the unknown.* 'Put it this way,' he said. 'They didn't find a soul in any scans. Not in my brain, not in my heart, not in my blood, not in my spine, not in my bladder. If I have a soul, it's in hiding.'

'Energy of soul never-ending. Something one feel, not see. My father met the Dalai Lama and ask him: "How can you know the soul exist if you cannot find it in body?" And the Dalai Lama think for long time and answer: "Does time exist inside broken clock?" When clock stop, time still continue. Time is its own keeper.'

'Your father met the Dalai Lama?'

She nodded. 'For me, body is temple, and somewhere inside, unique soul or energy exist.'

If Jack had been a Humanist he'd have felt affronted by her belief in the scientifically unprovable, even if her view was based on thousands of years of popular tradition. But as someone sitting on the fence, someone innately interested in the humanities rather than Humanism, he was struck by her faith and conviction in just the same way he'd been moved by the chaplain who'd sat by his bedside in hospital after the spinal tap. However, he thought to himself, if my body is a temple, my soul is bound, gagged and tortured somewhere else in the building. 'I suppose as a Buddhist you'd say I must have accumulated a lot of bad karma in past lives to be in such a bad state in this one? Maybe I was Jack the Ripper.'

Jin-jing shook her head, laughing. 'Now down to business.' She explained the types of treatment in such an authoritative and calm way that he wanted to believe they'd work. She asked him to remove his clothes and lie on the table. She left the room while he undressed down to his boxers. He made himself comfortable on the treatment table.

Jin-jing knocked and re-entered. She asked to see his tongue and made a note of its colour and appearance. 'I'm guessing it's furry,' he said, but Jin-jing gently touched his shoulder, asking him to relax. She measured the pulses in his wrists and ankles with warm fingertips. She moved around the table touching, holding or pressing softly down on various parts of his body, seeming to focus most attention on his stomach. 'Your feet cold,' she said, 'but stomach most cold and damp. Skin clammy.'

'Too much cheese in my diet?'

'Energy not moving around body.' She pressed her palm down on his stomach again, leaving it there a while. 'No fire in belly.' She made notes in her file. 'I give you only little acupuncture today. I suggest meeting weekly for next five or six week, fortnightly after, if you wish to continue and there is progress.'

'I'm hoping some of the pain will go, and I'll feel more energised.'

'I can't make promise,' she said, taking a needle and carefully placing it in the lobe of his ear, close to the opening. 'Breathe in, breathe out,' she said. 'Breathe in, breathe out.' She twisted the needle and he tensed.

'Sometimes sting. Breathe in, breathe out. Breathe in, breathe out.' The needles in his wrists stung the most, making him hiss. 'Good. I'll leave you now for five or ten minute, allowing needles time. Relax. Close your eyes. Focus on breathing. Slow and rhythmic. Breathe in, breathe out. Good.'

As promised, ten minutes later she returned. After she'd removed the needles she re-took his pulses saying they were stronger and more regular. She was pleased, as the needles had already had a mild, positive effect. She left the room again as he re-dressed.

He paid in cash, saying, 'I'm curious. Do you know what element I am out of the five?'

She looked up from her laptop. 'I have good idea confirmed after treatmen on table. You are earth elemen.'

'Earth?'

'You are stomach,' she said.

'Stomach?'

'Stomach and spleen big part of earth elemen. Stomach, spleen and gall bladder digest, refine and feed body. It is solar plexus powerhouse. Stomach important for nurturing body, mind and soul. You need fire in belly. Energy too slow in solar plexus. Next time I concentrate on stomach to improve flow. It's said an army march on its stomach, no? The way to a man's heart is through his stomach, yes?'

Jack smirked. 'I once went out with a comedian called Collette Farr. She said the best way to a man's heart was through the third and fourth rib. Going through the stomach takes too long, by which time the police have caught up with you.'

Jin-jing giggled. 'She tough woman. She go too far!'

'Collette was very funny back in the 80s. Hard-faced, hilarious. She's married now with three kids. So...I'm a stomach.'

'But your wife a tree. When I meet her at MS centre, I'm sure she wood elemen. She strong personality, and provide strength to others.'

'Alice is a tree, and I'm a stomach. Why can't I be a tree? I really like trees.' He looked out of the window at the waving silver birch.

'You complemen each other. Earth and wood. You are earth that nourish tree, and Alice nurture you in return?'

'Before I go, Jin-jing, can I ask whether the treatment you used on your patient with Lyme disease worked?'

'I don't know,' she said. 'I think once organism in body long time it always there. One need to accommodate. As Lao Tzu said, life is series of natural and spontaneous changes, don't resist them, that only create sorrow. My client stopped treatmen after a few month. She feeling stronger and had more energy but move away and see a private doctor for antibiotic. Naturopathic remedies better, but she want antibiotic.'

'You don't like antibiotics?'

'Very bad for stomach, intestine and bowel. They kill good bacteria. I know natural alternative; special herb from South American jungle that do same work of antibiotic. I will find information and bring to next session.'

'Thank you so much, Jin-jing.'

'It was nice seeing you,' she said, shaking his hand. 'See you next week and put fire in belly.' She smiled, making her dark eyes sparkle. 'You have colour again. Pale as ghost in waiting room, but pink as piglet now. This is good.'

Bus to Berry

The acupuncture seemed to boost Jack's energy. He wasn't sure if this was the placebo effect of *wanting* the treatment to alleviate his symptoms, but he was buzzing. Milling around the shops, mingling with so many other shoppers sapped any newfound strength, though, and soon he retired to the bus station with a mild headache.

When the double-decker arrived and the doors hissed apart, he climbed the steps to the upper deck in the hope of more panoramic views. The bus lurched through suburb, village and hamlet, expanding into open countryside. He saw sheep, horses and donkeys, a converted windmill and undulating farmland. Half way home, the bus slowed and a smartly dressed lady got on carrying a small terrier under her arm. Instead of taking a lower deck seat, she climbed the stairs, and the driver was courteous enough not to accelerate away before she sat down.

At first, Jack was miffed; he liked travelling alone on the upper deck, losing himself to his imagination without distraction. Quite often, he'd take out a notebook and jot down ideas. Some of these would grow into comedy monologues. Despite having the entire upper deck to choose from, the old woman decided to sit in the empty seat directly in front of him, planting her dog in the space beside her and keeping a firm hold of the lead. Now and then, the dog, looking impossibly old, wriggled about and turned around on its seat, staring at Jack. After a few minutes of this, Jack couldn't resist stroking its grey muzzle.

The old lady turned her head, saying in a refined accent: 'I'm sorry. Is Henry bothering you?'

'Not at all.'

'He was my husband's. I take Henry everywhere.'

'I couldn't take my collie on a bus,' said Jack. 'She's too bouncy.'

'Would you mind me asking you a question?' she said, turning fully around. She was fine-featured, though her eyes were heavily hooded and lines were deep in the corners of her mouth. 'I'm going to Tankerton to the funeral director, but I don't know where he is. Somewhere on the high street I'm told.'

'I'll tell you which stop to get off.'

'Most kind,' she said.

As the bus trundled on they talked more about living by the sea. 'My husband was a great lover of water,' she said. 'In a past life he must've been a fish, but we bought a house in the countryside and

205

lived there together for forty years. Quite odd of us in retrospect, don't you think?'

'Never too far from the sea, though?'

'We visited Tankerton a lot, my husband and I, especially on warm, sunny days. But you know, we never noticed a funeral directors. A neighbour told me about them. She said they're a good local family and have been burying people for generations. Have you heard of them, the Berry family?'

'I've only seen their shop. I haven't lived here long.'

'Ah well. I made an appointment to see them about the funeral.'

'I'm sorry,' said Jack.

'Oh no, my dear, don't be. The time comes when these things must be arranged. Sometimes you have plenty of notice, other times it's lickety-split. Yes, Tankerton is the right place to go this time.'

'Still, it must be difficult burying your husband after so long together.'

She laughed. 'No, my dear, I buried my husband six years ago. The funeral is mine. This way I get everything the way I want.'

The dog settled down, curling into a ball on the seat, burying its face in its paws.

Thirty seconds before reaching her stop, Jack pressed the button and pointed out where the funeral director's was. 'If you get off here and cross there, it's a few yards from the circus, the roundabout.'

'Oh yes,' she said. 'I see. You've been most helpful young man.' As the lady rose, her dog jumped down and she picked him right up again.

'It was nice meeting you.'

'Likewise,' she said, holding onto the steel bar and negotiating the first step. 'Goodbye.'

The first thing Pandora did when Jack walked through the front door was sniff out Henry the terrier on his fingers. As he closed the door he noticed a blue NHS logo on a white envelope on the doormat. He tore it open, walking from the hall into the lounge. The letter was from the doctor's surgery advising him that his recent blood test was ready to be discussed. He was about to dial the surgery, but noticed a red light flashing on the answer machine. A rare message from Lauren, telling him their Uncle Dicky had sadly just died from a heart attack.

Jack phoned the doctor's surgery and spoke to an administrator who told him the letter was routine. She put him through to her colleague who asked for Jack's name and date of birth before checking the system for recent blood tests. 'Here it is,' she said. 'It says negative.'

'Negative for Lyme disease?'

'If that was what the test was for, then yes.'

'Doesn't it say what the test was for?'

'Hold on a moment. Yes, the test was requested by the locum Dr. Oiseau and done by the microbiologist Dr. Cleaver just before Christmas?'

'And it's definitely for Lyme, definitely negative?'

'Isn't this good news?'

Jack remembered things he'd read online, that tests for Lyme were unreliable, especially basic tests, and particularly the longer you had the infection because the bacteria removed itself from the bloodstream and hid in hard-to-get-to places like the brain, liver, heart and joints. Blood tests looked for antibodies and some people didn't produce them because the bacteria evaded their immune systems. Some experts believed the bacteria actually hid in the lymph nodes, tricking the body into thinking it didn't have an infection at all. It really was a clever organism, this Borrelia, like an alien from a Ridley Scott film. 'Can someone find out what type of test it was, please?'

'I'd ask Dr. Greaves, but she's on holiday and wasn't the one who requested it. I'm curious myself now. We don't get many Lyme tests. I'll telephone the lab this afternoon and call you back as soon as I know anything.'

The administrator called back within an hour. 'I managed to speak to the microbiologist. A certain Dr. Cleaver?' She sighed. 'I had a difficult conversation. I'm afraid I couldn't find out what test was done for Lyme.'

'Why not?'

'Because Dr. Cleaver refused to say.'

'Refused?'

'Well, when I mentioned your test, he blew up at me, shouting: "Who do these people think they are?"'

'What does he mean *these people*?'

'He said too many patients think they know better than him, wasting his time. So he wasn't going to tell me what your test was.'

'I need to speak to my GP.'

True or False?

It was obvious to Jack and Alice that Dr. Greaves wanted to draw a line under Lyme disease. She sat with her arms folded across her chest saying she knew very little about the illness and the blood tests were entirely baffling. Nonetheless, negative usually meant negative in her medical experience. 'It's a pity you didn't take a photograph of your rash. We have a doctor here with a specialism in skin diseases.'

'With respect,' said Alice. 'We've gone way beyond skin complaints. If Jack had raging acne you'd prescribe antibiotics without a second thought, but you seem unwilling to treat for Lyme disease even though it's a thousand times more dangerous than spots.'

'I cannot treat you with antibiotics,' the doctor said, directing her comment at Jack. 'If the microbiologist can't find evidence of infection, my hands are tied.' Seeing his obvious frustration and disappointment, she added: 'But I can order further blood tests. Something called a C6 Elisa and a Western Blot?'

'Excellent,' said Alice, having already done research. Although still unreliable, these tests were far more specific for the antibodies to the Borrelia bacteria, particularly the C6 test. 'So, if they return positive will you treat Jack with antibiotics?'

'Let's see what comes back,' the doctor said.

Alice threw herself into work and Jack spent an inordinate amount of time researching Lyme disease, especially testing, diagnosis and treatment. He took regular breaks from the computer, resting in the bedroom upstairs or on the new sofa in the lounge. The more he discovered about Lyme, the more he realised that clinical and medical experts looked down the wrong end of the microscope. Instead of examining patients for clinical signs and symptoms, they tended to diagnose on the basis of blood results alone; a process fraught with inaccuracy.

Jack and Alice were called back to the surgery to discuss the results. 'Well, Mr. Mann,' Dr. Greaves said, 'your C6 Elisa returned positive for Lyme.'

Alice rubbed his arm. 'I knew it.'

'But the Western Blot was negative.'

Jack looked anxiously towards Alice, then back at the GP. 'What does that mean?'

'I've discussed it with Dr. Cleaver and he says your Western Blot was a *true* negative, and your C6 Elisa was a *false* positive, and doesn't recommend treatment.'

'What?' Alice shrieked. 'So Jack has all the clinical signs and symptoms of Lyme, now he has a positive blood test but it's a "false" positive?' She used her fingers as apostrophes. 'What if I suggested the Western Blot was a "false" negative?' She used her punctuating fingers again. 'Who decides what is and what isn't "false"? The microbiologist is interpreting what's "false" and what isn't to suit his own purposes.'

'I'm sure he wouldn't do that, Mrs. Mann.'

'When Jack asked what that first blood test was, the microbiologist refused, saying, "Who do these people think they are?" We were entitled to know, but he took our right away. When that first test returned negative he interpreted it as a "true" negative.' Punctuating fingers. 'But when the C6 test returns positive, he says it's a "false" positive, and when the Western Blot returns negative, it is a "true" negative. Can't you see that something isn't right here?'

Dr. Greaves pursed her lips.

'We're grateful to you for commissioning these tests,' Alice continued, 'but there's a question mark over interpretation. All we want is treatment based on clinical signs and a positive C6 blood test. My God, the only other way to find the bacteria is by dying and having a pathologist cut the organs out of your corpse.'

'Now, Mrs. Mann, that's going too far.'

'Is it? Are you not within your rights to ignore Dr. Cleaver's recommendations and treat Jack empirically? Diagnosis is *your* prerogative and *yours* alone. Microbiology should be secondary. That's what the NHS guidelines say. All we're asking you to do is follow your own guidelines.'

'Without further evidence,' she said, 'I cannot treat. It's now on record. A consultant has concluded there is no evidence of Lyme.'

'Come on,' said Alice, getting to her feet. 'We're wasting our breath. But we're not giving up. This isn't the end of the matter.' She banged the door shut, saying loudly: 'The Hippocratic oath states that a doctor should never knowingly do harm. Sometimes doing nothing is tantamount to the same thing.'

In the car on the way home she looked across at Jack. 'Greaves is frightened. Frightened, that's what they all are these days. Doctors too frightened to make decisions by themselves.'

'I'm properly screwed.'

'Over my dead body you are, Jack. If Greaves wants more evidence, we'll get it. I've been rooting around the internet. There's a clinic in Surrey that specialises in Lyme disease tests. I'll call them tomorrow.

'It's Dicky's funeral tomorrow.'

'You're too shattered to go, aren't you?'

'I promised Lauren, and Aunt Helen.'

'Lauren doesn't know what it's been like for you these past six months. If you explained…'

'She thinks I'm not pulling my weight with Mum.'

'Jack, we've been going through hell. Not once in the past six months has Lauren called to ask how you are.'

'She did.'

'Ok, she phoned once, Jack, when she believed you'd had a stroke, and then she flew off to Lake Garda!'

'She sent me that get well card, and a good luck in your new home card a fortnight ago.'

'Jack, she's your sister, not a pen pal. Ernie flew half way across the world to see you. I'm sorry, but when you got ill Lauren contracted ostrichitis. The sick shouldn't be checking up on the healthy, it should be the other way around, especially family.'

'Not all families are the same, Alice. You're an only child. You have a different bond. Anyway, Lauren is driving Mum to the funeral, and I should go too. Uncle Dicky was a lovely man. I'd like to be part of his send-off. You stay here if you like and I'll catch a train.'

'No chance,' she said. 'I don't want you falling under it'

Mystery Mann

Uncle Dicky's funeral day was bright and crisp. Richard Ward (Dicky to family and friends) had lived in Sussex most of his adult life and worked for the same pharmaceutical company for thirty years.

During the drive across, sun flickered through tangles of trees and Jack had flashes of childhood trips; he, Lauren and Ernie sitting together in the spacious back seat of their father's old Zephyr. Uncle Dicky and Auntie Helen were always welcoming, treating them as honoured guests. Each visit began with warm embraces on the doorstep of their detached, mock Tudor house. Crustless sandwiches were followed by a roast dinner, and copious amounts of alcohol for the adults. While the grown-ups caught up with each other in the lounge, Jack and Ernie played in the garden. They kicked a ball, threw a Frisbee or took turns at the crease of an imaginary cricket pitch using a tennis ball. Who could forget that unforgettable summer when Jack's Dad and Uncle Dicky got loaded, rolled up their sleeves and joined in? Jack was batsman, Ernie was wicket-keeper, Dad was bowler, Dicky and Lauren were outfielders, Mum and Aunt Helen were spectators.

'Hey, let's use a real ball!' Dad shouted, grabbing one from Dicky's shed. He spat on the red leather and rubbed it down his trouser leg like Botham. 'Here it comes, kid,' he said, taking a run-up. 'Watch out for spin! Step in and smash it!' shouted Ernie. And that's exactly what Jack had done, cracking it with force, the ball fizzing through the air and thudding through the kitchen window, scattering the birds from the trees and showering the kitchen lino with glass. 'Oh crap,' said Dad. 'Brilliant,' said Ernie. 'That's what you call a six,' said Uncle Dicky.

That's what becomes of you in the end, thought Jack, a colourful story from the past, a precious jewel taken from the vaults of your memory bank, lifted from the safety deposit box of love. It was odd how every childhood visit appeared sunny in Jack's memory, as if it had never rained on Dicky's parade. Even the Zephyr's leatherette always felt hot on the backs of his legs. By the time of Jack Snr.'s death, the visits to Sussex had dwindled and the skies of the early 1980s seemed impossibly dark. Dicky had come to stay in Muswell Hill, offering his grieving sister support. Jack remembered, after his father's funeral, being walked around the garden by his uncle and being told never to hesitate phoning or visiting. But only once had Jack taken his uncle up on the offer; in his teens, when he felt at a crossroads. Should he go to drama school like his mother, or study literature at Oxford? And Dicky had taken him to the local pub, The Huntsman, bringing him beer and listening patiently to his teenage ramblings. 'Follow your heart, Jack,' is what he'd said. 'But remember your head has a role to play too. You're young. There's plenty of time to act. Besides, Oxford opens doors. It's a sort of club. A man can't succeed in life unless he is part of something bigger than himself. He needs a club to protect himself.'

Pulling into the drive of the mock Tudor house, Jack saw Dicky's face in his mind; rosy cheeks, kind, eager eyes, like mirrors of Estella's. Yet after only a few phone calls and letters, Jack had lost touch. When they did meet, man to man, Uncle Dicky insisted on calling him "my little Jack-in-a-box" as if time had stood still.

Auntie Helen came outside with a pained smile. She kissed Jack and Alice, and ushered them up a step into the hallway where it seemed poor Uncle Dicky had collapsed and died from his heart attack. Not much had changed since the last time Jack visited, apart from the addition of a double-glazed conservatory, but it was the faint smell of tobacco that rekindled flashbacks. Dicky had been a pipe-smoker up until his last year of life, after which he'd become a secret pipe-smoker, hiding a stash in his office. The house, although clean and spotless and filled with fragrant flowers, still bore the sweet aroma of his Clan tobacco.

Jack wandered into the front room. His mother was seated in an armchair sipping tea shakily, looking blankly up at the faces, her mouth parted as if to ask a question that never came. Lauren was standing by a redundant fireplace, bolt upright and poker-faced. If Estella's three children were to be given nicknames in adulthood, Jack thought, they might be Ernie the Aspirational, Jack the Clown, and Lauren the Secretive. And yet, oddly, after the short church service and even shorter cremation it was Jack who'd be labelled the Mystery Mann.

Before the funeral, guests were invited in to see Dicky in his coffin. It was set on a trestle in the dining room, a blanket of sun half covering the box. Estella was the first to enter, aided by Lauren. Whilst they were there, Jack was asked if he wanted to say goodbye to Dicky too. Although he'd prepared a valid excuse (he'd like to remember his uncle just the way he was; warm and soft, not cold and stiff), Auntie Helen's tearfully poignant question tipped the balance. 'Well, of course,' said Jack. 'It's been far too long.'

'He died right where you're standing,' said Auntie Helen's sister, Claire. 'Snuffed out like a candle.' She snapped her fingers. Jack thought she'd been on the sauce rather early for a seventy-year-old, it not being quite mid-day.

'It's the way my Dicky would want to go,' said Auntie Helen. 'No hanging around.'

Jack's mother came out from the dining room blowing her nose on a handkerchief, Lauren with an arm around her shoulder. Jack wrapped his arms around them both, squeezing. 'He was my only brother,' said Estella, leaning on her cane.

Alice, surprisingly unsqueamish about bodies (alive or dead), linked Jack's arm and led him from the dark hall into the light where the dead man was waiting. They crossed the room to the open coffin and peered in as if looking over the edge of a precipice. Uncle Dicky's hands were by his sides. He was dressed in a neat tweed suit and waistcoat, white shirt and red dickey bow; though it wasn't his attire that drew their immediate attention but his buttoned-down eyes, forced-shut mouth, and the waxy yellow-grey pallor of the skin.

'He looks good,' said Alice, not knowing what else to say.

'Hello there, Uncle Dicky,' said Jack, hands clasped behind his back. 'Sorry we haven't seen you in a while.' His uncle's grey hair had been parted neatly to one side and his moustache had been impeccably trimmed. 'God, he loved his dickey bows, didn't he?'

They stood there for a few minutes, staring in silence, jumping slightly when Auntie Helen spoke behind them: 'It's okay to touch. He won't bite.' She stretched out a hand and lightly brushed her husband's face with her fingertips. 'Such a handsome man. Somehow they've made him look ten years younger.'

'Yes,' said Alice. 'He's very handsome.'

'Eighty-one years old and barely a line on his face.'

Jack stared. His uncle looked as if he'd been pumped up at the gas station, removing all crow's feet, laughter lines and creases. His cheeks were puffed out as if he was about to blow a raspberry.

'Look at me,' said Helen. 'I'm nine years younger and full of lines.'

'You're not,' said Alice, squeezing Helen's hand. 'You're beautiful. You and Dicky made such a lovely couple.'

'Everyone said so,' said Helen, voice breaking.

Jack reached out, making contact with his uncle's left hand, the wedding finger emblazoned with a tasteful silver ring. His skin was as cold as stone. Like a baby, Jack held onto the little finger, and said:

'Goodbye, Uncle. Goodbye and safe journey.' *My little Jack-in-a-box*, he heard his uncle say, at which point his own throat started to close.

Aunt Helen invited them into the study. She took a white envelope from a drawer in the writing desk. 'Dicky expressed a wish that each of his nephews and nieces should be given a gift, so don't hold up your hand in protest, Jack. Take it. It's a little something for a rainy day.'

'Only if you insist, Auntie. Thank you.' Jack pecked her on the cheek.

'Lauren said you've been unwell. That you've been in and out of hospital? What exactly is it?'

'Therein lies the problem,' he said. 'There is no *exactly*.'

Alice looked at Jack in desperation. From her recent experience of telling colleagues at work, it was hellishly difficult describing what was wrong with her husband, yet she'd felt compelled to explain. Despite her best intentions, her medical and clinical explanations always morphed into a diatribe on missed opportunities, misdiagnoses, blah blah blah, and that was before she'd got to Lyme disease, by which time her listener's eyes had glazed over. 'It's complicated,' she said. 'We think it's a chronic infection of the central nervous system.'

'How in heaven's name did you acquire such a thing?'

'Just walking the dog. I was bitten by an insect.'

'Arthropod, not an insect,' Alice corrected.

'The bacteria wreaked havoc. My brain got inflamed, damaged. I couldn't walk for a few months. At one point I lost the feeling in most of my body…but you don't want to hear all this today of all days.'

'Is it curable?'

'That's what we're trying to find out,' said Alice. 'The NHS won't treat, so we're forced to go private, though we haven't given up hope of being treated when we've proved this really is Lyme disease.'

'Lyme disease?' said Helen.

'It's rare,' said Jack.

'Though not as rare as Public Health UK would have you believe, Helen.'

'Oh I wish Dicky was still alive. He knew a thing or two about diseases and treatments, you know…from work.'

'We have an appointment at a clinic next week,' said Alice.

'Jack, you do have the look of someone a bit haunted. Lauren didn't say it was this bad.'

'I guess she didn't want you to worry,' said Jack.

'Please, excuse me. I have to do a few things before the cars arrive?' Helen left the room and Alice followed, offering assistance.

Jack opened the envelope amazed to find a cheque for £2,000. Good old Uncle Dicky. He slumped into his uncle's chair and cast his eyes over the bookshelves; books on birdwatching, gardening and sailing. There was a small TV in one corner, beside it a shelf full of CDs and DVDs. Classical in the main, marching band music, chamber orchestras and concertos. It was then he noticed that all the DVDs were Jack Mann tours. In fact, Dicky had a full collection, all lined up in chronological order.

'He used to watch you non-stop,' said Claire, appearing in the doorway, gripping a full glass of wine. 'He loved watching you making people laugh. He watched those DVDs a hundred times, never tiring of your impressions.'

Jack got out of Dicky's chair. 'I'm sorry for not coming down to see him more often.'

'That's alright. Dicky could see you every night in his study. Will your mother be okay? It must be tough for Estella.'

'Mum might not remember the events of today by tomorrow. You know, because of the dementia?'

'I know,' Claire said. 'It's a horrible thing, isn't it, what time does? Enjoy it while you can.' She saluted with her glass. 'Because the only hope we have of understanding the meaning of life is to accept there's no hope of understanding meaninglessness. There's nothing before us or after us. There's only us.'

The funeral service was delivered with minimal fuss to a crowd of twenty people. Just before the coffin was carried into church, Jack was handed a slip of paper by his aunt; a tiny eulogy that was a breakdown of the jobs Dicky had done. Perhaps it was Helen's way of understanding her husband's life, but jobs shouldn't define a person in their entirety. Life isn't a CV or an interview. However, even such a dry eulogy had Jack close to choking at the pulpit. Looking out to the gathered, eyeing the coffin in the central aisle, he wanted to add warm, amusing childhood memories and bring colour to the cheeks of his uncle's life, like the cricket ball incident, but he stuck to the bald facts.

The drive to the crematorium was long and winding through countryside, the trees bleak and bare. The funeral cortege arrived late for its timeslot. One of the funeral directors walked up to the main entrance, examining a timetable posted on the wall. Aware Jack was watching him, he turned and said: 'It's all getting a bit bunched, but not to worry, the next one is one of ours too so we'll still have a few minutes.'

A few minutes?

The funeral directors ushered the party into the characterless building, coffin first. Aunt Helen had arranged for Brahms, a favourite string section that hummed low through distant speakers. Jack sat beside his mother and sister, placing an arm around Estella's shoulder when she became upset. The priest said a few comforting words and a prayer at the lectern, the automated curtains closed around Dicky, and that was that. Done and dusted in less than ten minutes, by which time another coffin and grieving party were waiting outside the main entrance. No sooner had Dicky's crowd left through the side door than the next body was going headfirst through the front. And, standing outside in the frosty February air making small talk with mainly strangers, Jack noticed there was yet another funeral cortege arriving on the concourse. It was less of a crematorium and more of a drive-thru McDonald's.

The reception was at The Huntsman, which apart from new "no smoking" signs was little changed in decades. Staff directed people towards a small bar at the back, connected to a private area that normally acted as a breakfast room. Tables and chairs had been moved to the perimeter. Soon, these tables were covered with hot and cold platters of food. Auntie Helen had hired a DJ for the afternoon and he played records Dicky had liked from the 1950s and 60s; Jazz and a smattering of rock n' roll. Whatever happened to his musical taste after the 1960s was a mystery. Dicky went from Billie Holliday and Bill Haley straight into 17th century harpsichord.

Dotted around the bar and breakfast room were photo albums. Most of the images reflected Dicky's childhood, adolescence, engagement to Helen, their wedding, honeymoon, holidays and fragments of their blissful forty-nine-year life together. Dicky smiled in every scene, and that, said Helen, was the best way to remember him. In one of the albums there were photos of Jack, his brother and sister, father and mother from some of their visits in the 1970s. How skinny Jack and Ernie looked. How sullen Lauren, even as a toddler. Claire appeared at his shoulder, wine glass in hand. 'You see what I mean now about time…what it does?'

'Life was much simpler back then.'

'Well, as a child I guess it was,' she replied, hiccupping.

'Maybe things can be simple again, if we want them to be?'

'Like a second childhood you mean?'

Jack glanced across the dance floor towards his mother who was being helped to her feet by Alice and Lauren.

'I'm sorry, Jack. I didn't mean your mother.'

'It's funny,' he snorted. 'If we live long enough, we turn into the children we once were, just as Shakespeare said.'

Claire glugged her wine. 'I wouldn't use that as part of your next stand-up routine, hey, Jack?' The vowels and consonants collided on her tongue. Her eyes were glassy. A few more sips and she'd be under the table, or dancing on it. The more drunk people get, thought Jack, the funnier they think they are, and the more oblivious they seem to their audience's affected smiles, muted snorts and badly-timed laughter. People who didn't know him well often proffered funny stories as if he was on the lookout for a new gag. He felt one coming directly at him then in the form of Claire's jabbing finger and exaggerated mouth. 'Now I've got something really funny to tell you…'

Before she got going on her non-sequitur story of how she nearly lost all of her fingers in the blades of a lawn mower because of six afternoon gin and tonics, Jack excused himself. He looked around the pub for Alice who seemed to have disappeared. And so too had his mother and Lauren.

He found Alice standing outside the ladies' toilets. She explained that Estella had had a mishap and Lauren was changing pads. Five minutes later, Lauren emerged, linking arms with Estella who looked pale and confused. 'All done,' Lauren said.

'You okay, Mum?' Jack tried to place an arm around her shoulders.

'It's all been too much,' said Lauren. 'This happens all the time, only people don't see it. Good job I came prepared.' She led their mother slowly along the corridor.

Jack gently caught hold of his sister's sleeve. 'I'll get you a drink from the bar. What are you having?'

Lauren glanced over her shoulder. 'You've forgotten…I'm driving?'

'So am I,' said Alice. 'What about a coke, orange juice or coffee?'

'I'm fine,' she said.

'Lauren,' said Jack. 'I want to help.'

'I know,' she replied, leading their mother into the breakfast room.

'Have you said much to your sister today?' whispered Alice.

'Small talk. Why?'

'Well, I told her about your tests, the hospitals, the scans, going private, everything.'

'And what did she say?'

'She said, "I'm sorry to hear that".'

'She has problems of her own, Alice. I think she's depressed again. Remember that time we took her in all those years ago, when she nearly quit teacher-training? Sometimes I don't recognise her at all. It's like what T.S. Eliot said about reaching the age of twenty-five. By that time you have to reinvent yourself.'

'Jack, she's almost forty. If Lauren hasn't reinvented herself by now it's too late.'

'I don't think it's ever too late.'

'We should go before the night draws in. The roads will get icy. Give it another hour, then leave?'

Jack sat with Auntie Helen who flicked through photo albums. She pointed at the wedding pages. 'You were a big favourite with Dicky.'

'I feel awful for not visiting enough. I failed him, and you.'

'We all have separate lives to lead. Dicky knew that. He lived a long, healthy life and made me impossibly happy.'

Jack pecked her on the cheek and stood up.

'Before you go, can I tell you *why* Dicky took such a special interest in your life rather than in Ernie's or Lauren's? I think it was after that tour you did in Canada. Dicky said, "There's something a little different about my Jack-in-a-box, isn't there, Helen?" And I asked what he meant by that, and he said, "Jack's a bit of a mystery isn't he? I'm not sure anyone really knows who he is". He said you were so busy being everyone else with your impressions that you might not know who you really are. He said you didn't share your real self on stage. You were a persona, a mystery man.'

'I've stood in front of thousands and told them all sorts.'

'Dicky said, "I'm jealous of my little Jack-in-a-box. When a man's a mystery to those closest to him, he'll remain a mystery well after he's gone. People will say, who was Jack Mann really? Jack will live on in people's memories for longer, like a myth, Helen. Like an unanswerable question, a riddle, a legend. I'll just die and people will say, oh Dicky, he was a decent sort of fellow".'

'Uncle Dicky will live on in my memory for all sorts of reasons, Aunt Helen. It was a privilege to have known him. And there's nothing wrong with being a decent fellow.'

She smiled. 'I wanted you to know that Dicky thought you were a wonderful mystery.'

'Thank you,' he said, sadness swooping like a swallow into the ruins of his heart. Jack had never wanted to be a mystery, a riddle or an unanswerable question. Though being a legend would be quite nice.

As he was about to leave, Jack noticed his mother was getting agitated, her eyes locking onto his. The DJ, who'd been maintaining complete radio silence out of respect for the occasion, suddenly spoke out: 'The next song's been specially requested by Estella Ward, Dicky's only sister. Those still on the floor, stay and smooch a while. All you wallflowers grab a loved one.'

Estella was on her feet trying to negotiate her way around the chairs, almost toppling, and Jack caught her by the elbow. The unmistakable Hammond organ and first piano keys of John Lennon's

"Jealous Guy" sounded through the speakers. Jack remembered it being played in the old Muswell Hill house a week or two after his father's death; his mother's sad lifting and replacing of the stylus on the grooves of the vinyl. Estella had told him it was his father's favourite Lennon number. Jack imagined the song hid a special meaning for his parents, perhaps even recovery from an affair.

He helped his mother onto the parquet floor, stooped to take her gently by the waist and hand. The difference in height was striking, as if old age had shortened her spine, vertebra by vertebra, month by month. They were not cheek-to-cheek, but cheek-to-chest. 'Oh, Jack,' his mother cooed. He'd never been much of a slow dancer, even at sixth-form discos, but there wasn't too much to it; hold gently and sway from side to side. She sang how she was dreaming of the past, and that her heart was beating fast. She tightened her grip. She said she had lost control. She hadn't meant to hurt him. She was sorry that she made him cry.

Jack was surprised she remembered so many of the words, although patients with dementia sometimes found chinks of light in the darkest of rooms through music and melody. He'd seen it happen at the nursing home when musicians played well-known songs from musicals and his mother joined in, rekindling memories of her own time on the stage.

Jack and Estella didn't stray far from the original spot on the dance-floor, taking baby steps to the right, then to the left, moving slowly in an imperceptible circle. She was feeling insecure, she said. 'You might not love me anymore.' Jack tightened his hold.

During the whistled verse, accompanied by sweeping strings, Jack glanced over his mother's shoulder and smiled at Alice. She was holding his coat in her hands. 'I was trying to catch your eyes,' his mother said, looking up at him. 'Thought you was trying to hide. I was swallowing my pain.' Jack felt a lump rise to his throat and a stinging sensation in his eyes. Perhaps it was the music, or the words, or the fact that his mother was singing them. He slowed down, gently rocking her from side to side, whispering how lovely she looked and how she hadn't lost any of her moves after all this time. 'Thanks, Jack,' she laughed. 'You're still a good mover.'

When the song faded out, he took great care leading his mother back to her chair. Her face beamed. Alice brought Jack's coat across and he bent down to kiss his mother on the cheek, saying, 'I have to be going now.'

Her expression shifted from contentment to confusion. 'Why ever would you do that?'

'Because it's quite a long drive back to Kent.'

'There he goes again,' said Estella. 'You don't live in Kent.'

'There *who* goes again, Mum?' asked Lauren, shrugging her shoulders at Jack.

'I should have guessed,' said Estella, giving Alice a tasty glare.

'Should've guessed what?' said Jack.

His mother folded her arms across her chest, eyes full of spite. 'Go with *her* if you must.'

'Really sorry,' he said. 'Take care, Mum. I'll see you again soon. Goodbye.' He tried to kiss her cheek but she turned away.

Lauren got to her feet and gave Jack a hug, whispering in his ear: 'Mum thinks you are *Dad* and Alice is *the other woman*? You are the spit of Dad you know.'

'Oh,' he said, uncertain of how to respond. 'Well…look after yourself then, Mum, and you, Sis.'

Outside, the low sun was making long shadows of the conifers that lined the freezing car park. Jack got into the car seat, shaking his head and reaching for his belt. 'I'm glad we came, but my life's turning into a car crash.'

'What?' said Alice, reaching for her seatbelt.

'Well, I come here for my mother's brother's funeral; Uncle Dicky's wake. It turns out my uncle didn't really know who I was. I'm a complete mystery. For a split second I'm terrified Aunt Helen might solve the mystery by revealing I'm actually Dicky's son, not my Dad's, like I'm in an episode of *Eastenders*. Minutes later, I'm on the dancefloor with my mother who thinks she's dancing with her dead husband. She believes my wife is one of her husband's lovers. Meanwhile, my sister Lauren, like a seething, hungover Lauren Bacall, sidles around the scene as if she's hiding a switchblade in her shoe. I can't decide if my life is turning into a Dickens novel or a badly translated Greek tragedy.'

'Would you rather be an amoeba in a pond? Now belt up.'

'No, you belt up,' he said.

'No, you belt up.'

'No, you belt up.'

And they could laugh again, leaving the tragedy and mystery behind.

The Arrowhead

Although the name of the private clinic suggested round huts with thatched roofs from the Iron Age, Jack expected the cutting-edge Arrowhead Clinic to be more like a futuristic set of low-slung integrated pods he'd seen in episodes of *Space: 1999*. As Alice's Sat Nav guided them in to the docking station (car park), however, the clinic turned out to be neither Neolithic nor space-age but a ramshackle, refurbished old church nestled beside the M25 motorway in Surrey. There was a central bell tower, bearing no bell.

'It doesn't matter what it looks like on the outside, it only matters what they do on the inside,' said Alice, reading his disappointment.

Jack pictured Dr. Who's Tardis, wondering if time could be turned back.

Online reviews of the clinic were promising. Anyone scouring the internet for long enough, of course, as Jack and Alice had, might have stumbled across suggestions of malpractice or accusations that the medical director was a charlatan. But on the whole, the clinic appeared to have helped more patients than it had harmed, and those it had helped were full of the highest praise saying the Arrowhead had saved their lives.

It practiced environmental medicine, specialising in the diagnosis and treatment of allergies and associated illnesses. Included within this broad field were pathogenic diseases spread by insects and ticks. The Arrowhead had been treating Lyme disease for more than a decade. Although they did most of their allergy-testing in-house, blood samples for Lyme were sent to labs in other countries such as America; countries with a longstanding history of managing the disease. The Arrowhead treated Lyme patients with intravenous antibiotics, sometimes for months. For some experts it was the only way to cure patients with "chronic" Lyme infections. For others there was no such thing as "chronic" Lyme.

As someone who'd never used a private clinic before, and someone who'd actively advocated saving the NHS from creeping privatisation even during a Labour government, Jack was in two minds about using the Arrowhead, but the clinic might prove once and for all that he had Lyme disease. He could go back to his GP with evidence and she could treat accordingly. There was hope, and there should always be hope, particularly in purgatory. With the £2,000 Uncle Dicky had left him Jack could pay for tests, but first he had to have a consultation costing £200 per hour. Money never used to be an object for Jack and Alice. If they wanted something they'd get it. But since buying Seagull House and running into a massive overspend on the redevelopment (funded on credit in lieu of the now cancelled *Mad Infinitum* tour) things were extra tight.

As they climbed out of the car Jack caught a strong smell of flowers, which was strange given it was February. 'Alice, you're not wearing perfume are you? Only that email specifically said no one coming into the building should use deodorants, scented soaps or perfumes because it might affect patients with allergies.'

'I forgot,' she said, approaching the main door. 'I doubt Chanel No.5 will set alarms ringing.'

They walked anxiously into reception, gave their names and were politely asked to take a seat in the waiting area just down the corridor. The appointment was with Dr. Aziz, an Egyptian man who'd trained in London. He was experienced and widely travelled, so it said on the clinic's website.

A young, bearded man walked slowly through the waiting area, dragging a trolley with a drip bag hanging from it. A tube ran from his left arm. He put money in a water dispensing machine, pressed a button and picked a bottle from the tray. 'You pay for water in the private sector,' he said, smiling towards them. Then he shuffled down a corridor out of sight.

'£200 an hour per consultation, five consults a day makes a grand,' said Alice. 'Five days a week makes five grand. Four weeks makes twenty grand a month. That's £200,000 a year if you take two months off as holiday. How many consultants did you say there are at this clinic?'

'Five,' said Jack. 'That's a million pounds a year between them. Then factor in the profits from tests and treatment, which is north of four grand a month, that's without accommodation or food.'

'Jack, it's your health, not an all-inclusive holiday. Besides, the clinic gets Lyme patients from all over Europe. They wouldn't come all this way if they didn't think it was worth it, would they? Sometimes you have to pay for specialist treatment. And anyway, if you do have Lyme disease you're going to be treated on the NHS. But we need the tests first.'

Just as she said this, a group of Italians emerged from the corridor, talking among themselves animatedly. They sat down in a dark-haired, olive-skinned huddle near the bottled-water dispenser.

Jack noticed there was nothing on any of the walls in the Arrowhead, making the place feel unlived in, personality-free, or bland. In NHS hospitals the walls were smothered with medical information, posters, or reproduction art; normally flowers. Although once a church, the building had been modernised and extended in all directions leaving no physical trace of religious observation; no nave, apse or altar. The clinic reminded Jack of a derelict grammar school he once broke into with his childhood friends: large windows, high ceilings, wide corridors, walls and woodwork requiring a fresh lick of paint, and chipped vinyl floor tiles.

A young woman entered the waiting area, also dragging a drip trolley behind her. She was emaciated, her paleness exacerbated by huge bug sunglasses, and Jack realised he was still wearing his shades. Like someone from a Hollywood rehab clinic, the woman stared doubtfully through the glass at the bottled water, changed her mind and disappeared down another corridor. 'It's time,' said Alice, checking her watch. She picked up her handbag and walked Jack along the corridor to the consultant's room.

Dr. Aziz was sitting behind his desk, elbows resting, fingertips pressed together in a pyramid. He introduced himself and asked Jack to tell his story. He made copious notes, stopping Jack now and then to re-establish the dates of tests and diagnoses. Alice had brought all their paperwork and referred to the details.

'So, let me summarise,' said the doctor. 'You went walking in Wales with your dog. Days later you got an unusual rash. Weeks after, you developed a painful neck. Months later, you developed flu-like symptoms, unexplained fevers and fainting. The following summer you developed pins and needles. Then you had what you call a "neurological meltdown" followed by a series of diagnoses that were later retracted, and you now have a non-specific diagnosis of Clinically Isolated Syndrome.'

A perfect summary, but this had taken up half of the consultation. That was £100 and this information could have been sent by email.

Dr. Aziz asked Jack to remove some of his clothes and lie on the bed. He took his blood pressure, pulse and temperature. Occasionally, he'd break away to his file on the desk scribbling notes. *No pallor, icterus or cyanosis. Temperature 36.5, 5 amalgam fillings, 4 gold fillings. Thyroid normal. No lymphadenopathy. Lungs normal and clear with a peak flow rate of 630 L/mim. Pulse regular at 88/min. Blood pressure 124/80. Abdomen soft, non-tender and slightly obese. Fundoscopy normal. Pupils reactive.* He asked Jack to stand again, conducting a short series of neurological tests, all of which Jack had done before. *Plantar responses flexor and vibration sensation normal.*

No nystagmus. No ataxia. Cranial nerves normal. Romberg negative.
Then he said he was going to test for fibromyalgia.

'Fibromyalgia?' asked Alice. 'ME?'

'Your husband said he suffers from extreme fatigue and chronic pain. It won't take long, and might help with a full diagnosis.'

He pressed firmly on various parts of Jack's body, using his knuckles as probes. First the backs of Jack's legs, then the front of his thighs, then the lower back, top of chest, upper arms and neck. Jack made noises as the pressure applied started to increase. The amount of pressure applied seemed directly proportional to the lack of patient reaction. Jack thought he might end up with bruises. It was like a game he'd played at school, testing endurance; an odd variation on Chinese Burns. At one stage, Dr. Aziz got frustrated, puffing hot air through his nostrils as he held Jack still with one hand and dug in with the other. Registering Jack's lack of reaction, the doctor strode over to his desk and leaned across it. Jack thought he might be looking for something more effective, like a baseball bat, but Dr. Aziz only leaned over to make more notes. *Beighton score: 0 out of 9.* He returned to Jack, pressed again, hard for good measure, on the back of Jack's neck and sat down behind his desk, making more notes. *Fibromyalgia tender point score: 13 out of 18.* 'You don't have fibromyalgia,' he said, looking up. 'You're on the scale, but not high enough to diagnose. It's quite common with Lyme disease.'

'So it *is* Lyme disease?'

'All in good time,' the doctor said, leaning back in his chair. Jack glanced at the clock on the wall. The hour was up.

'You were never given any antibiotics?'

'No.'

'That's not true, hon. You were given a short course of penicillin after the bite and the rash.'

'How long for?'

'No more than five days,' she said.

'And you were later prescribed steroids for five days also?'

Jack nodded. 'For MS.'

'That's a pity,' said Dr. Aziz, 'because there's a strong indication of Lyme disease. A short course of antibiotics would've done little, and may have made things worse. Steroids were a mistake too. They suppress the immune system making it easier for the bacteria to reproduce. Steroids also skew blood tests for Lyme because they affect the body's ability to produce antibodies to infection.'

'If this is Lyme,' said Alice, 'what tests can we have?'

'It's not as simple as that, Mrs. Mann. A tick is a dirty needle and can carry more than Borrelia bacteria. There might be co-infections like Bartonella, Babesia, Ehrlichia; a whole host of nasty things. But we can test for all of these too, as well as the main critter. My only concern is that if this is Lyme, you've had it a long time. It's what we call chronic Lyme neuroborreliosis and is naturally harder to treat.'

'But it can be treated?' asked Jack.

'We've helped a number of chronic Lyme patients over the years. Many of these patients' symptoms have gone into remission, although it can be a long process to full recovery.' He went on to describe the full range of tests on offer including something called PCR, looking for the DNA of the Borrelia rather than just human antibodies to it.

'How long will it take to get blood results back?' asked Alice.

'We FedEx samples to America and Germany, to some of the most experienced labs in the world. They email us the results. No more than two weeks. Then we have another consultation to discuss, either in person at the clinic, or over the phone if you prefer.'

'And you think this is definitely Lyme disease?' said Jack.

'Almost certainly, to be confirmed by blood tests.'

'What if the tests return negative?'

Dr. Aziz thought for a while. 'A negative test doesn't preclude Lyme.'

'How much do blood tests cost?' asked Jack.

'The ladies in the finance office can tell you that. They're not cheap, but what price can you put on your health?'

Jack and Alice had no intention of paying for antibiotic treatment at the Arrowhead Clinic but they would pay for the tests, no matter what the cost.

'I'll book you in for bloods this afternoon. That gives you time to have refreshments in the canteen, and talk to the ladies in the finance office. I suggest a full panel, PCR, Melisa, Western Blot, and screening for co-infections. It's best to look for everything. You never know what you might find.'

Jack was surprised to discover the consultation that was meant to be an hour had turned into nearly two, and wondered if this would be added to the bill. He needn't have worried. Dr. Aziz didn't charge extra for extended, excitable first consultations.

There were sandwiches, salads and biscuits in the canteen, nutless and gluten-free, but Jack and Alice only wanted coffee. The woman behind the counter said the chef was in today and if they cared for something more substantial he could rustle up a beansprout salad or vegetarian hotpot.

They sat down at a table and shared a bar of chocolate and a bag of crisps from Alice's bag. Whilst sitting there, discussing the consultation, they noticed the young bearded man they'd seen earlier, still dragging his drip trolley along. Although most of the tables were unoccupied he pulled up a chair at theirs, saying, 'Do you mind if I eat here?' He introduced himself as Luke and said he'd been coming to the Arrowhead for three years. He wanted to know more about Jack's symptoms, nodding each time he heard anything similar to his own. He wanted to know about the mistakes, saying he too had been misdiagnosed with MS. Luke had had brain lesions on MRI scans, sensory deprivation, tingling in his hands and feet and all over the back of his head. 'We're very similar,' he remarked, tucking into his beansprouts. 'Definitely Lyme.'

'How long have you had it?' asked Alice.

'Six…maybe seven years?'

'Did you have a rash?' asked Jack.

Luke shook his head, forking food into his mouth, chewing and swallowing. 'Only about 50% of Lymies ever get the rash, man.'

'Stiff neck?'

Luke nodded. 'Fatigue, fevers, flu-like stuff.'

'Couldn't you get treated at an NHS hospital?'

He laughed. 'My tests returned negative. The NHS won't accept there's a problem. There's too much at stake.'

'Too much at stake?' asked Alice.

'Think about it. The tourist industry's worth millions. All that countryside and parks. Who wants public notices saying beware of infected ticks?'

'I guess not,' said Jack.

Luke took out his mobile phone. 'There's ticks in my garden. Look…' He scrolled through some photographs and showed them a tick he'd found on a rose petal in his back yard in Yorkshire. 'They're all over the UK, everywhere. Lyme's an epidemic. But it's all secrets and silence, man, like Aids in the 80s.'

Although heavily bearded, which added a few years to his face, Luke was too young to remember how terrifying the initial outbreak of Aids was back then, but Jack and Alice remembered it, even down to the grave, monolithic TV adverts narrated by John Hurt: "There is now a danger that has become a threat to us all. A deadly disease, and there is no known cure."

'The Center for Disease Control in America,' Luke continued, 'is the most conservative institution in the world regarding diseases, right, but even they upgraded Lyme from 30,000 to 300,000 cases a year. In Germany it's 60,000. In western Europe it's 200,000 a year. But here in Britain it's under 3,000. How is that? We're living proof, sitting here, aren't we? We're not on any Public Health UK database. Lyme's not just ticks and spirochetes, man. It's a can of worms.' He explained how Lyme was probably the result of government bio-warfare research on Plum Island, America. A man-made stealth pathogen. By the 1970s, he said, it found its way out of the research facility into the community. 'Plum Island's less than ten miles from Lyme, Connecticut, man. Where the disease really kicked-off?'

Alice shook her head. 'That Otzi, that 5,000-year-old ice man they dug up in Europe? They found Borrelia in him.'

Luke nearly choked on his rocket leaves. 'That's what they want you to think. That it's been around for thousands of years. But this new Borrelia is something else. Fact. It's harder to treat than TB. Fact. They experimented on infected mice and macaques, and after a year of antibiotics the Borrelia was *still there*. Fact. The bacteria changes itself when under attack, turning into these impregnable types. Fact. They lie dormant, and drill into nerve cells and move to the brain. Fact. They're harder to beat than syphilis or leprosy.

'Look,' he sighed, 'this probably sounds far-fetched, like something out of a sci-fi film, but science backs it up. The bottom line is that Lyme is selling homes, wrecking relationships, losing jobs, losing lives. Nobody tells you this stuff, but it's a fact. Some Lymies end up killing themselves. They can't afford treatment, can't handle the symptoms, or the stigma. Last year, I met this lecturer in the canteen. About your age. He was sitting in your seat. He went off a week later and hung himself from a tree.'

Alice placed a hand on Jack's, and asked Luke how much the treatment costed.

'Depends. I had a three-bedroom house, now I live in a one-bed flat. I had a full-time job in advertising, now I work freelance. I come here for a month's treatment, six days a week, staying in a hotel. Every eight months I do this, to keep on top of the infection. In total, accommodation included? I've probably spent 20 K in three years.'

Alice's jaw dropped.

'It's not just the infusions, it's the electrolytes, probiotics, nutrients and immune system boosters. That's a grand a month. You don't have to have all that stuff, but I'd take it first time around or you'll end up with diarrhoea or C Diff.'

'Does it work?' said Jack.

'You should've seen me three years ago, man. I could barely walk. I needed a stick just like you. The mental fog was so bad I couldn't remember the alphabet past the letter K. I was so tired I slept twenty hours a day. I was dying, and the NHS kept saying, "You've got MS," but I knew better.'

'How?' said Jack.

'The fact my blood tests came back positive from America, and all my symptoms matched Lyme, and I saw a GP privately. You're probably where I was three years ago, man. The UK tests aren't as precise as those in America. America's been testing longer.'

'So, even if my Arrowhead tests return positive, the NHS still won't treat?'

Luke shook his head. 'I can't think of a single person who got positive tests abroad who was treated with antibiotics in the UK, other than those treated privately. Some go to America. Flights and accommodation, six months treatment, that's upwards of 50K.'

'It might just be easier to have MS,' said Jack, deflated. 'At least they can slow it down.'

'No, man,' said Luke. 'I'm much better. Get the tests done, see what comes back. Eat healthy. No sugar, no gluten, nothing processed. Think anti-inflammatory.' He pushed his empty plate into the centre of the table. 'Excuse me,' he said, patting his drip, 'I need a new bag.' They watched him move gingerly towards the corridor. Before disappearing, he turned and gave a Vulcan sign of forked fingers, saying, 'Live long and prosper.'

'This is a minefield,' Jack whispered to Alice. 'All from a tiny bite. How can something as small as a full stop cause a problem so big it can't be fixed by a giant the size of the NHS?'

Blood flowed freely into four vials. The nurse put them in the chiller waiting for collection by FedEx. Jack asked how long it would take for them to get to the American lab. The nurse said 24 hours. Jack's samples were being sent along with another three patients' blood. And tomorrow there'd be another five patients arriving for the same tests.

From where he was sitting, Jack looked around the makeshift ward that had once been a private chapel. Light shone through a large, solitary stained-glass window depicting a biblical scene; a man standing beside his own tomb, the name Lazarus glittering beneath his feet. Two beds were given over to the taking of blood. Five others lined a far wall filled with pasty-faced patients attached to drips. On Jack's way out, the young woman with the bug sunglasses stared blankly up at him, looking like a sad human insect. Infected arthropods were turning human beings into insects. Jack prayed in his head for salvation.

Dr. Aziz's blood tests included haematology, biochemistry profiles with electrolytes, a comprehensive Lyme panel, co-infection panels and a Lyme MELISA evaluation. Combined with a one-hour consultation, these amounted to a few pounds shy of Uncle Dicky's

£2,000. *Another beginning,* Jack thought; *the beginning of another long and twisted road.*

It was only later, on the motorway home, that Jack realised he might have been staring the future in the face when he'd looked into Luke's ominous eyes. 'I have to be careful,' he said, 'or Lyme will take me over like it has him.'

'You're not going to turn into Luke,' said Alice. 'We're realists, not conspiracy theorists, or freedom-fighters from outer space.'

'Luke Skywalker,' said Jack in his best Darth Vader voice: 'I sensed something. The force with him is strong.'

Do You Want the Good News, the Bad News or the Good News?

The day before the Arrowhead results flopped through the letterbox Jack received a phone call from Gerry. It had been weeks since they'd spoken. Their catch-up conversations were being eroded and replaced by those between Alice and Francesca. Any news about Gerry now came through Fran's filter and Alice's interpretation; a kind of third-hand friendship, or love by proxy.

According to Alice, Fran's pregnancy wasn't going too well, which was an understatement. There was a 50/50 chance their baby would have Down's syndrome. A consultant noticed disproportionate shortness in the foetus's legs on a scan and the only way to be sure was to undergo amniocentesis. Fran and Gerry didn't want to put the baby's life at risk, so decided to take their chances, knowing they'd love the baby regardless. 'It'll probably be due to their combined age of 96,' said Alice. 'Age increases likelihood.' Jack imagined Gerry at sixty-something waiting at the primary school gates beside other parents, some of whom would be young enough to be his grandchildren.

Jack had called a few times offering moral support, but Gerry was getting unpredictable about answering his mobile. Jack had also called Gerry's home phone but he was usually out and Jack had to have the tricky conversation with Francesca. Things had become sticky ever since Frangate, and though their conversation was cordial, it was inorganic.

So it was a pleasant surprise that morning to see the number of the Ravenscroft Comedy Agency on the telephone display. Gerry was calling from London, though in a very bad mood. There was none of the usual preamble, cutting straight to the chase: 'Jack, do you want the good news, the bad news or the good news?'

'I dunno,' said Jack. 'That sounds suspiciously like a bad news sandwich to me.'

'The good news is that I've got fresh information from Interpol about Hernandez.'

Jack's stomach flipped. He hadn't heard that name in years. 'Hernandez? Your ex-accountant Hernandez? Who ran off with £300,000 of my money?'

'Yes, the same Hernandez who fled to Mexico City with a million quid of *my* money, a lot of which was *yours*. Yes, *that* fucking Hernandez. How many other Hernandezes do you know?'

'Interpol *phoned* you?'

'Of course not. It was the Fraud Squad. They received a report from Interpol.'

'So, after all this time, they've finally found Hernandez?'

'Fifteen years too late, but yes they found the double-dealing Mexican bastard.'

'Does that mean we get our money back?'

'The bad news in that sandwich you mentioned earlier is that they found him naked, face down in the Mojave Desert with a cactus rammed up his arse and a bullet hole in the back of his head. And I hope that cactus really hurt. I hope it was a million pounds' worth of hurt.'

'Gerry, the Mojave Desert isn't in Mexico, it's in California.'

'What is this, an ordnance survey test? I don't care if he was found in the Mojave *Wasabi* Desert. He's dead, okay?'

'What about our money?'

'Zero. Zilch. Zip. Nada. Kaput. Capiche?'

'Nothing? What did he do with it all? You could buy a million tequilas or a palace made of burritos with that sort of money.'

'Interpol said his bank account was cleaned out before he bit the dust. He was involved with some Mexican cartel boss; gambling, prostitution, drugs, people-trafficking, the works.'

'So, these guys were sending out a message? He got into bed with the wrong sort of people?'

'Jack, I don't care if he got into bed with Ken bloody Dodd as long as he still had our money stuffed under his mattress! I couldn't give a damn about that bloody Mexican now!'

'Gerry, you keep saying it, but Hernandez wasn't Mexican.'

'Of course he was, Jack.'

'Hernandez was from Hampstead Heath and educated at Eton. He studied accountancy at the London School of Economics before he took us to the cleaners.'

'He was 100% Mexican, Jack. He had a Mexican name, a Mexican girlfriend and they fled to Mexico City with nearly every penny I had. I'm calling him a fucking Mexican even if he wasn't!'

'This is bad news. I could do with the cash. We've overspent on the house. I never thought I'd hear that man's name again but I must've been clinging onto the hope I'd get the money back.'

'I'm sorry,' said Gerry. 'Our lolly's propping up a meth lab now.'

'You should front a programme on the telly, Gerry, called *Breaking Bad News*.'

'I'm glad you can still see the funny side.'

'Am I laughing?'

'Jack, listen. Do you want to hear the other piece of good news? I'm not sure this will be good news, unless you're up for it.'

'Up for what?'

'It's not as good as finding £300,000 down the back of your sofa, but I've wangled a spot for you on *Celebrity Come Dine with Me*.'

Silence.

'It's a sort of cookery programme.'

'Gerry, I know what it is. Lyme gives me brain fog but it hasn't wiped out my entire memory.'

'You cook food badly for some celebrity guests and they insult you, then they cook badly for you, and you insult them, and then you all lie down on a bed...not all at the same time of course, or sit in a taxi, and you hold up scores out of ten and say something witty or nasty to camera. The winner gets £5,000 for their chosen charity. What about that MS centre you talked about? Besides, it would be excellent profile, Jack. You've been off the scene a while.'

'I'm sick. I'm having tests here, there and everywhere. Even if I had the strength, I can't cook. Chilli or roast chicken, that's my lot.'

'Celebrities don't cook. That's what's funny. You say your oven blew up, you microwave some fish fingers, or send Alice out for a takeaway, or better still get Alice to cook everything for you *incognito*.'

'Gerry, even if the cameraman in my kitchen doesn't know who I am or what I look like, and Alice wears a fake beard, he might still wonder why Jack Mann has mammaries.'

'Look, filming's penned for July and I need to let them know this week. I thought of you first. You could show off your lovely new house by the sea?' He paused a moment. 'Or I could always hand it to John Cockshaw.'

'Cockshaw? Since when was he part of the Ravenscroft empire?'

'Since last month. I schmoozed him over lunch at the Groucho.'

Silence.

'He's still an utter knob but he does have good connections, and new material. He's going on tour later this year.'

'Look, I'll do *Come Dine with Me*. Maybe I'll be better by summer.'

'Good man. That's the spirit. That's what I like to hear, the word "Yes".'

'Who else is on the programme? You know, who are the other celebrities?'

'Oh, they don't tell you that, dear boy. That's the whole point. The element of surprise when you open the door and a bunch of grinning idiots hand you bottles of wine and you spend the next twenty minutes standing in your lounge dressed as Zorro trying to figure out who the hell they are.'

'Right,' said Jack. 'So there won't be other comedians?'

'Shouldn't think so. Too many cooks spoil the broth. Too many comedians fart in the Jacuzzi. It will be some forgotten TV presenter from the 1980s, and a model-turned-actress with pneumatic tits and a permatan, and maybe an eccentric old singer; you know, like that Agga-do-do-do, eat a pineapple, grate my shoe sort of novelty songwriter. He was on last month.'

'You're not really selling it to me, Gerry.'

'I don't have to,' he said. 'You've already bought it. I sent our agreement to the production company half an hour ago, so now you'll have to get better.'

Blinded by Science

LYNCH-LABS, USA

PATIENT: **JACK MANN**

SEX: **M**

Test Name: **Lyme Immunofluorescence Assay (IFA)**

Result: **40 (EQUIVOCAL)**

Test name: **LYME IgM WESTERN BLOT**

Result: **POSITIVE** (according to lab criteria)

18 kDa, **31kDa, **41kDa, 58kDa, **83-93 kDa

(**NEGATIVE** according to CDC criteria)

Test name: **LYME IgG WESTERN BLOT**

Result: **NEGATIVE** (according to lab criteria)

31 kDa **INDETERMINATE, **39 kDa **INDETERMINATE**, **41kDa **POSITIVE**.

(**NEGATIVE** according to CDC criteria)

Diagnosis should not be based on laboratory tests alone. Results should be interpreted in conjunction with exposure risk, clinical symptoms and patient history.

WOLFSDAMM LAB, GERMANY

Positive reaction to Borrelia burgdorferi sensu stricto p41 antigen (confirmed in morphology). Presence of Borrelia garinii p41 antigen (not confirmed in morphology).

Result: **EQUIVOCAL**.

At first, Jack couldn't make head or tail of the numbers, abbreviations and asterisks. The American results included an *equivocal*, a *positive* and a *negative*, but according to the Center for Disease Control the tests were *not positive*. The German lab had concluded *equivocal* with evidence of two specific strains of Borrelia: sensu stricto and garinii. Garinii was widespread across Europe. So, by some criteria Jack *definitely* had a Lyme infection and it was currently active, not historical. By other criteria he only *might* have Lyme, and by other criteria still he did *not* have Lyme (active or historical). But, the bacteria were either in his body or they were not, weren't they? Why would Jack's body produce antibodies to Borrelia if the bacteria weren't there?

Copies of the results were sent with a letter requesting a further consultation with Dr. Aziz. Jack decided a phone consultation would be easier, cheaper and faster than booking an appointment. He made the call at the appointed hour and Dr. Aziz said that in his opinion the results were highly indicative of Lyme disease.

'And these tests are reliable?'

'Greater than 94% specificity. Also, you were given steroids that can abrogate results. To put it another way, Mr. Mann, these are strong indicators. You have five bands of antibodies in your IgM Western Blot that suggests the infection is currently active. It explains your symptoms.'

'So, it's true. I do have Lyme disease.' Jack wanted to leap out of his chair and punch the air; his illness was no longer unexplained. It had a definite cause, a name, a possible cure.

'I advocate four weeks of intravenous antibiotics, six days a week, see how you react, and go from there. You might require repeat treatments.'

'Can you put this in writing, Dr. Aziz?'

'I can, but it might be sensible to have a fuller consultation at the Arrowhead Clinic.'

'Dr. Aziz, I want to go back to my GP. I can't afford thousands of pounds of private medicine. Besides, the NHS should treat now there's hard evidence.'

After a momentary silence, Dr. Aziz spoke: 'Mr. Mann, I doubt anything I write will convince your doctors to treat with IV antibiotics. Looking at your records they failed to treat you with oral antibiotics even though you had a positive test result. Although these new results show highly probable infection, I think you'll have greater difficulty than you imagine.'

It was just as Luke Skywalker had warned.

'No,' said Jack. 'It won't be the same for me.'

No Mann's Land

Dear Dr. Greaves,

I had the opportunity to review Mr. Mann over the telephone last week. He told me he continues to feel fatigued in a disproportionate manner and that his peripheral neuropathy is increasing in intensity. The results of all his investigations are now to hand and we discussed these. I explained to him that considering the fact his IgM Western Blot for Borrelia burgdorferi is positive and Borrelia burgdorferi IFA and MELISA results are equivocal, it is highly recommended that he have treatment with at least intravenous Ceftriaxone 2g daily for 4 weeks, along with nutritional supplements and probiotics, plus biofilm breakers and other supportive measures to address his oxidative stress within the body. He will require further monitoring of his haematology and biochemistry levels during this protocol. Please find in the list below.

*500ml Ceftriaxone 2g

*Therbiotic Factor 1, 1 daily

*Therbiotic Factor 4, 1 daily

*Nutrient 950, 2 capsules 3x daily

*VegEPA 500mg, 3 capsules 2x daily

*CoQ10 120mg, 1 capsule daily

*Artesunate, 20mg 4x daily

In addition, I have recommended that Mr. Mann have a nutritional consultation with one of our clinical nutritionists and that he have a consultation with me every 4 weeks whilst on the treatment and with his blood results.

With kind regards,

Yours sincerely,

Dr. Prem Aziz

Physician at The Arrowhead Clinic

Dr. Greaves read the letter three times before Jack and Alice came to their appointment at the surgery. She'd also seen copies of all the blood tests undertaken at the Arrowhead Clinic. As expected, Jack and Alice made a persuasive case for treatment, but therein lay the problem, as she explained: 'All I can do is contact the neurologist and ask him to decide our next step. If he agrees, we'll start immediately.'

'Why contact Dr. Rama?' asked Alice. 'The letter's addressed to you, and you have Jack's full medical records. I don't understand.'

Dr. Greaves leaned forward. 'You must know, Mrs. Mann, that intravenous antibiotics carry risks. The GMC, the government, the whole world is cracking down on antibiotics, and these recommendations of yours come from a private clinic, not a consultant in the NHS.' She picked up Dr. Aziz's letter, reading again. 'And what's all this stuff?' She pointed to the list. 'Nutritional supplements? Biofilm breakers?'

'The most important part is the antibiotics,' Alice said firmly. 'The other recommendations are to support the body during treatment.'

Dr. Greaves placed the letter on her desk. 'If Dr. Rama agrees, we'll start treatment, but I'm not sure about the add-ons. I've faxed him this letter and the blood results. He'll know how to interpret. To be honest, I'm a complete novice when it comes to Lyme disease. And speaking of which, this letter doesn't actually state that you have Lyme disease?'

Alice rolled her eyes. 'An infection with Borrelia burgderfori *is* Lyme disease.'

'Still, odd he doesn't state it in black and white.'

'With respect, this is zebra black and white.'

'When will you hear back from Dr. Rama?' asked Jack.

'I've asked him to telephone me this week. As soon as he does, I'll contact you.'

Jin-jing Li poured sea salt into Jack's navel and placed a small cone on top. She lit the taper with a lighter. 'As before,' she said, 'you let me know when it feel hot or burn.' She returned to her seat and made notes about the needles in his knees, between his toes and in his wrists. Smoke coiled upwards from his navel, smelling as sweet as cannabis resin. Gradually, as the taper burned lower he began to feel the heat. He let it burn and radiate a little longer before alerting Jin-jing. She pinched it out with her thumb and forefinger. Then she pressed her palm against his soft belly and remarked that it was warm. 'Fire,' she said, smiling. She removed all of the needles, threw them into a bin, and asked him to roll onto his side. She placed a cupped palm under his navel to catch the flakes of salt. She re-took pulses in his wrists and ankles. 'Pulse fast when you come, but slower, more balance now.'

Jin-jing left the room allowing Jack time to get dressed. He sat at the table waiting for her to return. He guessed his pulse would have been fast because he was angry about the delay in getting a decision from Dr. Rama. The neurologist said he couldn't make a unilateral decision regarding treatment for Lyme disease. He was seeking advice from the microbiologist Dr. Cleaver. If Cleaver accepted the Arrrowhead results, Rama would treat in accordance with whatever was advised.

Jack explained all of this to Jin-jing, and she was full of sympathy. She produced two small brown bottles from her satchel; tinctures called Banderol and Samento. She gave him a printout that explained something called "The Cowdon Protocol"; how to take the drops, building up from one to twenty drops over a period of weeks and then taken at full strength for eleven months. 'Powerful,' she said. 'Made from tree bark in Amazon. Tribes use as natural antibiotic. More in tune with body.' He paid for the bottles and she gave him another printout detailing a scientific study demonstrating that Banderol and Samento could kill Borrelia bacteria; at least in a Petri dish.

Conspiracies

It was clear from Dr. Greaves' defensive posture that something terrible was about to be announced. 'Dr. Rama has now deliberated with the microbiologist. Has he written to you with his findings?'

Jack and Alice shook their heads.

'I've spoken to him on the phone, and have also received a letter from Dr. Cleaver.'

'A letter from Dr. Cleaver?' said Alice. 'We've not received anything.'

'I'm afraid it isn't great news.'

'What do you mean *not great news*?'

Greaves scrolled down a few pages on her computer screen. 'Here it is. Oh, you weren't copied in. Sorry, it was sent two weeks ago. I'll print you out a copy, but will read it out first.' She started to read, and every word made Alice's heart skitter and Jack's stomach sink.

Dear Dr. Rama,

Re Mr Jack Mann

Thank you for the information on this patient. Having read the material I can say that there is no convincing evidence to contradict my earlier view that this patient is not infected with Lyme disease.

There is, as I suspect you are aware, a large industry dedicated to the notion that there is a conspiracy to under-diagnose chronic Lyme disease, particularly in the USA, but increasingly in the UK and Europe.

The American tests reported are marketed by a Californian company, which although licensed by some states, is not recognized by the CDC (the US Federal Public Health Authority), nor has it fully satisfied the FDA. There are numerous reports of "over diagnosis", and a recent critical review in the New York Times. They rely on "internal validation", and have rejected papers comparing their tests to established methods.

I would advise this patient that there is no evidence he has Lyme disease and that prolonged intravenous antibiotics cannot be justified.

Yours sincerely,

Dr. I Cleaver MB ChB MRCPath

Consultant Microbiologist

Cc Dr. Greaves

Having read the letter aloud, Dr. Greaves leaned back in her chair waiting for the expected bomb to go off. For once, however, the Manns remained silent and open-mouthed as if they'd just borne witness to a catastrophic natural disaster. 'So,' she said, 'that's what the microbiologist thinks.'

'I can't believe it,' said Jack, holding his head in his hands. 'It's just what Luke Skywalker said would happen.'

'Conspiracy?' shouted Alice. 'What the hell is he talking about a conspiracy?'

Dr. Greaves shrugged her shoulders.

'I can tell you right now the only conspiracy is the one you've just read.'

'I feel like I've been pushed over a cliff,' said Jack.

'Did you hear that, doctor? Pushed over a cliff.'

'I'm suicidal,' he said, eyes turned down to the carpet.

Dr. Greaves looked at him sorrowfully, saying nothing.

Alice spoke up. 'The American tests are more sensitive and more specific than any UK lab other than Porton Down. I know because I've spent days researching it. Frankly, we're shell-shocked. We're not conspiracy theorists.'

Dr. Greaves nodded, as if in agreement. 'If I'm honest, I'm surprised myself by the tone.'

'I was not part of a conspiracy when I rushed Jack into A&E three times. Jack was not part of a conspiracy when he thought he was dying. Inflammation in his brain wasn't a conspiracy. His constant pain isn't a conspiracy. Traipsing into this surgery time after time for eight months trying to get to the bottom of a mystery illness that is devastating our lives is not a conspiracy. For eight months all we've done is place our faith in you, our consultants and our health service.'

Dr. Greaves kept nodding.

'Whatever we've been told by experts we've accepted unerringly: stroke, brain tumour, MS. But they were all wrong. For eight months my husband has been shoved from pillar to post, getting sicker and sicker. We've spent time and money handing you evidence on a plate. Then this one consultant, this Cleaver, who has never even seen my husband, writes a single letter and the whole process collapses, turning my husband suicidal.'

'My hands are tied,' said Dr. Greaves.

'With respect, you won't treat Jack because you want Dr. Rama to make the decision for you.'

Dr. Greaves's back arched. 'That's not true.'

'Yes,' said Alice. 'And Dr. Rama won't treat because he wants Dr. Cleaver to make the decision for him. It's like a game of pass the parcel bomb.'

Dr. Greaves folded her arms. 'They're the consultants and I must take their advice.'

'That's not true either,' said Alice. 'Jack is *your* patient. It's *your* decision, regardless of what any consultant thinks.'

Dr. Greaves leaned forward. 'Mrs. Mann, consultants far more qualified than me are saying this is *not* Lyme disease. You could pursue treatment privately, say at the Arrowhead Clinic?'

'Privately? That would cost thousands. Treatment on the NHS would be a fraction of the cost. Jack hasn't worked since last August and it doesn't look like he'll be returning to work any day soon, does it? He's sick, he's depressed. Did the tick that bit him differentiate between the public and private sector? Did the bacteria transmitted from its gut into Jack's bloodstream tell the difference?'

'It's only a suggestion, Mrs. Mann.'

'I've read horrible things about what can happen to people with Lyme disease in America,' said Alice. 'But I believed treatment in this country would be based on clinical evidence, not unreliable blood tests. Everyone goes on about prioritising clinical evidence, even on the NHS website, but you won't treat on a clinical basis.'

Dr. Greaves didn't respond.

'No. So we have an NHS blood test that indicates infection, but *still* you won't treat. We buy expensive private tests from the USA and Europe that prove definitively that Jack *has* a Lyme infection, and then we're told by a micro-nerd we're part of an international conspiracy. Well, guess what, Dr. Greaves: there is a conspiracy. It's as plain as the nose on your face.'

'I think we should go, Alice,' said Jack, getting to his feet and leaning on his father-in-law's cane.

'Not before Dr. Greaves prints us a copy of Dr. Cleaver's letter.'

'Of course.'

She handed the sheet to Alice who scanned it briefly, still reeling with incredulity, but there was the word in black and white: *conspiracy*. The ink was smudged and the letters had run. Alice waved the piece of paper in the air. 'This is the conspiracy.' She looked at it again, noticing the familiar blue and white logo at the top. She noted the logo at the bottom too; a family of five blue, genderless matchstick people, one in a wheelchair, underneath, the words: ***Putting patients first***. No doubt hatched from some PR think tank. 'Putting patients first,' Alice scoffed. 'I used to believe that, Dr. Greaves. When I had two miscarriages and then my first baby died, the NHS was kind to us. It was a real *service*.'

'I'm sorry to hear about these things, Mrs. Mann.'

'When I had a hysterectomy a few years later, suspected cancer, the doctors and nurses were brilliant. The NHS saved my life and I was incredibly grateful for this *service*.'

'We try our best to help.'

'But the way Jack has been treated…he was never put first. It's as if he got funnelled through the wrong door, forever lost inside the bowels of an alternative NHS, until he was crapped out the other end. It's not a *service* any longer, it's a *system*, Dr. Greaves. A broken National Health *System*.'

Dr. Greaves stood up, inviting them to leave the room.

'I'll write to Dr. Cleaver and Dr. Rama and change their minds.'

'That's completely your decision,' said Dr. Greaves.

'There you go again,' said Alice, face flustered, eyes reddening. 'It's always someone else's decision.'

'Come on, Alice.' Jack took hold of her arm.

'Crap will hit the fan,' said Alice, 'and when it does everyone had better take cover.'

Jack wrestled her hand from the doorknob and led her down the corridor into the car park. Her mascara had run. He leaned his stick against the bonnet of the car and cupped both hands around her face, kissing her damp cheek. With his thumbs he smudged away her tears. 'I'll write to Cleaver and Rama. You've got enough on your plate with work and your parents.'

'We'll split it,' she sniffed. 'You have Rama, but I definitely want that microbiologist Cleaver.'

They sat in the car for a few minutes until they'd recovered from the shocking appointment, and disappointment. Alice took Jack's hand, asking, 'You're not really suicidal, are you? Tell me you're not thinking of doing something stupid, like that time in Fulham? I don't know what I'd do…'

'I'm miserable, Alice, but I'd never do anything silly.'

The Lyme Wars: War of the Words

Jack wrote slowly on the computer, taking regular breaks on the sofa. Since becoming ill he'd been wrapped in a strange mental fog which meant he couldn't concentrate on words for any great length of time. The letter he wrote to Dr. Rama would ordinarily have taken a day, but it took him a week, and was substantially rewritten by Alice before sending.

Dear Dr. Rama,

I'm grateful to you for keeping me informed of decisions made regarding Lyme Borreliosis, but am hugely disappointed that despite recent positive tests for the disease (and a well-documented clinical history) you will not treat me with antibiotics.

As you know, my symptoms are mainly sensory with no motor involvement. I've measured zero on the EDSS scale at every consultation since my neurological problems started. Isn't such a presentation unusual for someone with MS? I had an abnormal sensory evoked potential (quite common with Lyme Borreliosis), and mildly elevated protein in my spinal fluid (also common with Lyme). My sensory symptoms have persisted without remission for nearly 300 days. You'll know better than I, but it seems uncommon for someone who might have MS to have unremitting symptoms without motor involvement, and for so long? Yet, it is incredibly common for patients with Lyme Borreliosis.

According to the Health Protection Agency: "76% of Lyme cases in the UK were found to be in the southern counties of England" (I live in a southern county). "The diagnostic peak was between June and October" (My first clinical sign of infection was in July). "The highest attack rates occurred in people between the ages of 45 and 64, followed by those aged between 24 and 44 years" (I was in my mid-40s). The HPA also states that the "diagnosis of Lyme is primarily **clinical**", not serological. In the early stage of infection an expanding rash is usually enough to diagnose and treat with oral antibiotics. A stiff neck with a history of an unusual rash can also be enough to treat. But at neither time were my physical signs recognised or treated, and left untreated too long the bacteria can take hold and spread, causing untold damage: inflammation and lesions in the brain, peripheral neuritis and sensory radiculitis (tingling, numbness, burning pain), all of which I've suffered since August last year. Some genus of Borrelia cause neurological damage in mid-late stage Lyme. My blood results from Germany in February this year indicated the presence of Borrelia garinii. Garinii is a strain found exclusively in Europe, including the UK, and causes neurological damage.

Dr. Cleaver made no mention of these German results in his letter to you. American laboratory tests showed positive for Lyme Borreliosis, but Dr. Cleaver failed to mention these in his letter too. His letter says more about personal and political opinions than it does about clinical decisions. Political opinion has no place in professional diagnosis. Contrary to Dr. Cleaver, I don't believe my results should be so easily dismissed and discarded. His decision to introduce the words "conspiracy" and "over diagnosis" is ill-judged. He is misinformed, and his motives might be construed as an attempt to undermine a legitimate investigation, simultaneously undermining the relationship between a patient and his GP. I have never thought of the clinical investigation of a differential diagnosis as a "conspiracy".

It should also be noted that many of the Lyme blood tests available on the NHS lack sensitivity. According to the NHS Map of Medicine, the ELISA and Western Blot tests have a "poor" combined sensitivity of only 56% and "better tests are needed". Dr. Cleaver fails to mention this in his letter too, and also the fact that there are numerous reports of "under diagnosis" of Lyme disease as well as "over-diagnosis". In the absence of any other firm diagnosis, I believe there is strong *evidence to suggest Lyme Borreliosis. During the diagnostic process, there has been an overreliance on blood tests to discover this notoriously difficult-to-find bacterium, Borrelia. According to the NHS, "there may be down regulation or modification of surface antigens to evade the body's immune system" in Borrelia infections. It is possible that during the long and exhausting process, going as far back as the initial bite and expanding rash, that delay, misdiagnoses and inappropriate treatment affected my immune response putting the accuracy of all future blood testing at risk.*

During our last consultation, Dr. Rama, you told me that if any new symptoms arose you'd agree to treat me for MS. You showed me a list of available drugs on your computer screen; a life-long and very expensive regimen. Yet it seems impossible to receive a 3-4 week course of IV antibiotics based on the possibility of a bacterial infection; a relatively inexpensive treatment, especially should it prove successful. I understand that there are disadvantages in having IV antibiotics over a four-week period, but feel strongly that the potential advantages far outweigh these.

In the light of these facts, I'd be very grateful if you'd reconsider your decision not to treat, taking into account my full clinical history. There appears to be a logical trail, and clear footprint of Borrelia. You were very open to the possibility of Lyme as a differential diagnosis when it first raised its head in the winter, and I hope you'll agree with me that there remain more arguments for a diagnosis than against, and approve treatment accordingly.

Thank you for your time.

Yours sincerely,

Jack Mann

Alice took less time with her letter to Dr. Cleaver, based on fastidious night-time research. At first, she'd thought of making a formal complaint. Cleaver's letter had brought the medical profession into disrepute, deliberately undermining a patient's credibility. How could they ever see Dr. Greaves again? Their GP would think they were time-wasting cranks.

Dear Dr. Cleaver,

I'm writing on behalf of my husband, Jack Mann, who is too sick to respond. I write regarding a letter you sent to Dr. Rama which was copied in to our GP (Dr. Greaves)

Given that Jack is normally copied in to all correspondence, may I ask why you decided to exclude him from your letter? Jack waited and waited to hear if your review of his private blood tests would lead to a treatment plan for his Lyme disease. Eventually, we visited our GP, discovering you had come to your conclusion, only you hadn't the decency to tell Jack, the patient.

Our GP read your letter to us. We were shocked, undermined and disempowered. Jack said he felt "pushed over a cliff". It seemed to us that your letter served to discredit him in the eyes of his consultant and his GP, and the fact you didn't copy him into your correspondence reinforces this view. Clearly, Jack wasn't meant to see it.

I suggest, Dr. Cleaver, that your professional opinion has been influenced by personal bias regarding what is unhelpfully called the "Lyme Wars". As a patient, Jack has no position on this schism, nor should he suffer because of it. He should not be stranded in no-man's land, caught in the professional cross-fire from opposing sides.

The purpose of this letter is not to contest your professional opinion. It is to say that any diagnosis of Lyme neuroborreliosis should be a clinical decision, informed by your view of the microbiology, but not bound by it. You, however, draw a conclusion from your own blood tests and nothing else, ignoring Jack's clinical history, signs, symptoms and exposure risk to tick-borne diseases (all of which are there on record).

Your letter contains inaccuracies and is selective in the information it provides, purporting to be objective and factually accurate. Your statements about the American lab link unrelated facts and are misleading. These "facts" are clearly intended to influence the opinion of other doctors involved in Jack's case, not only with regard to diagnosis and treatment, but in relation to their view of him as a patient, which is unforgiveable.

There are scientific and medical views contrary to those you present as singular and definitive. Indeed, some of these views are endorsed in formal NHS documentation mapping the diagnostic and treatment protocol for Lyme disease, but you have chosen to ignore that. Why?

You imply that Jack thinks he is the victim of a conspiracy. He does not – or perhaps, I should say, he did not, until you used such an inflammatory word in a diagnostic assessment of a patient's blood tests results.

You say that the American lab is inaccurate and not licensed in all US states, but this is untrue, as you must know. You'll see from Jack's blood tests that he was positive for Lyme disease. Even if you do not accept private tests as the basis for diagnosis, surely his bloods give weight to his clinical history (rash, stiff neck, chronic fatigue, flu-like symptoms, neurological damage and neuropathy)? To an educated layperson this seems significant. We want to ensure that no stone is left unturned. You, on the other hand, seem determined to close minds rather than ask questions. You hammer the final nail in Jack's coffin with a reference to a "recent critical review of the lab in the New York Times". No – this is a ten-year-old opinion piece that was actually even-handed. Why did you misrepresent it? Why did you use it to undermine a patient in the context of making a formal diagnosis?

I am sure you will be thinking: "Who on Earth do these people think they are?" I hope that you are, because we are exactly that – people. Human beings with names and not just patient numbers. Over the past eight months Jack has had several diagnoses of what seems to be a mystery illness. Early symptoms were diagnosed as unconnected minor ailments from allergic reactions to insect bites to pulled muscles, UTI infections to possible kidney stones, and even over-excited nerves due to too much strimming in the garden! When his neurological symptoms became so severe he was admitted to hospital he was given a definite diagnosis of stroke. This was overturned to one of neuritis. Then he could have had a brain tumour. Then he definitely had MS. Then he definitely didn't. So, there we are. In limbo.

You can see that the same evidence can produce several different diagnoses from a number of medical professionals that now amounts to no diagnosis at all. But I ask you: what if Jack has undiagnosed Lyme disease? What if his untreated condition progressively worsens leading to greater, more permanent damage? It doesn't offer much hope for a future life. Are you comfortable with that conclusion?

You know that short courses of antibiotics coupled with high dose steroids will have impaired Jack's immune response too, and produced false negatives. Why haven't you acknowledged this?

Your letter says that there are no grounds for prescribing long-term antibiotics, that the patient should be categorically told he does not have Lyme disease. On the first point, Jack is not asking for long-term antibiotics. He is asking for treatment as recommended by the NHS which is "21 days of IV antibiotics, or longer for neuroborreliosis if recommended by a Lyme specialist" (though, of course, he has not been assessed by a Lyme specialist in the UK because he has never been referred to one, should one exist within the NHS).

Surely, empirically, it must be worth trying antibiotic treatment for Lyme Neuroborreliosis if there is a probability it could help Jack regain his health and his life?

Jack will be following this up with his GP and Dr. Rama.

I await your response to the questions raised.

Yours sincerely,

Alice Mann (on behalf of Jack Mann)

The letter Jack received from Dr. Rama suggested a consultation to explore further differentials, including Lyme disease. *I agree with your concerns regarding Lyme Borreliosis* he wrote.

'Why does it take subliminal messages of legal action to make people sit up and take notice?' said Alice.

Nothing at all came back from the microbiologist Dr. Cleaver.

Positivity and Patience

'You get no apology,' said Jin-jing, dropping the acupuncture needles into a bin. 'Too dangerous. Never apologise. While you wait for Rama consultation you try Amazon tinctures, Banderol and Samento?'

Following the Cowdon Protocol, Jack diluted drop after drop of the Amazonian tree bark into filtered water, slowly building up the concentration day by day. The brown substance was slightly bitter on the tongue. When he held up the glass of water and looked closely at the diluted solution he could see small particles floating around like miniscule fish scales.

After just one week, barely on more than five daily drops, Jack started to feel much worse; pounding heart and headaches. Flu-like symptoms surged through his body sending him back to bed. His neuropathy was exacerbated making sleep virtually impossible. During the day, overwhelming fatigue forced him onto the sofa. He was starting to live in his pyjamas, wandering Zombie-like from kitchen to sofa to bed. He texted Jin-jing to cancel his next acupuncture session explaining what was happening. He told her he was having strange nightmares about fighting snakes in trees.

Jin-jing texted saying he was having a Herxheimer reaction: *As antibiotic remedy start to kill bacteria, there is "die-off". Good sign Jack. Bacteria release toxin in body but this last no longer than few days. Stay on same dose. When symptom settle build up again. Snake is Borrelia maybe? Drink hot lemon juice first thing in morning. Great detox!*

A week before his showdown with Dr. Rama, still taking the Amazonian remedies, Jack gradually started to feel stronger. Certainly, his legs were less rubbery and his vertigo wasn't so pronounced. The headaches too had lifted and he was able to take Pandora on small walks.

On the upper deck of the bus on his way to see Jin-jing, he realised for the first time in more than half a year that his hands and feet didn't hurt as much. Usually, he'd resort to placing his palms on the cold window to leech out the heat, but now his hands were resting on his lap, only mildly irritated.

Sitting opposite another patient in the waiting room of the acupuncture clinic, however, the searing heat re-emerged making Jack's hands and feet feel raw, as if scalded in boiling water. He hung his head down onto his chest, exhausted and in defeat.

'Hello, how are you today?' said Michael Wasser, striding into the room, face aglow, manic eyes roving from Jack to another patient. 'You're looking well. How are the rainforest remedies?' He was standing with a poker-straight posture, shoulders back, hands on hips, eyebrows flexed in anticipation of a positive answer.

Jack wasn't sure how to respond. Although the rule wasn't posted on the noticeboard, he got the distinct impression from previous visits that no one was allowed to be pessimistic in Wasser's company, particularly if he asked you how you were, and especially if you were in the company of another patient.

'Well,' said Jack, 'this morning was the first time in ages I could actually make my own breakfast, and take my dog for a walk.'

'Excellent,' said Wasser, beaming, and nodding at his next appointment.

'Yes. I actually had a shower without falling out of the cubicle.'

'Good, good. Energised. Jin-jing will be pleased.'

'And for the first time in nearly nine months, just for a couple of hours anyway, I didn't notice the horrible pain in my hands and feet.'

'Wow! That really is good, isn't it, after only a couple of weeks?' Wasser clapped his hands together in delight.

'But just now,' said Jack, 'this afternoon, sitting here, everything came back; the fatigue, the pain, the mental fog. I'm right back where I started.'

The grin slid from Wasser's face.

'I had half a day when everything was almost normal. You know, how things used to be before the Lyme disease? And then, bam! Back where I started. I just want more than half a day, that's all.'

Wasser's face grew mean, more flushed, almost puce. He re-placed his hands on his hips. 'Well, what do you want exactly?' His eyes roved from Jack to the other client and back again. 'It's one day at a time.'

'I know that. I'm grateful for a couple of hours, but I don't know if the tree bark is a placebo effect. I'd like to have just one full day without pain.'

Footfalls sounded on the staircase and Jin-jing helped a patient out of the front door, returning to the waiting room and leaning on the doorjamb.

Wasser sighed. 'What is it with some people?'

'Sorry?' Jin-jing looked up at him, concerned by his tone.

'You need to have a word with your client,' he said.

Jin-jing looked over at Jack who shrugged his shoulders. 'You mean Jack?'

'Yes. Jack,' he said. 'Your client wants to run before he can walk. He wants everything in one day, Jin-jing, like a child. You should have words with him about positive thinking and patience. What are the watchwords of recovery, Jin-jing?'

Jack glanced across the room at the other patient, feeling as if he was being made an example of. Maybe Wasser was a scientologist, like Tom Cruise. You could never contradict him in front of anyone because he was a charismatic demi-god or magician. Jin-jing might be Wasser's pretty assistant and Jack the lump of flesh to be cut in half and put back together.

'Positivity and patience,' said Jin-jing, smiling in an embarrassed way.

'Yes. Positivity and patience, that's it! We can't expect miracles in minutes or even months. You'll have to re-educate your client, Jin-jing. Positivity and patience.'

'All I said, Jin-jing, is that I had a couple of good hours out of the last *nine months* and I wish I could have just *one whole day* without pain?'

'Yes, you did,' said Wasser, 'but it goes deeper than that.'

'What does?'

'Life,' said Wasser. 'In life, is your glass half full or half empty?'

'What?' said Jack, glaring under Wasser's pseudo-psychotherapeutic spotlight. 'That's a cliché, Michael.'

'Because at the moment you are definitely glass *half empty*.'

Jin-jing smiled but it came out a frown. 'Let's go up,' she said, walking into the hall.

Jack got to his feet, a little punch-drunk. He wasn't going to let Wasser have the last word. He didn't come to acupuncture for arguments. Positivity, yes, but not at the cost of public ridicule. As he stepped forward into the doorway, coming shoulder to shoulder with Wasser, he knew he had to respond but couldn't think of anything. And then, just as he thought he'd have to let it go, something Jack Snr. once said leapt to mind. He looked Michael Wasser deep in the eyes and said: 'You're something of a philosopher, Michael, so you'll probably know about the ancient eastern wisdom passed down generations for millennia regarding emptiness?'

'No, what?'

'Wisdom that says the true path to *nirvana* can only be found in *emptiness*. So, if I'm half empty, I'm half way to paradise.'

It was as if a bell rang out ringside: *ding-ding*. Michael looked bewildered as if struck in the jaw, Jin-jing giggled to herself and Jack followed her up the stairs to the treatment room.

During acupuncture Jack apologised for getting upset, and Jin-jing apologised for Michael's behaviour. 'He too positive all the time, but always mean well.'

'I'm not sure if he had what I have he'd be so positive.'

'You looking tired today, Jack.'

'It's all the energy I'm using to fight the system. It's hard enough battling Lyme. I'm exhausted, and so is Alice. But we have our consultation with Dr. Rama next week and we'll see what happens.'

'Earlier, a few weeks ago, you said something about having Buddha?'

Jack nodded. 'It's in my Zen garden. Well, it's not exactly been Zenned yet.'

'I remember,' she said. 'And you meditate in garden, and talk to him?'

'I used to, but that stopped a few months ago. Buddha isn't listening.'

'How you know?'

'Well, I talk, he listens. I talk, he listens, like a blunderwall. That's as far as it goes. I don't think he likes me. I may as well talk to a plant pot.'

'You must believe,' she said, smiling. 'You remember to give present to Buddha?'

'Do you mean like at Christmas or Easter..?'

She shook her head. 'Any time present. A flower from garden? I give my Buddha gift every weekend; a rose, sometime just petal.

Something to offer and he can touch or feel or smell. Something from life.'

'I see,' said Jack. 'Like quid pro quo.'

'Try, and see what happen.'

Jack laughed.

'What so funny?' she said, stepping around the bed, removing the needles.

'Oh, it's my gardener, Graham. I asked him to cut back our tamarisk. He refused because it hadn't yet flowered, and the bees love tamarisk flowers. He said, "Be kind or be nothing at all".'

'Always good to help bees. Insect keep humans alive.'

'Except ticks,' said Jack. 'And mosquitoes. They maim and kill people.'

'Ah yes, excep ticks and mosquitoes with nasty things in them. But even then, they have role in life too?'

Jack raised an eyebrow.

'Be kind or be nothing at all?' she said.

Jets of air puffed through his nostrils. 'You know, I never thought of that. Maybe everything, no matter how big or small, no matter how good or evil, has a purpose, even if it's only to talk about what that purpose might be.'

Chronic

Everything was coming into leaf in the garden at Seagull House. The twiggy traces of winter had gone, replaced by filling branches and a myriad of greens. The sea breeze was more westerly too, warmer and gentler. Young birds flitted from bush to shrub to tree, from buddleia to silver birch, lilac to lavender and hawthorn to holly: bickering sparrows, busy blackbirds, darting tits, noisy ranks of starlings marching in rows across the lawn, waddling wood pigeons and preening collared doves. Now and then, a bright-chested robin flew down from the tamarisk to feed from the bird table close to the wooden veranda, or bathe in the birdbath beside an old kidney-shaped pond created by the previous owner. Above all of these, seagulls swirled high on thermals, coming down to roost in the nooks and crannies of rooftops, including a pair on Seagull House. This idyllic, meditative scene was a far cry from Jack and Alice's old maisonette in Fulham that had a small yard backing onto a kebab shop. They'd rarely see a single bird there; perhaps a scrawny pigeon or sickening sparrow.

A Tankerton neighbour had told Alice that the previous owner of their house, an elderly lady of ninety-two called Agnes, had spent most of her springs, summers and autumns sitting at the rear of her home admiring the wildlife. She'd positioned her chair roughly where Jack was now sitting, although he was a metre higher on the new veranda. Agnes had died two feet from her own front door, dragging a green recycling bin out for collection. Jack had Agnes to thank for their mature, abundant garden and variety of planting, and for the pond that brimmed with newts. Even Graham, a gardener with more than twenty years' experience, had been impressed. There'd always be something flowering, he said.

Jack was sitting on the veranda, wearing sunglasses, dressed in his pyjamas and 1940s silk dressing gown he'd bought many years before from a vintage clothes shop in the Mission District of San Francisco. He thought about what Jin-jing had said about giving Buddha a gift.

Bleary-eyed, he trudged around the garden looking for a flower, but despite what Graham had said about all-year-round blooms, none had yet appeared and he didn't want to pick new buds. In their absence, Jack didn't know what else to give Buddha that could be touched or felt or smelled from life, so he decided to offer something more radical: dried mealworms usually left out for the robin that hung around the tamarisk and Zen garden. Jack tipped some worms into

Buddha's palm. Then, he sat down in the arbour facing the stone statue, waiting.

A few minutes later, the robin flitted down from a tamarisk branch, landing on Buddha's large head, twitching, looking left and right as if crossing a road. Jack remained stock still staring, and the robin fluttered to the palm of worms, pecking one, taking it in its beak and flitting to the tree again. And so it repeated itself, this scene: tamarisk to Buddha to tamarisk, branch to head to palm to branch. Soon, other birds cottoned on. A blackbird, or was it a thrush, barged in on the feast, eating worms that had fallen onto the pebbled ground.

Jack did this each morning after Alice went to work, if it wasn't raining, and the robin grew used to his presence. Shyness was overtaken by boldness and soon the bird sat for longer on Buddha's head, giving Jack time to take a photograph with his phone. He wondered if this could be the same robin from the garden of the Bunker; the robin that had sat on Buddha's head, the robin that followed Jack over barbed wire to the railway tracks.

He showed Jin-jing the photograph, and she said: 'You see. Offer present, and Buddha give something back.'

'I think it might have something to do with the mealworms?'

She tutted: 'Now you *are* being half-empty. In China, robin mean good luck. Angel watching over you.'

It was around this time that Jack thought he might be going mad. He wasn't sure if it was a neurocognitive problem brought on by Lyme; by that small tick bite. He recollected an Edgar Allan Poe story called "The Gold-Bug" where a man went insane after an insect bite. But if Jack remembered it correctly, the man hadn't gone mad at all, had he? Having being bitten by the bug, didn't the man find a fortune in the heart of a tree? But that was fiction. In reality, Jack learned that many Lyme victims weren't finding fortunes, they were losing them. Some were hanging themselves from trees. Anxiety, depression, insomnia, thoughts of suicide. Lymies around the world were taking their lives, and Jack didn't want to be one of the casualties.

To offset his darkest feelings and fill his emptiness, he took to drinking. Why not have a few drinks? Trying to gather his thoughts up like leaves each morning was proving impossible, with or without a hangover. They were not crisp individual thoughts; more of an indistinguishable mush. Not only was he now sitting in his arbour in the Zen garden most days, even in drizzle, still dressed in his pyjamas, dressing gown and sunglasses, he was also talking to Buddha as if the giant statue might reply; drunken, one-sided conversations about anything and everything from the weather to old jokes, from past doctors to new research on Lyme disease. Occasionally, these conversations lasted hours. He wondered if the compulsion was born out of isolation and loneliness or just a symptom of chronic illness.

Since falling ill, he hadn't been to a single social function other than the opening of the new theatre with Alice, and the Christmas panto, both of which he'd left early. He'd not gone to dinner parties in London, and there'd been quite a few invitations. He'd not even been on the excursion to Brighton to visit Gerry and Fran's new baby, May. Alice had gone by herself and he had spoken to them all on the phone from the comfort of Seagull House. This was what he had to do time after time; Alice would visit friends and he'd speak to them on the phone. Do that too often, and friends gave up on you, or forgot you, and eventually all invitations dried up. When you lose interest in the world around you, he'd come to realise, the world reciprocates. As he once said on stage: *A man who sticks two fingers up his nose is a comedian. A man who sticks two fingers up someone else's nose is an alternative comedian. A man who sticks two fingers up to the world is a fool.*

But the mystery surrounding his illness and its chronic nature, the fact it had been going on for so long without remission, had isolated him. Some friends didn't know what to say anymore and stopped phoning. They'd got bored of hearing the same old story without a happy ending. Others, he suspected, believed he was mentally ill, that he was an attention-seeker and just making it up; that he had "Mann Flu" and should "Mann up". He should pull himself together, like a pair of curtains.

Things had become strained with Alice. Her life had been turned upside-down too. She never mentioned it, but was fed up of sleeping by herself. A beautiful master with a six-foot bed, and no master slept there. Instead, he slept in a guest room upstairs or in the makeshift bedroom/study on the ground floor. She accepted it took him hours to get to sleep and understood he got up in the middle of the night, pacing to distract himself from the pain. She knew the heat from her body was unbearable to him. But important physical things were being lost: contact, affection, intimacy. Sex had stopped since Glyndebourne. Jack was too fatigued or in too much pain. Alice just wanted to be held like she used to be held.

It wasn't only that; Jack's whole personality had shifted. He was guarded, private, secretive, cut off, disconnected. He was paranoid and hypersensitive. Whenever she suggested doing something social he'd recoil into his shell. She'd ask each evening: 'How are you? How's the neuropathy tonight? On a scale of one to ten, how bad is it?' The answer was always the same stoical lie to protect her from the truth: 'It's okay. It could be worse, Alice.' And then one awful night, he'd drunk a bottle of wine before she'd got in and she'd asked him the same questions and he'd snapped: 'Don't ask me how I am anymore! Just know that I am!' She'd cried, saying their relationship was falling apart. It was, she said, as if she was perpetually treading on eggshells. It was, he replied, as if he could hear himself cracking under her feet.

Jack always had Pandora, of course. She was therapeutic to stroke and never asked difficult questions. She'd show him how she was feeling through actions, not words; like digging holes in the lawn, as if trying to escape. Sometimes she'd sit beside him in the arbour looking where he looked, wondering what the hell was so fascinating about an inanimate stone object. Whenever the robin flew down to Buddha's head it must have looked to her as if an evil spirit or red lightbulb had flashed to life and she'd run at it, scaring it back to the trees.

Sometimes, when the statue didn't answer, Jack walked over to it, half-tipsy, slapping the stone-cold face. 'Not much of a talker, are you? You gotta *help* me out here. You gotta *help* me *out of* here. Take me to nirvana, give me a glimpse of paradise, even if only for a minute. Show me the path or issue me with some words of wisdom, or any words at all? You're not much of a Buddha if you can't offer me that at least. I've known you all my life and you've never offered a single word of support. I've taken you from a pitiful concrete yard in London and given you a peaceful Zen garden to meditate in. I've given you your own personal robin, a good luck angel. Not a twinkle of thanks in your eyes, not a grain of gratitude. I give up.'

One afternoon, Jack was so drunk he got down on his knees and begged Buddha: 'Help me if you can I'm feeling down, and I do appreciate you being around, help me get my feet back on the ground, won't you please, *please* help me?'

'Sorry,' came the reply, making his heart leap.

It was a woman's voice coming from the other side of the bamboo fence. 'I've heard the things you've been saying. I'm not snooping, it's just-'

'I'm rehearsing,' said Jack, getting to his feet.

'Please don't take this the wrong way, but I know a very good therapist who works in London, and she has a second home locally. She might be good to talk to?'

'No. Thank you. I was…practicing a monologue for radio.'

'Marjorie,' she said, 'but everyone calls me Madge.' A hand appeared at the top of the screen and he felt compelled to shake it. 'Number 29, on the seafront, called *This'll Do*?'

'I know it,' he said. '*Seagull House*. One street back.'

'You've built an amazing home.' An awkward silence followed. 'Well,' she said, 'let me know if you want those contact details of my friend. She's brilliant, and so non-judgemental.'

'I'm fine,' said Jack. He slumped down in the arbour and closed his eyes. Behind them he imagined Jin-jing saying, *first Buddha give you robin, then he offer you name of non-judgemental therapist; maybe Buddha speak louder in action, not word?*

The Sympathy Well

It had been a while since Jack had contacted his brother in America. Months had passed with only a handful of text messages. Jack's last text to Ernie had been about Lyme disease, informing him of the latest diagnoses and possibilities or impossibilities of treatment. Ernie had responded by trying to sound clever, referring to two weeks' treatment with basic minocycline or doxycycline. He also said the writer Amy Tan, who lived in California, had Lyme disease. 'If Ernie researched Amy Tan properly,' Alice had said, 'he'd realise Amy Tan was ill for years before anyone treated, and she still didn't make a full recovery. She has to eat special mushrooms.'

Since that text everything had gone quiet. Jack didn't like to bother his brother too much. Ernie's marriage was "on the skids" or so Lauren had said at Uncle Dicky's funeral. He was going through "a mid-life crisis" which Jack translated as "having an affair". Certainly, things between Ernie and Ariel were strained, Lauren had said. News about Ernie always seemed to arrrive via Lauren. She had a hotline to Ernie that Jack sometimes envied, but he understood Ernie liked to play their little sister's big brother, helping her out financially as much as anything else. Lauren took cheap holidays to San Francisco, for example, and she'd babysit her two nephews in the Nob Hill house. Ernie even paid for her flights.

One Sunday afternoon, after a short walk along the seafront, Jack stretched out on the sofa half-watching a football match on TV. He wasn't that interested, dozing, having intermittent conversations with Alice who was preparing a late afternoon lunch/early dinner that she called "linner". She walked over to the coffee table and handed him a bottle of beer. 'I know you shouldn't drink, but it's a Sunday, the sun is shining and what the hell...?' She went back to the kitchen. Jack heard a cork popping, a glug of wine being poured and the sizzle of onions. The aroma of garlic wafted into the lounge.

Jack drank from the bottle and smacked his lips. He wrote a text to Ernie: *Quick update. NHS will not treat despite positive blood tests. Have complained and have another consult soon. Meanwhile, having acupuncture and treating Lyme with Amazonian tree bark and Japanese algae! Love to you and everyone in SF! Jack xxx*

He finished the bottle of beer and put it on the table. He placed the mobile on his stomach. Alice was singing something he couldn't quite recognise; was it from *A Star is Born*? "The Man That Got Away"? There was a free-kick on the telly. He watched it come to nothing and closed his eyes, listening to Alice's singing. She was always singing on Sundays. Maybe her mother used to sing to her on Sundays while they were cooking the roast. Jack heard the half-time whistle and adverts. Pandora wandered in, licked his hand and lay down by the sofa with a soft groaning noise. There was a crackle and the smell of seared lamb. Pan returned to the kitchen and Jack's mobile phone vibrated on his stomach; a lengthy reply from Ernie. As he read it, his heart nearly burst out of his chest. A rushing sound blocked out Alice's singing. Everything stopped. It was like that time he was in a car crash, pulling out of a T-junction and was shunted sideways by a truck.

He put the mobile down on his stomach thinking a stranger must have got hold of Ernie's phone. Or that Ernie was drunk. Maybe he'd just had a row with Ariel? Perhaps Ariel sent the text using Ernie's phone for mischief? Possibly it was one of their two sons playing a sick joke?

But it wasn't a joke.

'Can you smell the bacon?' Alice called from the kitchen, humming a different tune. Jack picked up his mobile and re-read the text message, thinking he was going to be sick.

Jack, read this twice because I'm gonna say it only once. Not interested in details of your health any longer! Been there, visited you, you only contact about ur health nothing else. Done the research, given you my thoughts on the matter…you have no real interest in me

*or the boys...despite the fact you are a godparent. The boys don't
know u from Adam! Sad! These r the questions u should be
asking...What are they doing...How am I? How's Ariel? What does
she do for a job? How's life in Nob Hill? What's it like running the
legal side of a complex real estate firm? Why is it that Lauren and I
appear to be the only ones actively worrying and doing anything for
Mum? Just maybe you need to worry less about illness and spend more
time living a life. Remember, I've been seriously ill but this was not my
life! I didn't broadcast my news. Two brain scans and lumbars, then I
got on with my life. I'm not interested in what label my tie is or what
brand of wine I prefer! I'm interested in living now. Harsh as this may
seem, as insensitive as it may seem, refute and complain, get second,
third, fourth opinions, for goodness sake don't let this take over your
life! ...Get working, get touring, get mobile! Support Lauren in
supporting Mum! ...You're a kind and witty lovely bloke with a great
sense of humour and an amazing wife. Get on with life!
Ernie*

When Alice walked in to the lounge she knew by the wobble in
Jack's voice something bad had happened. She worried at first it might
be a new symptom, and he tried to explain.

'But what did Ernie say?'

He handed her the phone. 'Does that sound like my brother to you?'

Alice perched on the arm of the sofa. 'My God,' she said. 'What the
hell did you send him?'

'All my love.'

She read the chain of texts, shaking her head. 'What a shit!'

'I can't believe it, but it's true, I'm not imagining it?'

She had to read it three or four times herself to be sure. He watched
the words forming on her lips. For ages they tried to decipher the
message. Why would Ernie say such things and in that tone of voice?
What does he mean by this, and by that? Who the hell does he think he
is?

'I guess it ain't called "Nob" Hill for nothing,' said Jack.

'I'm calling him right now.' Alice dialled and put the phone to her
ear. Her eyes darted left and right as if searching for Ernie's face.

'He's not answering. Gone straight to voicemail.' She tried again and the same thing happened. She left a message asking him to call back. Then she sent a text asking him to explain himself. She said he'd dropped a bomb on their house and Jack deserved an explanation. When nothing came back, she called their landline and that went straight to voicemail too. She left a message.

Two hours later, they were sitting at the dining table barely able to taste their linner, and drinking too much wine for a Sunday evening. They took turns reading the message again, line by line. 'He's a first class bully,' said Alice, 'and Lauren has something to do with this. She's been badmouthing you. It's clear in the message.' She phoned Lauren; straight to answer machine. Alice left a message asking her to call back, it was an emergency.

'You're better off without them, Jack.'

He sighed. 'I've lost my entire family and all I did was send love.'

He called Ernie the next morning, and the morning after that; still no reply. He re-read the text message. In hindsight he understood that it was definitely written by Ernie. There was something about the phrasing that was so him. Ernie when he lectured his two sons or thought he knew better than anyone else in a room. Ernie, the opinionated overbearing patriarch. Perhaps when their dad had died and Jack and Lauren were so young, and Ernie had stepped up as the impromptu father figure, that was when this part of his Moses personality had developed; laying down his Ernie rules and laws. But from memory, that was when Ernie had been so supportive. That was when Ernie had become the Super Mann of the family.

After a week of no replies, Jack stopped calling. The letter he composed took five days to write. It wasn't just the length, it was finding the right words. With the cognitive cloud messing up his thoughts it was difficult enough writing anything as simple as a shopping list. Having sealed the envelope, he telephoned one more time, hoping to speak to his brother of forty-five years, but the drawbridge was still pulled up in San Francisco, so he posted the letter first class, half vindicated, half regretting the moment the letter slipped through his fingers into the post box.

Dear Ernest,

This letter shouldn't come as a surprise. You can't send such a text message to your brother without expecting a response, especially if you run away from the explosion after the bomb's dropped.

I must reply for a number of reasons, not least because you refused to answer your phone or Alice's texts. Only you will know the reasons for writing and sending your message. I won't waste any time working out if it was meant to be a big brother lecture or plain and simple bullying. What I do know is that instead of encouraging me to get a life, you have happily trampled all over mine.

The hardest thing to accept is that you don't understand my illness or its consequences: unremitting pain, brain damage, chronic fatigue. I'm sorry you went through a hard time with migraine. I sent you texts of support at the time. But you simply can't compare our illnesses, Ernie. For one thing, you went into remission after a couple of months, whereas I have lived with mysterious and terrifying pain for the greater part of a year. You were admitted to hospital and had a couple of brain scans (both clear). I was rushed to A&E three times unable to feel most of my body and had numerous brain scans (all abnormal). I couldn't walk, was pushed around in a wheelchair. I was admitted twice to stroke wards. Now I either have Lyme disease or I have a 50% chance of developing MS inside four years. You on the other hand are living a normal, unaffected life. This will be hard to swallow, but compared to what I have been through, am still going through, and am likely to go through for the rest of my life, you had a stroll in the park.

The fact that you compare our experiences is a measure of how badly you understand what went on, and is still going on. This is regrettable and upsetting because I tried my best to keep the family informed, and, like you, without too much 'broadcasting'. Either I was unclear about the severity of my illness or there was denial on the part of individuals, or I just didn't 'broadcast' on the right wavelength. You sent a text saying everything would be fine, even though I'd been told I'd had a stroke at the age of 44. Admitted for a second time for a second stroke, you sent me a text: **Have you had a bed bath yet? Ask the nurse for a moisturising rub too!** *Our family seems very good at denial using humour to mask harsh realities.*

Your horrible text suggested I'm selfish, that I don't care about you, your complex work as a real estate lawyer, your wife, your children, or your life in San Francisco. That is **not** *how I feel. Of course, I do stand guilty as charged for not visiting much, and the truth is I'm sorry about that, but I don't think it deserves an attack on who I am as a person, or opinions on how I should live my life. We all make decisions that have repercussions, like pebbles in ponds. Your decision to move to SF means it's difficult for you to see Mum. I don't blame you for making that decision. It's your career, your family and absolutely your life. You are free to do whatever you want with it. Just as no one tells you how to live your life, don't tell me how to live mine.*

Time has moved on a great deal since we were children. We're all middle-aged and the intensity of communication has changed between us, if not broken down altogether. That's life, and with such changes priorities inevitably alter. When Alice was told she might have ovarian cancer some years ago, and the only way to be sure was to remove all of her reproductive organs, I thought she might die. The only family member to telephone was Mum. You knew about the operation because Mum told you. I blew a fuse because I thought you cared about Alice, but the truth is you didn't call. It simply didn't affect you. I never wanted to bring this up. I had filed it under ancient history, but your text tried to make me feel guilty about your life, your wife, your kids etc. When my wife was going through the tossed coin of life or death, you looked the other way. So, don't lecture me on caring. Your text says ten times more about you than it ever did about me.

God only knows what possessed you, Ernie. I'm not sure I know you anymore. Your well of sympathy has run dry because my illness has *lasted too long for you. You had time to think your words through, time to write your text, time **not** to send it...but you chose to send it and sod the consequences. I will always love you as my brother because of the blood and history we share but I'm not sure about respect.*

Before I finish, I want to return to the worst inference in your message. I won't accept that I'm not worrying about Mum or Lauren. That is false, plainly insulting, and so far from the truth it makes me sick. I see Mum as much as possible, talking her care over with the care home manager and offering Mum emotional support. When I can, I do my utmost to get there, but I'm genuinely ill. Lauren must be doing incredible things helping Mum, which I acknowledge and admire her for, but she has never discussed the situation with me even when I tried to speak to her at Dicky's funeral. And neither have you, come to think of it, until your out-of-the-blue outburst. Lauren had the perfect opportunity at the funeral, but did she broach the subject? No, it was small talk as usual, and that's what our family have done so well for the best part of fifty years. I'm not sitting in judgement (perhaps small talk is the glue that binds families together) but somehow we have been conditioned to put up and shut up, and when we do decide to talk seriously it manifests itself as blame or the transference of guilt. The fact right now is that I'm ill, can't drive and live a five-hour round trip to the nursing home by car. It is not an excuse; it is a fact.

I held back from writing this letter at first, because I hoped you'd phone or write to explain. After only a few days I realised you weren't going to contact me because your stubbornness and pride meant more than your brother. Now that really is "sad!" The days turned into weeks, and nothing. I realised then that you're not the brother I once knew, trusted, respected and looked up to. The brother I once knew wouldn't have dropped a bomb and run away.

If you're interested, despite everything I am trying to put the pieces of my life back together. My tour is on hold but I hope to do it one day. I see an acupuncturist every fortnight who tells me I should turn all the negatives in my life into an opportunity for change. So, ironically, I want to thank you for sending me your text message, Ernie, and providing me with the opportunity to 'broadcast' the truth to you in all its awful glory.

I wish you a long, lucky and healthy life.

Jack

Cornered Cats

The first thing noticeably different about the meeting with Dr. Rama was the presence of a senior nurse. Having received Jack's letter weeks before, Rama had sought advice from the clinical lead, Dr. Solomon, and Solomon had advised him to have a witness. Although Dr. Rama had more than fifteen years' experience as a consultant, he'd never got close to being involved in a dispute with a patient, nor a complaint, and definitely not a potential lawsuit. This time, however, he felt vulnerable.

Earlier that morning, after he'd brushed his teeth and proudly sharpened his pencil moustache in the mirror, he'd meticulously gone through all of his notes on Jack Mann. Although mistakes had been made, particularly during primary diagnoses, Dr. Rama had little to do with them. The biggest mistakes had been made by other consultants, most notably Mr. Swan who no longer practiced at the hospital. Dr. Rama had, however, made his own small admin error regarding a mix up with MRI scans and King's College in London. This, he told himself, was very minor and based on a ridiculous workload. Since his appointment, he'd been handed the case files of more than half of

Swan's patients, and that was on top of his existing list. Not to mention his teaching at the med school. Somehow, Jack Mann had slipped through a lot of torn nets, but Rama had not been the fisherman. Before the consultation, Dr. Rama had discussed the matter briefly with the senior nurse. His Dictaphone would be all ears too, quietly lying on the desk mid-way between himself and the Manns.

He asked Jack whether he minded the nurse being present during discussions. The Manns looked surprised but agreed without any fuss. In light of Jack's letter, and after a thorough re-examination of his case, Rama maintained that his conclusion was still a diagnosis of Clinically Isolated Syndrome with probable demyelination, cause unknown. However, he was now prepared to look at other differentials including Lyme disease. The Manns appeared to settle more comfortably in their seats, as he'd expected. He said he'd commission new blood tests for sarcoidosis, HIV and syphilis too, explaining that all of these were very unlikely to return positive. 'I have a patient with sarcoidosis, and believe you me you do not want it.'

'What about new tests for Lyme?' asked Mrs. Mann.

'I'll come to that in a minute,' said Rama, feeling pushed around. 'Lyme is the least likely diagnosis, but as you say there has been one positive in the past, and your symptoms have not gone into remission, so we'll do more tests.'

The Manns glanced at each other triumphantly, as if winning a small battle.

The truth in reality (after a long discussion had been had between Dr. Rama and the microbiologist Dr. Cleaver) was that Jack Mann's blood would be sent to the government's Porton Down facility in Salisbury. Still smarting from Alice's letter, Cleaver had explained to Rama that the Manns were barking up the wrong tree with Lyme disease. If the patient's blood came back positive for Lyme from Porton, Cleaver said, he'd eat his own bicycle! Rama had asked why he was so confident, and Cleaver said the testing kits at Porton were no different to the ones he used in his own lab. 'You'd have to have a raging infection to test positive,' he said. 'The world and his dog seem to *think* they have Lyme disease when in *fact* they have an illness that boils down to some random undetectable virus that's confused the immune system. Or, more likely, the patients are part of some mass hysterical nocebo effect or psychosis. You know; nut-jobs or Lyme loonies. Ten years ago I'd get maybe fifteen or twenty requests a year for Lyme tests,' he said, 'and each year I might have one positive result, normally from someone who'd contracted it abroad. Now I get fifty requests a month from GPs who say their patients haven't travelled further than their garden gates. Each test is £40!'

'What about Jack Mann's rash and radiculoneuropathy?' Rama had asked.

'I wouldn't go down that road,' said Cleaver. 'That way lies madness. Who's never had a rash in their life? If this is a Lyme infection, it would've showed on his previous tests as longstanding, i.e. in his IgG antibodies. It wouldn't show as a current infection in his IgM. He would have seroconverted from IgM to IgG. The patient's never been IgG.'

'But what about the use of steroids mentioned in their letters?' Rama had asked. 'Can steroids abrogate tests?'

'I stick by everything I said in my original letter to you,' Cleaver said.

'And what about the positive foreign blood tests?'

'Bogus microbiologists and money-makers preying on the afflicted,' said Cleaver. 'There is a conspiracy, sadly gaining momentum year on year in the UK, that despite numerous negative tests for Lyme a patient can still have it, even after taking long-term antibiotics. They call it "chronic Lyme" when there's no such thing. The residual symptoms are the damaging effects of an historical infection, not active Borrelia. Or it's an autoimmune issue. Cyberchondriacs spend too long online, and too much money getting private tests. The internet is full of psychosomatics, lunatics and quacks. What they want is a magic wand to fix everything, but sometimes there is no explanation, no fix, no cure. Tough, but that's life. If I were you I'd not bother with more testing, but in light of the letters and this blame culture we seem to have inherited from America, and the fact that he's still in *your* care, you'd better go through the motions. No doubt he'll be impressed by the fact tests will be done at Porton, the top secret laboratory. Kid him along. Watch his face when you mention Porton Down.'

Dr. Rama did watch Jack's face when he mentioned Porton Down. The patient and his wife both seemed impressed, or was it relieved, optimistically squeezing each other's hands. "Impressed" or "relieved" was not the nomenclature when Dr. Rama suggested another MRI of Jack's head and spine with gadolinium. "Concern" was the patient's reaction that quickly turned into "horror" when Dr. Rama mentioned another lumbar puncture. 'Belt and braces,' Rama said. 'We'll check your spinal fluid for antibodies to Lyme.'

'Will it be done on the neurology ward?' asked Jack, a quiver in his voice. 'Only it was a disaster last year on the stroke ward.'

'It will be done by a qualified neurologist on our new Swan Ward,' said Rama. 'So, if that's everything, I'll send you up to phlebotomy. The MRI and lumbar should take place in the next couple of months. If, as expected, everything remains unchanged I'll sign you off. There'll be no need for another consultation. I'll write with the results and copy in your GP.' He briskly filled in the request forms, including one for Porton Down, and slid them across the desk.

Getting the hint the meeting was over, Jack and Alice stood up. There was no shaking of hands, only a mild thank you from them and a nod of recognition from him, but no smile.

They walked out into the corridor and the nurse closed the door behind them. She waited a few seconds, then whispered, 'From what you told me, Dr. Rama, I thought they'd be lions when they were more like frightened pussy cats.'

'Cornered cats show their claws, Fiona,' he said, sighing. 'Now, I need five minutes to collect myself before you show the next patient in. Will you kindly take this out of my sight?'

The nurse lifted Jack Mann's heavy patient file from the desk and tucked it under her arm. Dr. Rama clicked off his Dictaphone and removed his jacket. The scent of pine from his morning shower drifted across his nostrils and he looked down. Chest to waist, the front of his pale blue shirt was dotted with dark clouds of perspiration.

Genie Bottles and the Cryborg

The build-up to the argument about drinking happened in early June. It started with word that Jack's blood samples had gone missing somewhere between the phlebotomy unit at the local hospital and Porton Down, Salisbury. Jack and Alice had been waiting by their letterbox for weeks and now Jack had to start the process all over again. On the bright side, Dr. Rama had telephoned and said the tests for sarcoidosis, syphilis and HIV had all returned negative, as he'd suspected they would. He said he'd not contact them again about the Lyme results until they'd been formally discussed with Porton Down, and Dr. Cleaver.

This unexpected and disappointing news seemed to blow a fuse inside Alice's head, and set light to a fuse wire connected to a bomb inside Jack's. What had Cleaver got to do with this anymore? He'd insulted them in his letter and wrecked Jack's chances of being treated, and he hadn't even had the decency or courage to reply to Alice's letter. Dr. Rama also said that he wanted all of the results in front of him before discussing Lyme disease, and the MRI and LP procedures were not due to be done until August; eight weeks away.

No amount of persuading or pleading could speed the process up, or, as Dr. Rama phrased it, "alter the realities of a national health service under extraordinary pressure". Dr. Rama was also going on holiday from mid-August, so they shouldn't really expect to hear back from him until early September.

September?

The prospect of waiting another two and a half months for the rest of the tests to be done, results processed, discussions had and decisions made was almost too much to bear. Seagull House was fast turning into Jack's personal drinking den and Alice's shattered dream. Whenever she returned from work, there he'd be, still in his dressing gown, unshaven, wearing sunglasses and sitting in his tatty leather armchair, or lying flat out on the sofa, a glass of wine on the coffee table or in his hand, with a "this is only my second glass" look in his eyes. She knew he'd downed an entire bottle, had opened a second and drank two more glasses making it look as if it was the first bottle of the night.

After a few weeks of this, Alice took to counting the number of empties piled up in the recycle bin; that was if Jack hadn't deliberately smashed the glass to oblivion. She pointed out to him that each Saturday she was buying a case of wine and there was rarely more than one and a half bottles left in the chiller come the following Friday. She had worked it out, she said, and if she was drinking no more than two glasses a night (and sometimes none at all because of early morning meetings), that meant Jack was downing eight or nine bottles a week all by himself.

'Well, I have to escape this misery somehow, Alice. It softens the edges.'

'But it makes your pain worse the following morning, hon, doesn't it?'

'I have a hangover every morning whether I drink or not. It's just the way it is. The bloody Lyme fog. The bloody drugs.'

'I wasn't talking about hangovers, Jack. I was talking about polyneuropathy and fatigue.'

'And what would you know about it?'

'It's costing us a fortune. I've had to stop shopping in Waitrose. I'm thinking about shopping at Aldi.'

He laughed. 'Well, what a First World problem to have.'

'While you're pickling your liver and swimming in a sea of self-inflicted misery, think of the cost why don't you!'

He lifted his head from the sofa. 'Self-inflicted?'

'You know what I mean. This drinking. It's not good for you, or our bank account. All of our savings have disappeared. I'm overdrawn each month. I can't remember when I last bought new clothes. We haven't been on a holiday for nearly two years! I'm starting to ask myself, what's the point and purpose of life anymore? It's joyless. It's one constant run of bad luck.'

'Welcome to my world. Lyme world…according to Sod's Law.'

'Great,' she said, 'now you're slurring.'

'Alice, I know you mark the wine bottles in the fridge with your lipstick like some fucking FBI agent. Do you think I'm blind?'

'And why do you think I do that?'

'It's not *why* you do it, it's the fact you do it at all. I thought you'd understand. I need something to help me through each god-damn day. All this waiting, and waiting, and waiting, and never getting any better. How are you feeling today, Jack, when it's all so fucking obvious how things are today. They are like they are every other god-damn fucking day! Self-inflicted?'

'I didn't mean it like that. I meant drinking to excess.' She pulled at her hair. 'Look at you. Look at us. Look at me.' He looked out of the window. 'I said look at me!'

He still looked out of the window.

'I'm going to Mum and Dad's.'

'Of course you are. Good old Moms and Popsicles.'

'But before I go, I want to say this. Don't ever think I don't care about you, Jack. I love you and my heart breaks for you every day. You know that?'

His eyes remained glued to the outside as if he was watching a soap on TV.

'I'm tired. It's hard work for me too. Nothing, nothing like it is for you, I know. Sometimes I'm scared. Sometimes I'm angry with the world, angry at the doctors, angry with your brother and sister, but I can't slide inside a bottle looking for a genie. I have to keep going, and so do you. Sometimes I'm just upset. Please don't ever think that means I won't do whatever it takes to support you. Haven't I shown that? Let's not fall at the last hurdle.'

Jack's eyes started to soften and glitter in the evening light coming through the window.

'Sweetheart, please don't take it out on me, please don't think I'm not there every step of the way. Some steps are just a bit harder.'

The Mann floodgates opened.

It was a rare event. Somehow, Jack had mastered the art of tear control. Alice had seen it happen many times. His eyes would moisten and threaten to spill tears down his cheeks, and he'd suck them right back in with anti-gravitational force. Even when she took him to see *Les Mis* and the song that always made her cry ("I Dreamed a Dream") was sung, and the mascara ran in rivulets down her face, and Jack's breath was stuttering and his eyes were moist, he did what he always did; he tapped his tears, reining them in as they teetered on his lashes. She called him a "cryborg"; a robot that wanted to cry but couldn't, unless seriously provoked. Only when Hunter died did she feel the full force of his personal tsunami. Jack could go years without crying (even during the hell of the past ten months and she hadn't seen any tears except her own), but storing things up so long only meant that when the Mann dam finally broke, it broke big, and here were the signs again; his stuttering breath and moist eyes staring back at her.

He tipped his head down and tried to say something but his throat was closing. 'Everything breaks my heart. Dad. Hunter. Mum. Ernie. Lauren. I've lost Gerry, I know it. I can't lose you too, Alice.'

She ran to him and wrapped her arms around his shoulders. 'Ssshhh. Ssshhh. Ssshhh.' He was making incomprehensible noises, a Mann-wail or shrieking Mann-baby. And what do you do with a crying baby but hold and rock him from side to side, saying everything will be okay, and Ssshhh, it's alright, and Ssshhh baby, around and around in circles until the sobbing stops, the breathing steadies, the ribcage settles. 'You'll never lose me, Jack. Never.'

After he'd calmed down and wiped away his tears, she smiled at him. In an attempt to melt the melancholy, she said, 'Jack, I hope you're not going to do any of this on *Come Dine with Me*.'

He refused to let go of her hand. 'Do you mean the drinking, the swearing or the meltdown?'

'How about we start with the drinking?'

Oranges and Bananas

Mr. Swan was the last person Alice thought she'd ever see again, especially in a now rare trip to Waitrose. For weeks after he'd misread Jack's MRIs, prescribing unnecessary steroids and pointing her husband down a long and disastrous road, Alice had fantasised about what she might do or say if she ever saw him again. Sometimes, in her imagination, it was a verbal confrontation ending with her having the final word. At other times, she had her hands wrapped around his scrawny neck and her right knee thrusting into his balls. Whatever her revenge fantasies might be, she always regretted not making a formal complaint about Swan to the board of hospital trustees. She should have told them how Swan had made mistakes because of his student doctors, and one in particular; the bright, confident bombshell with the expensive shoes.

And here he was; the bearded Mr. Swan, relaxed, dressed in white tennis shorts, Fred Perry t-shirt and trainers, standing in the fruit section looking profoundly at the bananas, with oranges already in his basket.

You couldn't make it up, thought Alice. Hadn't his very last words to Jack been to eat plenty of oranges and bananas? Should she say something witty, cruel or ironic about oranges and bloody bananas? Should she educate him about the great MS imitator, Lyme disease?

Alice pushed her trolley close behind him. She should have been concentrating on collecting the things Jack needed for his *Come Dine with Me* cooking night: finger food to go with the Aperol cocktails, red onions and lentils to go with the grilled sea bass starter, feta, flageolet beans and cherry tomatoes to go with the slow-roasted lamb; the finest filtered coffee, sea-scented candles, bouquets of tall flowers, and numerous herbs and spices. Not to mention a chocolate cheesecake, just in case Jack's own attempt failed on the night. But right now, all

Alice wanted to do was push her trolley at ramming speed into the hairy stilts that Swan called legs. The opportunity was a gift from God.

At the very last second, she veered off course towards the herbs and tomatoes. What good would GBH do now? What good could ever come from attacking this god of consultant neurologists? Alice bit her tongue and headed off in the opposite direction. Swan was in the past, where she should leave him. She wandered the aisles filling her trolley with groceries, unable to shake the image of Swan from her mind. Without realising it, she was tossing cans of tomatoes on top of crackers with an unconscious force, as if raining them down on Swan's head.

Twenty minutes later, in the wine section, Alice saw them together; Mr. Swan and his beautiful trainee from Singapore. Swan's hand brushed against the back of the young doctor's tightly-fitted tennis top, dropping down her spine to her short, white, grass-stained skirt, lingering there. Her long, black shiny hair was loose and relaxed-looking. She raised a hand to Swan's back, the other pointing to the chardonnay. Swan and his latest conquest, younger than him by at least forty years, were all smiles and laughter.

Alice could no longer resist. She left her trolley by the champagne and stomped over. Her blood pumped fast. 'Excuse me,' she said, and Swan turned his head in surprise. She looked him directly in the eyes thinking he might recognise her.

'Sorry,' said the young woman, moving to Swan's side, thinking Alice wanted to get to the chardonnay.

'You probably don't recognise me, Mr. Swan.'

He took in her features with his dark brown penny eyes trying to recall when or where or how they may have met. For one awful moment he thought she might be someone from his ex-wife's circle of friends, perhaps from her old book club, but then surely she would have called him Geoff, not Mr. Swan. He shook his head. 'No, sorry, should I?'

'*Alice Mann* ring any bells?'

He examined her face again, eyes darting, memory turning over. 'Sorry, you'll have to be more specific.' He smiled and put his basket on the floor.

'Wife of *Jack Mann*?'

'Mann?' he said, stroking his beard. 'No, still can't...'

'You diagnosed him with MS last October?'

'Forgive me, madam, I've diagnosed thousands of patients with MS. Last October you say?' It was the month he retired from the NHS, and something clicked. 'Oh, yes, yes, possibly. Jack *Mann.* Comedian fellow?'

'Yes,' said Alice, temper surging. 'You'll remember Jack too,' she said to the young woman, 'because you were present at the same consultation.'

'I think I remember,' she said.

'And how is Jack?' said Swan. 'Well, I hope?'

'*Well, you hope?* It's funny you ask because firstly Jack doesn't actually have MS.'

'Oh? How's that?'

'Because you misread his MRI scans.'

'Pardon me, I never misread scans.' He folded his arms across his chest. 'And I've seen a great number of them.'

'Oh you did, Mr. Swan,' she said, voice ratcheting.

'Look,' said Swan's sidekick, taking up a defensive posture. 'We need to do some shopping and we don't investigate old cases in supermarkets.'

'Old cases?' said Alice, laughing hysterically. 'Well, you don't mind investigating this old case.' She thumbed over her shoulder at the sixty-something consultant. 'On the basis of the mistaken reading, Mr. Swan, you misdiagnosed MS and Jack's condition worsened.'

Swan said nothing, fearing the patient called Jack may actually have snuffed it.

The beautiful trainee doctor tutted. 'Let's go, Geoff.' She picked up her basket of noodles, natural yogurt and salad.

'Mr. Swan, Jack's been in and out of hospital ever since.'

'I'm sorry to hear that,' he said, encouraged by his young girlfriend to pick up his basket and walk away.

'He can't work. He's in pain night and day. He was discussing suicide with his GP last month.'

'I'm sorry, we have to be going,' said Swan, not before snatching a bottle of wine from the shelf.

'And it turns out that Jack has Lyme disease,' said Alice, following them down the aisle.

Swan stopped in his tracks. 'Lyme's disease? That's rarer than hen's teeth. Who said it was Lyme's?'

'No one said it was *Lyme's*, Mr. Swan, because experts call it *Lyme* disease, not *Lyme's* disease.'

'Geoff, let's go,' insisted the young woman.

'Jack tested positive in an NHS test, and in private tests. Porton Down laboratories are looking into neuroborreliosis, Mr. Swan.'

'I'm well aware of what neuroborreliosis is, madam.'

'Are you really?' snapped Alice. 'Because you weren't aware of it when you examined Jack on the stroke ward, when you commissioned MRIs and a lumbar puncture and evoked potentials and forgot you'd even commissioned them. You weren't aware of Lyme when you looked through Jack's patient file. It was all in the clinical history, everything. But you didn't look, did you, Mr. Swan?'

'Say nothing, Geoff,' his sidekick said. 'She's probably recording this.'

'I've nothing to hide,' said Swan. 'I'm very thorough in my investigations.'

'You missed all the classic signs of Lyme and Jack had every single one. You saw things that weren't there instead, like an enhancing MRI when there wasn't enhancement.'

Mr. Swan looked confused. 'No enhancement?'

'No enhancement, confirmed by Dr. Rama, Dr. Solomon and by senior consultant Mr. Knox at King's in London.'

'If you don't leave us alone,' said the panicky young doctor, 'I'm going to call store security.'

'It's alright,' said Alice. 'There isn't a Kalashnikov in my trolley. I've said what I wanted to say, except for one last thing.'

'You'll have to be quick,' said Swan, tapping his foot nervously. 'We have somewhere to be.'

'I should let you know, Mr. Swan, I've made a formal complaint against you for malpractice.' This wasn't true, but she couldn't help wondering what his face would look like, and how he'd squirm after hearing such news.

'Have you indeed?'

'It's with the board of trustees as we speak, and they've agreed to investigate your mistakes.'

'Well, they'll not find any I can assure you,' he said. 'Now, if you don't mind…'

Alice let them pass and watched them scurry away. She called out as they reached the tills: 'Now you know what it feels like to have a sentence hanging over your head, *Geoff*! Oranges and bananas, *Geoff*! Oranges and bananas!'

Come Dine With Me Post-Mortem

Jack spent three days and nights flat out in bed following the filming of *Come Dine with Me*. It had all been too much; four evenings with complete strangers, making small talk and pretending to like their homes and their cooking. He'd drunk too much over the week and probably said things to camera that he'd regret, but he'd given it his best shot, for charity.

During the days leading up to the culinary celebrity showcase, Alice had shown Jack how to grill sea bass and slow-cook lamb shanks and carefully bake chocolate soufflés. During the practice run, he'd managed to cremate the fish, sink the soufflés and undercook the lamb. He thought plan B would be a better option (soup, casserole and cheesecake), but Alice was having none of it. The cameraman would surely want to film Jack walking around Whitstable and Tankerton and using the local fishmonger's and butcher's, along with the establishing shots of him standing in the harbour, sitting on the Slopes, and as many beach hut close-ups as possible. Millions of people would see their seaside home on TV and Alice had spent an entire weekend cleaning Seagull House from top to bottom. She'd rearranged framed photographs and artwork too, placing seascapes on most walls.

The letter that came from the production company had been vague and mysterious, not revealing who the other guests were or where they lived, specifying only that there'd be three other dining guests and Jack would be the last celebrity to host, after which the winner would be announced by him and the £5,000 prize paid to their charity of choice. Guest 1, it was revealed, wished to host their evening along the theme of "James Bond", which Jack and Alice both agreed would be a doddle. Jack could wear his tux and do impressions of Sean Connery and Roger Moore. All he had to do was stay sober, compliment the host's home and eat whatever food was placed in front of him. He should also try not to get into any fights. Guest 2's chosen theme of "Comic Book Heroes" was a little more problematic in the costume department, but Jack could do a pretty decent baritone impression of Michael Keaton's Batman. Guest 3's "Rock Gods and Goddesses" was trickier still, Jack settling on Bono from U2. He owned an old biker's jacket, could buy pink wraparound sunglasses and did a mean impression of Bob Geldof that could just as easily be presented as Bono if he played around with the attitude and the tone, and mentioned the United Nations.

Jack's theme would be "Comedians". A bit unadventurous, he realised in retrospect, having seen what everyone else was doing. He was a comedian himself, but was well-versed in impressions of others: Laurel and Hardy, Tommy Cooper, Eric Morecambe, Billy Connolly, Ronnie Corbett, not to mention Robin Williams. He owned a fez, fake beards and various sets of glasses and teeth. All he had to do on the final night was make people laugh and cook better than the disaster of his rehearsal.

The first three nights merged into one in Jack's exhausted brain. The chauffeur arrived and took him to the home of Guest 1 who lived in a penthouse apartment in Chatham. Jack hadn't known penthouses existed in Chatham. Guest 1 was Dawn who was half-drunk by the time she served the first course of prawn cocktail, and was slurring, rambling and giggling by main course. She'd initially found fame as a burlesque dancer who was talent-spotted and did "a bit of acting" in early episodes of *The Only Way is Essex*. Then she recorded a single. Then she was the cover girl for various beauty products and men's magazines. Only 29, Dawn was botoxed to infinity. Her lips were not so much bee-stung as anaphylactic. Her breasts were bronze balloons. She forgot which Bond girl she was meant to be and served up a burnt pheasant pie. She said she had a deep interest in history and her favourite period was the Anglo-Saxons and King Alfred. Jack made the worst pun ever suggesting Dawn should appear in The Only Way is Wessex, which made her laugh so much she almost choked on her shop-bought pistachio ice-cream. Dawn was already out of the running. Nonetheless, Jack gave her a generous 5 out of 10 for effort, holding up to camera a large white card in the back of the cab.

Guest 2, Jean-Paul Pierre, former magician, general knowledge nerd and TV gameshow host from the 1990s, came as Dr. No the first night, with a fluffy fake white cat strapped to his arm. Guest 3, the most mysterious of Jack's three competitors, was called Elisha (singer-songwriter for Goth rock band, The Hooded Crow), and came as Solitaire, the Bond girl in *Live and Let Die*, complete with Tarot cards. Jack played Roger Moore to her Jane Seymour all evening, making everyone laugh. Elisha, an ethereal, spiritual person, did Tarot card readings for the guests. Oddly, she messed up Jack's reading and refused to do it again. The beautiful Elisha might be real competition. She was cool yet friendly, in control yet relaxed, amusing yet demure. *Delisha Elisha.*

The second night Jack was driven to Jean-Paul Pierre's detached Georgian house; something of an impressive country pile. Jack's Batman impression went down well, though the plastic costume grew shockingly hot after the first hour. Jean-Paul Pierre (who it turned out had no French connections) had been a genuine celebrity in the late 1980s and early 90s, judging by the copies of *Hello!* magazine he and his wife appeared in, now framed and proudly hanging in sequence around the downstairs lavatory walls. Jean-Paul came as Thor, smashing an enormous inflated mallet down onto the table whenever anyone disagreed with him. He hosted well, thought Jack. His food was pretty good, though perhaps too spicy. Dawn, bursting out of her Wonder Woman outfit, couldn't eat any food due to her hangover from the first night. Elisha, dressed in a black leather catsuit, ate some but hid lots under her knife and fork, and the sly look she gave Jack indicated she wouldn't score highly. For entertainment, Jean-Paul put on a magic show using his wife as his glamorous assistant. It was jolly, but not a winning performance, especially when one of Jean-Paul's real cats took fright and crapped on the beige dining room carpet. In the cab, Jack held up a generous 7, saying the cat had stolen the show, and by that he meant Elisha. That wouldn't go down too well with Alice when the programme was eventually broadcast.

On reflection, Jack knew he'd been too quiet that second evening; fatigue and brain fog were setting in and he hadn't been up to his usual witty repartee. Since the onset of Lyme disease, he no longer had the stamina for back-to-back evenings like these, or even back-to-back conversations. It was all too easy losing the thread of a story told around a stranger's dining table. So the third night would be tough at Elisha's. But, he told himself, and Alice reminded him, there was an important prize at the end of it for the therapy centre. And Gerry would think it was all good publicity whether Jack won or not.

Elisha's house, up an isolated dirt track in the middle of the countryside, was a Tudor-style country mansion in need of TLC. Jack noticed, looking up at the leaning chimney, that perched on top was a witch-on-a-broomstick weathervane. The door knocker, just about to fall off, was a gargoyle's head. When Elisha opened the door, Jack's eyes popped out on stalks. She was wearing the shortest, tightest, leather minidress ever sprayed on, torn purple tights and thigh-length PVC boots. Her hair, no longer sleek rivers of raven-black, was dyed blood-red and backcombed into a mountainous hedge, like Robert Smith from The Cure. Like him too, her lipstick was crimson and smudged as if applied with a chamois leather. 'Go girl!' Jack said in his Bono accent. But he didn't have a clue what rock goddess she was meant to be.

When Elisha was in the kitchen clattering pans and saucepans, and the guests were standing in the front room drinking, Jack asked if they knew who she was being. Jean-Paul, who'd come as Jon Bon Jovi but looked more like George Michael in his denim jacket and blond wig, insisted Elisha was obviously playing Cher. Dawn, who'd actually come as Cher but looked more like Alice Cooper and was totally crestfallen nobody had noticed, said she thought Elisha had come as herself from her band The Hooded Claw. Jack pointed out that it wasn't The Hooded Claw, it was in fact The Hooded *Crow*. "The Hooded Claw", he said, was from *Ripping Yarns*, a 1970s BBC comedy series starring Michael Palin. Dawn had never heard of it. Jean-Paul, hot on his special subject (popular culture), reminded Jack that the episode in question was actually called "The Curse of the Claw" *not* The Hooded Claw, and there was nearly a falling out over the title. Anyway, said Jean-Paul, it's the height of narcissism to come as yourself at your own themed dinner party. And Jack thought, oh dear, I'm coming as myself tomorrow; maybe I'll have to rethink the comedy costume.

Elisha's food was strange and not exactly seasonal. As the courses kept coming through a hole in a wall, the more Jack realised everything was very Halloweeny for July: pumpkin soup, homemade red carrot bread with sparklers sticking in it, sausage and bacon surprise (the surprise being there wasn't any sausage or bacon, only meat substitute and lots of carrots, herbs and potatoes). Dessert was the oddest thing Jack had ever seen on a platter; a bible-black blancmange with "spider" ice-cream and ice cold sticks of fudge that the host called "fudgicles". She plied everyone with booze so they'd get too drunk to remember they'd eaten some hippy rock chick's children's party food. They might also forget the walls of her house had ornate, spray-painted spiders' webs, healing crystals on the coffee table, and dream-catchers suspended from the ceilings. Elisha's bedroom walls were black as soot and her bed was a large scarlet heart apparently pulsating, until they all lay on it discovering it was a water bed. Her wardrobe was schizophrenic: black or red leather outfits with slits, metal straps and fastenings, or long-sleeved, flowing velvet gowns in a kaleidoscope of different colours.

'Have you ever heard any of The Hooded Claw?' asked Dawn, as they walked to a ramshackle barn for the gig.

'It's Hooded *Crow*,' Jean-Paul reminded her. 'They had a top ten hit in the late 1990s.'

'And we're going to hear some of it now,' said Jack, as he took his straw bale seat.

Later, back in the relative quiet of Seagull House, the tinnitus was so severe Jack could barely hear what Alice was asking. He kept shouting his responses above the ringing in his ears. 'What was her house like?' said Alice. 'What was her band like?'

'It was so loud the neighbours called the police! And that's saying something, because the nearest neighbours lived half a mile away!'

'Was Elisha any good?'

'She's got a lovely voice, but it didn't really match the Nirvana drums and thrash metal guitars! Couldn't understand a word, until she did a cover of Suede's "Still Life"!'

'Still Life is *our* song,' she said. 'What did you give her?'

'Eight!'

'Eight? That's high.'

'Her food was odd, yet quite funky!'

'You fancy her, Jack Mann.'

'I do not!'

'Okay,' said Alice, 'let's see if she returns you the favour tomorrow night, shall we?'

The final night of *Come Dine with Me* arrived. Jack wanted to spend the whole morning in bed recovering from the cumulative effects of socialising and forced funniness. Over three nights he'd covered his entire repertoire of impressions with a few spontaneous ones thrown in. His neuropathy was off the scale. Fatigue had him pinned to his mattress in the guest room. But the director telephoned early to confirm the film crew would arrive between nine and ten. Jack would have a camera in his face for twelve hours, and as he discovered looking in the bathroom mirror, his face was a sorry state: bloodshot, bleary eyes, and saggy skin the colour of corn-fed chicken.

Alice took a day off work to "arrange" Seagull House. She set the scene of a seaside idyll replicating those she'd seen in coastal magazines. She'd bought new bathroom towels in nautical shades. Shells and driftwood collected from the beach over the course of three weeks were carefully staged on mantel pieces, shelves, side tables and sills. On the wooden railings of the veranda she hung a pointing sign that said "Beach". When Jack was dressed, she tidied the guest bedroom, evaporating his presence. She made it look as if they slept together in the master. She gave the whole house a final hoover and polish.

The bell rang and Alice let the cameraman and director in. The cameraman walked around the house checking the quality of natural light in each room. The director sat down with Jack and Alice at the kitchen table with coffee, explaining the timetable. Satisfied with the light, the cameramen joined them. He was in his fifties and the director was no more than twenty-five.

Alice left soon after ten, reminding Jack to light the sea-scented candles in the lounge and dining area before the guests arrived at 7 p.m. She kissed him on the cheek, squeezed his hand and wished him good luck. She was going to spend the rest of the day at her parents' flat. Jack didn't know how he was going to last the distance without her.

The director wanted quick establishment shots of Jack living in Seagull House. 'Mann about the house,' Dave Lamb, the funny voiceover guy would add during later editing. Then he wanted local everyday scenes: Jack walking along the sunny seafront, Jack strolling past beach huts and moored sailing boats, Jack sitting on a bench eating an ice-cream at eleven in the morning, Jack sitting at a table outside a café drinking coffee and reading a newspaper, Jack talking to complete strangers, smiling and giving the impression of a likeable local celebrity.

That had never been Jack's way. He usually kept his head down, never made a fuss, didn't want to be recognised, and as he was rarely on TV no one knew him from Adam. The director didn't like him wearing sunglasses, so he removed them, squinting in the daylight. Then he wanted Jack wandering around the hustle-bustle of Whitstable high street, picking up sea bass from a cheeky fishmonger, and shots of him collecting lamb shanks from the butcher on Tankerton high street. For once, Jack noticed, the butcher was all smiles for the camera when most often he was quite a sullen, tight-lipped sort of person. It is not true what they say about the camera never lying, he thought, there is something in the lens that compels people to smile unnaturally for posterity.

Jack wasn't smiling. He was his usual grumpy self. Ironically, the director seemed to love this, thinking it was his stage persona. If Jack cracked a smile it looked done under duress, like Tony Hancock waiting impatiently in a long queue at the post office, or Peter Cook unable to get a drink in a busy saloon bar. Jack imagined the repetitive voiceover during editing: 'Crack us a smile, Jack. A smile's not too much to ask.' Jack would be made a parody of himself.

By the afternoon it was mayhem. The kitchen island was stacked with ingredients. Alice had put things in careful order but Jack lost the ordering as soon as he removed them from the cupboards and the fridge. It was a sea of fresh herbs and spices. The cameraman filmed him slicing onions, peeling garlic cloves, prepping the fish and the lamb. He filmed him tossing the lentil, bacon and red onion salad. Jack's hands were red raw and burning. He was worried the camera would pick it up, or the voiceover would joke about the number of times he appeared to run them under the cold tap like someone with OCD: 'If he washes them one more time, they'll run down the plughole.'

Everything was going to plan. By late afternoon the lamb was in a huge casserole dish slowly cooking and beginning to fill the house with mouth-watering aromas. Jack set the table for three courses. He had plenty of time to change into his evening wear which he hoped would steal the show, themed as it was: "Comedians". The director wanted to cover the sartorial transformation and had the cameraman stand at the bottom of the stairs showing Jack walking up in his ordinary jeans, black t-shirt and trainers. Thirty minutes later he filmed

Jack posing at the top of the stairs dressed in a full clown outfit: oversized pantaloons with red braces, zany orange hair standing on end as if his fingers were plugged into a socket, size fourteen flipper feet, a grease-painted mouth and enormous red nose. Jack stood there doing jazz hands before pretending to fall down the stairs. It was so realistic the director ran forwards to clutch Jack's elbow. Finally, the director must have thought, something to laugh about. 'Careful, Jack,' the voiceover would say, 'we don't want you ending up in hospital dressed as Krusty the Clown.'

The guests arrived and Jack led them onto the veranda for Aperol cocktails. The sun was warm and bright. Jean-Paul was dressed as Charlie Chaplin complete with bendy cane and jaunty bowler. Poor Dawn got the wrong end of the stick and came as Cruella De Vil, who she'd always considered as funny. The voiceover man would have a field day with that mistake. 'I couldn't think of a famous female comic,' she said.

'Dawn?' said Jean- Paul. 'What about *Dawn* French? The Vicar of Dibley?'

'Oh yeah,' she giggled. 'Duh!'

Elisha's hair was black once again, and pinned up. She had painted on two thick black eyebrows, and a fat, oblong moustache filled her upper lip. She was wearing a dinner suit with impressive tails, saying it was her brother's. She'd always loved *A Night at the Opera* with Groucho Marx. Now and then she waggled her big cigar in people's faces and did an American accent that oscillated absurdly, Jack thought, between Ronald Reagan and Jimmy Carter.

Being the perfect host, Jack took Dawn's fake Dalmatian coat and flip-flopped through the house to the hall, hanging it on a peg. Pandora followed the coat, wagging her tail.

When Jack popped another bottle of bubbly, Pan barked madly, to the amusement of everyone. 'I see you have that bitch well-trained,' said Elisha in her oddly presidential voice. Jean-Paul waddled up and down the veranda with a practiced twirl of his Chaplinesque cane.

'So, Jack,' Dawn said, 'why've you come as Ronald McDonald? We having McNuggets for dinner?'

'No,' he said. 'McSeabass, McLamb shanks and McSoufflés.'

'McWonderful,' Elisha said, in her strange voice.

Whilst Jack busied himself in the kitchen, panicking over the fish and worrying about getting the grill to the correct temperature, his guests took a tour of his home, starting upstairs. The cameraman followed them, leaving Jack to himself for the first time in eight hours.

Everyone loved Seagull House. They appreciated its location, gushing over the master's bedroom balcony and partial sea views. They moved from room to room stopping to comment on art, photographs and personal objects. They noted how pristine everything was, including the ensuite bathroom. They were most impressed with a photograph on the landing showing a much younger Jack Mann shaking hands with the Queen backstage at the London Palladium. Next to this, a photograph of Jack with famous actor Jim Carrey and chat show host David Letterman. Beside this, Jack with the ventriloquist Keith Harris and his puppet duck, Orville, signed, with a message: *"I wish I could fly way up in the sky..."*

By the time the sea bass was cooking the guests were back downstairs snooping in what appeared to be a study or occasional guest room. There was a folding bed standing against one wall squeezed between a writing desk and a small flat screen. Books lined two of the walls floor-to-ceiling, mostly poetry and fiction, and lots of books about John Donne. On the wall above the desk was a large picture frame holding two delicate paper masks of Laurel and Hardy in fading 1930s red and blue. The comedians wore fezzes with stickers attached saying Carnaval de 1935 no SAO LUIZ. 'They're original,' said Jean-Paul, 'from *Sons of the Desert*?'

'Let's have a good nosey,' said Dawn, opening the drawers of the writing desk. There didn't appear to be anything of interest: pens, paper and printer ink cartridges.

Jean-Paul delved further into the last drawer and pulled out a framed handprint. He laughed. 'No doubt somebody else famous.'

'If it is,' said Dawn, 'they must be a midget or an oompaloompa.'

'Jack says the starters are nearly ready!' shouted the cameraman, and they closed the study door behind them.

The sea bass was almost a triumph, Jack forgetting to squeeze fresh lemon juice before serving. Also, Dawn said she didn't really like fish, and left half on her plate. Jean-Paul pointed out that she herself had served prawn cocktail during her soiree and Dawn took great pleasure in explaining to the general knowledge champion that prawns were not actually fish, but crustaceans. She made up for the fish by eating most of the shop-bought olive bread and downing more Sauvignon Blanc. Elisha, no longer in character, said she made her own bread at home and was disappointed Jack hadn't made it himself. That was at least one point lost.

As queen of slow-cooked meats, Alice would have been proud of Jack's lamb shanks in red wine with flageolet beans, cooked tenderly and falling from the bone, served with a sprinkling of feta cheese, roasted cherry tomatoes and fresh oregano, complimented by an expensive, chocolatey claret. Not a single word of criticism. Maybe points gained.

Elisha, noticing his fatigue, collected up the plates for him. Jack carried them out and placed them on the counter beside a full sink. He put the soufflés in the oven and set the timer when laughter suddenly erupted from the dining room. Pandora was stealing the show in his absence, or she'd jumped up and stolen the bread. He hastily flip-flopped to the dining table. 'What's so funny?' He leaned on the back of a chair staring into the camera lens.

'Your oompaloompa!' screamed Dawn, now so drunk she was rocking in her seat, her rolling eyes watering. Jack looked down at Pandora thinking Dawn was talking about his dog.

'The midget man!' roared Jean-Paul, taking encouragement from Dawn. He lifted the framed handprint up from under the table.

Jack stared at it.

'Who is it?' said Jean-Paul, spluttering. 'One of the Krankies or the Diddy Men?'

'Put it away,' said Elisha.

'I've heard of shrunken heads before but this takes the biscuit,' he said, slapping his leg.

'Here,' said Jack, flip-flopping around the table with his hand out.

'Not until you say,' said Jean-Paul. 'C'mon, what's the big deal?'

'*Big* deal!' Dawn howled, holding her sides. '*Big* deal!'

'Switch it off,' Jack said, glaring at the cameraman.

'We're only having a joke, Jack. We're being comedians!' said Dawn, trying to fit Jean-Paul's bowler over her large head.

'Well, who is it?' said Jean-Paul, handing the print over.

'My son.'

'Your son?' said Jean-Paul. 'But you said you didn't have children.'

'He was our only son, Hunter, but he died straight after birth. The nurses suggested a handprint to remind us of him.'

Dawn's clownish expression turned to shock as if slapped in the face with a kipper.

'Oh my God, mate,' said Jean-Paul.

'Are you okay, Jack?' asked Elisha, getting up from the table.

'I'm fine,' he said. 'I'll just pop this back in the study and then we can have dessert? Maybe filming can start again in a few minutes?'

The cameraman nodded.

Jack flip-flopped to the study, sat down in the chair and put Hunter's little handprint on the desk in front of him. Alice wouldn't have minded leaving it on the wall for the whole world to see on TV, but Jack felt it was too private. The handprint no longer made him cry. At first, yes, the sight of Hunter's tiny hand that had been too weak to curl around his outstretched finger had made him weep buckets. It reminded Jack of Hemingway's shortest ever story: "For sale: baby shoes, never worn". At first too, he cried at the memory of Hunter looking into his eyes and seeming to smile, moments before he stopped breathing. Of all the things, laughing gas. Laughing gas. Laughing gas. Months, then years passed, and now all Jack wanted to remember was what might have been a smile on his baby son's face.

The evening was ruined, he knew that. He'd have to muddle through and hope no one minded going through the motions. He returned to the dining room apologising for the change in atmosphere. Elisha hugged him. 'I'm fine,' he said 'it's you lot I'm worried about. This is a night for comedy. After dinner I'll perform a small piece from a tour of mine called *Mad Infinitum*. It's likely to bore you rigid so you'd better start enjoying yourselves right now.' He re-filled their wine glasses and tried to lift the mood with a few jokes and impressions including Loyd Grossman, saying, 'And who do you think lives in a house like this…?' The guests laughed, but he recognised pity in it.

He returned to the kitchen realising that the timer was no longer counting down and the soufflés had risen, sunk and were now crisping. Nonetheless, he rescued them with double cream and ice-cream. He also brought in the shop-bought chocolate cheesecake. Everyone made exaggerated noises of pleasure and satisfaction, overacting for the camera, or Jack's benefit.

Jack's routine had them laughing more naturally, he thought, though he knew from decades of experience that his guests weren't his true target audience or demographic. Despite this, Jack gave it his best shot, throwing in some more popular, recognisable impressions including Hugh Grant and Michael Caine. When he stopped after only fifteen minutes, the audience generously hooted for more and he obliged with a skit on Tony Blair, George Bush, Arnold Schwarzenegger and Clint Eastwood.

After coffee, the guests were filmed individually upstairs lying on one of the beds giving their comments and marks. The director fanned out £5,000 in cash under a silver-domed platter. Jack sneaked a peek at the hundred fifty pound notes.

Everyone was directed into the lounge with glasses of champagne. They chatted excitedly in anticipation of the final result, though Dawn looked the least confident. Jack was handed a scroll. He was asked to stand up and read out the results. He untied the scroll, saying in his best Bruce Forsyth voice: 'Good game, good game.' And everyone laughed. 'In last place is…' he looked around the faces one by one for dramatic effect, '…Dawn. So sorry my luv, so sorry.'

'I can't cook,' she said.

Jean-Paul patted her on the knee.

'And in third place…is…nice to see ya, to see ya nice…Jean-Paul.'

'Bugger,' he said. 'Was it my cat crapping on the carpet?'

Dawn kissed him on the cheek.

Jack opened the scroll further, too far this time, glimpsing who'd won. Elisha beamed up at him. He'd suspected from the very start it would be down to those two.

'In second place is…I'm so sorry my darling, I loved your black blancmange and fudgicles…in second place is…Elisha!'

She smiled nonchalantly and got out of her chair. Jean-Paul and Dawn cheered, getting to their feet. 'Well done,' they said, kissing him and shaking his hand. Jack threw the money into the air; something of a convention on the programme. Encouraged mainly by Dawn and Jean-Paul, he opened another bottle of champagne, removed his flippered feet and joined in an unplanned conga around the ground floor of Seagull House. Great shots for the end of the programme, which the director said would be screened September-ish.

Before catching their cars home, each guest gave a final piece to camera in the kitchen. The director and cameraman said their goodbyes on the doorstep. They confirmed that nothing regarding Jack's son would be broadcast.

Elisha was the last to leave and sat at the kitchen table with Jack while her driver finished his cigarette on the driveway. She said she was glad he'd won, that he was the most entertaining host, and his food was *just about okay.*

He laughed. 'I hope I was judged on the food. I'd never want to win anything out of pity.'

'Put it this way,' she said. 'Dawn can't cook, shouldn't cook. Jean-Paul can cook, can't host. I can cook, can host, but having the police shut down my gig blew it.'

'No comment,' he said, ears still ringing from the noise of that night.

'Whereas you pulled it off, Jack. Even dealing with something awful like that.'

'Things happen we can't control. You just have to suck it up.'

'You remember my tarot reading?' she said, 'when I wouldn't do a second reading for you the first night?'

'How could I fail to remember? You clearly picked up the skull and cross bones and didn't want to alarm me with news of my imminent death.'

'Exactly,' she said.

'You did?' he said, choking on his coffee.

'But it wasn't *your* death, I realise now. It was from the past, or the future past; coming here tonight and finding out about Hunter… you know…the cards are subtle like that.'

'They move in mysterious ways.'

'Give me your hand,' she said. He held it out. 'Lovely and warm.' She examined the palm. 'I'm making up for the Tarot.'

It was odd sitting in the kitchen dressed like a clown, his palm being read by a sexy Groucho Marx. She moved her fingers across his skin, tracing the lines and curves, and noticing fateful intersections. 'Now, Elisha, if you see sudden death again I'm gonna have to ask you to leave.'

She ignored him, dissecting the signs in his palm. When she was ready, she lifted her eyes. 'I see a dolphin,' she said, matter-of-factly.

'A dolphin?'

'A very sad dolphin…but he is free.'

'I don't know any dolphins, happy or sad in Whitstable,' said Jack, pulling his hand back. 'I think the sea air has gone to your head. Aren't you meant to make things up about the future? Tell stories?'

'I don't make things up,' she said.

Elisha gave the driver the thumb's up through the window and he switched his engine on. 'Before I go, can I ask why you agreed to be on this silly programme? You don't seem the kind of man to watch daytime TV.' When he didn't reply, she said, 'Because as far as I can make out, Dawn will be appearing in a new series of TOWIE, Jean-Paul is on some quiz thing on SKY, I'm releasing a new album in the autumn, so what are you promoting, a comeback tour, a book or something like that?'

He shook his head.

'You're giving the money to an MS centre…do you have MS? God, sorry, that's too personal. I thought maybe, you seemed very tired and unsteady..? I just wondered, but shouldn't have asked.'

'I did it because my agent thought it'd be good for my profile, but there's no tour. I did it for the MS centre. It helps so many people and they need a new building. To be frank, I could do with the money myself, but there you go.' The cab driver bibbed his horn. 'Your carriage awaits, Groucho,' he said, gesturing with a clownish bow.

Her eyes flashed at him. 'Shall we remain friends do you think?'

'Hey, you're the fortune teller. You tell me,' he said. Then he kissed Groucho Marx goodbye on both cheeks.

The Buddha of Tankerton

Trips to Jin-jing Li became three-weekly. The acupuncture treatments became shorter than discussions about meditation. One week, Jin-jing undertook no acupuncture at all, focusing instead on breathing techniques and posture. She taught Jack how to clear his mind of everyday thoughts and concentrate on his breathing, and what his body was doing. She said anyone could meditate anytime, anywhere. She suggested yoga classes, and knew a brilliant Alexander technique expert. Perhaps Pilates and "Mindfulness" classes would be useful too.

She asked how things were going with Buddha and he reported that things were still going slow. Jack had been giving Buddha gifts of fresh flowers almost every morning. In late May and early June it had been tamarisk flowers, sometimes complete with honey bees. He said that he sat in the arbour watching life happening, closing his eyes and listening to the warm buzz. He told her that one of the days he'd got very close to meditation. It was as if he was lifted out of himself. He said this was about the time Buddha communicated strange words of wisdom.

Jin-jing was fascinated. 'What Buddha say?'

'I opened my eyes too soon, and Buddha said, *yf thou doe knotte close them, howe will thee evere hath them open'd?*'

'Ain' that wonderful? Maybe he mean open third eye?'

'Having released him from his vow of silence for forty years, Buddha won't shut up. I sit in the arbour, close my eyes and focus on my breathing, clearing my mind, and he speaks. I ask him things in my mind and he talks, though it's just gobbledygook.'

'Like what?' said Jin-jing.

'Not long ago, Buddha said, *ytt ys easier to faken one's lyfe thanne to faken one's death.*'

'Wow.'

'Also, *respecting deathe ys knotte to bee confus'd with disrespecting lyfe.*'

'Morbid.'

'*Lyfe ys some tymes knotte meant to bee enjoi'd, onlie endur'd.*'

'This true,' she said.

'*In tyme of crisis brave men doe knotte aske questions, they doe answer them.*'

'True again.'

'*A familee tree doth split in two halfe waye through a lyfe.*'

'I heard that somewhere.'

'My family has been split in two half way through my life, Jin-jing.'

'What else he say, this Buddha of Tankerton?'

'Buddha says, *a wyse man knoweth his owne limitations; a wyser man fyndeth waies to overcomen them.*'

She nodded. 'I like this Buddha. What weird voice, though.'

Jack laughed. 'That's the peculiar thing. He speaks to me with this late sixteenth-century twang. It's hard to explain, but it's as if John Donne is speaking to me.'

She shook her head. 'John Donne is speaking to you through Buddha of Tankerton?'

'Somehow, Buddha's turned into a metaphysical poet. He says, *yn the kingdome of the minde the thirde eie ys kinge.*'

'Hmmm,' said Jin-jing, writing it down in her notepad.

'When I ask him a question, he comes back with another, like a riddle or a Zen koan. He doesn't like being asked questions, though. *Whatte use ys mie answer to a wronge question?* he says. *Doth thou beliefe thys to bee trowe because thou doth thynke ytt, or doth thou thynke ytt trowe because thou beliefe ytt? Change ys the onlie constante yn thys lyfe, whye would'st ytt bee any different after?* He got angry with me once and said, *whatte parte of happienesse doth thee knotte understande?'*

'He a bit like Mike,' she said, meaning Wasser, her business partner and now boyfriend.

'Buddha tosses these things out at me at random, like *ytt ys easier to picke holes yn a fabrick thanne yt ys to menden them. Prooving peeple wronge doth knotte meen youe hath prov'd youreselfe ryghte. Thou hath nevere reallie liv'd untill thou hath nearllie dyde. The trowe value of a personne's lyfe cannot bee measured bye howe muche theye hath lov'd, onlie bye howe muche theye hath beene lov'd.'*

'Isn' that T.S. Eliot…?'

'*The reede that swayeth yn the breeze doth knotte breake yn a gayle. Bettere to hath liv'd a longe lyfe and dyed after a shorte sicknesse than vice versa. Deathe doth love a loser.'*

'Ain' that song lyric?' said Jin-jing, putting her notepad down.

'I think Buddha's more out of control than me! *A hearte, lyke an egge, becomes nothinge yf ytt ys nevere broken.'*

'Beautiful,' she said, scribbling it down. 'Maybe you are hearing the real Buddha of Tankerton?'

'*Were thou wakinge from a dreame, or dreaminge of a wake?'*

'What wake he talkin' about?'

'I was a bit down this one day, Jin-jing, and I asked: How long do I have left? and he replied, *thou hath the reste of your lyfe, of course.'*

'Clever clog,' said Jin-jing.

'*Lyfe ys a storie nevere written. All you can doe ys playe your parte yn yt.'*

'Cod philosophy.'

'Codpiece philosophy more like. *The onlie man unafraide of dyinge ys already deade. Showe mee the man unafraide of deathe, and I schalle showe youe his grave.'*

'He so morbid your Buddha of Tankerton.'

'D'you think I'm transferring my neuroses onto a stone statue, Jin-jing?'

'What does it feel like to you? Is it come from you, or Buddha?'

'Does it sound like words of wisdom to you?'

She shrugged her shoulders. 'Good he feel he can talk, even if don't make sense?'

'True,' said Jack, 'but sometimes I feel like taking a sledgehammer to him.'

'No! Must not harm Buddha!'

'I think he's depressed because his soul is trapped. No one wants to come back as John Donne stuck in a stone. I mean, how long would you have to live in a stone…forever? I think he wants me to finish him off.'

'You very hyper today, Jack.'

'It's the relief of getting the MRI done and that second lumbar puncture. All I have to do now is wait for Rama to get back from his holiday. He's going to assess all of the results including the blood tests. Everything hinges on these.'

They embraced after Jack's final week of acupuncture and he noticed a bump in Jin-jing's tummy. She said she was three months' pregnant with Michael Wasser's child.

See You Next Tuesday

My father-in-law customises everything to suit his and his wife's many needs. That's admirable in my opinion. He has a lot of time on his hands and likes to tinker. Personally, if I had so much time in retirement I'd spend it in cafes, bookshops, galleries, pubs and restaurants or jaunts to the seaside, or trips abroad. But my father-in-law customises his slippers, his spectacles, and his wife's kitchen apron. He customises the switches on the cooker and the dishwasher.

He customises the indicators on the fridge. When he's finished customising the inside of a building, he customises the outside. His block of flats is shared by ten other residents who are vehemently opposed to any sort of change, but he starts building a ramp for his wife at the main entrance and a meeting is called by angry residents. Fists are thrown. Well, maybe not fists, but custard tarts and vol-aux-vents.

His car is rigged up out of old wires, train-sets and toilet rolls to detect hidden speed cameras on the roadside. 'I'm not spending hundreds of pounds,' he said, 'I'll build my own for a third of the price.' Amazing really, to think he has the knowledge to actually do that. You sit in his front passenger seat now and the dash is like the star ship Enterprise. A sort of Blue Peter version. Going anywhere in the car takes forever because he's got to engage all of the gadgets, alarms and flashbulbs before take-off. His wing mirrors have wing mirrors that have wing mirrors on, even though he doesn't tow a caravan. The volume on everything is switched to maximum because of his poor hearing. You're sitting next to him in the car ship Enterprise and you pass a speed camera. Five seconds later, the car is ringing and rocking with alarms, the lights are flashing, he has to pull over to the curb to regain control of the steering. And I say, 'What's the point of having speed camera detectors if they only notice one after you've passed it?' He didn't like me enquiring, just said it was working perfectly fine until I got into his car, like I brought a curse down upon him. He uses this accusation frequently whenever things he's built don't function according to his high standards, and I'm there to witness the failure. He deflects the failing onto me: 'It was all fine, Jack, until you walked into the room/showed your face/opened your mouth.' He's blameless you see. It's the way it's always been. He's the silverback, and no one blames the silverback. I'd never blame him; he's like the father I lost at the age of fourteen.

[*Mann About the House* Tour, 1998]

By the end of August, still waiting for the letter from Dr. Rama, Jack's fingers were chewed down to stumps and he'd grown a full beard, half of which was Captain Birdseye white. The barber called him the "Monochrome Mann". 'Men your age normally look distinguished with a beard,' he said, 'salt and pepper mixed, not split in half. Maybe you shave it off?' That's exactly what Alice wanted him to do. 'It makes you look sixty,' she said. Alice's father saw the beard and said: 'You can't trust a man in a beard; shows they're hiding something.' And Jack replied, 'Okay, so what was Jesus hiding?'

Although riddled with disabilities and diseases and forty years older, Jack's father-in-law was now fitter than Jack. How the tables had turned. Alice's dad was a mystery to modern medicine, and to the DVLA. Now in his mid-80s, Alan was still allowed to drive, even though he had four prangs a year. His peripheral vision had deteriorated so badly he couldn't see kerbs or soft verges, driving slowly on the central white lines and screaming at on-coming traffic to Pull Over! Get Over!

So what was Jack doing sitting beside Alan in the car ship enterprise this week, going to a mobility scooter shop of all places? It had been Alice's idea, to get Jack out of the house for a few hours, in the process helping her father choose a scooter for her now chronically disabled mother Pat.

As anticipated, Alan wanted a full range of choices and prices set in front of him before making a decision, and that meant driving back and forth to different mobility shops across half of Kent, and participating in excruciating conversations with shop owner after shop owner. Jack pointed out to his father-in-law that it would have been wiser to have taken Pat along to try out the scooters herself. Alan said it took half an hour getting her into his car and half an hour getting her out, and he wasn't going down that road today.

Instead, in each shop, Jack was the one sampling the scooters, sitting in shop windows wondering how the hell he ever got to this point in life. In truth, he'd recently wondered if he should invest in a scooter himself, to take Pan out on longer walks, but there was a part of him that denied Lyme and its disabling effects. Sitting in one shop window, aboard a trendy three-wheeler designed to look like a Harley Davidson, complete with chrome wing mirrors, Jack wished it could have been a real Harley and he'd crash through the window and ride off into the sunset, leaving everything and everyone behind.

'So, you like the least stable one do you?' Alan said with distinct disapproval. 'Four wheels surely? Pat couldn't fit her bottom on the seat, Jack. Let's go back to that first place again.'

It was en route to the first shop, driving at an optimum fuel-saving speed of 50 mph along a dual carriageway, when an unseemly incident occurred. As they were approaching a busy roundabout, an open-topped Mercedes flashed past at 70mph, the drum and bass of hard-core rap blaring in its slipstream. The three men were wearing baseball caps turned the wrong way around.

'Rap and baseball caps,' snapped Alan. 'That's the problem. Everything's imported. German or Japanese cars and American pop culture.' He tooted his horn to make the point and the driver gave him the bird. Alan didn't see it because of his poor eyesight and he was concentrating on the road.

'Alan, you've driven Fords all your life and they're American.'

'Yes, but they're made in Birmingham.'

'Those baseball caps are probably made in Birmingham.'

'No, they'll be manufactured in the Far East, in a sweat shop.'

The roundabout was chock full of traffic because of the summer holidays. This allowed time for Alan to pull up beside the Mercedes. All three men looked over at him and started to howl and hoot. Fortunately, Alan had all of the windows up to conserve air-conditioning, so was unaware of the mockery. But as they were waiting for a gap, Alan looked across, winding his window down. He shouted at the hoodlum in the passenger seat: 'I'm surprised you can concentrate on the road with all that racket!'

Jack sighed, hoping the crew hadn't heard it above the noise. As the traffic started moving and the Mercedes shot off with screeching tyres, the passenger shouted back: 'See you next Tuesday, old man!'

'What did he just say? Was that a threat?'

'What are you doing?' said Jack.

Alan was racing to sixty. 'I want his number plate. He threatened me. "See you next Tuesday" he said. You're my witness, Jack!'

The car jerked, confused by the sudden burst of speed and automatic gear changes. Alan increased to seventy, weaving in and out of traffic. His speed camera detectors kicked in, making alarm bells ring. Alan switched them off, leaned over the steering wheel and screwed up his eyes like Mr. Magoo, focusing on the car ahead.

'Slow down, Alan!'

'Can you see their reg?'

'It wasn't a threat.'

'What if they actually know where I live and turn up on my doorstep next Tuesday? How would you feel then?' Traffic was building and slowing again, and Alan got closer to the Mercedes.

'Alan, it was an insult, not a threat, and quite a polite insult in a way.'

'Damn right it was an insult; making threats to an older, wiser man, but they're not getting away with it. Mark my words!' The road narrowed into a single carriageway and Alan pulled up behind the Merc. 'You get the last half, I'll get the first,' he said, muttering letters and numbers. 'Even better, take a photo with your phone.'

'Alan, they weren't threatening a drive-by shooting; they were calling you a c, u, next Tuesday. Do I have to spell it out?'

'What?' He glanced over, disgust growing in his eyes.

As the soft-top started pulling away, Alan roared through his open window, 'SEE *YOU* NEXT TUESDAY, YOU MOTHERFUCKERS!

It demonstrated two things to Jack: 1. The world was full of surprises. 2. Under enough duress anyone could say or do things completely out of character.

Easy Rider

A few days before the letter came from Dr. Rama, Jack received an unexpected surprise. Alice led him blindfolded onto the driveway of Seagull House, and stood him next to the garage door. Pat and Alan were behind him almost unable to contain their excitement. As Alice pushed the up-and-over door, Jack heard a pleasurable groan come from his mother-in-law. Alice removed his blindfold, singing, 'Ta-da!'

Sitting next to the bubble-wrapped, gold-framed mirror was the Harley Davidson-inspired mobility scooter. Alice had tied a large red ribbon around it making a big bow at the front. At first, Jack remained rooted to the block paving. 'Oh my God,' he finally said, stepping closer.

'Easy Rider,' said Alan, beaming. 'After you sold your car we thought you needed a new set of wheels.'

'You can take it along the sea,' said Pat. 'Or go shopping. It comes with a basket.'

'She's fully charged and should give you a good eight hours or more. There's a two-year warranty.'

'Sit in it,' said Alice, removing the ribbon.

'Thanks so much,' said Jack. 'So, you were just having me on last week, looking for a scooter for Pat?'

'Oh no,' said Alan. 'We bought a four-wheeler for Pat, and this one for you.'

'Al got a deal on two,' said Pat, shuffling forward with her walking sticks.

'You didn't have to tell him that, Mum!'

'It's okay,' said Alan. 'I got a very good price on Easy Rider. A large reduction as it was ex-display; the one you sat on in the shop window.'

They watched Jack ride it out onto the driveway and do a few circles. 'Pretty nippy for a little scooter,' he said, not knowing what else to say. He looked up at Alice. 'How did you ever get it in the garage without me knowing?'

'When I took you to the cinema, Dad had the keys. It was partly my idea, and partly Dad's. It's just we noticed that you've been so tired, and after selling your car…well, it's easier than walking.'

Jack rode around in another tight circle.

'Why don't you take it for a spin along the seafront?' said Pat.

'I'll bring Pan,' said Alice.

'We'll be heading off now, love,' said her father. 'You enjoy your new toy.'

Along the seafront, Jack asked if Alice would like a go. He felt too self-conscious. They travelled a couple of miles all the way to Whitstable and back, taking turns. Pandora didn't like the sound of the electric motor, nor the fact she couldn't sit in the seat. When Jack gave it maximum throttle she charged alongside, barking.

After parking it in the garage at home, Jack gave Alice a kiss. 'It's not something I'd ever imagine buying for myself. It took me by surprise.'

'Are you sure you like it? Only you're a bit quiet.'

'What's not to like?' he said. 'It's black, my favourite colour. It's called Easy Rider. All I need is a bandana and some weed. Dennis Hopper eat your heart out.' The truth was, when he'd seen the ribboned scooter in the garage and realised it was his present, he'd wanted the earth to open up. The scooter was goodbye to able-bodiedness. He'd become one of the people he'd once felt sorry for, passing them on the seafront or the high street. One of the old people generally overlooked by the healthy, or made to feel invisible.

In a gesture of positivity after dinner, Jack said he wanted to sleep in the master bed; an opportunity to be closer to Alice. But once again at three in the morning, having had no sleep, his hands and feet on fire, and riddled with anxieties about pending results, he slid out of bed and tiptoed downstairs to the kitchen with Pan. He ran his hands under the cold tap for a few minutes and retired to the study, hands inside wine coolers. He looked up at Hunter's tiny ink handprint framed on the wall, and saw Hunter's first and last smile in his mind. All of a sudden he hated hands; Hunter's, his own, everyone's. He wanted to chop off his hands. He wanted to take the largest, sharpest knife from the kitchen and cut his hands off. But if he cut one hand off, what would he possibly use to cut the other one off with? Would he bite it off? No, what he really needed was a guillotine. Chop off his head and be done with it.

Death Knells and Dolphins

Dr. Rama's letter arrived during the middle of a dramatic thunderstorm. The intermittent rumbling continued throughout the morning into the early afternoon, so deep and resonant that with each drumroll the schoolchildren of the local primary school could be heard screaming in the playground. Oddly, there was no lightning to accompany the thunderclaps. After weeks of wall-to-wall sunshine, bubbling clouds and stultifying humidity, the heavens finally opened.

The letter was damp from the postman's bag. Jack tore it open before leaving the hall and read two short paragraphs with shock. Rama's letter was not addressed directly to him but to the microbiologist Dr. Cleaver, and his GP. Jack had only been copied in.

Resigned to his fate, he took the letter into the living room, sat down on the sofa and re-read the shattering details. The MRI showed little change, except perhaps for unexpected "healing" of the brain lesion adjacent to the right lateral ventricle. That was good news, wasn't it? Bad news: the lumbar puncture continued to show **inflammation** and **oligoclonal banding**. Other bad news: unfortunately, the spinal fluid sample was not tested for antibodies to Lyme as originally planned, but given the Porton Down screening test and more specific immunoblots from the Rare and Imported Pathogens

Laboratory in Salisbury were **negative for Lyme**, spinal screening was deemed unnecessary.

In view of these results, Dr. Rama wrote, *and the fact that there is no serological evidence of Borrelia burgdorferi infection (Lyme), I am now signing this patient off from my care. There will be no further investigations unless new symptoms develop. Thank you for your support and assistance Dr. Cleaver.*

Dr. Rama
MD, FRCP,DM, FEBN

Jack looked closely at the results, comparing them with those from America and Germany. Some of the Lyme antibodies Jack had tested positive for in America hadn't been assessed in the test kits used by the Porton Down lab. But this looked like the final word. It was the end of the road; over a year pursuing truth and treatment only to be abandoned again; betrayed even. Jack was right back at the beginning, only this time he knew it was the beginning of the end.

The first decision he made was not to tell Alice. She'd only want to complain about discrepancies in blood testing. She'd want to know why the decision to treat still seemed to be up to a microbiologist who'd never seen Jack in person and knew nothing about his clinical signs and symptoms; a consultant whose mind had been made up before the Porton Down tests were commissioned. A positive Porton Down result would have contradicted his own results. It would add up to a conspiracy in Alice's mind. She'd want to know why antibodies to Lyme were not searched for in Jack's spinal fluid. They'd been commissioned by Dr. Rama after all. Did someone put a last-minute stop to the test or was it once again an oversight on the part of a broken system? It would be a never-ending cycle of complaints and questions, and *never ending* was the last thing on Jack's mind. It was time to alight from the sickening merry-go-round.

The decision was not one, but a series of considered thoughts and actions taken over the course of a week. First, he made lists for and against suicide. He decided that if there were twice as many reasons to end his life than to continue it, he'd follow through. Even in childhood, Jack had been a compulsive list-maker. Before going on holidays he'd list all of the things he'd spend his money on: slot-machines, ice-creams, crisps, roller-coaster rides etc. Planning for a holiday was better than the holiday itself; pleasure captured in anticipation and expectation as much as in the actual reality.

Today was a day of different lists. A list of all the things he'd be throwing away and all the things he'd gain by doing so. It turned out to be a struggle of *Hamlet* proportions. To be or not to be. Jack reasoned, what greater philosophical question in life is there than whether or not to kill oneself? And the battle turned into a resounding victory for acting out his death-wish, not just because it would end his suffering; it would also end Alice's.

Once decided, he made a list of all the people he'd like invited to his funeral. He threw that in the bin. What did it matter? He made a list of the music he'd like played at his funeral. Was there room for "Love is All You Need", "The Fool on the Hill", Suede's "Still Life" and, as the red velvet curtain folded around the coffin, Max Richter's "The Consolations of Philosophy"? Or should it be Waits's "I'm Still Here"?

He realised whilst drawing up these lists, that this was what lists did; they made the future real. Lists were shorthand wish-fulfilment. These final lists were meant to dissuade him from a possible course of action, but instead they realised the truth of it. It was no longer 'now or never' but 'now and forever'. His lists created order out of chaos, like commandments. Lists did that, they stamped order on things. Lists focused the mind on what was required. Whether tablets of stone or on the back of an envelope, commandments or shopping lists, a list was a coda to live by and a basket of consumables. Lists were dreams made concrete. They might be things to aspire to before one dies (a "bucket" list). Jack realised all of the things it was too late for him to achieve: to own the vintage deep blue Maserati he'd seen parked on the forecourt of a local showroom; a boat, dry-docked at Tankerton sailing club; a beach hut, kayak, apartment in San Francisco, villa on a remote Greek island, heated swimming pool, Jacuzzi…all the things he'd never enjoy or experience on a list that Jack now called his "fuck it" list.

Jack researched the best ways to kill oneself, although this would obviously come down to personal preference. Many men opted for the rope, like David Foster Wallace. A few women fancied the blade, but Jack preferred the idea of gently slipping off to sleep like a hamster going into hibernation. He had amitriptyline in the house, but nowhere near enough to be sure of death. His father-in-law, though, had a stash in his hallway cupboard large enough to kill a herd of buffalo.

Whilst online, Jack came across sad stories and headlines, statistics and academic papers. He discovered that each year across the world a million people killed themselves. Between ten and twenty million people tried to. In the UK, there were 6,000 suicides a year. It was the biggest killer of men up to the age of 49, and men accounted for three-quarters of all suicides. "Under extreme pressure", he read, "women talk, and men walk." Male suicide was highest among those aged between 40 and 59. Most were clustered between 40 and 54, just like Jack. He'd die an average statistic, then. He read that he was a "remaindered man", a man inhabiting "a place of neutered uselessness". He was part of a "sandwich generation", a man caught between "the baby-boomers and Generation Y". These men were lost souls. 13 men killed themselves each day of the year; unlucky numbers for poor lost souls.

Jack went to his Zen garden and sat in the arbour closing his eyes, meditating, ruminating on disconnectedness. His breathing calmed, his body relaxed and he spoke to Buddha: 'Everything seems connected, except me. No family to talk to, no friends either, really.'

Buddha said, *looke closelie and youe schalle see, that youe are the onlie reason every thynge ys connect'd.*

Jack wasn't sure who or what Buddha was anymore. He'd hauled the stone monolith from place to place like a ball and chain to the past, to a lost childhood, to a lost father, to a lost child. And Jack asked him: 'What was it in life that made a hermit of my heart? How is it I know nobody, yet nobody knows me? I will die a complete mystery to anyone who thought they knew me, just like Uncle Dicky said.'

Buddha replied: *a mirrore doth knotte telle youe whoe youe are, onlie whoe thee myghte bee.*

'What the hell does that mean? Stop talking in riddles. This is not a case of losing the will to live, it's simply finding a way to die.'

And Buddha said, *deathe ys soe long-lived. The present ys a gifte thatte keepes on giving.*

Jack's confusion turned to rage: 'I'll ask one final question, Buddha! Before I smash *thee* to fucking pieces with a club hammer! You encourage living in the moment, to enjoy the experience of now, this present, but what if the present is one of suffering? If you say one more time that life is to be endured and not enjoyed, I'll smash *thee* and leave *thee* to the snails as a rockery.'

Buddha declined to answer.

It took only a few minutes to retrieve the club hammer from the garage. Jack's father-in-law had tidied everything up in boxes the day he left the mobility scooter. Jack locked Pandora in the house and marched off to the Zen garden. He crunched across the shingle and stood in front of Buddha, tears pricking his eyes. He raised the hammer high, saying goodbye, crashing it down on the outstretched hand; the hand meant to protect. The blow landed hard on Buddha's wrist, cracking the hand clean off, landing on the gravel. 'What do you say to that, Buddha?' He glared at Buddha's serene smile. 'So on your head be it.' Jack raised the hammer again, his hand shaking and shooting with pain from the first clean contact. He held the hammer there, hand hovering above his head just below the branches of the tamarisk. As he was about to crash it down onto the carved hair, the robin flew from a thick stem to the Buddha's head. It twitched and chirped. 'You'd better fly or be mashed,' said Jack, but the robin was unmoved; an angel protecting the protecting Buddha.

Jack lowered his arm, dropping the hammer onto the shingle. Still the robin would not move. Jack knelt down before the Buddha, moved his fingers to the bird, only inches away, and it flew back to the tamarisk. Jack looked at the lonely stone hand on the pebbles, its palm up, fingers closing around thin air as if making a blessing or benediction, or so it seemed. Jack felt a pang of guilt, but what was done could not be undone, John Donne. He picked up the severed hand. It was heavier than expected. Disconnectedness, he thought. He aligned it with the wrist. A clean break that could be fixed, reattached with cement. What did it matter now? What did Jack care? What protection had the Buddha ever provided for him, or for himself come to think of it? Jack laid the hand in Buddha's lap and went in search of a flower. He plucked a young, perfumed rose from his favourite climber. He returned to the Zen garden and placed the rose in the broken hand on Buddha's lap. He picked up the hammer and returned it to its box. His hand ached at the wrist, and spasms of pain shot right to the elbow.

His hand still hurt the day he stole the drugs from his father-in-law's cupboard. He said he needed to use the loo and disappeared into the hallway, leaving Alice and her parents to tea, custard creams and conversation. Alan was a meticulous man; order in all things, especially pharmaceuticals. The left side of his adapted walk-in closet was dedicated to Pat's prescriptions and over-the-counter medicines. Alan's were stacked on the right side, alphabetised. Amitriptyline was close at hand. Alan had packets of unopened prescriptions. Jack stole a dozen or more, and secreted them inside the pockets of his jacket and jeans. He went to the bathroom and flushed the loo in pretense, returning to tea in the lounge. His cup rattled in his saucer, but no one appeared to notice.

Three days before his plan was executed, Alice told Jack she thought it might be good news they hadn't heard back from Dr. Rama. The long delay could be a good sign, she said. They might be debating the best treatment for him. He agreed, unwilling to tell her there'd be no treatment. Soon, there'd be no Jack to treat.

He made sure the last few days were as sweet as possible for Alice. Despite fatigue and burning agony, he took her out for dinner at a seaside restaurant. Despite everything that had happened, maybe even *because* of everything that had happened, he said he loved her more than the Earth itself. They stared into each other's eyes like the two lovers had done the first time they'd met in San Francisco. He asked her what she saw in his eyes, and she said it was difficult as his pupils were too expanded, but she thought she saw the future. And what did he see in hers? He said he saw only her, only Alice.

That same night, for the first time in many months, he tried to sleep in the same bed as his wife. They talked most of the night, lying in each other's arms. As dawn approached, Alice finally drifted off to sleep, and he crept downstairs in search of the wine coolers. If anything, the pain was increasing, confirming with each passing minute that he was doing the right thing.

As if he needed more encouragement, the next evening he was sitting in the study flicking aimlessly through TV channels and caught sight of a dolphin in a documentary. Jack thought of Elisha and what she'd read from his palm; a sad dolphin, but it was free. The story unfolded: Jason, a baby dolphin, was rescued from the Pacific Ocean after his mother was killed by a fisherman. At the training facility, a scientist taught Jason human language. The scientist swam daily with him in a number of different pools, feeding him, playing with him, bonding with him; laying down trust. As he grew into a juvenile Jason thought the scientist was his mother. Through a series of recordings there was audible proof Jason could count, squeaking: *One, two, three, four, five*. He could repeat some of the alphabet as spoken by the scientist, and he was an excellent impressionist. After a few months, phonetically-sounded letters became words. Soon, Jason could say "Mommy" and "Jason", usually for a fish or a game. Then he could say "Love". And then, spontaneously, after a game, but no fish at all, Jason said: "Jason Love Mommy, Jason Love Mommy". And that's when the story turned ugly.

Word leaked to the military. They said Jason had been taken illegally from the sea and started legal proceedings to have him removed. Despite resistance and numerous appeals backed by famous celebrities, Jason had to go. The morning before strange men took him away, the scientist swam with Jason one last time and tried to explain. She held him and stroked him. She said she loved him and reassured him that everything would be okay. The men came in the afternoon with a tank not much bigger than the dolphin. It looked, Jack thought, like a coffin. As Jason was lifted from the pool into the water-filled tank, he was heard saying *One, two, three, four five*. And then, just before they replaced the lid, thinking it was a game, he giggled: *Jason Love Mommy*.

Ordinarily, it would have made Jack catch his breath, heave his diaphragm. He'd have failed to hold back his Mann-flood. But in the study, the night before he planned to take his own life, he felt nothing but emptiness. His well had run dry. The story concluded; months later, one morning at the army facility, Jason was found dead at the bottom of a tank of water. A man said Jason had simply taken the decision not to swim to the surface anymore, allowing water to fill his blowhole and lungs. Jack felt nothing but conviction. The day before Jack did it, he bought Alice two gifts: an artist-made seagull, and a necklace; hanging from its chain, a perfect silver dolphin.

For Whom the Bell Tolls

Alice was up early and dressed for work. She had back-to-back meetings and wouldn't be home until six or seven, all of which suited Jack's plans. He'd have all the time in the world to shower, take Pan on a final walk along the seafront, recover from the exertion, and then write his last letter to Alice. He would lock up Seagull House one last time, and go out again to the Slopes, pockets full of pills.

Alice hadn't wanted to wake him, standing outside the guest room door, whispering bye. He didn't want it to end behind closed doors, and groaned in acknowledgement. She went in and sat on the edge of his bed. She patted his leg. 'Maybe today we'll hear. I just have this feeling something will happen.' She was talking about the overdue letter from Dr. Rama that had arrived a week before and was nestled in a box-file in the study named "Jack in a Box". The box that had the smell of a freshly dug grave. 'It's much colder today,' said Alice. 'We've gone straight into autumn.'

As she was getting up to leave she leaned in and kissed him on the cheek. She made to go and he grabbed her hand, holding her there in front of him, her face inches from his. He wanted to savour her image, take it with him, store its details in his memory: large, kind eyes and naturally inquisitive expression, lips slightly parted, hair wild and falling like a curtain onto his cheek. 'One more kiss,' he said. Her breath was minty and sweet, her perfume floral, lingering in his room long after she was gone.

He wrote a final letter. Completing it used up every crumb of cognitive power and concentration, not to mention emotional control. He didn't want to be like the many others who departed this Earth without an explanation, leaving loved ones wondering for eternity.

Dear Alice,

You'll know already how much the past year has been an unimaginable hell, beginning at Glyndebourne when the nightmare first took hold. We came so far, got so close to a cure, but ours was a pointless journey through a maze of walls, barbed wire and trap doors of a broken system, only to end up where we started. Thank you for nearly saving my life, chickpea, but I can no longer endure the pain, torment and uncertainty. Forgive me for what I'm about to do, but nothing destroys the human spirit faster than pain, except the knowledge it is never-ending.

A letter came from Dr. Rama a week ago. Sorry I didn't tell you. It's at the top of a file marked "Jack-in-a-Box". It contains every document relating to my illness and is now the weight of an albatross. Dr. Rama has abandoned me. I have gone from "this charming right-handed professional comedian" to "this patient". He copied me in to a memo addressed to his esteemed colleague Dr. Cleaver whom he thanks profusely. Between them, Cleaver and Rama have drawn a line under their diagnosis, and driven a nail through the lid of my coffin. When you're trapped inside chronic illness, abandoned by those who have the power to set you free, desperation strangles hope, and living without hope is like sailing a sea with no shore.

My decision hasn't been taken lightly. I decided that if Dr. Rama's response was another cul-de-sac it'd be my dead-end, and after the letter came I planned my escape. I raided your parents' cupboard and stole a heap of your dad's amitriptyline. There should be enough to send me to sleep. Please don't blame them. Alan and Pat will give you support, as too will Gerry. A lovelier friend one could never find in life. No one I've loved or cared about should blame themselves (God knows, I wasn't the perfect husband, son, brother or nephew. No man is perfect). If you must blame something or someone, place it at the door of a broken system. Show my file to the coroner. Coroners investigate suicides and pathologists perform post-mortems. Instruct them to look closely in my brain and heart for Lyme disease. Ask our GP or Dr. Rama, or that other neurologist Mr. Swan to attend the post-mortem. Though dead, it might still give me quiet satisfaction knowing they are there to bear witness. In any case, a post-mortem is in the public interest and may help others who suffer the same plight as me. May their gods bless and help them. Because going through the processes of early, mid and late-stage Lyme, praying for salvation, hoping for a cure, was like straddling two escalators moving in opposite directions. One an ascending, slow, juddering Jacob's Ladder; the other, a rapid descent into Dante's Inferno.

Alice, please don't view this as cowardice. It's my only way out, and I'm not afraid to leave. Death is life's natural way of saying goodbye, no matter how unnatural it seems. It feels peculiar, though, to die younger than my Dad who also took his life. Who knows, maybe his name, my name, our name "Jack Mann" was cursed; not so much a mid-life crisis as a mid-life catastrophe!

That's not to say I haven't felt blessed to have spent a quarter of a century with you. My life with you has been extraordinary and I take solace in the memory of it. If and when things get black, remember the

318

first time I made you laugh. I carry that smile in my heart to this day. Remember our chance meeting in San Francisco and going to the comedy club in Nob Hill, not telling you I was on the bill. And all those wonderful martinis we downed at the Top of the Mark with the spread of the glittering city all around us. And the love we made at my brother's house. That was the beginning of a twenty-five year love affair; a quarter of a century of loving and being loved by you.

Invite anyone you like to my funeral. Do what you want with my body and anything else I materially owned. You were everything, now everything is yours. You might like to invite Jin-jing Li. Acupuncture did nothing for my neuropathy but I enjoyed talking to her. For someone so young she is very wise. It must be Buddhism. She believes in reincarnation, of sorts, and I have a feeling she might be right. I have this fluttering sensation in my stomach as if a bird will fly out of it. Remember when we did that charity parachute jump and our buddies readied us by the hatch, and our stomachs were in knots? We were too afraid to let go of one another's hands, but jump we did and flew like eagles. The feeling was wild and weightless. If I do have a soul, it might flee this body and become someone, some thing, somewhere else and this might not be a tragic end, only a beautiful beginning.

When something's so badly broken it cannot be fixed, there's nothing to do but move on. In my case, to another world. Truth is, I'm not sure who Jack Mann is anymore. It's like I'm living in his shadow. Lyme disease invaded his body, ransacked his mind and stole his identity, but it shall not have his soul.

Before saying goodbye, I ask one more thing of you, Alice. That is to try and live by the mantra "Be Kind or Be Nothing at All". It was something Graham the gardener said last spring when I asked him to cut the branches of the tamarisk in the Zen garden. He refused on the grounds the tree hadn't flowered. Every tree should flower, he said. Bees need flowers. Be kind or be nothing at all. It resonated inside me like a tuning fork for months. It's so simple yet so profound, and probably the hardest thing to carry out in life. I once joked on stage that the word "humankind" was an oxymoron. Remember? Back when I was too cynical. In reality, if a human cannot be kind he cannot be much of a human. The mantra must first be applied to yourself, Alice. You must allow yourself to flower again. The last year has been unkind to you too. I know what you're like for self-punishment. Be kind to yourself. If you want to leave Seagull House and move back to London, you must, you should. If you want to stay by the sea, all well and good, but don't let me or the memory of me affect your future. The same is true of love. Obviously, it will be impossible to love someone the way you loved me (!) but loving another isn't outside the realms of possibility. He may not make you laugh the way I did, or call you "chickpea", or know that tickling place you hide so well, or hold you the way you love to be held. But there are other routes to comedy, different ways to love, alternative nicknames to be called, and he may hold you in a way that isn't unpleasant. What I'm saying is, loving another doesn't mean you didn't love me.

Okay, my time has come. I'm sorry, Alice. I must go. This bird must fly.

All my love as always, forever.

Jack

PS They will find my body on the Slopes, on a bench facing the sea and the setting sun.

After he'd written it, he lay down, exhausted. He took the model seagull with him to the master bedroom and set it on Alice's bedside table. He placed the new dolphin necklace wrapped in a pretty box beside the gull and his letter.

The time eventually came to say goodbye to Pandora in the hall. When he reached for his coat she thought he was taking her out again and threw herself against the front door, whimpering. In a different frame of mind Jack might have thought she was trying to stop him.

He decided to take Easy Rider. His legs were wobbly, his vertigo was horrendous, and the bench he wanted to die on was at least a mile from Seagull House. He'd scooter his way up to the high street to what he jokingly referred to as the "nearest and dearest"; an excellent, but pricey wine merchant. He'd buy a chilled bottle of champagne to help wash down the pills.

He opened the garage and sat on the scooter catching his reflection in his mother's large, gold mirror. The bubble wrap had been removed. The frame was half-painted off-white, and a paint pot was sitting on the floor with an unwashed, stiffened brush balanced on the lid. Alice had never been a completer-finisher. Jack was. He stared at his reflection in the mirror. Who was that tired old man staring back at him from that mobility scooter? Not the old stand-up, Jack Mann, surely? Scruffy beard, bug sunglasses, dark woollen coat and Chelsea boots. He remembered what Buddha said about a man in the mirror not being who he was, only who he might be. He cracked a smile and pulled his best Robert De Niro face, summoning the voice and words: 'Are you lookin' at me?' Then, the famous line from Scorsese's *King of Comedy*: 'Better to be King for a night than Schmuck for a lifetime!'

The scooter wasn't fully charged, but there was enough juice to get him one way. He rode out onto the driveway and closed the garage door. A neighbour walked across the road. Ron was a bit of an eccentric. Long since retired as a pilot, he'd become a collector of American memorabilia and drove a classic 1970s American cop car around the neighbourhood. For some reason he also had a 1930s American water hydrant planted in the centre of his lawn. He pointed up at the roof of Seagull House saying two gulls were nesting. 'They're lodged in the nook of your chimney,' he said. Jack was well aware of the gulls. From his bed he'd often heard them scrambling around, taking off and thudding as they landed early in the morning. 'I can see them from my upstairs window,' Ron said. 'There's an egg, which is weird in mid-September. They normally hatch in summer and are fledged by now.'

Jack looked up at his chimney and saw one of the gulls on the nest. He didn't mind birds using his roof, but some people detested gulls, seeing them as vermin. Ron was one of those people, which Jack always thought mystifying for a pilot. Surely his neighbour could appreciate the amazing flying ability of these birds? Ron was always saying the same thing about gulls. Don't feed them or you'll be inundated with the critters. The acid in their poo will burn clean through the paintwork on your car. They carry diseases. 'Once they've paired up,' he said, 'they mate for life and you'll never be rid of them. I've got a gun and can shoot them if you want.'

'The gulls have been around for much longer than us,' Jack replied stonily.

'I don't know about that,' said Ron, 'and I've lived here for nearly twenty years.'

'I have to go,' said Jack, signalling departure with a twist of the throttle.

The scooter made a high-pitched whine as it bobbled along the high street. Jack rode on the pavement past the shops, rekindling thoughts of bus journeys to acupuncture, and how the premises seemed connected, spanning a whole life. As he was passing "Tankertunes", one of a once dying breed of second-hand record shops now being re-born, Jack noticed a new sleeve in the window display that had replaced David Bowie's *Ziggy Stardust*. The twelve-inch single cover looked like a childish representation of chaos or an apocalypse; people, animals and houses uprooted by a hurricane, flying in the sky like confetti. Talking Heads' "Road to Nowhere".

His mobile rang out. 'Where are you?' asked Alice. 'I called the house six times and no answer.'

'I'm giving the scooter a proper test-drive on the seafront.'

'I was worried, Jack.' Something was the matter with him. Although it was nice to be taken out to dinner and told over a candlelit meal how much you are loved, there'd been an odd finality to his conversation. And when he'd looked into her eyes and said he'd seen only her. And when she'd looked into his swollen black pupils, she'd seen the future. 'Have you eaten?'

'I'm about to buy fish and chips.'

'I'm jealous,' she said. 'I had a tuna sandwich from the canteen. Okay, I have to go to a meeting now. Don't stay out too long, Jack. It's cold.'

'It's not too bad,' he said, coat tails flapping in a strong easterly. 'Love you, Alice.'

There he goes again, she thought. *Love you,* when his normal sign-off was *see ya later.* He hung up suddenly before she had time to say she loved him back. She would have called again but was already late for a meeting with her chief executive.

Jack travelled the length of the high street and parked up outside the wine shop. He asked for chilled champagne, two bottles; the best they could muster. The owner was delighted, lifting his most expensive bottles from the chiller. He rolled them in noisy wrapping paper and put them in a brown carrier bag. 'Having a celebration?' he said, taking Jack's card. 'Someone's birthday?'

'Quite the opposite,' said Jack. 'Have you got any Marlboro red top?' Reds being his father's preferred choice.

'Red top?' The owner slid a screen across revealing the many brands that, to the untrained eye, looked identical. He picked out a packet of cigarettes. 'By law, they're no longer red,' he said. 'But this one showing a woman coughing bright red blood into a brilliant white handkerchief is probably what you're looking for.'

'And some Swan Vestas?'

From the wine shop, Jack hobbled into the Berry family funeral directors. He tried booking his funeral but it turned out to be harder than expected. 'When did your loved one pass away?' a young woman asked from behind a counter.

'Well, he hasn't exactly died yet,' said Jack.

'I see. But it's good to plan ahead, isn't it?'

'Yes, normally it is. But it's my funeral.'

'I'm so sorry.' She wouldn't have said it was uncommon for people to come in off the street and make their own funeral arrangements. In fact, only a few months ago there was an elderly lady with a pet dog who came in. But like that lady, those customers tended to be older than this gentleman. She always thought it sad anyone had to do this for themselves. It was like asking a man to dig his own grave.

'I'd like the black horses and carriage, exactly like the ones in your window display, only a lot bigger than model size.'

'Of course,' she said, laughing awkwardly. 'The horses are so beautiful with their black plumes. They create a splendid scene on the day.'

'I see them pulling me all along Tankerton seafront, like Churchill-on-Sea.'

'I'm sorry, this seems rude, but when are you likely to be dead...I mean desiring the horses and carriage?' When he hesitated, she said, 'You know, a kind of ballpark, because they get booked up more often than you'd think.'

'That's difficult,' he said, scratching his head. 'There's going to be a post-mortem, and that won't be straightforward.'

She looked puzzled. 'Okay, the best thing to do is give me your details. And who will be dealing with the process after you've...after you are...after...'

'My wife Alice.' He wrote the details down.

'Here's a brochure of all the services we provide, and the rates. We have a website, so if you or your wife want to look at that, and then when you're ready to go we can get the ball rolling.'

Jack thought about fish, but stuck with a small portion of chips. Food of any sort would slow down the effects of the alcohol and drugs, but it was approaching half past three and his growling stomach had different ideas. Champagne, cigarettes and chips; not what the doctor ordered.

He trundled across the road, past a tennis court, across another road and onto the Slopes. He rode along the grass to his final destination, parking up beside the bench dedicated to the memory of a sea captain. Jack got out of his faux Harley and sat down in the middle of the bench. He popped a cork, realising he'd forgotten to bring a glass. He'd have to swig the frothing champagne straight from the neck like a high-class wino. He opened the packet of steaming chips and picked out a couple. All the salt was at the top of the bag and all the vinegar was at the bottom, but they were the most delicious chips in the world. This was exactly what he'd bought the day Alice moved into his flat in

Fulham, and it was what they had when they moved down to the rented Bunker, and it was what they had the day they moved in to Seagull House too. But somehow, those chips never tasted quite as good as these.

The sea wasn't too choppy. What waves there were moved from right to left cresting diagonally to shore, and brushing against the wooden groins. Three rows of colourful beach huts stood their ground in the gentle bluster like sentries. The Slopes were bereft of people. The wind had put them off. Seagulls rode the blustery thermals, weaving in solitary circles above his head. Noisy terns ran across the grassy bank easing into the air and taking turns on the tops of street lamps.

Half way through his chips, Jack felt full. He tossed a few to the terns and large gulls swooped down making squawks, screes and gracks. He thought of the little gull he'd bought Alice and the one she'd bought him, now sitting together on her bedside table, and how pathetic they were in comparison to the magnificence of the real things. How clean and white their chests. How bold their yolky beaks with red dot. He wondered about the egg on the roof of Seagull House and was struck by the simple sadness that he'd never see that hatchling hatch and fledgling fledge.

He took out the packet of cigarettes and tried to light one with a match. The wind blew it out, so he tried again, and the wind blew it out. Ten matches later he took a deep drag, choking and spluttering. He took a few more drags realising he liked the bittersweet taste and effect of clouds rolling around his mouth. He could get used to tobacco again, just like that. But what did compulsions and addictions matter now, a few smokes on an autumn afternoon at the dying embers...at the fag end of a day in the life?

A young boy walked along the beach below. He was the age Hunter should've been. Jack watched him pick up stones and skim them across the smooth shallows. It seemed in that moment that each stone represented a life, or life in motion; the way the stones skipped and danced, finally disappearing under the surface, leaving only circles within circles. How important those leaps and landings were, those ups and downs, those brief kisses between pebble and water. They were the defining moments in a life, weren't they? The turning points that determined direction and longevity. Some lives had the worst of all trajectories; one short arc and *plonk*. Not much between start and end, just like Hunter's. His infant face loomed large in Jack's mind, his death never more than a stone's throw away from memory. Dear little Hunter, dear son. Laughing gas. Laughing gas. Laughing gas. The boy down on the beach was perfecting the ancient art of skimming now. His stones tap-danced at length across the water, leaping and landing in countless kisses; longer, more eventful lives, perhaps. Though in the end, in time, all stones must sink to the sandy sea bed.

From his coat pocket Jack took out the first amitriptyline packet; twenty-eight 10mg pills. He popped them out of their foil two at a time and washed them down with wine. He'd need to swallow hundreds at this rate, and decided to pop all of the pills into his pocket and grab handfuls. Some were 10mg, others 20s and others 50s. They got mixed up like Smarties in his pocket, and in his stomach. He had to make sure he'd swallow enough. Research online had raised questions over the wisdom of overdosing on these tricyclics. Not enough and you could throw up and have seizures. Too many, but still not enough, you could go into a coma for days, losing most of your memory and you'd still be here with all your problems. When was enough enough? Two thousand or three thousand milligrams? He'd just have to swallow the lot.

Onto the second bottle of champagne and a gram of antidepressant down, he started to feel effects. The sea was coming in and going out of focus creating a soft seasickness. An uncomfortable pressure had developed in his stomach, in and around his sternum; not bloat, more like a finger prodding and poking from the inside. The sky, once a glorious and uniform pink, was swirls of technicoloured Constable clouds. A bird flew across them the size of a pterodactyl, or was it a plane? A sea fret was developing. The lone boy who'd once skimmed stones across the skin of the sea now charged through the shallows lost to an enveloping mist; a cold, cold fog. Jack's pocket no longer bulged with meds, only half full, and he grabbed another big handful and threw them into his mouth. He took another swig of champagne and tipped his head back, swallowing. He thought about his two previous suicide attempts; at the turn of the millennium in London, and more recently at the Bunker just before Christmas. 'Third time lucky,' he burped, 'touch wood.' He tapped the slats of the bench, remembering how he'd tapped his father's oak desk all those years ago in the Fulham maisonette during an interview with the *Observer*, just weeks before Alice gave birth to little Hunter. Third time lucky for her had not proved to be so. He held his hands aloft realising that the pain was draining from them like blood, and he smiled, saying, 'Finally.'

Alice had called the home number twice without reply. She'd called his mobile too, leaving a message: *Break in meeting. You okay? Are you out with Pan? Are you in garden office? Are you asleep? xxx*

Tired, sleepy on his bunk bench, limbs of lead and head of feathers, Jack sensed gulls marching around him. One flew up to the chip packet and pulled it towards the ground. Jack tried to catch it before it fell, but his reactions were comical. It was pandemonium. Turning his head from left to right took an age, jerking in stop-motion. Seagulls all over the place, in the air swooping, on the bench scrabbling over his legs. Chips. Jack shooed the gulls off with flailing arms. His arms moved in slow-motion, juddering to a halt. They appeared as if they'd divided and doubled into two pairs like the arms of Da Vinci's "Vitruvian Man" trapped in a perfect circle. *Vitruvian Mann*, he thought, nearly falling from his bench.

Alice's meeting was coming to a close when an accountant raised another question on budgets. She was getting desperate. Something was wrong. She felt it in her bones and in her stomach. She kept her phone on her lap under the table waiting for it to vibrate with Jack's message. It did vibrate and she glanced down; her father wondered if she was popping in after work.

The sea fret rolled inland, creeping up the bank, cold and getting colder. Jack pulled the collar of his coat up but couldn't stop shaking, as if his spine had turned into a shard of ice. He took another gulp of pills and wine, throwing his head back, swallowing. When was enough, enough? Objects were spinning in his view. The world was turning. Although he could still see Essex across the Thames estuary, he was sitting at the edge of the universe peeking through a veil. He looked down at the shore in awe of the shifting shape of shingle, thinking: *how strange it is, that change never changes*. He lay as flat as possible on the bench, knees slightly raised to fit his feet in. He was losing the feeling in them.

A foghorn blasted far out at sea and Jack felt something soft slide across his face. Hand or wing? Fingertips or feathers? There was a definite presence. 'Who are you?' he said in the mist. His words sounded slurred and alien; his tongue swollen and useless.

A mature seagull stepped out from the fog and stood before him, staring down its beak. It was larger than the rest, its eyes more hooded, the yellow of its bill more yellow, and the red dot was as bright as a bulb.

Jack lifted his head and screwed up his eyes. 'Who are you? Jonathan, Livingstone or Seagull?'

The giant gull raised a wing and fanned it out wide, as if a gesture of welcome.

'Bird, Man or Birdman?' said Jack, sitting up. 'Are you a figment of my imagination?' He laughed. 'Am I?' His phone vibrated and he fumbled it out of his pocket, unable to focus on the screen. He tried to slip it back inside, but the phone fell onto the grass at the webbed feet of the strange bird.

'*Grack*, what's the difference between God and a consultant?' asked Birdman, deadpan. He strutted back and forth, as if on a stage.

'I dunno,' said Jack, 'what's the difference between God and a consultant?'

'God doesn't think he's a consultant.'

Jack laughed generously, and the giant gull took an exaggerated bow. Almost in silhouette, Birdman closed his wing over and bent down to peck at the phone. Straightening up, he said: 'It does a seagull good to see a soul in silhouette.'

'Huh?'

'I said, *grack*, it does the soul good to see a seagull in silhouette, *grack*.'

'I thought that's what you said.'

'And it's nothing to be frightened of, *grack*.'

The premature night sky had turned violet, and still the sea-fog rolled ashore gobbling up the seafront café and swallowing parked cars. Distant people disappeared into the peasouper. Jack grabbed more pills and shovelled them in. 'Want some?' he said, laughing at the giant gull who stood there motionless, the three white dots on its black tail-feathers pronounced like ellipsis. More wine spilled over Jack's mouth and down his front. 'I'm tired. I just want to close my eyes,' and the gull seemed to blink and nod in the dusky light. Birdman turned its back as if to walk away. 'Don't leave me!'

'I'm not leaving you, *grack*,' Birdman said, looking over its shoulder. 'I'm calling our brothers and sisters.' He threw back his head, opened his beak wide and made a *scree scree scree*. And out from the fog flowed a flock.

The foghorn blasted. Jack lay down again, closing his eyes, trying to focus on a new world with his third eye. But his third eye was not as it usually appeared. Normally, when he meditated in the Zen garden, the eye was small, soft and wobbly in the middle of his brain, like frogspawn. But now it hung out of bed on a loose stalk of tissue swinging like a pendulum in an empty cave. Through this engorged and monstrous pupil Jack saw primitive shadows on walls and Alice standing alone among them. A pale hand reached out to her from the blackness; Buddha's hand, cracked at the wrist. Jack tried to open his eyes but they were glued. Then, to his horror, he saw a different kind of darkness folding around him; a timeless, infinite cloak of space. And it hit him like a train.

'I don't want to die.'

'Why not, *grack*?' Birdman said.

'Because it would be the death of all my dreams.'

-PART SIX-

All that we see or seem is but a dream within a dream.

Edgar Allan Poe

For a second you see – and seeing the secret, are the secret. For a second there is meaning. Then the hand lets the veil fall and you are alone, lost in the fog again, and you stumble on toward nowhere, for no good reason! It was a great mistake, my being born a man, I would have been more successful as a sea-gull or a fish.

Eugene O'Neill, *Long Day's Journey into Night*

Through the Fog

Alice drove at breakneck speed through the woods. She telephoned Jack on her hands-free, without reply. She called her parents who said they hadn't heard from him all day. She phoned Gerry who hadn't heard anything from Jack in weeks. She put her foot to the floor taking the bends at high speed, then crawled through rush hour jams at traffic lights and roundabouts. Finally, through a strange and thickening fog, she made it home. Pandora barked. There was no sign of Jack. Alice called out his name. She moved from room to room downstairs, calling, then upstairs, shouting, and found a letter addressed to "Chickpea" on the bedside table.

A woman walked along the Slopes. Her cocker spaniel ran in and out of vision in a thickening veil of mist. The dog approached a bench, chasing off gulls, but some stubborn birds remained unmoved on the wood. The woman came closer, noticing a man laid out. Such a fool on the hill in this weather. Was he a down-and-out? She looked more closely. Chin to toes, the bearded man was dressed in grey and white, all feathered and covered in beaks. The bodies of twenty gulls rippled, grackling and grumbling. The poor man's face was deathly pale, eyes closed, a foolish grin on his lips. She shrieked: 'Are you alive? Are you dead? Are you only sleeping?'

With no response, she set her dog on the gulls, yelling at the top of her lungs, but none of those bench birds budged. Instead, as if in a Hitchcock film, they glared, hissed and squawked. More gulls swooped down from the sky, dive-bombing and pecking at the woman's scalp. The cocker was turned over, its belly bloody from darting beaks. The woman ran into the road, waving down a car. The driver swerved and accelerated away. 'It's a horror film,' she told herself. She got out her phone and called emergency services. 'Yes, dead, or dying on the Tankerton Slopes! And the gulls are eating him!'

Alice sped along the seafront, peering anxiously over the dash and through the fog trying to see benches. As she reached the far end of the Slopes she saw the lights of an ambulance parked up on the grass, the hazards blinking. She mounted the pavement with force, leapt out and ran. She made out the fluorescent jackets of two paramedics pushing a gurney into the back of a vehicle. She cried: 'Stop! Jack! Wait!'

'You know him?' a paramedic said.

'I'm his wife.' She looked down. Jack was unconscious, his mouth covered with an oxygen mask. She grabbed hold of his hand. Ice-cold.

'Took us ten minutes fighting off the gulls,' another paramedic said. 'Is that yours?' He pointed to the car on the grass.

They placed another blanket over Jack's legs. His chest was bare where CPR had been administered. 'Follow us. He's overdosed.' The paramedic held up the evidence. 'Eight or nine boxes, with alcohol.'

'His heart's sluggish, his temperature's low,' said a female paramedic, pushing the gurney further inside. 'Do you know how long he's been out here?'

Alice shook her head.

'Well, someone said your husband was being eaten. The girls at the centre thought we had some crazy old bird, but you want my opinion? Your husband's a degree off hypothermia. The gulls saved him from freezing to death.'

'Don't look so worried,' said the female paramedic, getting into the back of the ambulance. 'But we must go.' The driver banged the rear doors shut and raced around to the driver's side, responding to his crackling radio. Then the fog was filled with the sound of a wailing siren.

Alice discovered at the hospital that Jack had regained partial consciousness in the ambulance, but hadn't said anything in the seconds leading up to his first seizure. His heart had stopped during the fit and the female paramedic administered CPR again. Once admitted, a crash team worked around the clock dealing with three further seizures, each one longer and more violent than the last. Finally, after a fourth, a decision was made by a senior registrar, neurologist and anaesthetist to medically induce a coma; a last resort to reduce damage to Jack's brain. He was in a "critical but stable" condition. Vital organs had nearly shut down, but Jack was able to breath for himself, his blood pressure and heart rate were satisfactory, and his touch reflexes were sound.

Stabilised, Jack was moved to the intensive care unit where Alice sat with him before the team ran further tests. Tubes, cables and wires ran out from him to bleeping monitors and machines. A tube in his nose fed him active charcoal. An oxygen mask hissed over his nose and mouth, but there was no ventilator. She held his hand, pleased to feel warmth in his skin again. She spoke to him in whispers, fighting back tears, telling him everything would be fine. Everything would be okay. When she returned to the relatives' room, she crumpled into her father's arms.

An hour later, a doctor came carrying a grave expression. There were signs of heart block and arrhythmia. If Jack had swallowed all of the amitriptyline, he should actually be dead, so it was all a bit of a mystery how he'd survived. He was in a dangerous situation regarding his brain and heart, not to mention his liver. 'The toxic load is high,' the doctor said. 'We can move him to King's in London, or have a specialist come down, but all we can do now is keep our fingers crossed.' He was about to leave the room but turned and asked: 'How did Jack get hold of so many drugs?'

Alice stared at her father. 'He smuggled them out of my cupboard,' said Alan.

'You have *this much* amitriptyline?'

Alan shrugged. 'I don't like using them, they make me drowsy.'

'I ask because the boxes the paramedics found were past their use-by dates; prehistoric even. I'm hoping the chemical effect will be less harmful to Jack. Only time will tell.'

Alice left a message on Lauren's answer machine: *Jack has overdosed and in a coma. Doctors say we must prepare for the worst.* She didn't call Ernie in America. Initially she'd wanted to dump a great big steaming guilt-trip on his doorstep, but couldn't bear the thought of Ernie's name or the fat face his name conjured, let alone speak to him. Ever since that text he'd sent, not a word, not a phone call. No sorrys. No explanations. No peace offerings after his textbomb had been dropped.

Lauren raced to the hospital from Muswell Hill. Alice offered her an invitation to stay. A guest room was already made up. From there, Lauren telephoned Ernie who said he was on holiday in Bermuda trying to save his marriage, but he'd fly over as soon as he could. Lauren cancelled all of her supply teaching and helped around Seagull House. When Alice was with Jack, Lauren tidied the place, fielded calls and walked Pandora twice a day. She made herself useful in the kitchen making omelettes, salads and soups, for which Alice was grateful.

Husband in a Coma

Days passed, and Jack remained stable. When he was out of immediate danger he was moved into a smaller room in ICU where relatives could spend private time with him. Having stayed a week at Seagull House, Lauren felt she'd outstayed her welcome, giving apologies and making a final visit to the hospital. She kissed her brother's bearded cheek and squeezed his hand. 'Won't be too long before you're cracking jokes at my expense again,' she said, fighting off tears.

Ernie flew over from San Francisco, coming straight from the airport, luggage still in hand. Alice had to resist slapping his jet-lagged, super-tanned face. Instead, she maintained a cool distance, politely bringing him up to speed with the situation.

Ernie felt the frostiness, and then the heat as if he'd actually been slapped. 'You don't have to worry. I'm staying in a hotel. If it's okay with you, though, I'd like to visit each day?'

'Perfectly understandable,' she said. 'He is your only brother.'

Ernie arrived at the hospital the next morning and Alice let him have plenty of time with Jack. She stood outside, looking through the glass wall. The door was ajar and she overheard Ernie telling Jack about his impending divorce from Ariel. A lawyer was working on access to his boys and alimony. 'It's pretty amicable. We're just about friends.' There was a moment when Alice's heart nearly burst, listening to Ernie's yarns, taking Jack back to their earliest days in Muswell Hill: school, scouts, the local football team, girls and records. Ernie stopped himself, leaned in and said in his brother's ear: 'Jack, I can't reverse time, but if I could I'd go back and delete every word I sent in that text, and then I'd take you to San Francisco. There are Lyme doctors in the Bay. You could stay with me a few months. You and Alice, while you get treatment. Maybe I can do that for ya, when you get outta this hole?'

Ernie bumped into Alice as he tore from the room, tears streaming down his face. She called after him but he ignored her. She asked him to stop walking away, following him all the way into the car park to his rental car. 'I heard what you said, Ernie.'

'I'm sorry, Alice. If I'd known this would happen…'

She turned him around to face her. 'Jack was angry, but he didn't do this because of you. He did it because of Lyme. Is it true about the doctors in San Francisco?'

'I have the details right here in my pocket.' He tapped his bomber jacket. 'I found the best Lyme-literate doctor in town, called Lindberg.'

'Come here,' she said, eyes filling, and she wrapped her arms around him.

Collette, the nurse assigned to Jack, was friendly and considerate, regularly explaining how things were going. She said she'd call if there were any changes in his condition. It was Collette who washed Jack, carefully turning him from time to time to avoid bedsores. She explained that Alice should talk to her husband as if everything was normal because there was a possibility he could hear her. She should try to sound positive too. When the doctors and consultants were happy, probably in a matter of days, they'd withdraw the barbiturate and he'd regain consciousness. Since inducing the sleep, Jack had had no more seizures, so things were going to plan.

Alice took turns by his bedside, sharing the vigil with her parents and Gerry who drove over from Sussex. She showed him Jack's letter, which he'd have preferred not to have read as it was so sombre and personal. Alice told Gerry she'd been in touch with a Lyme awareness society and a support group. She'd been forced to contact the local newspaper too over a laughable story that Jack was an alcoholic, half-eaten by gulls. A photo lifted from an old website showed Jack in his younger days, below it a photograph of a local lady pointing angrily at her cocker spaniel's stitches. Alice told the journalist Jack had tried to kill himself because he had Lyme disease and could not get treatment. The seagulls had little or nothing to do with it. If anything, she told the paper, Jack was *saved* by the gulls.

The phone never stopped ringing. Messages flooded voicemail. Not just familiar voices from the past, but newcomers too. Radio journalists, magazine editors and TV producers wanted to run features about Jack Mann the comedian, and what happened to him. Well-wisher letters and cards streamed through the letterbox. Everyone wished Jack a speedy recovery. Others sent prayers. For someone who thought he was alone, Jack had a lot of support, even from complete strangers.

It was all Alice could do to keep sane during the waiting. If she wasn't by Jack's bedside talking, holding his hand or reading him newspapers, she was fighting his corner outside in the real world. She wouldn't fail him. That's how she saw it, and that's what she thought Jack would expect her to do; to raise awareness, not just about Lyme, but how difficult it was to diagnose and treat.

Behind the closed doors of Seagull House Alice frequently cried. Her crying became a deluge when she took a call from the Berry family undertakers asking if Jack was still alive. It was the palpable emptiness present in their dream home; the sheer lack of Jack. Though she fully understood why he'd done it, she was shocked and sometimes felt betrayed that he'd gone through with it. Without Jack, every noise in the house amplified and echoed: a creaking floorboard became the rumble of thunder, the pop of the toaster a pistol, the ticking of the hallway clock the moving hands of Big Ben, and Pan's paws on the decked veranda became the pounding of an elephant. It was as if Jack had been natural soundproofing, as if when he had been at home she'd never noticed any other sound.

Her boss was full of sympathy, giving her a month off. Alice wondered if she'd ever go back. She'd sell the house and move back to London and old friends, maybe. There were people to talk to from work, of course, but she wouldn't call them intimates or friends. They were fine to share a polite conversation, but not a deep secret, anxiety or fear. And, as she'd noticed months before all this, the longer Jack was ill, the shorter their sympathy survived. People avoided her and the subject of Lyme. She called it "crossing over the street" syndrome; chronic sickness could turn close friends into vague acquaintances. Alice didn't blame anyone; she understood that people had their own lives to lead, that most lives didn't touch those of others outside the primary family unit. Nonetheless, it was eye-opening to witness at first hand, the way people avoided the subject for so long. It was just a hard fact, she realised, that when things go well for you, you are a magnet to the iron filings that make up your circle of friends. When things go bad, the filings begin to drop away as if de-magnetised. And when things go from bad to worse, any remaining filings are actively repelled. Yes, she concluded, it's not that people are bad, it's more that they aren't very good beyond a crisis. Then again, she thought, most people want to escape the misery of their daily lives, not experience the agony of someone else's.

It was comforting having Gerry over; joking, making meals, almost making her smile again. Though Jack seemed to hover above her in the ether casting a dull shadow, it was a blessed relief to have someone close to talk to under that cloud. When Alice and Gerry walked along the seafront, it was restful, enjoyable even. They avoided the benches, going in the opposite direction where it was less manicured, wilder and more windswept. When Gerry left, Alice was miserable again.

Soon, Ernie would make his way back to America too. He stayed one night at Seagull House and showed his indomitable Super Mann spirit, listing positive futures: 1. Jack wouldn't die, he was a fighter. 2. Jack's Lyme would be treated in America. 3. Jack would stay in the Nob Hill house. 4. Alice would stay too and they'd eat out every night at fancy restaurants all over the city. 5. They would take a trip up the coast to the Sonoma valley and go on wine-tastings, like the good old days.

With the list-making, and the way he looked and sounded, it was as if her husband was home again. When Ernie was showering, humming to himself, it was like Jack was physically back and she yearned for him. The morning Ernie left, Alice stood on the tips of her toes to kiss him goodbye and found herself willing him to kiss her on the lips, which he did, and she pulled away, slapping him full on the face, but Ernie read her signs, pulling her into him and they fell onto the sofa making love. Then they put their clothes back on, never saying a word.

Collette phoned Alice's mobile late one evening with disastrous news. During the latest reflex tests Jack had reduced responses bilaterally, hands and feet. Neither did he respond to freezing water tipped into his ears when there should've been an automatic reflex. Jack's pupils were reactive, but nothing like as pronounced as before. 'I only just discovered it speaking to the doctors.'

'I'm coming in,' said Alice, mentally putting on her coat.

'That's the reason I'm calling, Alice. Mr. Knox is coming down from King's in London. He's bringing a specialist in neuroimaging with him.'

'I want to speak to this Mr. Knox.'

'He wants to talk to you too. He's asked if you can bring in Jack's favourite CD?'

Alice cast her eyes over their joint music collection. They hadn't bought anything for years, usually downloading digital recordings. The CD collection was a complete mess, no longer in accordance with the alphabet, a genre or theme. She liked it ordered, but Jack must have shoved them back willy-nilly. Even in a hurry, Alice realised that she generally liked what Jack called her "wailing women" and he liked what she called his "moaning men". These men included Cash, Cave, Cohen, Dylan, Waits and Young. Whereas her women included P.J. Harvey, Laura Marling, Joni Mitchell and a variety of cabaret singers and West End stars. She saw a pile of CD cases without CDs inside; a cardinal sin for a control freak like her. They were all Beatles' albums. She went over to the player and discovered CDs sitting on top of a speaker, and one was still in the player itself.

The Machine in the Ghost in the Machine

Alice stared through the glass screen at the MRI scanner. The lower half of Jack's body was outside the machine, feet to waist in a blanket. She wanted to hold his hand. Against the senior registrar's wishes Alice had been invited in to the control booth by the maverick neurologist Mr. Knox and his Japanese colleague, Dr. Ono, both of whom had travelled down on the fast train from London. Dr. Ono didn't look like a regular consultant. He was young, had dark shoulder-length hair and was carrying a guitar case in his hand like a busker from the underground. Mr. Knox introduced him as one of the world's leading authorities on MRI imaging and comas. He'd trained in Kyoto and Tokyo and taught at Columbia, New York. His last book, *Conversations With the Unconscious*, had been a New York Times bestseller, outselling *The Woman Who Mistook Her Husband For a Twat*. 'Dr. Ono is due to finish a short secondment at King's, so we're lucky to have him here,' said Knox.

Dr. Ono familiarised himself with the control room, discussing it with the radiographer. He asked if the Beatles CD could be recorded simultaneously with the imaging. He asked if he could "live-mark" whenever he saw something potentially interesting, and the radiologist showed him the switches. 'This is quite an old model, Mrs. Mann, that's all,' he said, 'and the timing is everything. In a functional MRI scan we're looking for increased blood flow and oxygenation. We play Jack's favourite album through his headphones - and *Revolver* is a great choice might I add - and we look for physiological reactions in his brain. The music acts as a stimulus or starter pistol, and we see how many runners there are, or not. Can we have the music on in here on low?' he asked the radiographer.

'Are you a Beatles fan too, Dr. Ono?' the radiographer replied, trying to sound hip.

'Haven't you heard?' Ono said. 'Everyone in Japan loves the Beatles, but I'm not related to Yoko Ono.'

'*Revolver* was Jack Senior's favourite album,' said Alice. 'It was released the year Jack was born. His father played it during the second half of the pregnancy.'

'Well, it beats whale music, doesn't it?' said Dr. Ono, making Alice smile. 'And it has great emotional resonance, which is the most important thing.'

The radiographer got out of the way and Dr. Ono took his seat, looking at a screen. 'If and when I see anything of interest I'll mark it, but Mr. Knox, if you see anything tap me on the shoulder and I'll mark that too. Now, if I'm not mistaken, *Revolver* is about forty minutes long so we can listen to the whole thing, but I'd suggest everyone sit down and be as silent as possible so I can concentrate. The only two people who can talk are me and Mr. Knox.' He smiled at Alice. 'It'll be all acronyms and neurospeak anyway, Mrs. Mann.'

The scanner started and then the music. "Taxman" came and went without a single mark. The anti-climax was etched on Ono's face. "Eleanor Rigby", no mark, but a point of Ono's finger at Jack's brain on one of the monitors.

Dr. Ono glanced anxiously at Mr. Knox. 'Jack might not like the first two tracks,' Ono said to calm Alice down. She was pressed into her swivel chair, arms tightly folded around her middle.

"I'm only Sleeping". Mark. Mark. Mark. Mark. Dr. Ono pointed to a particular part of Jack's brain on the monitor. 'Strange, don't you think, Mr. Knox? The voxel load right there?'

Knox leaned in. 'Hmmm. MPFC.'

'And here, the precuneus, look.'

'Yes, rather peculiar.'

'MPFC is the medial prefrontal cortex, Mrs. Mann,' said Ono. 'The precuneus is associated with episodic memory and happiness. The precuneus is the time-machine of memory, the cave of imagination, the store room of wishful thinking. It's unusual for activity here when just playing a song. The MPFC is known for self-reflection qualities, decision-making, human anticipation of the future, that sort of thing. Psychologists are fascinated by these areas. If only Carl Jung were alive today to see these new scientific discoveries.'

'Maybe Jack's saying he's *only sleeping*?' said the radiographer, receiving a sharp look from Mr. Knox.

'He does have a point, though, Roger,' said Dr. Ono. 'Different songs can mean different things to different people. Every unconscious experience is unique.'

"Love You To". Mark. Tap on the shoulder. Mark.

"Here, There and Everywhere". Mark. Mark. Mark. Alice listened to the lyrics, feeling a personal resonance throughout the song and its final words: *I will be here, there and everywhere.* She was close to tears.

'I entirely understand,' said Dr. Ono, nodding.

"Yellow Submarine". No marks.

'I'm neutral over Yellow Submarine too,' said Dr. Ono, smiling again to reassure Alice.

"She Said She Said". Mark. Tap on shoulder. Mark.

"Good Day Sunshine". No marks.

"And Your Bird Can Sing". Mark. Mark. Mark. Mark. 'Now look at that,' said Dr. Ono to Mr. Knox touching the middle of Jack's brain on the screen.

'The size of it,' said Knox.

'Calcification or cyst?'

'Either or neither. Definitely not a tumour.'

'It's the pineal gland,' Dr. Ono remarked to Alice. 'Don't look so worried. It's probably a benign cyst. We've seen all of the earlier MRI scans and I would have noticed by the outline. The size of Jack's pineal gland is quite extraordinary. It should be the size of a garden pea; seven by six by three in a normal adult, but this is what...double that?'

'It's a marrowfat,' said Knox, rather amused with himself. 'Definitely engorged, and look at the great vein of Galen, Dr. Ono. Why is the pineal body so excited?'

'Is this bad news?' said Alice, getting butterflies in her stomach.

'No, no,' said Mr. Knox. 'I'm just not quite sure why this has grown since the last MRI... which was done when...last month?'

Alice nodded. 'It makes melatonin, doesn't it?'

'Indeed,' said Dr. Ono. 'Melatonin is produced in darkness and promotes sleep. Light slows down the production. The pineal body controls Circadian rhythms according to the season.'

'Jack's a terrible sleeper,' said Alice, 'so it's ironic he can't wake up. Could he be producing *too much* melatonin if the pineal is large?'

'It's not quite that simple,' said Mr. Knox. 'Dr. Ono, I'm not aware of any research suggesting the amount of melatonin produced is proportional to the size of one's organ, do you?'

Dr. Ono shook his head, trying to focus on the monitors. 'Which organ are you talking about, Mr. Knox?'

Knox gasped at the flippancy. 'Pineal, Dr. Ono!'

'Pineal is midline, dead centre,' he said. 'Too difficult to biopsy from a living patient.'

'And this growth, it seems too recent,' said Mr. Knox, scratching the top of his head.

'Of course,' said Dr. Ono, 'devout Hindus believe the pineal is a third eye. They say if Shiva's third eye opens it will herald the end of the physical world.'

'The human third eye is pure science fiction,' said Knox, getting frustrated with his esteemed Japanese colleague who he'd never known to spout such unscientific mumbo-jumbo.

Dr. Ono went on: 'The pineal has perfect singularity. It sits by itself. Every other part of the brain has two of its kind, called duality. Buddhists say it is the site of the sixth chakra, a metaphor for mindfulness or higher consciousness. The sixth chakra is also believed by some to be the centre of dreaming or visions.'

'Dr. Ono, as you well know, the pineal gland is a *vestigial eye* that died out millions of years ago through biological evolution. I think only some reptiles and sharks have a parietal third eye.'

Alice interjected, because she thought it might have relevance: 'Jack's dad, Jack Mann Snr., he wrote a sci-fi novel called *Humalien* in the 1970s. It was about a creature that was a third human, a third reptile, and a third bird, and it had a third eye.'

Mr. Knox stared at her. 'This is just what I mean about science fiction, not science fact, Dr. Ono.'

Dr. Ono ignored him. 'Philosophers like Descartes believed the pineal was the seat of the soul, the place where intellect meets body. Descartes thought there had to be a little man sitting or standing inside the human brain interpreting the pictures received from the external world that were filtered onto the retina. They called him *Homunculus*, "little man", from the Latin.'

'Seventeenth century ignorance,' said Knox. 'I very much doubt there's a little man, or indeed a little woman sitting inside Mr. Mann's pineal gland, no matter what its size. We are scientists, aren't we, Dr. Ono? Not philosophers?'

'We are indeed,' said Dr. Ono. 'But jump to 1966 and what are we doing? We are putting little men inside a human being to investigate the pathology of a mysterious disease.'

'*Fantastic Voyage* was a film!' said Knox. 'And Raquel Welch didn't find any little men.'

Alice imagined these were the frivolous conversations consultants might have over one-brandy-too-many in The Athenaeum, not in the control room of an MRI scanner, and certainly not in front of a wife so concerned for her husband's life.

The rest of the album played with fewer and fewer marks or taps on shoulders, increasing again dramatically with "Tomorrow Never Knows", Dr. Ono's favourite track. 'That squeaking you hear at the beginning that sounds like a seagull?' he said. 'It's actually one of the Beatles' laughter recorded and played back at double-speed. Who'd ever have thought human laughter could sound like a gull? Anyway, Jack's responses are predominantly MPFC again,' he said, reclining in his chair. 'Seat of planning, thinking and anticipation. The human brain. There's nothing more mind-expanding than the mind-expanding mind. Did you know,' he said, directing his question at Alice, 'there are a thousand trillion neurons in the human brain? A quadrillion neurons.' He took the *Revolver* CD out of the machine and held it up in front of her. 'If this CD was just one neuron in your brain, you'd have enough CDs to stack them flat, one on top of another, and be able to reach the sun, and another stack to come all the way back down to Earth again. Physiologically locate consciousness, the self, the ghost in the machine, and you've outdone Einstein by solving the greatest mystery of mankind.'

'Find the machine in the ghost in the machine and you've won the Nobel Prize,' said Knox.

'Sorry,' said Alice, 'but can I ask if Jack's responses show anything?'

'Too early to say,' said Knox.

'You're probably right,' said Ono, 'but if it's any consolation, Mrs. Mann, I've seen hundreds of coma MRIs and some of them provoke little or no response at all, so there's hope.'

'That's not to say Jack will come out of his coma any time soon,' said Knox.

'Sadly, this is also true,' said Ono. 'It's unusual for a patient with an induced coma not to regain consciousness after the infusions are stopped. It's possible the tricyclic has caused damage. On the other hand, the prognosis for a patient in a coma brought about by an overdose is normally good, isn't it, Mr. Knox? Jack's a puzzle, but we'll look into it and give an opinion next week.'

'I'm incredibly grateful to you for doing this, and at such short notice.' Alice got to her feet and shook their hands. 'And thank you for letting me sit in.'

'There's a reason for that,' said Knox. 'Dr. Ono, do you want to do the honours?'

'Of course,' he said, getting out of the controller's seat and gesturing with a sweep of his hand. 'Please, Alice. The mic is here. Flick it up like this and you can talk to Jack.'

'I wouldn't know what to say. I've said everything to him over and over in ICU.'

'You'll find something,' said Ono. 'What was the first joke Jack ever told? He's a comedian, right?'

'Jack's not a one-liner stand-up. There's never any punchline. He tells funny stories using impressions.'

'I see,' said Ono, not seeing at all. 'Then tell Jack a short story for a few minutes. We'll leave the room. Jack's all yours.' Dr. Ono smiled at her kindly and Mr. Knox did an unexpected bow as if he was the one from Japan. 'It's all being recorded,' said Dr. Ono. We'll examine Jack's responses at King's.'

Alice waited for the radiographer to leave, then flicked the switch and spoke: 'Hello, Jack. It's only me. Alice. You must be pretty sick of me talking to you day in, day out. It's you who tells the stories and are funnier. I hope you can hear this somewhere in your head, and in your heart.' The words echoed in her own head and came out of her mouth like a message she'd leave on an answer machine. All she wanted was for Jack to pick up, to reply. 'It's so strange to be talking to your feet through a glass window and looking inside your lovely brain at the same time. Hey, you'll be able to brag how big your pineal gland is when you're better! What plans and dreams are you hatching in that third eye of yours? A trip to San Francisco? I hope when the neurologists examine these scans they'll see the Blackpool illuminations. They're really clever and should help us understand why you're not coming out of your big sleep. Maybe, before they've even figured it out, you'll be sitting up in bed eating your breakfast and telling me all about your fantastic journey, and I can, well, I can be happy again. Oh, Jack,' she said, 'you stupid, stupid man. Please come back to me. I will always love you, no matter what.'

Mann Versus Machine

True to his word, Mr. Knox telephoned Alice from King's. It was already late October, weeks into Jack's coma, and there'd been no signs of consciousness. Alice took a deep breath as he explained the results.

It was both good news and bad. There were clear neural patterns that showed Jack was able to respond. He was putting up a bloody good fight. Jack had responded well to stimuli of music, songs and especially to Alice's voice. All very encouraging, Knox said, as some coma patients had poorer reaction speeds. However, the responses happened in unexpected places, as if Jack's brain was confused or disorientated. They'd expected the emotional centres to have flared when Alice had spoken into the mic, but they hadn't. It was the decision-making or future-planning frontal lobes that engorged, and oddly, the pineal gland too. Knox said in his view this meant Jack did have brain damage, though it was unclear how much had been caused.

Alice's heart sank.

Dr. Ono held a slightly different opinion, Knox said. He was more of an expert regarding coma patients, and it might be prudent to accept his view that Jack's brain was actively seeking a way out of its difficulties, as if sleepwalking through a maze searching for an exit from the unconscious. The MRI definitely showed that Jack's Default Mode Network was fully active, which meant his mind was wandering. He was probably remembering the past, or imagining the future, or constructing a narrative from those two. Dr. Ono had seen it before a few times, so there was still hope.

Alice's heart lifted again.

Knox and Ono concurred that Jack had a 50% chance of regaining consciousness, though the odds dwindled each day he remained in a coma without communication or improvement in sensory reflexes. Knox said Jack could be experiencing a "delirium of negation"; something called "Cotard's syndrome". He might be thinking he was dead, or that he didn't physically exist. Then Knox raised the spectre of permanent partial consciousness; the nightmare scenarios of "persistent vegetative state" and the rarer "locked-in syndrome". It would be remiss if he didn't mention them, he said.

'But what about all the activity shown on the MRI?'

'Sadly, sometimes it is a case of the lights are on but nobody's at home, Mrs. Mann.'

Neither Knox nor Ono had got to the bottom of Jack's enlarged pineal gland; only an autopsy could determine that. Not a tumour, not a cyst, and definitely not sudden calcification; a plain and wonderful mystery, Knox said. 'There isn't a single recorded case of a patient's pineal gland growing to double its normal size inside one month…until now.'

Alice was by Jack's side, half asleep in the sunshine spilling through the window, when he made the initial choking noise. At first she thought she'd imagined it, and then she thought Jack was finally coming out of his coma, and shouted excitedly. By the time Collette arrived, Jack was having a convulsion. Then he stopped breathing. A crash team arrived, surrounding him, giving CPR, using a defibrillator, restoring a heartbeat. A ventilator was set in place. Intubating tubes were inserted into Jack's nose and throat, and taped down.

Once he was stabilised, Alice sat by his side again, listening to the regular sound of the machine that breathed for him. She spoke as if nothing had happened, but knew in her heart of hearts it was the beginning of the end. A series of poor reflex tests followed. No pain responses. His feet were dead. Pressure applied to his sternum provoked nil response. When his nose was pinched, nothing. His pupils had temporarily blown but were readjusting, just about reacting to piercing torchlight. Most worrying of all, the consultant said, there'd been no reaction at all when he'd stroked the corneas of Jack's eyes with a piece of tissue. 'Everything is failing, Mrs Mann. Poor brain stem signs, his heart is slow, irregular. I'm sorry but I think you must prepare for the worst in coming days.'

'I can't bear to see him like this any longer,' she said in tears.

'Mrs. Mann, there is never a right time or a right way to say what I'm about to say. The decision is yours, I understand that. All I can do is give my medical opinion. And my advice to you is that you should go home this weekend and think about what you said just now. You can't bear to see your husband like this any longer. Maybe your husband wouldn't want to be seen like this for much longer himself? You may decide that enough is enough for this life; that your husband is allowed to go. At the moment, and ever since he was brought in, there have been no external signs of communication. Jack cannot speak, eat, swallow, or breathe unaided. It is not much of a life.'

Alice looked at her husband's sad face. The only sign of life was in his beard; the way it seemed to grow exponentially between each hospital visit. 'I've made my decision,' she said.

These were the hardest days of all; watching people saying goodbye. Although Ernie said he'd fly over again, Alice convinced him not to come. There would be a coroner's report and a post-mortem and these would delay the funeral. Ernie would surely want to attend that. And besides, what they'd done at the house was wrong, wrong, wrong. He cried down the phone. Lauren was the same; tears and devastation by the hospital bed. Estella was too confused to understand, and like a child was upset by everyone else's tears.

Gerry was broken in pieces and spent the last two nights with Alice at Seagull House. He'd known Jack for the longest time, and despite losing touch over the past year was already stricken with grief. He damned himself as a useless friend. In twelve months, he'd telephoned Jack fewer than a dozen times and sent a couple of text messages. And latterly, he hadn't even asked how Jack was feeling. Gerry said, 'It's like someone has thrown a punch to my stomach and ripped out my heart. And the irony, Alice, is that his DVDs are flying off the shelves. I can't keep up with orders. Amazon sales are red hot. *Mann in Black* is the fastest-selling stand-up DVD *ever!* Just imagine the sales after he's *really* dead! Christ, sorry, Alice, that came out wrong. My timing's always been awful. What I meant was, you'll have financial security.'

The evening before it was due to happen, all the paperwork signed off and agreed by two independent consultants, Gerry and Alice took a rare break from the hospital. Gerry needed fresh air and a cigarillo, and Alice needed time to think things through one last time: was she doing the right thing? Could Jack still awaken from this nightmare?

They drove back to Seagull House and walked Pan along the Slopes. This time, quite bravely in Gerry's opinion, they sat on the bench where Jack had effectively taken his life; the sea captain's bench. Pan jumped up between them and Alice gave her a kiss on the top of her long snout. The three of them looked out beyond the beach huts, over the estuary to Essex on the left, and to the wind farm on the right. Alice wondered if she should commission a new bench for Jack with words of remembrance: *Jack Mann, beloved husband and comedian.* The thought nearly crushed her. What if he came out of his coma tonight, and she wasn't there? Should she give him more time? 'I blame myself, Gerry. I didn't do enough. I should have complained sooner. I failed him.'

'Nonsense. No one could have done more.'

'When I see him lying there in hospital, I think he'll suddenly open his eyes and everything will go back to normal.'

'That's only natural.'

'Jack's still here, though, isn't he?'

'Physically, but he's not *really* here.' Gerry looked glumly out to sea. 'This is all so wrong. This Lyme disease, what it did, what it made him do. Jack has no life, no future, but you do, Alice.'

'I keep thinking, I dreamed a dream that ended in catastrophe. It's odd sitting here. I can feel his presence even though he's in ICU. I asked if I could bring Pandora in, you know, but a consultant said it was a health and safety issue. Jack would want to see her. He used to call her his "Velcro bitch" because she never left his side.'

Gerry patted her hand. 'Why don't we take Pan in, and to hell with health and safety? What will they do, call the police? She's Pandora, and Pandora unleashed all the evils upon this world, but what was left in the box, Alice?'

'I'm all out of hope,' she said, knocking his leg with hers.

'I'm telling you,' he said, getting worked up, 'if a man can't have the people...or the pets he loves by his bloody side when he dies what's the point of existing? Alice, if you want to bring her in, there isn't a single person on this Earth who can stop us.'

-PART SEVEN-

His eies will twinckle, and his tongue will roll,
As though he beckned, and cal'd his Soul,
He graspes his hands, and he puls up his feet,
And seems to reach, and to step forth to meet
His soule

John Donne, *The Second Anniversary.*
Of the Progres of the Soule

Humour can be dissected, as a frog can
but the thing dies in the process and the innards are discouraging to
any but the pure scientific mind.

E.B. White

Seeing For Oneself

Two porters lifted the body onto a gurney and Collette placed a fresh linen shroud over it, tucking the corners lightly in around the calves, heels and shoulders. The porters guided the trolley down to the mortuary in the basement. En route, one of them listened to Talking Heads on discreet earphones, to the obvious resentment of the other, much younger apprentice. 'We're on a road to nowhere,' Neil hummed as the trolley moved along the artery of Main Street. 'There's a city in my mind, come along and take that ride…baby, it's alright.'

Arriving at the mortuary, Neil switched the music off, leaving his earphones in. He said to Octavian, the disgruntled mortuary assistant who officially, and at work parties, preferred to be called an anatomical pathology technologist or APT: 'One stiff, direct from ICU. Time of death, three and a half hours ago. We would've brought him down sooner but his wife wouldn't let go of his hand. We had to tear them apart like clams. I know you like the bodies down in good time.'

'It's about core temperature, preservation and possible infection,' said Octavian.

'Anyway,' said the young porter, 'Collette's tagged him on the ankle. There's a lot of hoo-ha over this one, so Collette told me. Complaints, coroner, post-mortem.'

'Bit late for coroners and complaints, isn't it?' said Neil. 'Horse already bolted. DIY dead. Overdose, clear as custard.'

'Which one is Collette?' asked Octavian.

'The blonde,' said Neil.

'She hasn't washed him or removed any of the PICC lines?'

'No,' said the apprentice, 'but the tubes in his mouth are gone.'

The mortuary assistant glared. 'That shouldn't happen until the pathologist has seen everything in situ!'

'Hark at 'im,' said Neil. '*Silent Witness.*'

The apprentice porter looked around the chilly metallic room. In a way, taking bodies down to cold storage was the easiest job in the world, like moving furniture around a house. But pushing live patients in wheelchairs and beds was preferable. You can talk to them and cheer them up. What can you say to a corpse? Maybe, he thought, that's why Neil always plays music, to block out the awkward silence? There were already at least four other cadavers laid out on trolleys under white sheets, the peaks and troughs of their noses and toes reminding the apprentice of a snow-capped mountain range he'd seen on a post card from a long-lost pen friend. 'All waiting to be washed and bagged up?' he said, trying to sound unaffected and cool, but shivering in his thin grey polyester uniform.

'Jesus, Octavian, you're slacking,' said Neil. 'It's backing up in here like Operation Stack.'

'We are short-staffed,' he said, taking the paperwork and ticking off a couple of boxes. 'So, have all personals been removed?' Octavian lifted the sheet a fraction and looked at the second finger of Jack's left hand. Sometimes the rings are taken off by relatives or removed just prior to post-mortem. There was no ring.

'The widow asked for everything. Real cut up she was,' said the apprentice.

'Not as cut up as *he's* gonna be,' said Neil, tapping the trolley and cackling.

Octavian gave him a disapproving look and ticked boxes on the pro forma. 'I'll contact the coroner and see which pathologists are available. The autopsy will have to be done in the next three days before any decay or possible deterioration of evidence. You can leave him with me now,' he said, taking legal possession of the body.

When the porters had gone, Octavian removed the winding sheet and gave the body a quick once over. The first thing he always did before all else was make sure the person in his charge was 100% dead. He'd heard of a pathology assistant at a nearby hospital who'd failed to feel a cadaver's carotid artery or shine a light into the black wells of the pupils before putting the body in a refrigerator, only for a tapping noise to come from the chamber half an hour later.

Jack Mann had no pulse and no pupil reactions. His expression was relaxed, an easiness death commonly bestowed upon the faces. Jack Mann wouldn't have a facial anatomy, Octavian knew, but if he did, under his skin one would find muscles that offered up clues to this person's attitude to life, or personality. During his anatomy training, he'd been told to maintain a safe psychological distance from each cadaver as it came through the door, but sometimes a face brought out tenderness in him. If Jack's face was anatomised, Octavian was sure he would find strengthened laughter muscles. The development of particular muscles around the mouth, eyes and forehead; the *zygomaticus major* and *minor*, whose function was to spread the corners of our mouths to a smile. Octavian had seen these muscles in various anatomy classes. Well-used *zygomaticus* during a lifetime of laughter made the muscle thick and well-defined. Sometimes, it would be shrivelled to little violin strings suggesting years of misery with nothing to laugh about. Other facial muscles also hinted at personality, attitude and life experience; a knitted brow from the overuse of the *corrugator supercilli*, or *levator labii* of the upper lip providing a snarl, or the concentric fibres of the *orbicularis oculi* arranged around each eye like Saturn's rings used for blinking and squinting and leading to crow's feet. *Frontalis* raises the eyebrows in horror, dismay or shock. *Orbicularis oris* puckers the lips for a kiss. *Depressor anguli oris*, conversely, beneath each corner of the mouth, pulls the lips down into a frown. All of these muscles, thought Octavian, are so fragile under the skin.

After the body was checked over and a brief report made for the preliminary record, the orifices were sealed with pads and plugs. Then Jack was wheeled through to the refrigerator units and placed in number six.

Dr. Constance Farr would perform the autopsy on Jack Mann the next day, requiring the largest theatre as there were going to be a number of witnesses present. Octavian was pleased it would be Farr. Connie was one of the sensitive pathologists who treated the dead with respect, as he did himself. Quite often he assisted her during autopsies and she'd explain things to him as if he was less of a mortuary assistant and more of a qualified diener. She knew of Octavian's professional interest and would ask him to have a look at slices of organs under the microscope. Dr. Farr would hand him organs like the heart or the liver, and ask him to weigh them and replace them back into the cavities, even though this should be the diener's job. Farr once fired an insult at one of her dieners for replacing a woman's heart upside down in her chest. One day, she might let Octavian hold a brain. He knew the human body was a marvellous instrument or machine, that was undeniable, but there was no greater magnificence than the brain itself; the nerve centre, the mainframe for so much that happened within the machine. It held the key to so many secrets locked inside, perhaps a skeleton key to the soul, the spirit; that unpindownable jelly that tells us who we are, or who we are not.

I have beene a snoweflake and a giante, donne and undonne like a lace on a shoe. Yet no one hath seene a partickle of mee. I am the silver screene behind the mirror'd christall glasse reflecting thee, seene and unseene, beene and not beene. I am the quintessence of the quintessence of the quintessence of thee, regressus infinitum. The size of a graine of sand or poppy seed in the pockett of the pineal gland, itselfe the size of a pea, lyes mee. In daies gone bye I wouldst' move naturally from here to sternum, the gladiolus, sword protector of thy beating heart; or playe in the pouch of the stomack making butterflies dance.

In a tighte circle doe I sleepe nowe this nighte, anticipating dawn, though there bee noe naturalle lyghte, lying at the roote of the pineal, that slumber ringe. Though sleepe ys nothinge I doe easily, travelling aboute, night-walking, sleep-talking to thee, Jack Mann, withoute sweet replye. Though I bee nothinge and every thynge bee, I doe knotte possesse fingers or hands to tickle your minde or knocke at your heart as yf doors that ope wide. Trapp'd inside, prisoners entwin'd as wee muste bee, ys stille the olde curiousitee of catte, loyaltie of dogge, agilitiee of batte and catchabilitee of flea, that seems still to suck at mee. I am a barren angell. Thou ys colder nowe, I knowe, in thys necromancer's tombe. But thys ys nothinge, Jack Mann. Thys ys nothinge. Remaine here nowe, for thou art soe beautiful.

Pitie mee more, as thou hath lefte mee alone to live in thys carkasse. Pitie the starveling soule caught 'twixt lyfe and deathe and nowhere to goe. Feel howe I cling to the insydes of darknesse, a babe at a milklesse breste. When I doe goe, I shouldst knotte knowe, but into that bryght lyghte I suppose, and was ancientlie tolde, that which I have only distant memorie of. I hath noe bodie but thine's. I am noe bodie but thee's. So for nowe, I doe staye at home.

I could'st knotte save thee, yet thou could'st knotte kill mee too. Lyfe ys cruele, deathe sodaine. I am alle a broken compasse pointing northe, easte, southe and weste, somewhere loste and craving kingdome, shape, a bodie to bee put in, a house to heate, a feaste to share. I am a monkee with noe mate, a fish-hooke withoute baite. I am deepe in your shallowes, unhappyness in your hollowes. I am a man in a mirrore. Invisible inke written on the page of thee. Of thee I am a blank palimpsest. I am one whoe noe longer ayges. The 'y' in lyfe, the 'oh' in love, the 'you' in you. Though I cannot conceive tyme as any thynge precise, or that ytt holdes some specialle qualitie, theye doe say ytt comes and goes lyke tydes, and waites for noe mann. I am the soule of thee, the spheare of mee, a buoy beached by roughe tides, and schalle floate againe, in tyme. Ys ytt knotte saide that what doth knotte kill thee makes thee stranger? Hee, hee, hee.

I did enjoi the tyme of youre lyfe, and soone I schalle hath the tyme of some one else's. Onlie nowe counts for nowe. I doe knotteth knowe a then or schalle be, hath little memorie of those whoe came before. I cling to you like a memorie but doe knotte have one I may truelly calle my owne. Nowe and then, I sense a subtile heate rise from your sinewy thread and settle behinde your eies. Moving from pineal to heart to stomack, that crossroads, there ys stille lyfe, lyfe stille. Yf only I could'st prove it. Whye I am nothinge more than a cruste of breade already eaten and digeste, noe more alive than deade in peristalsis. And yet, I could'st journey on, bee some one, some thynge. I have noe pulse, noe heart to pumpe bloode, noe braine to conceive thoughte, yet I still feele a movement in our bodie, thynke of yt lyke love that lies waiting in thy bed. I feel ytt in the humours, vapours and spleene that *could'st noe longer feel melancholia, onlye mirthe and wit. To wit, yf a soule doth have a soule, mine should smile righte nowe. Seeke wee then our selves yn our selves. I am the smile yn this tragedie. Ys knotte the rarest essence of rose laced in its thorne? But howe can'st I laughe without laughing, withoute airey lung or curling lip? Thou hath gone, like a name cast in miste. Looke closelie, though, and your name doth reappear in cloudes. What lyttle signe of us past is left lyke a fishy in a stream, or a birdie in the aire. As ys knowne to thee, there ys philosophie in this consolation, and consolation in this philosophie.*

Though I should'st knotte feele, having noe hearte, yt ys broke. I am knotte sure of righte from wronge, cannot sing a deade man's song. Soon I schalle come out and bee gone. From a memorie I doe not possesse, ytt ys jumping from a bridge into a rivere noe one knowes exist'd. Ytt ys deepe and wide, youe cannot see land on any side. Alle you knowe ys youe must swim or flie through water, that you are happye yn thys struggle, for ytt ys your rivere, and your rivere alone.

Dr. Constance Farr arrived in good time to perform the autopsy. Autopsy, as Octavian knew, meant "to see for oneself", and Dr. Farr would see very well for herself this morning as Octavian had just had powerful new lights fitted in the large theatre. The draining table and scales gleamed, though soon enough they'd be spoiled by two-day-old unoxygenated, coagulated blood, the colour of black cherries.

As the coroner had intimated to Octavian, there'd be other witnesses in the theatre: a neurologist called Mr. Swan, recently retired from the hospital, the deceased's GP Dr. Greaves, and yet another neurologist called Dr. Rama. The first thing that happened at this most eventful post-mortem was the argument that ensued between Dr. Farr and all three witnesses. She asked what they were doing there. Mr. Swan and Dr. Rama said the deceased had requested it in a letter before his death and the deceased's widow had signed consent, and besides, they were both curious. 'And what about you?' she asked Dr. Greaves.

'The same as them,' she said.

Dr. Farr nearly exploded. Normally a placid pathologist going about her procedures with skill and precision, she was pacing the theatre, rippling in her scrubs and gloves, the naked cadaver of Jack Mann waiting on the table for the diener's knife. 'None of you should be here,' she said. 'I don't care what your reasons are. In my notes it clearly states that each of you is under investigation by the Trust.' She turned to Octavian. 'You didn't just hear that by the way.'

He nodded. 'I heard nothing, mam.'

'I didn't know I was under investigation,' said the GP, panic spreading through her body.

'It's not an investigation, only a foolish complaint, all unfounded,' said Mr. Swan. 'Isn't it, Dr. Rama?'

'Correct,' he said.

'The coroner approached us, not the other way about,' said Mr. Swan.

Dr. Farr shook her head in frustration. 'Octavian, get Peter on the phone right now.'

There was a phone in the corner, attached to the wall. Octavian dialled the external number, waited to get through to the coroner's office, asking for Peter Witliss, and handed the phone over to Dr. Farr.

She explained her call, listened to his reply, and then she hit the roof: 'I don't care about any of that,' she said, looking around the theatre. 'We can't have the *named* doctors watching the flaming autopsy, Peter. What the hell would that look like? No, this is a balls-up, Peter. I'm very, very surprised this got sanctioned. What?' She listened again, impatiently tapping her foot. 'Well, I couldn't disagree more. It's *my* post-mortem, *my* jurisdiction and in *my* professional opinion they should be asked to leave.' She drummed her fingers on the counter, listening. 'Good.' She handed the phone back to Octavian. 'Right, thank you for coming to this post-mortem,' she said to the audience, 'but your presence is no longer required. You may leave.' When there was no activity, she walked across to the main door and opened it. 'Please. Thank you.' And out the three doctors walked, mumbling to themselves. 'Most extraordinary,' she said to her diener. 'Now, shall we begin?'

Octavian switched on the draining table. Blood was drawn from the body and drained away, gurgling as it went down. Octavian handed across the long needles and watched the vitreous liquid being sucked from the eyeballs. In an anatomy class not that long ago, he'd been told that the only parts of the human body that communicated directly with the sun and the stars were the eyes. Photons of natural light reaching the retina had been born eight and a half minutes before in the core of the sun. After birth, the photons streaked past Mercury and outran Venus on the way to Earth where the multicoloured scatter was then funnelled through the cornea and lens, caught in the net of the retina where protein bent and fired a nerve leading to full perception of one scintilla of light. But not here, thought Octavian. Not under artificial light. And not in a dead man's eyes.

Dr. Farr spoke into the microphone that dangled above the table: 'Examination of skin.' She rolled the body over, and back again, eyes roving the surface for signs of trauma or disease. 'What's this dark mark?' She leaned in. 'Clippers, please.' She shaved the chest hair just above the heart, remarking, 'Octavian, my spy glass.' He handed it over, waiting to discover the mystery. 'Tiny tattooed letters inside a small heart,' she said, staring through the lens. 'A heart inside a heart, and the name *Alice*. Almost impossible to see. Touching, don't you think?' She lifted one of the cadaver's arms. 'Here too, on the wrist, on the pulse point, another tattoo.' She turned to Octavian, puzzled. 'You didn't notice these?'

'No, but it said on file he had acupuncture before death?'

Dr. Farr laughed. 'As opposed to acupuncture *after* death? And were the acupuncturist's needles full of ink? Did the needle-points spell the word *Hunter* on his wrist? And what's this on his shoulder?' She examined it under the spyglass 'Seems incomplete. A bird of some sort? A seagull?'

'There's no such thing as a seagull,' said the diener.

Blood samples were taken and stored in vials. The abdomen was sliced in the usual "Y" from shoulders to belly button. The layers of hardening skin split open, revealing the buttery subcutaneous fat and connective tissue. These were pulled back by the diener. The muscle smelled like raw lamb. The rib cage was now fully exposed and the intestines protruded, smelling pungent. The diener got the buzz-saw going and approached the breast bone with relish, until Dr. Farr leaned in, saying, 'Not today, I have the worst possible headache. Save it for the cranium, but not the sternum. Get the cutters out would you, Octavian.'

He handed them over to the diener. Not one of Farr's usual assistants. A bit brutal in practice, or so Octavian thought, having seen his handiwork before.

I knowe knotte what awaites. I come out from my pineal place, floate downe to sternum and solar plexus. Though I doe knotte possesse feare, I feare the outside ys coming, so sticke to the gladiolus. No thynge breakes through that.

Crack! I flee the bodie, flying to lyghte, a spheare yn space, a miniscule orb bouncing from surface to surface at great speed settling then yn a corner, highe up. Though I possesse noe eies and noe ears, I see and hear them, and knowe what they doe. I bear witnesse to the witnesse laid bare. A man should'st be envied, not pittied. Bee kinde to him, bee kinde or bee nothinge at all.

The diener separated the rib cage with another crack. Dr. Farr examined the appearance of the heart, speaking into the microphone above the table. 'No signs of stenosis or aortic regurgitation.' She felt around the heart, neatly cutting and lifting it out.

What noyse thy heart makes! Murmur of gull, dove or night-crow? Noe mouthe to ope, noe tongue to speake withe, "This ys nothinge," I whispere. "This ys nothinge, Jack Mann."

Dr. Farr handed the heart across to the diener who weighed it and placed it in a plastic tub for further examination of the valves, and later dissection. Meanwhile, Octavian sucked blood from the chest cavity. Down it went into the gurgling drain.

The lungs were snipped out and placed in a sink to test buoyancy. 'Not a heavy smoker,' said Dr. Farr.

The lungs were about to be sliced when the telephone rang again. Octavian tore off a glove and answered. Dr. Farr asked him to hold the phone to her ear this time, and he heard the whole conversation:

'Sorry, it's me again, Connie.'

'What's this about, Peter? I'm not half way through the post-mortem.'

'You haven't dissected, have you?'

'Any second now. Why?'

'I've had a call from Public Health UK.'

'Peter, I'm up to my elbows. Can't it wait?'

'Porton Down contacted PHUK.'

'So what?'

'They want the patient's organs *before* dissection. They wouldn't say what it was about, Connie. They just sent an email. Porton is doing the pathology on this one. They're sending a courier to collect the brain, heart, liver, stomach, gall bladder and testicles.'

'Testicles?'

'They're carting them off to Salisbury for examination. It's about possible infection.'

'There was nothing in my notes about infection.'

'Lyme's disease. It's not contagious, but they suggest you mask up. No dissection. Just remove, store in tubs and they'll collect. Ask that Bulgarian mortuary chap to put them in a chiller. He can sign off the papers when the courier arrives.'

Octavian sighed. Although he'd left Bulgaria ten years ago, to some he'd always be "that Bulgarian chap" with the anachronistic name that he was actually very proud of because it was the birth name of the first Roman Emperor, Augustus, the designated heir of Julius Caesaer.

'I'm flabbergasted, Peter. I'm a pathologist, not a bloody butcher. What's so important about this patient's organs?'

'Bit of a mystery, Connie.'

'What about cause of death?'

'The pathologist at Porton will confirm cause of death and return the organs to the morgue.'

'Peter, this is unethical. Have the relatives been informed?'

'I have no idea,' he said, getting flustered. 'I'm just following orders.'

Octavian replaced the receiver.

'You'd better mask up too, Octavian,' Dr. Farr said. 'I had no idea of possible infection. Twenty years a pathologist, hundreds of autopsies, never seen anything so cloak and dagger.'

'Still,' said the diener. 'We could wrap this up in under an hour.'

Farr looked at him disdainfully, which pleased Octavian. She extracted the stomach, spleen and liver. The diener placed these in large boxes, and Octavian put them in fridge number six. The testicles were carefully sliced off and provided with their very own bollock box. When it came to the brain, Farr asked Octavian if he knew whether there was going to be an open casket at the funeral, and he nodded. 'Pity,' she said, 'not because I like to go in through the front, I just mean if these organs don't come back from Salisbury this poor man's going to be as hollow as The Wicker Man at cremation. You or the undertaker will have to pack him out like "Penny-for-the-Guy". None of his suits will fit. And we don't want him to look like Frankenstein either.'

The diener placed a white towel over Jack Mann's face before slicing into the back of the scalp. After twice failing to pull the scalp forwards over Jack's face Dr. Farr took over, carefully cutting away connective tissue with a scalpel. 'A fine head of hair actually,' she said. 'My husband would be jealous.'

This was always the most surreal part of the autopsy, thought Octavian, when the hair from the top of the head was pulled down to where the face should be. Jack Mann looked like a bald werewolf.

A head saw was used to crack open the cranium, not the buzz-saw. A putty knife was then used to prise open the lid, revealing the brain. When the calvarium was lifted it sounded like two coconut halves tapping together or horse hooves clip-clopping on cobbles. With a quick snip away from the brain stem, the brain emerged in Dr. Farr's hands. 'You wanted to hold a brain, Octavian?' she said. 'Don't drop it though, will you.' He placed his hands together receiving the unexpectedly heavy brain from her when the telephone suddenly rang and he almost dropped it onto the floor.

Dr. Farr snapped off her gloves. She pulled her mask down and picked up the phone expecting it to be Witliss. 'Everything of Mr.

Mann's is now in boxes, Peter, apart from his brain.' She glanced over her shoulder. 'That's literally in hand.'

'Excellent,' said an unfamiliar voice.

'Who is this?'

'Mr. Knox from London. And you are..?'

'Dr. Constance Farr, pathologist-turned-butcher.' She looked at Octavian who was carefully planting the brain in a plastic tub full of formaldehyde.

'I'm senior consultant neurologist at King's,' said Knox.

'Bully for you,' said Farr. 'And why you are interrupting my port-mortem?'

'It's about a certain brain you have in your possession?'

She snorted: 'I must be on Candid Camera.' Her eyes darted around the room sardonically. For a moment, she thought she saw something lurking in one corner, near the ceiling, but it could have been a trick of the light; something so small and round, like a tiny black dot. 'So, where's the camera? Inside one of the cadavers? Where's Jeremy Beadle? Inside a cooler? Come out, come out wherever you are.'

'Jeremy Beadle died years ago,' said the diener, 'and I'm really hoping he isn't still in a cooler.'

Mr. Knox said, 'I'm sitting in my office on the Denmark Hill campus. I wanted to talk to you about the patient's brain. How far into the autopsy are you? I'd be grateful if you didn't cut through the pineal gland. Nothing must happen to Mr. Mann's pineal gland *until we have seen it at King's.*'

'This has got to be a joke,' said Farr, looking around the theatre again.

'I've sent a courier on motorbike. He should be with you in under an hour.'

'Porton want the brain along with all the other organs, Mr. Knox.'

'I was promised the brain!' he shouted.

'Well, you'll have to speak to Porton, not me. I'm just the humble bloody pathologist.'

'Dr. Farr, this pineal is extraordinary.'

'Not my concern. Now, I have another post-mortem to conduct. Goodbye.' She returned to the corpse.

'Want me to start stitching up?' said the diener, but she seemed lost in thought. 'Dr. Farr?'

'No, I'll deal with the cranium,' she said.

Should'st I staye yn the pretious lyghte withe them, or goe backe inside the darknesse with thee, Jack Mann? Connect'd withe silken thread, I flee to where your braine did once nestle. Bodie withoute minde ys but a mummy.

Dr. Farr replaced the top of the cranium, matching up the two pieces perfectly. She gently pulled the scalp back into position, removed the white towel, revealing the man's bearded face again. She stitched along the original line of incision, hiding it well among the man's hair. She did this loosely. If and when the brain was returned, it would be easier to unpick. 'If you can do the rest,' she said to the diener. 'Though not too tightly. All the organs will need to pop back in when Porton have finished with them.'

She stood back and leaned against the counter, watching the diener suturing the Y incision from shoulders to belly button. "Why?" was exactly the question in her mind. Why the sudden change in protocol? Why *this* man? Why were different institutions fighting over his body parts?

When the stitching was complete, Dr. Farr walked over to the corpse and did something she'd never done before. Octavian was quite sure of that. Professional distance was always maintained during her work (corpses had once been living, breathing, thinking, feeling human beings after all). Neutrality was maintained at all times, and there was certainly no religion. This time, though, she placed her hand on the man's right shoulder as if he might be her own brother, and said: 'God rest your soul.'

Ytt doth ecchoe insyde the soule of mee, insyde the cave of thee, Jack Mann. Our ruinous anatomie, these immedicable harmes. Wee are yn fantastik chaosses, teare-floods and through-shines, push'd to the colde darke tombe againe. Why, this ys hell, nor am I oute of ytt. Yf I have beene and gone and schalle bee, why am I soe loste without thee?

I move aboute the durty foulenesse, the undulations and knottie riddles of the bowels, up through space, clinging to the rock face of thy ribs, to sternum, the gladiolus I must goe and reste; to that broken sworde.

On Funeral Eve

Alice spent most of the night before the funeral sitting beside Jack in the study talking to him, occasionally stroking his face. The undertakers had done a splendid job given the delays with the post-mortem. They'd cut Jack's hair the way he liked, except they left it a bit longer than normal to cover the stitching and staples. They'd trimmed his beard and he looked as distinguished as a professor of English. They'd applied light make-up to disguise the deathly grey pallor. He was dressed in his best black linen suit, black t-shirt and black slip-on boots. The Mann in Black. No shirt and tie, which he'd always regarded as stuffy. His eyelids appeared only lightly closed as if about to spring open, though that might have been her imagination. His jaw, mouth and lips were set in soft repose not unlike the subtle, serene smile on the face of Jack's Buddha in the Zen garden.

Jack had been embalmed, but the Berry family undertakers hadn't overdone it as others sometimes did. He didn't look bloated. He didn't appear to be blowing a raspberry like his Uncle Dicky. No, her beloved Jack looked at peace now, asleep, and if mourners coming tomorrow wanted to see him they could visit him here in the study, one of his favourite hiding places when he was alive. Jack's coffin was set safely on a strong trestle. The lid lay against the writing desk. Pandora weaved in and out of the legs looking up at the coffin, sensing her master and wanting to jump up and lick his face.

Although Jack usually planned things off the hoof, Alice realised her husband had given his own funeral a lot of thought: the Berry family undertakers, the casket (a simple softwood), even horses and a carriage to carry him away the next day, trotting around the seafront before going to the crematorium for an extended service. No flowers, but instead donations to the local MS therapy centre. No church. No priest. No ashes to ashes; although Jack had selected that as one of his songs to be played, along with The Divine Comedy's "Gin Soaked Boy". Alice had consulted Jin-jing Li regarding a Buddhist speaker, and she'd recommended a monk near Dover who agreed to do some readings from the ancient masters including someone called Vairacchedika. Death as renewal, not conclusion, the monk said on the phone. Gerry would read an excerpt from John Donne's poem, *The First Anniversarie. An Anatomy of the World. [To the Praise of the Dead, and the Anatomy]* that Jack had left earmarked on his desk in the study:

Wel dy'de the world, that we might live to see
This world of wit, in his Anatomee:
No evil wants his good; so wilder heyres
Bedew their father's Toombs with forced teares,
Whose state requites their los: whils thus we gaine
Well may wee walk in blacks, but not complaine.
Yet, how can I consent the world is dead
While this Muse lives? which in his spirits stead
Seemes to informe a world: and bids it bee,
In spite of Losse, or frail mortalitee?

Or had he earmarked *Metempsychosis*, "The Progresse of the Soule"..?

Alice would speak of personal memories. Everything was written down, and she had only to say it without crying.

Gerry and Francesca were expected to arrive early in the morning, bringing their baby May with them. Fran said she'd help Alice prepare the food, making sandwiches, heating sausage rolls and quiches, mixing up some simple salads; enough to feed the expected twenty family members and friends. Could be twenty, could be more. The telephone had been ringing non-stop for days with deepest sympathies, and Alice hadn't been able to keep up with who could come and who couldn't. There were at least thirty cards on mantels, sills and shelves.

Ernie was staying at Lauren's flat in Muswell Hill, helping her with their mother. Poor Estella; first her husband, now her son, both killing themselves in their forties.

The night before the funeral passed slowly, and Alice didn't know what to do with herself. She couldn't leave Jack alone, but neither could she stay there in the study all night with so much tidying to do. She should have taken her parents up on their offer to help, but she wanted one last night alone with her beloved Jack. She placed Hunter's framed handprints inside the coffin beside Jack's arm. She didn't want Jack to make his journey alone. After two hours of talking to him and dozing and drinking wine, she ransacked their CD collection. She remembered what Dr. Ono had said about neurons stacked up like CDs reaching the sun and returning back down to Earth.

The more she drank, the more morose she became, playing her "wailing women": Camille O'Sullivan, Ane Brun, Florence + The Machine. And then she played Scott Walker's "If You Go Away", crying. Finally, she came to the song that made Jack the cryborg almost cry all those years ago at the theatre in London; "I Dreamed a Dream" from *Les Miserables*. She played the film version starring Anne Hathaway and drowned herself in the words, sing-shouting her misery. *You spent the summer by my side...and you were gone when autumn came...* Half way through the song, at a mini-climax, Alice belted it out and Pandora took it as a sign to howl. It was a wild, primeval sight and sound that Jack would have relished. Only Major Tom had ever howled like that. Alice played the song five times, even louder, and took Pan into the study where she howled again for her master in his coffin.

At around three in the morning, she finally went to bed. Tears in her eyes, she kissed Jack on the forehead before closing the study door, and despised herself for leaving him alone. She hadn't brought herself to place the lid over his lonely face, and left a light on for him too.

I schalle miss the lovelie anagram of this ideott's face too. But hee ys knotte quite alone, Alice. Dry your spungie eies. Jack stille has mee, and I ys hee. Alas, true griefe ys shee, teares tangled yn the sunbeames of her hair; his magique braine noe longer thinkes, that beating hearte has been ecclips'd, as much use nowe as a sun dyall to a grave. But hee soules language understood; the elixir of good love hee drank; twas knotte a foolishe phantasie. It was knotte rubbidge, but boundlesse Galaxie.

Alice lay awake visualising her husband's body parts being sliced and diced. She'd felt at first vindicated by, and then furious with Porton Down's pathology report. It stated there *was* evidence of pathogenic Lyme infection. Borrelia spirochetes were found in Jack's brain, gall bladder and testes. In light of this (and the fact Jack's previous blood tests had all returned negative from the same facility) Porton was now reviewing all serological testing for Lyme disease and advising GPs across the UK to favour clinical diagnoses. Alice could take solace; Jack hadn't died in vain. Something positive had come from his tragedy. But in conclusion, the pathologist stated, Jack had not died from the infection, mortality explained by simultaneous organ failure and brain death due to tricyclic toxicity: a simple overdose. The report took into account Jack's medical history, emphasising his depressions. The pathologist noted in this respect that Jack had attempted suicide before, in 1999. The coroner agreed that there was no need for further investigation.

Alice had given an exclusive interview to Siobhan Lafferty; the same journalist who'd run a feature on Jack eight years before. She devoted a double-spread and gave it the title, *The Tragedy of Mann*. Alice provided photos of Jack "before and after" Lyme: Jack running the London marathon, Jack sitting dishevilled on a mobility scooter. It's ironic, said Alice, the illness is called "the great imitator", a disease that led to the death of my husband, a great imitator himself. Lyme is labelled "an invisible illness", she told Siobhan. Loved ones and medical professionals doubt the validity of the sickness, opening the door to accusations of mental instability or psychosis. Jack's symptoms were blatantly visible, so obviously physical, she said. He ticked every physiological box and fought the disabling effects to the bitter end. Anyone who knew him would say Jack was a fighter, a survivor, not a quitter, but with Lyme he was under attack on too many fronts: pain, physical disorientation, psychological trauma, and on top of these an endless struggle persuading health professionals of the truth; the same people who abandoned him. It was a slow-moving, diagnostic shambles from start to end, she said. Jack and I were experiencing a monumental earthquake and most of the fault lines ran under the hospital. Imagine having all the symptoms and signs of MS and receiving none of the sympathy, understanding or treatment. Allowing a person to go down a path of progressive neurodegeneration when he could be treated is unconscionable, she said. Jack had always been an advocate for public health services, but the irony to crown all ironies was that his consultants were more resistant to the possibility of Lyme than Borrelia bacteria are to antibiotics. Lymies are diagnosed too late or not at all, throwing them into the hands of expensive private doctors. NHS consultants seem to have their hands tied, so they have to say "this is not Lyme". Nothing comes out of their budgets. It's the patients who go bankrupt. You see, Jack was torn to pieces bit by bit, not just by Lyme, but by human hands. Who'd have thought something as small as a poppy seed could destroy a person's life like that? It's the stuff of nightmares, horror films. There are thousands just like Jack in the UK. Hundreds of thousands in America, Canada, Australia. Millions worldwide. Something has to be done, she said. New research, reliable diagnostics, better education, and political change. Only with these things, she concluded, only then can we avoid the tragedy of yet another Jack or Jacqueline Mann.

Mr. Knox claimed the famous pineal gland with Alice's full consent. What use was it to Jack now? He wouldn't need to produce melatonin where he was going. A consultant with a specialism dissected the gland and discovered a most remarkable thing. For the first time in a human being there was evidence of a "parietal" third eye. Not a lens as such, but certain retinal and corneal structures akin to an ordinary eye. Such things were usually found in fish, sharks and lizards, Knox said, though a fossil of a Russian bird from ninety million years ago also had a pineal sac. Jack was some sort of evolutionary throw-back, he said. Some sort of bird-man. It was BIG news, not only for neuroscientists but for philosophers and parapsychologists and those with an interest in, dare he say it, the *spiritual*. Perhaps now, he said, there *was* evidence of a machine in the ghost in the machine; the substance of "self" or the soul.

Though she thought she'd never sleep, her mind a whirl of memories and misgivings, Alice drifted into unconsciousness in the master bedroom, her balcony door slightly ajar to hear the tide. She was woken by a terrifying dream that needed no explanation: Jack burning alive at a crematorium. She rushed downstairs to check on him and he was sitting upright in his coffin, staring at her. In his teeth flapped a fish, its tail dripping saltwater. She screamed, and Jack screamed at her screaming. He dropped the fish into his lap and said: 'It came from the sky.' She looked where he was looking, up at the ceiling, and another fish plopped to the floor, landing with a thud, its mouth making "Oh"s. Then another fish came, and another, and another at great speed as if spewed from a trawler's net. Pandora scampered around barking at the fish rain. Crabs, oysters, lobsters and crayfish crashed to the floor. Alice looked at Jack, shocked to discover his head was gone, replaced now by a seagull's, and it was laughing: *grack grack grack, scree scree scree.*

A foghorn sounded and Alice awoke just before dawn, her nightdress damp at the chest; a dream within a dream from too much wine, worry and sorrow. There was a noise in the ceiling; the scrambling of gulls on the roof. They were dropping food caught from the shoreline. Her neighbour Ron had spoken of a nest and an egg, though she hadn't seen them from her windows. And anyway, no seagull hatched in October when the north wind blew cold and continually.

The Big Day

All Alice had to do was hold it together. For weeks now, even before Jack took his life, she'd almost drowned in a sea of tears. Floods happened when she least expected; standing at a deli counter or supermarket till, in the bathroom of her parents' flat, putting the lead on Pandora in the morning. Soon, these outpourings joined up like canals of misery encircling her, and she contemplated taking her own life; times when she found herself missing him the most, like looking in the wardrobe at his empty clothes that still had his shape in them. One night she took one of his favourite woollen jackets from the wardrobe, put it on and held herself in his arms. She re-read his last letter, the passage where he asked her to go on, to flower again, to find new love, to move away from the sea even. She was signed off from work with depression; a dark shadow that kept her in the cold and which she'd never fully experienced before. Everyone said it was her expression of grief, of loss, and would soften with time. But for what seemed like ages, her grief was a fever breaking into a sweat of sad memories; all the things she and Jack had shared and would never share again. She just had to get this day over with, without any big scenes.

Alice took a call from the actor Jim Carrey who was currently shooting a film in Hollywood. Jack and Jim had been phone pals at the tail-end of the 90s, but the relationship had fizzled out. The film star had just heard the sad news. Why, Jack was one of the funniest guys he'd ever met, he said. As a Buddhist himself, he thought Jack had stored up enough good karma with comedy to come back as whatever he wanted in the next life. He said spirituality was about the end of all suffering and that Jack was no longer in any pain. Jack was no longer locked inside his brain. He was free.

The foghorn sounded sad as the mourners arrived in dribs and drabs in the seaside drizzle. Family and close friends came first. Gerry with Fran who was holding May in her arms, all bubble goo-goos and gurgles. Alice's parents were next, Alan pushing Pat in a wheelchair.

Ernie and Lauren escorted their frail mother Estella into the hall. Magda, the nursing home manager, headed straight for the food.

The intention was to have light snacks and drinks at Seagull House before going off to the crematorium, and from there to a local pub for lunch and what you might loosely call a celebration of Jack's life. Donations to MS and Lyme charities were appreciated, though some mourners still brought bouquets of flowers. Some of these the Berry undertakers would lay on the top and sides of the coffin inside a majestic black carriage standing behind two magnificent black horses with plumes. No one ever thought Jack would want to be taken to the crematorium in a hearse more fitting for state funerals. It was all an odd sort of dream, thought Alice, light-headed from lack of sleep. Intermittently, she led people to the coffin in the study. Some mourners didn't want to see Jack's body lying in wake, politely declining. Alice thought they must have heard about the unusual post-mortem and feared Frankenstein was waiting for them.

Family did say their goodbyes to Jack. Ernie said: 'Hang in there, buddy.' As if he might still be alive. Following Ernie's lead, Estella said to her dead son, 'What are you doing sleeping in here? Come on, get up.' And Lauren said: 'You'll be just fine, Jack.'

Most people preferred not to touch Jack's body. It was so with Jack's former friend and fellow comedian John Cockshaw, who stood there frozen before the open casket. 'Jack, you fool,' he said, in his Kenneth Williams "mockney" accent. 'Stop muckin' about.' Alice couldn't get over how young John looked. She hadn't seen him for fifteen years, and he hadn't visibly changed. Perhaps, he'd had a face-lift.

Jin-jing arrived. Now mid-way through her second trimester, there was a well-defined bump resembling a smooth egg beneath her black dress. She came with her husband, Michael Wasser. Jin-jing wasn't afraid of death. She held Jack's hand, smiling at him and wishing him well on his journey. She turned to Alice and said: 'Jack is an old soul, been around long time and going somewhere else now.'

An ambulance pulled up outside the house and Gerry alerted Alice. At first she thought it might be for a sick elderly neighbour, but then three men got out of the back. Two made it down by themselves and the third, in a wheelchair, used a ramp. Slowly, they made their way along the road to the drive, and she thought she recognised the man in the wheelchair. 'Mrs. Mann,' he said. 'I'm sorry, I didn't realise how ill your husband was. Me and my two friends wish to extend our condolences and deepest sympathies.'

Though Christmas was still two months away, Alice thought they would make excellent wise men. She knew the man in the wheelchair: Dr. Skelton, the old Time Lord. He used to have a terrible stutter, but that had resolved. David, the Ugandan businessman, was no longer jaundiced. If anything, he looked rosy. 'Forgive us, Mrs. Mann,' he said, tears starting in his eyes. 'I knew Jack for such a short time, but will never forget his single act of kindness. He was a decent sort of fellow. A fellow of infinite jest.'

'How did you know about the funeral?'

'We free kept in touch,' said Stan, the retired plumber. He stepped forward and shook Alice's hand with a firm grip. He was thinner, fitter, with no visible signs of stroke. 'The Docta saw yer on the telly.'

'But how did you know where Jack lived?'

'I have contacts at the hospital,' said Skelton, tapping his nose.

It was all so unreal, as if the Time Lord had taken his two friends back to a time when they'd been healthier and happier. 'How well you're all looking,' she remarked.

'Time Lords don't age,' said Skelton. 'We just alter appearance.'

She shook her head in puzzlement, and looked further down the road at a fresh stream of people making its way towards the house. 'What's all this?'

'More gate crashers,' said Gerry.

Alice recognised the manager of the MS centre, and the MS nurse who pushed Stevie, the ex-soldier. Jack's ICU nurse, Collette, was there, and chatting her up was Jack's old university tutor and Donne specialist, Professor Bird. There were friends from the alternative comedy circuit, the pubs and clubs of the 1980s and 90s. The producer of *Come Dine with Me* said he'd pull his programme, but to his delight Alice requested only a dedication to her dead husband. Jack's Aunt Helen arrived with her sister Claire, already inebriated and hectoring strangers with notions of age and time. Luke "Skywalker" turned up direct from the Arrowhead Clinic, dragging a drip stand alongside him.

Mr. Knox was next to show, carrying a special glass presentation case containing Jack's pineal gland, or what was left of it, as small as a flea. He said he represented the whole of King's College in London. 'Dr. Ono sends his deepest sympathies, and apologises, but he's currently touring Japan with his cyberpunk band, The Jung Ones. Alice, I also have something very important to give you from Dr. Ono...' He reached inside his jacket pocket and took out a manila envelope, but replaced it when he saw how busy she was with mourners. Graham the gardener shook her hand, his honest, open face reminding her of the mantra: *be kind or be nothing at all.* It was all so surreal. Someone strange called Octavian arrived saying he knew her husband "inside out".

Soon, Seagull house was bulging with mourners, all with little or large stories about Jack Mann, neighbours included. Ron, the seagull obsessive, someone called Madge from a seafront house. An attractive lady threatened to steal the show, dressed head to toe in white, her long dark hair pinned up in a frizzy nest, a curly slick of grey running down one side like a streak of lightning. Her lips were painted black. She looked like the bride of Frankenstein, and introduced herself as Elisha. She'd met Jack on the *Come Dine with Me* programme. She complemented Alice on her dolphin necklace, then asked if she could see Jack in his coffin.

Elisha stood beside the body, tears in her eyes. She reached out and touched Jack's wrist. 'He was such a loving man,' she said.

Not lovely, but *loving.* 'He was,' said Alice, prickling.

Letting go of the wrist suddenly, Elisha smiled, saying, 'There's still life.'

'That was *our* song,' said Alice, distracted then by a commotion in the hallway. A long queue had formed outside the cloakroom, and Alice barged through. The door was locked, so she knocked loudly three times.

Stan the plumber opened up. The whitewashed floorboards were covered in bits of wire and cables. He'd stripped her new combi boiler to pieces. 'The wiring's back to front,' he said. 'Makin' a terrible noise it was. Don't worry, I'll 'ave it fixed in time for the creamatorium.'

Gerry helped make extra sandwiches in the kitchen as the crowd milled around the house, the veranda and the rear garden. 'I expected twenty or thirty,' said Alice, 'but there's more like eighty. They just keep coming, like a stream of unconsciousness.'

'We should have sold tickets,' said Gerry, annoyed at the swelling ranks of rubberneckers and hangers-on. He looked through into the lounge, over the heads of everyone. He was holding two plates of food, trying to recognise faces. 'Blow me!' he roared, thrusting plates of cheese and tomato sandwiches into the hands of Alice's father. 'It's the damn Mexican!' He barged through the crowd screaming at the top of his lungs: 'Hernandez!'

'It can't be!' Alice cried. She watched Gerry bound across the room towards a dark-haired, well-dressed gentleman standing by the hallway door. It was difficult seeing his face through the throng. He looked familiar, but how could it be Gerry's old accountant? Interpol had confirmed his death. The Mexican would have to be Lazarus. Pandora sensed something, barking with purpose.

The mourners parted, making a path for Alice. By the time she reached Gerry he had both hands around the throat of Dr. Rama, not Hernandez. Gerry had him off the floor, pushed against the wall. 'Hernandez, you thief! You come here on the day of Jack's funeral! What the hell do you think you're doing?'

Dr. Rama's eyes were watering and bulging, his pencil moustache distorted by Gerry's fingers, his short legs kicking cartoonishly. Alice got hold of Gerry's arms, pulling them down. 'It's not Hernandez! It's Jack's neurologist!'

'Where's the dough? Where's the bullet in your brain? Where's the cactus?'

Michael Wasser charged across the room, tearing Gerry away from Dr. Rama. Gerry pointed his finger, shouting, 'Get the hell out! No, stay here, I'm going to call Interpol! Hold on, I don't have their number. Michael, keep a hold. I'm making a citizen's arrest!' He started to get his phone out but stopped short, looking at Alice. 'Jack's neurologist you say?'

Dr. Rama was bent double, hands on knees, gasping for breath. The small bald patch on the top of his head shone bright red like a bullseye.

'I don't know what you're doing here,' said Alice, and Rama looked up, straightening his tie.

Recognising the hurt in her voice, Gerry said: 'Right, you've ruined a man's life; you're not going to ruin his funeral too. Off we go.' He grabbed hold of one arm and Michael Wasser got hold of the other. Together, they frogmarched Dr. Rama into the hall, all the way to the front door.

'Wait!' shouted Alice. 'I have no idea why you came, Dr. Rama. You left Jack for dead. If you came to apologise, or explain, or offload your guilt, you're too late.'

Dr. Rama turned his head a fraction, looked her straight in the eyes and said: 'It's not too late, Mrs. Mann, because Jack isn't really dead.'

'It's true!' Octavian barked from the back of the room. 'He's alive!'

'What?' said Alice, turning to face the crowd.

'Show her the note from Dr. Ono!' Luke shouted.

'Oh yes.' Mr. Knox reached inside his jacket pocket and pulled out the manila envelope. He handed it across.

Alice dragged out a white card. One side bore a beautiful illustration of a lotus flower, the other had ancient calligraphic symbols that made no sense. 'It's in Japanese,' she said, and a titter rose up and moved around the room. Everyone laughed, laughed as if it was the funniest thing they'd ever heard. 'What does it mean?' cried Alice. 'What has Dr. Ono written?'

Everyone replied in perfect unison: 'A story told by the conscious has a beginning, a middle and an end, but a tale from the unconscious has many beginnings, lots of muddle and a bend.'

She stared at them, open-mouthed. 'We're figments of Jack's imagination?'

'Jack isn't dead,' they said, 'because it's only in his head.'

Whan the Berry man doth screwe down the lid, some thynge connect'd snaps 'tween us like a broken thread or promise, and I knowe thys ys ended. The shadowes, blacke as crowes, spille oute onto streets of glassie deepe redd. I spye the cavalcade goe bye. Yn here burnes a forgotten flame on a table where I flye moth-like, fluttering aboute the heate and lyghte in never-ending circles; only one does ende. My wynges catch lyghte lyfting mee up to a newe worlde. I am warme and comfort'd. A small hearte beats yn mee, and mee yn yt. Pineal, hearte and stomack here as yf nevere died and disappear'd. Ytt ys darke lyke nyghte, but dawn appears yn the cracks. I schalle bee awakt againe. Scree, scree, scree. And though I have loste almoste alle memorie of thee, Jack Mann, some where yn my soule of soules I knowe you are my favourite historie. I stille recall that melancholic thynge with clearnesse, soe cheerefully: a hearte, lyke an egge, ys useless yf yt nevere breaks. So I hatch. Naked, wette and colde. Wynges beat, beaks grackle. Lyfe ys againe.

Shaggy Dog Story

Gerry had a tight hold of the dog lead. Pandora pulled him frenziedly through the electronic hospital doors trying to keep up with her new pack leader, Alice, who marched past the porter's office. It was an adventure full of brand new smells, sights and sounds. Pan's long nose sniffed the ground and then the air as if searching for clues to the whereabouts of her true master, Jack. Her nutty eyes flitted left and right and then focused again on Alice.

She created quite a stir on the ground floor. Patients in wheelchairs pointed, exclaiming how wonderful it was to see such a shaggy dog. 'Look at the snout on it,' one man said. Others shook their heads and tutted, questioning its unhygienic potential. Germs in its paws, fleas in its fur, and what if it did something unseemly on the floor?

The excitement alerted a porter behind a glass screen. ''Scuse me, miss,' he said. 'Is that a PAT dog? Have you got a certificate?'

'She's well-behaved,' said Alice. Pandora scrambled and skidded on the slippery polished floor, panting, almost choking in her stretched collar.

'Can I see your certificate?' cried the porter climbing out of his chair. 'Has this been arranged through Infection Control?'

Alice pressed the button at the side of the lift. The door opened and she hurried inside. Pan and Gerry skidded in beside her. The door closed just before the porter reached it. He spoke into his walkie-talkie as the lift went up. 'Assistance required.'

The ICU door was locked. Gerry stood well out of the way of the camera mounted on the wall whilst Alice pressed the entry buzzer. Footsteps could be heard running up the stairs. Three security guards appeared, leaping two steps at a time, breathing heavily into walkie-talkies.

'Now then,' one of them said, waving both hands in a placatory manner. 'We don't want any trouble, but you can't take a dog into ICU.'

'No?' said Alice, 'Then watch this.' A buzzer sounded, the door clicked open and Alice held it ajar for Gerry and Pandora.

One of the security men made a move and Gerry raised a hand as if a black-belt in karate. 'Steer clear,' he growled and darted inside. Alice pulled the door shut, hearing a click. She rushed down the corridor towards Jack's room.

Collette was standing beside Jack's monitor, making notes on a clipboard. 'Gosh,' she said.

'Collette, help. We only need a few minutes.'

'I'll see what I can do.' She closed the door behind her and rushed into the corridor, bumping into one of the security men.

'We're here for the dog.'

'What dog?' said Collette.

'C'mon. The dog.'

'You must be imagining things.'

'It's in there,' said a guard, looking over Collette's shoulder and through the glass wall of Jack's room. 'It's sitting on the bloody bed.'

'Out the way, Miss.'

'The patient's life-support is due to be switched off in a few hours. His pet has been allowed one last visit.'

'First I've heard.'

'Well, if it's been arranged,' said a guard. 'One of us will wait, and escort the dog from the premises. How long will it be?'

'However long final goodbyes take,' said Collette.

Having jumped onto the bed, Pandora was now stepping all around it, sniffing the cables, wires and tubes. She nosed the tubes that masked the lower half of Jack's face, wagging her tail and plonking her bottom down. She glanced at the ventilator momentarily as if understanding the connection.

'Do you think she knows?' asked Gerry.

'She knows,' said Alice.

Gerry still had hold of Pan's lead and was standing on one side of the bed. Alice was standing on the other side. She noticed Collette's thumb's up through the internal window, and mouthed to her, 'Thank you.' Collette held up both hands, indicating ten minutes.

Pandora lay down beside Jack's left leg, making a huffing noise. Gerry let go of the lead and sat down in a chair. Alice took hold of her husband's hand, lightly squeezing it. 'We're here for you, Jack.' The dog's floppy ears pricked at the mention of his name. She raised her head, staring at Alice, and then put her chin down on Jack's lap.

'Jack Mann's best friend,' said Gerry, and Alice smiled at the simplest of puns.

'We're getting close to the end now, aren't we?'

They sat there for what seemed like ages, Jack unmoved and unmoving, Gerry and Alice looking from each other's faces and back to Jack. Collette passed by the internal window at regular intervals, first one way and then the other like a pendulum in a grandfather clock. Alice thought of the one in the hall of Seagull House and how it had stopped working the day Jack tried to take his life.

The ventilator pumped oxygen into Jack's lungs and removed the carbon dioxide. The heart monitor bleeped in a slow, regular rhythm. Combined with the hospital's heating, these things had a mild, soporific effect. Alice hadn't slept for days. She sat down and closed her eyes.

Gerry gazed at her sad, beautiful face. Although he'd never told her during all the years he'd known her, when her hair was this messy and her eyes were so black, she looked like Theda Bara.

Collette stopped by the window, indicating it was time. Gerry nodded. 'Alice, darling, it's time we took Pan home.'

Alice stood up and Pandora leapt to her feet. 'Well?' she asked Pan. 'Aren't you going to say goodbye properly?'

Pan lowered her head and licked Jack's hand. Her tail thumped the bed, and she kept licking. When the bleeps of the heart monitor started to accelerate Alice looked at Gerry, concerned. Pandora licked and licked as if softening a bone, and the heartbeat increased further.

'Alice!' shouted Gerry, staring at Jack's hand.

'My God!'

'He's moving his fingers!'

In the pandemonium, Pandora leapt from the bed, barking, and Alice pressed the buzzer. 'Jack!' she cried. 'Jack?' His eyes rolled under his lids, opening suddenly, sending Alice into hysterics. 'Jack! Jack, it's me! It's me!' He started choking on the tubes.

Collette ran in, shouting for assistance. Gerry pulled Pandora to one corner. 'Is he coming out of the coma?' Collette loosened the tape around Jack's nose and mouth.

'Jack, it's me!' cried Alice. 'You're awake!'

A doctor arrived. Jack gasped for air as if coming up from the bottom of a deep river. He stared blankly up at the ceiling, seeing something or someone. Collette placed an oxygen mask over his nose and mouth. Jack's pulse normalised. His heartbeat grew regular. He was breathing and looking around the room, confused.

A neurologist entered the room. The patient had classic signs of near brain death, yet here he was, already propped up in bed, and blinking. But this patient had been too far gone to come so far back. It was a miracle. He double-checked the readings; all normal. He shone a light into each of Jack's eyes noting prompt constriction. He tested sensory reflexes in the hands and feet, each within normal limits. 'Extraordinary,' he kept saying. 'Extraordinary.' He asked Jack some questions, but the patient was disorientated. The patient didn't know where he was or who he was for a while. 'What do you expect,' the consultant said to Alice, 'when you've been in a deep sleep for more than a month?' He turned and noticed the dog. 'What's *that* doing here?'

'*That* is Jack's beloved Pandora,' said Gerry. 'And if you knew your Greek mythology, you'd know that when all seemed lost, Pandora found hope.'

-PART EIGHT-

This to thy soule allow,
Thinke thy sheell broke,
Thinke thy Soule hatch'd but now.

John Donne

Hardships often prepare ordinary people for an extraordinary destiny.

C.S. Lewis

In Another Life

Jack was kept on ICU for a week. He breathed without an oxygen mask, could eat and drink unaided. He walked unassisted to the bathroom and showered without help. He was visited by Lauren and their mother Estella, then Jin-jing. Gerry drove over from Sussex twice, once with Fran and the baby. Jack seemed to recognise everyone by their faces but needed assistance with names, as if the details had been erased.

He was moved to a general ward and assigned a psychologist, a psychiatrist, and then a psychotherapist. They discussed what happened to him. He told them he could remember fragments, as if from a dream: bench, fog, foghorn and a giant gull. He told one therapist he'd seen himself dead on a gurney and fully anatomised, but hadn't seen himself actually die. He'd been about to go to his own funeral too, but that never happened either. He said he had seen these things as if from a distance, way up high. 'It's foggy. I saw myself dissected and my soul leap out of me. Am I a man with no soul?'

One therapist said these feelings weren't uncommon in patients with near-death, or out-of-body experiences. 'Seeing one's body from above is the brain's way of making sense of physical or psychological trauma. It's called "derealisation" or "terminal lucidity".' Jack told her it was more real than that; a part of him *had* died and a different part had been re-awakened or reborn somewhere else, possibly in an egg?

'Life is here waiting for you, Jack,' the therapist said. 'Life is worth it.' She discussed his neverending pain as if it were a pathological liar: 'Nothing lasts forever. Pain tells you it will last, but pain lies. Ignore it. Pain will go away.'

'Pain isn't imaginary,' he said. 'Pain is relentless.'

The therapist said, 'Because the pain still exists, what are the chances of you trying this again?'

Alice drove him back to Seagull House. As he got out of the car he looked up at the roof as if looking for the pair of gulls. 'They flew away last week,' she said, 'and they haven't come back.'

'Was there an egg?'

She shook her head.

The house was immaculate, except for sofa cushions thrown onto the floor by Pandora in anticipation of his return. 'Who's this?' said Alice, and Pandora leapt up at him. He bent down to her level letting her snuffle his face and lick his ears.

Letters and cards arrived daily, some from long-forgotten friends, others from complete strangers including members of the international Lyme community. Alice set the cards out on the mantelpiece and shelves. Jack didn't seem interested in them, saying he couldn't read. It was the brain fog.

Whenever she was out for longer periods, Jack wandered from room to room with Pan shadowing. He soaked up each space, lingering in the study most of all. A room full of books. He spotted John Donne among them and remembered things: *Yf the soule doth looke, sees the bodie ys a booke? Unable to express words makes man a grave of his thoughtes?* There were tiny hand prints framed on one wall, but he didn't know whose they were; something to do with hunting, or laughing gas? Seagull House felt oddly familiar, as if stills from a film he'd seen and half-remembered, as if sleepwalking through the past, like Rebecca wandering Manderley; as if there might be a ghost waiting for him, or he might be that ghost waiting. Fragments of feelings slowly joined up in him, revolving around a little coffin and a hearse.

Alice did most of the talking. In some of his longer silences she believed her husband had brain damage, not brain fog, though the neurologist said it would just take time for him to readjust. It was a miracle he'd survived at all. The biggest problem was his loss of memory. Jack was slow to react to the names of places, people and events that had once filled his past. He'd nod at her, but it was obvious from the vacancy in his eyes he hadn't recollected. She'd never say it, but her husband seemed to have come back from the dead as a cold and empty vessel, a blank sheet of paper or outline of a man; lobotomised, as if from *One Flew Over the Cuckoo's Nest*.

Jack slept in the guest bedroom because of his burning hands and feet. Although he and Alice were apart at night it was a far cry from the loneliness she'd felt when he was lying in a coma. When a foghorn sounded, she tapped the wall between them and called out: 'Isn't it wonderful to hear when you're safely tucked up in bed, Jack?'

'Yes,' he called, but something about that sound confused and terrified him.

In the mornings he hauled himself out of bed and peered into the bathroom mirror, seeing a much older man than he recalled. 'What's happening to you?' he asked his reflection. 'It's taken years off your life and added them to your face. This isn't you, Jack.' After showers he made odd words with his finger in the condensation on the screen: *glass lue*, *lass glue*, *gall sues*, *slug sale* and *guess all*. And one morning, he seemed to guess right: *seagulls*.

He spent a lot of time in the Zen garden, even though it was frosty in early winter. There was a stone Buddha in one corner. One of its hands was cemented onto its body in the wrong position, and the join was visible. The garden was quiet. Jack watched a robin flit through the branches of a tamarisk tree, coming down as if to speak to him. He knew it from somewhere, but couldn't place it in his mind.

One evening, in front of the log burner, Alice broached the subject of his suicide attempt. She told him he'd been found on a bench and some seagulls saved him from hypothermia. He had no recollection. There was a foghorn, he said, and this Birdman? He thought the Birdman was going to take him away. She showed him the local newspapers to make it more real. She mentioned Mr. Knox and Dr. Ono, and how they'd looked for signs of consciousness and she'd been invited into the MRI control room. She said it was the scariest moment of her life, except when he crashed in ICU. He shook his head, vacant-eyed. 'It feels like

I'm here with you but I'm somewhere else, like on that bench, or in an egg. How can that be?'

She lightened things up saying he had a most unusual pineal gland; twice the size of the average. He smiled, but it was shallow and unconvincing. She told him he'd been given a 50% chance of regaining consciousness, and that was before his breathing stopped. When she mentioned how the machine was going to be switched off, she cried, saying she feared she was going to lose him forever.

Sometimes, as in that moment, he'd stare at her like she wasn't the person he remembered living with; that she was only the *idea* of Alice, not the real one. And sometimes she'd look at him in exactly the same way.

The TV programme, *Come Dine with Me*, aired in November. Jack and Alice watched it side by side on the sofa. She finally got to see who the other guests were. The Goth Elisha was beautiful, but her rock band was awful. Dawn was sweet because she got everything wrong. Jean-Paul was very knowledgeable and warm. And Jack was the old Jack, not the man who was sitting beside her right now. On the screen he was funny and his impressions had the guests falling about. Jack was special, or had specialness inside him. That's who she had fallen in love with and married. When he appeared at the top of the stairs wearing the clown outfit, she just knew there was no way he could lose. Seagull House looked beautiful too. It was a lot of people's dream house and she was living in it for real. And there was Pandora on TV, following Jack like his shadow. And here Pan was right now at Alice's feet, cocking her head to one side when she heard her own on-screen bark. Pandora had brought hope, hadn't she? She had restored life, hadn't she? But right at that moment, Alice feared hope might just be wishful-thinking with bells on. Be careful what you wish for, her father had once told her as a little girl. The titles came up and Alice thought of how it could have been if things turned out differently.

The phone rang constantly after the show; Gerry first, then Sarah the manager of the MS centre, then Lauren. Jack's words on the phone were clipped and tired. He wasn't really sure who he was talking to without a face to place the voice.

Alice explained how wonderful Ernie was; how he'd arranged a treatment programme with a Lyme-literate doctor in San Francisco. Dr. Lindberg had a waiting list as long as the Golden Gate Bridge, but treatment was booked for March. Jack and Alice could stay at Ernie's old house in Nob Hill, keeping the costs down. Ernie had split up with Ariel. The house would be sold in the summer, after some refurbishment and redecoration. 'I'm going to help him with the painting,' said Alice, 'while you have treatment at the clinic. Jack, it will be good for you to be treated properly, good to be away from all of this, don't you think? Wonderful San Francisco, our city, where we first met?'

'Thank you,' he said, clearly not remembering where they'd first met.

'Gerry and Fran have agreed to take Pandora. I'm giving them the keys to Seagull House too. Fran was over the moon.'

'Which one's Fran again?'

'Mum and Dad can keep an eye on the house too. Don't worry about the money. They've given me some of my inheritance early. The most important thing is to get better, Jack. We'll do it *our* way in America.'

Ernie telephoned. He cut straight to the practicalities of the upcoming visit, Lyme treatment and logistics of staying in the Nob Hill house when it had so little furniture. Ariel had removed most of it, leaving only mattresses, an occasional table and some chairs. All mod cons were still in situ, though, Ernie said: refrigerator, cooker, TV. His sons were going to live with their mother and grandma for a while in L.A. Ernie was planning to sell the house, split the difference and buy a spanking new condo in the Mission District. For now, though, the house was all theirs until the summer when it would go onto the market and everything would change.

-PART NINE-

It is an odd thing, but everyone who disappears is said to be seen in San Francisco. It must be a delightful city, and possess all the attractions of the next world.

Oscar Wilde

On Nob Hill

The Nob Hill house in San Francisco looked as timeless as ever; a solid, post-earthquake, three-storey house with stone steps up to the front door and a small veranda overlooking the intersection of cable car tracks; a hop and a skip from the fancy Mark Hopkins Hotel. Ernie had had the exterior painted and repointed top to bottom. As soon as Alice and Jack walked inside, it became apparent how thorough Ernie's ex-wife had been with the furniture removals. Ernie had bought bean bags and dotted them around the bare living room in front of the old TV and bay window. Ernie and Ariel had fought over everything. The makeshift dining table and chairs were the only things he had held onto, besides the mattresses from his sons' dismantled beds.

Having spoken to Alice a few times in advance of their arrival, Ernie understood the situation regarding Jack's difficulty sleeping. He had set up separate bedrooms at the back of the house; single beds with brand new bedlinen. They were at the back, he said, because the cable cars got hellish busy early in the mornings and took a bit of getting used to. He'd forgotten that Jack and Alice had been here before, sleeping in one of the front bedrooms the first night they'd met, nearly 25 years ago. They'd loved the sound of the trolleys then, the ding-dings and metal catching on metal. Sleeping separately from each other now, they knocked the dividing wall between them when the trolleys vibrated past. From his window, Jack caught a tiny glimpse of the Golden Gate Bridge; the upper section, rusty red in a sky of blinding Pacific blue.

The first couple of weeks of treatment at the clinic hit Jack harder than expected. Lindberg said it was a classic Herxheimer reaction;

bacteria dying off as a result of intravenous antibiotics. All of Jack's original symptoms returned and were so bad he stayed a week at the clinic itself, wandering the corridors with a drip trolley attached to his arm, just like Luke from the Arrowhead Clinic. Dr. Lindberg said chronic Lyme patients often felt much worse before they started to feel better.

During the first month of treatment he was collected at the clinic by Ernie or Alice and taken back to Nob Hill where he'd go straight to bed or doze in front of the TV, unable to communicate. He had hallucinations during the day and terrible nightmares at night, but these subsided by week six. Two months in, there were some improvements in energy levels. By week eight Jack was more like himself, as if emerging from a shell. Some of his memory was returning too, aided by Ernie's photo albums and stories from the past. His brain fog was lifting. He ventured out by himself, and once walked all the way to Chinatown and back, stopping off at stalls, shops and teahouses. One woman there looked the spitting image of Jin-jing Li. Jack went to see an absurdist play with Alice too: Gogol's *The Nose*. It pleased and teased, ending romantically.

One evening, just before sunset, all three walked to the Mark Hopkins Hotel and took the lift to the summit, The Top of the Mark, where the views were stunning across the glittering city. They drank cocktails in the northwest corner, and Ernie regaled them with a story they'd never heard before, about Second World War soldiers drinking there before embarking, and soldiers' wives coming to watch their husbands sail off toward Japan, many of them soon to become widows. This corner, with its view of the Golden Gate and Pacific Ocean, became known as "Weepers' Corner".

One Sunday, Ernie and Alice took him to see the Golden Gate Bridge up close. Ernie parked the car and they sat on a knoll of scrub admiring the rainbow that appeared to straddle the bridge. Alice wandered off to buy an ice-cream from a vendor at the edge of the car park.

'What's with the scaffolding?' Jack asked Ernie.

'Anti-suicide works.'

Jack looked at him, gob-smacked. 'Well you could have said they were re-painting it.'

'So, what are you going to do now, Jack? I mean after treatment. What's the plan?'

'I'm going to get better.'

'And then back to stand-up? Kickstart the *Mad Infinitum* tour?'

Jack looked out towards the mouth of the Pacific and up at the great bridge that crossed to Sausalito. 'Well,' he said, 'tomorrow never knows. I'll cross that bridge when I come to it.'

'You always were such a wise-ass,' said Ernie, punching his brother's arm.

'Whoa! Watch my toggle!'

'You've had rotten luck, Jack.'

'That's life, that's what all the people say.'

'Yeah…but you've been through hell and come out the other side.'

Jack put his arm around his brother's shoulder. 'I'm the luckiest man alive. I've lived life doing what I always wanted, making people laugh, and had the love of a good woman…and the love of my family.'

The room Jack slept in had been Gus's; Alice slept in Ryan's. On Gus's wall there was a *Mad Infinitum* tour poster; the tour that never was. The poster showed Jack's head in convulsion, split three or four ways, meant to reflect the madness of having too many choices in the 21st Century. It was also an effective way of conveying the variety of impressions that were a staple of Jack's act. Jack remembered something Alice once said to a journalist about his impressions which had upset him at the time. She said it as a joke, drunk at the end of a national tour: 'Jack can do anybody, but doesn't do a very good impression of himself.' Jack didn't know now, whether he ever wanted to do another impression of anyone other than himself. He might grow to like Jack Mann, the former comedian. There was an opportunity for change; a chance to become himself, and no one else.

Late one night, lying in Gus's bed, feet hanging over the mattress, Jack heard a distant foghorn. It reminded him of the one he'd heard at Seagull House and it took him right back to the foghorn and the bench on the Tankerton Slopes. He could actually smell the muddy English sea. He tapped the wall and asked Alice, 'Did you hear that?'

She tapped the wall in reply. 'No. What?'

'The foghorn?'

'I don't think so,' she said. 'Aren't we too far away from the sea to hear a foghorn?'

'It's not a *sea*!' shouted Ernie from the other side of the house. 'It's an *ocean*! Now will you two lovebirds quieten down! I've got work at seven!'

'Did you hear it?' Jack shouted to his brother.

'No, Jack. Now will you guys sleep! This isn't the Waltons on the the goddam mountain!'

'Maybe I imagined it,' said Jack, turning over on his side.

'You're always making things up in your head!' shouted Alice.

'Why would I do that?' he called back.

In the corner of Gus's room there was a toy cupboard. Most of the toys had been taken away, leaving only boxes of puzzles and a few games. There was an old-fashioned Anglo-centricity to what was left, time-warped from the 1970s: Battleship, KerPlunk, Buckaroo, Golden Shot, Rebound, even the game Operate. Jack realised that these were not Gus's toys but the original games owned by Ernie when he was a child and still lived in Muswell Hill, not Nob Hill. He must have taken them over when he moved. Jack remembered sitting on the living room carpet with everyone at home; Lauren and his Mum and Dad, Ernie shakily lifting out plastic bones and organs with a set of metal tweezers without activating the buzzer. And Jack remembered with sadness one of his first ever impressions in imitation of that TV advert: *Here goes his funny bone!*

One afternoon, Jack removed the tatty, age-stained cardboard lid of Operate. He saw the prone cartoonish patient with his clown-red nose that lit up if you hit the metal sides. Batteries lay dead and smelly in their housing. Most of the compartments had lost their organs and bones too, but Jack was amazed to see the funny bone still in its correct place, although there was no such thing as a funny bone. It was, he knew deep down, the final part of the jigsaw; the last piece to be lifted into place, or lost.

-THE FINAL PART-

Life is a journey.
Death is a return to earth.
The universe is like an inn.
The passing years are like dust.
Regard this phantom world as a star at dawn,
A bubble in a stream,
A flash of lightning in a summer cloud,
A flickering lamp – a phantom – and a dream.

Vairacchedika 32 (Diamond Sutra)

The jewel centre of interest is the eye within the eye.

Jack Kerouac

Fog City

With the last session of IV antibiotics complete and a long list of medicines to take back home, Jack revisited old haunts with Alice and Ernie. Ernie had taken the day off. Alice was dressed up to the nines, wearing a long sparkly dress more suitable for an opera than a walkabout. The weather was fine and sunny, though not especially warm because of a stiff breeze from the Pacific. They went to City Lights bookstore in North Beach where Jack and Alice had fallen in love at first sight. Ernie had them hugging and kissing each other as he took a photograph. They walked into the nearby Vesuvio Café; the old Beatnik drinking den and favourite watering hole of artists and writers including Jack Kerouac.

Although he was under strict instructions not to consume alcohol, Jack felt well enough to have a few drinks. After all, in a couple of days he'd be home again in Tankerton, and didn't know when he'd return to America and see Ernie. Somehow, the two of them had managed not to kill each other in the Nob Hill house for three months. In fact, apart from a few minor skirmishes, they'd got on well, reconnecting and rebuilding a close friendship. It wasn't that long ago that Jack thought family was his saddest failure in life; the break-up of the Family of Mann. Now it was gluing itself back together.

They walked up to the counter at Vesuvio. The bartender, who sported a wonderful handlebar moustache, said: 'Welcome to the last chance saloon. What can I get you guys?' Alice caught sight of the drinks menu chalked on a board noting house cocktails, including a strange one called "A Fool in the Feathers", beside the better known "Jack Kerouac": *rum, tequila, orange/cranberry juice, lime, served in a bucket glass*. She ordered three Jacks.

They sat at the barstools watching the cocktails being made. The bar wasn't busy; it being ten past noon.

Alice raised her glass in the air and said: 'Here's to Jack.'

Ernie raised his: 'To Jack Kerouac and Jack Mann.'

Jack raised his: 'To Jack London and Jack Mann Senior.'

They clinked glasses.

Sitting on the counter was a strange contraption that looked like a large ornate glass juicer. It held a murky substance and hanging on the glass was an art deco notice saying: *genuine absinthe*. Vesuvio had a special license to sell it. Alice's eyes lit up, the way Jack knew they would. After finishing two Kerouac cocktails, Alice ordered an absinthe. Ernie and Jack declined, sticking to pints of Coors. Having not drunk much for three months Jack was already woozy, and Ernie wasn't an afternoon drinker.

The barman winked. 'Guys come in for a single hit. It smooths out the rest of the day.' He fiddled with the absinthe filter and tap as if he was making a coffee, then he drained out a glass, letting the absinthe run over a warmed spoon of sugar. 'Real wormwood, the kinda stuff they loved in Paris.'

Alice took a sip. 'Mmm. How long does it take?'

'You'll find out,' said the bartender with a knowing smile.

Jack swivelled around on his bar stool to get a better look at the art on the walls. The bar hadn't changed much in all the years he'd been away; only the art and the clientele. The sun still burst through the smoked out windows the same way he recalled. The scuffed wooden floor was the same. Some of the wacky decoration was unchanged. There was one thing different though, as he looked up towards the first floor. Suspended from wires was a large wooden seagull in full flight; very similar to the one Jack's father had bought him from San Francisco when Jack was just a toddler, the same one he kept all those years and hung up in Hunter's bedroom in Fulham, near the cot; near the cot that was never used. Whenever anyone came in or out of Vesuvio, the draft from the door made the gull's wings glide up and down. Jack wasn't in the business of buying any of this art. It seemed too abstract, and some of the realist stuff crudely drawn or painted as if the world was seen through a child's eyes. None of the pieces were seascapes either, so he didn't think Alice would be interested. 'I'll buy the giant gull,' he said, pointing up. 'How much?'

The bartender shook his head. 'Part of the fixtures and fittings. Sadly not for sale.'

'Just as well,' said Ernie. 'It wouldn't fit in your suitcase.'

Jack noticed when another few people came in through the door that the fog was getting up. San Francisco was living up to its name, Fog City. The wings of the gull flapped so violently they nearly clapped. For a second, Jack thought he saw a smile on the gull's beak. He was going to point this out to Alice but was struck instead by her own exaggerated grin and eyes like pin-wheels. 'Here we go,' said Jack out of the corner of his mouth, giving Ernie a little elbow.

'What?' said Alice, leaning on the bar, and taking another sip of absinthe. She giggled and span around on her chair. Her limbs were loose. 'Look at all the art!' she said, pointing across the room.

'All local artists, mam,' the bartender said.

Alice got off her stool and Jack tried to grab her arm. She ventured half way across the floor, eyes fixed on one particular abstract painting of a sunset. 'That's fantastic! Look at all the colours and what the artist is saying. Look, Jack!'

Jack was looking, but all he could see was the panic in the eyes of an older couple who were sitting directly under that piece, quietly drinking their drinks.

Alice wandered around the bar leaning across people to view the art at closer range. She moved from painting to painting unaware she was tiptoeing along the floorboards like a cat-burglar. She stopped at some pieces and held her chin like Rodin's Thinker. At others she cocked her head like a confused puppy. She moved along and shook her blonde locks, making a tutting sound. She was an art critic all of a sudden. 'I do not wish to represent man as he is, but only as he might be. Paul Klee,' she said, nodding at her own perfect recall.

The bartender leaned on the counter, saying, 'Now she's cookin'.'

Alice returned to the sunset painting behind the old couple. 'What do you think?' she said to the man sitting there.

He looked at her soberly. 'What do I think of what?'

'This!' said Alice, arm flying out, finger pointing.

'Well…' The man shifted around in his seat and looked at the sunset. 'It's good.' He frowned at his partner sitting opposite him.

'Just *good*?' said Alice, irritation in her voice. 'That's hardly a critique is it? *What's* so good about it?'

The man peered at the artwork again, shrugging his shoulders. 'The colours?'

'Yes, the colours,' said Alice. 'It has all the colours of the brainbow, but what else?'

After a hilarious silence, the man said, 'Well, it's…very…*real*?'

'Eggs-actly,' said Alice, nodding theatrically. 'It's absurd but very *real*. The way it catches the beautiful yet terrifying sunset so perfectly. This isn't good,' she said, folding her arms. 'It's magnificent! You have good taste, sir! *Real* taste. It's *real*, like my lovely husband over there!' She pointed across the bar and everyone looked at Jack. 'He's very *real* too! Although from where I'm standing he seems to have grown two heads and I don't know which one I'm going to kiss!' By now Alice had generated her own audience. Everyone was staring. 'My husband can see things, you know. He has the biggest pineal gland in the western hemisphere.'

'Alice,' Jack said. 'Why don't we sit down at the bar?'

She threw her head back, laughing. 'You're already sitting at the bar.'

'That's true,' said Ernie, slapping his brother's back.

'I think I'll dance now,' said Alice, spinning on the spot, arms outstretched, eyes closed. 'I'm in *The King and I*. I could have danced all night, could've danced all night…'

'It might be a good idea to fetch her back to the stool,' said the bartender. 'This bar ain't suited to windmills.'

Jack walked over and took her by the hand. Alice tried to lean him into a waltz but he kissed her cheek and led her safely back to the stool. 'Thank you kindly, your majesty,' she said, curtseying. 'I shall partake of another one, bartender.'

'You haven't finished the first,' he said.

She downed it in one and plonked the glass on the counter so hard it nearly broke.

'I don't think you need another,' the bartender said. 'You're doing just dandy.'

'I am, I am,' she said. 'The world is full of beauty, isn't it?'

'Sure is,' said Ernie, trying to contain himself.

'You're beautiful too, Ernie,' she said. 'Well, not beautiful exactly, more…handsome…in a sort of prototype for Jack kind of way.'

'Well, thank you very much,' he said.

The bartender laughed. 'In absintho veritas.'

'And your moustache, bartender, your big moustache is handsome too. Nonetheless, it does remind me of a walrus. Does it bother you, this walrus hanging on your lip? Or did it…just grow on you?' Her voice was loud and fast and everyone was captivated by the spectacle. 'You look like a friend of ours back in England called Gerry. If I say nice things, will you pretty please pour me another one of those absinthe things?' She tapped the filtration bottle.

'Let's give it a few more minutes, see how things pan out.'

'Okay,' she said. 'You wanna play hard ball. Let's see who cracks first.' Alice lowered her chin onto the backs of her hands on the counter and stared at him from under a dramatically creased brow.

An old, sensible-looking woman entered through the main door making the seagull's wings flutter in the draft. She walked up to the counter and looked over the top of her spectacles at the drinks menu. After a while, she said, 'Hmmm, I can't decide. What's this?' She tapped the absinthe filter.

'*Real* absinthe, mam.'

'What sort of effect does it have?'

'Ask the girl with kaleidoscope eyes,' the bartender said, nodding in Alice's direction.

Alice's head slowly turned, eyes spinning, a messy grin spreading across her mouth. 'It's like a liquid lucid dreeeammm.'

'In that case,' the old woman said, 'I'll just have an Irish coffee.'

After asking Ernie to keep an eye on Alice, Jack disappeared down a tiny wooden staircase that led to the gents'. It was just as he remembered; a dimly lit, dank basement. He felt a frisson of excitement, though, thinking how Jack Kerouac probably stood here peeing out cocktails that would someday be named after him. And Dad too, Jack Mann Snr., who no doubt stood here as a San Francisco Chronicle journalist and writer in the 1960s. He wished his father had lived long enough to have stood with him and Ernie and Alice at the Vesuvio bar. *Dead people and ghosts*, he thought. He remembered the beginning of *The Turn of the Screw* at Glyndebourne, and it sent a shiver down his spine. That horrible summer when the illness first took hold; how his left foot turned into a crab, the numbness in his left hand, and all the hell that followed, leading him now to San Franciscan fog, giant gulls, absinthe and liquid lucid dreams. Alice had said he was very *real*, but he wasn't feeling real. For the first time in over a year he felt no pain at all. His hands were not burning. They were quite the opposite; as cold as cod. His feet were frozen blocks. His soles no longer stood on broken glass or burning coals. This had to be the effects of alcohol, or was it a turning point? Although excited by the prospect of painlessness, he stopped himself believing; too much wishful thinking might herald its immediate return. He touched the door frame, saying, 'Touch wood.'

Half way up the stairs, he heard Alice's loud voice. She was holding court, a second shot of absinthe coursing through her veins and flooding her brain. 'Ssshhh! Jack'll be up in a minute! You know my husband is the funniest man alive!' Silence. 'Yes, he was on at the London Palladium! My Jack met the Queen, and Orville the Duck! And David Letterman! And Jim Carrey. He won *Come Dine with Me*! He'll be up soon! Wait and see! He's the funniest man alive!'

Jack hesitated on the narrow stairwell feeling a jolt of adrenalin; the way he used to when he first stepped onto stages in his early stand-up days. Back then, butterflies flitted in the net of his twenty-something stomach. Such feelings all but disappeared by his thirties, but now, here in Vesuvio, they returned. A foghorn sounded, making the butterflies scatter.

'He's been gone some time,' said the bartender.

'Maybe he's gotten lost,' came a stranger's voice, raising a titter.

'Ssshhh!' said Alice. 'I hear him!'

Jack's foot creaked the top step and he hesitated. He saw light through the crack of the jamb. He wondered how he'd ever live up to the billing of his wife's hyperbole. Her build-up was better than

Letterman's. Perhaps it would be easier using physical comedy like John Cockshaw used to on the old circuit. Tumble through the door into a heap on the floor like Charlie Chaplin or Norman Wisdom. Or should he do an impression? President Obama, Clinton, Trump, or former governor of California, Arnold Schwarzenegger? He could walk through the door pretending he *had* got lost, and say: 'Vair did you say the john voz again?'

Jack walked through the eager crowd of onlookers. All eyes were glued to him as he strode across the room towards the bar. He had a swagger at his hip, a stiffness to his shoulders, and walked partly as if he'd been riding a cattle-droving horse across the Midwest for sixty days. He smacked his lips and wiped an apparently parched mouth. He hitched up imaginary pants and leather chaps. He raised one dust-coated boot and plonked it down heavily on the foot rail hearing a spur jangle. He looked around the room, tipped back his imaginary sweat-stained Stetson, leaned one elbow on the counter and said to the bartender in his finest John Wayne voice: 'Hey, Joe! Set me up one of those wormwood things would ya? I'm gonna be Yul Brenner this afternoon!'

It was as if Jack could see tumbleweed rolling across the floor. You had to have been there, he thought, in the crushing silence. You had to have been party to that *King and I* song that Alice had sung. It wasn't the funniest line he'd ever delivered. It wasn't even the best impression he'd ever applied, but the walk wasn't too rusty, the intonation wasn't bad. But the joke hadn't landed. Silence gripped the room. In a rising panic, he looked around the blank faces like a virgin stand-up.

'How'd you know my name was Joe?' said the bartender.

'Why,' said Jack, not missing a beat, and still in character, 'don't you know I can see things? I have the biggest pineal gland in the western hemisphere!'

The bartender sprayed a mouthful of coffee over the counter. He dragged a towel from his shoulder and slapped it down making a *crack*! A solitary clap came from Alice. Ernie raised his glass of beer in the air and said: 'Is your glass half full or half empty, bro?'

'Let's just say I'm borderline optimistic, or half way to nirvana.'

Ernie laughed, and laughed, holding his sides as if they were splitting.

'Hey,' said Jack. 'It wasn't that funny.' His brother stopped laughing, but his mouth remained locked in an unusual rictus grin. He tugged at the corners, but couldn't straighten them out, as if he was having a bad trip. 'You been at the wormwood too, Ernie?'

Alice clapped faster. Another clap fired across the room, and more claps around the tables, and the clapping gathered momentum like a wave swelling and coming in to shore. A man beat a table with his fists, another whistled using his fingers. Another person howled, setting off a chain reaction of cheering. Jack remembered this: what it had been like when a joke landed, when a full set hit the mark. He remembered living, breathing, feeding from this guttural human noise, and his heart soared.

Music started on the speakers and Jack recognised it from The Beatles' *Magical Mystery Tour*. The bartender took a mic out from under the counter, tapped the head twice with his finger, and breathed *one, two, three* into it. He passed it to Ernie.

'Karaoke at Vesuvio?' said Jack, not believing his eyes.

Ernie stood up and cleared his throat, the unusual grin still planted on his face. Ernie had never been one for public shows and was actually tone deaf. 'I am he as you are he as you are me and we are all together...' he sang. For once in his life, in the right key. He looked straight at Jack, telling him he'd been a naughty boy, and had let his face grow long.

Alice joined in. I am the eggman, she said. They are the eggmen. She pointed at the bartender, calling him a Walrus, 'Goo goo g'joob'.

The main door opened. People came in wondering what the show was. A blast of cold Pacific air blew through, swirling and making the suspended seagull's wings jerk into motion, flapping as if its life depended on it.

Pornographic priestess, Ernie continued, boy you been a naughty girl, you let your knickers down... Ernie glanced at Alice, Joker smile still ironed on his face.

'Whoop!' Alice screamed, dancing, singing.

Ernie continued to belt out the words: Penguins. Hari Krishna. Edgar Allan Poe.

When the song was over, Ernie took a bow and thrust the mic into Jack's hand.

'You're having a laugh. Okay, what am I singing? The Fool on the Hill?'

'You know,' said Alice, a sparkle in her eyes.

When the brass section of a band started playing "Le Marseillaise" and he heard the drumroll running behind it, Jack relaxed. It was how he used to finish his sets in the late 1980s; first an impression of a resurrected John Lennon as the British prime minister, followed by this song. It was also the song Jack sang at his own wedding reception before taking the first dance with Alice. His wife and his brother stood either side of him now, swaying. They swung arms around his shoulders and waved their free hands left and right in time with the music: 'Love, love, love,' they sang. 'Love, love, love. Love, love, love. Love, love, love.'

Jack took his cue, singing nasally into the mic. Alice and Ernie pulled him tighter. The crowd began to sing. 'All you need is love. All you need is love. All you need is love…love. Love is all you need.' During George Harrison's guitar solo, all three tried doing synchronised leg kicks, only Jack couldn't find the energy, and his legs were leaden.

When the song ended, the crowd stood up, clapping and cheering. Jack, Alice and Ernie joined hands and took a bow. They let go of Jack's hands, taking a step backwards, leaving the floor to him.

Jack gave his trademark stage sign-off: 'You've been listening to Jack Mann, but please don't hold that against him. Thank you. God bless your souls, and goodnight.' Curiously, even after the din had died and the wings of the giant bird no longer beat above his head, Jack could still hear applause.

A foghorn sounded, stealing everyone's attention to the door. People hurriedly retook their seats. One by one, Jack noticed the smiles slip from their faces, and how the noise settled to a respectful, chapel-like silence. The door swung open, almost breaking free from its hinges, and fog rolled in, thick and low along the floor like dry ice across a stage; a stage set for a singer, not a stand-up. Jack noticed a lonely mic stand in one corner where the smoke pooled. 'So, Alice, what are you going to sing?'

She let go of his hand and drifted off towards the smoke. She stood behind the mic stand, face white and serious, her lipstick glowing bright red in the spotlight. She looked beautiful. The crowd murmured. Sleepy jazz started up on the speakers and Alice pointed at Jack, saying, 'This one's for you.' She cupped her hands around the chrome microphone, singing a dark lullaby to send a loved one to sleep. She sung about a night that was bitter, and stars that had lost their glitter, and the winds were colder, and then you were older.

Her voice was mesmerising, and more emotional than usual. She had a terrific voice and was forever singing songs from famous musicals, but Jack was struggling to identify this particular tune, even though he'd heard it many times. James Mason's haunted face flickered on the surface of his mind. He cast his eyes around the room, noticing how everyone was wearing jaunty black berets and black roll-necks. They were engrossed in Alice's drama, nodding in agreement. Some were smoking at their tables, and Jack wondered if Ernie had poured wormwood into his pint.

And all because of a man that got away, Alice sang, eyes glued to Jack.

He clicked his fingers. *A Star is Born! James Mason walks into the sea. Well, his character Norman Maine does. As one star falls, another one rises.*

'The writing's on the wall.' Alice pointed towards the door, or the wall with the sunset painting. She said a man had gone off and undone her, and their great beginning had seen its final inning.

Jack was unsteady on his stool, as if it was sliding along the deck of a rolling ship.

'Good riddance, goodbye!' Alice boomed. 'Fools will be fools…'

Jack stood up, staggering, the room listing. He swayed, but not to the music. As he fell backwards towards the ground, it was as if he was laid down by the soft strings of a web or a puddle of invisible hands. Alice built to a thrilling, tragic crescendo. Jack couldn't see her through the fog. Ever since the world began, she wailed, there wasn't anything sadder than...

The floorboards were uneven against his spine, gaps between them like the wooden slats of the sea captain's bench on the Tankerton Slopes.

Nothing sadder than a one-man woman, she said, who was looking for a man that got away...the Jack Mann that got away.

The singing stopped. The faces disappeared, and Jack realised: *this is nothing, this is nothing, this is nothing but wishful thinking.*

Jack opened his eyes and looked to where the ceiling should have been, seeing only fog and gulls. His limbs were immoveable and cold. Never rescued, never returned home, never flew to San Francisco? Here on the bench all this time? Months in minutes, seasons in seconds, lost in a forest of possible futures?

A giant gull dropped down from the sky, landing on the arm of the sea captain's bench. It examined Jack with wise, hooded eyes, padding up and down his body, turning in circles. It was doing a danse macabre or searching for something. Three brilliant white dots shone out from its black tail-feathers like an ellipsis. The gull tapped at the centre of Jack's forehead with its sharp, hooked bill and bright red spot. Tap, tap, tap, right between the eyes. 'Welcome back, *grack*!' Birdman said. Tap, tap tap.

In the fading light, Jack wondered if the things he'd seen happen could still happen. Perhaps a blanket of gulls to warm him, a curious lady to find him cloaked in birds, Alice running through the fog. And after that, who knew? Futures are full of infinite possibilities, aren't they? *Then again*, he thought, *it's possible that what becomes of you is what you always knew you'd become.*

Birdman appeared to nod.

'Goodbye,' Jack whispered; to whom or what he couldn't say. Even the word sounded strange, catching in his throat like a grackle.

The crashing tide rolled in under an ultraviolet sky. A foghorn blasted, joining the noisy flux and flow of seawater below. Jack listened to the wax and wane of it, his heartbeat slowing in sad synchronicity. Birdman trod down his shoulder onto his chest and pressed with its beak, prodding, probing. *This is nothing*, Jack told himself. *This is nothing*. Wings beat in a frenzy above his head, and mad flutterings came from all around.

'This is not nothing, *grack*,' Birdman said, taking flight into the fog.

For what seemed like an eternity, there was only peace and warmth. Jack craned his neck, looking down at himself. Everything about him was speckled, grey-white and feathered like a strange suit of duvet, or blankie of love. His head tilted backwards. His eyelids closed over, and he smiled, because he knew.

A dog barked in the distance, stirring the fledgling gulls into grackles and grumbles. As the dog drew closer, it growled, and a woman shrieked: 'Are you alive? Are you dead? Are you only sleeping?'

The gulls tensed, stiffening their gizzards. They threw back their heads, opened their throats and made such a tumultuous noise.

If you heard it, Jack thought, *if you ever heard it and weren't afraid, you'd swear the seagulls were laughing.*

Acknowledgements

Profuse thanks go to my wife Janice for her constant support during my battle with Lyme disease (effectively saving my life) and for her incalculable input into the writing and publication of *Anatomised*. I'm indebted to my editor David Chaproniere for his diligence and suggestions made at critical stages. Gratitude is extended to good friends and readers of early drafts: Craig Dadds, Angela Lubbock, Paul Hendy and Prof. Mike Cronin. Their advice and comments have been invaluable. I thank Tuscan artist Antonio Breschi for allowing the use of his original artwork for the cover.

During the writing of this novel I have come into contact with many people from the international Lyme community: professionals, patients, carers, writers and researchers. I'd particularly like to thank Natasha Metcalf (co-founder of Lyme Disease UK), Sandra Pearson (Lyme Disease Action), Allie Cashel (author of *Suffering The Silence*) and Sarah Bignell-Howse who was vital in my own quest for treatment. Along with the many patients I've met on social media, I owe them a huge debt for their positivity, insight and encouragement. Similarly, I offer thanks to the doctors who treated my illness empirically. I must also thank Karen Middlemiss from the Kent Multiple Sclerosis Therapy Centre. Lyme mimics many illnesses, including MS, and the people I met at the centre in Canterbury were inspirational.

Sadly, whilst writing this book, my parents John and Martha passed away, followed shortly after by my mother-in-law, Patricia Campbell. They were only ever loving and supportive. *Anatomised* is dedicated in memory of them.